Conference
TIME

L. L. CONRAD

ISBN: 978-1-4834-5753-6 (sc)
ISBN: 978-1-4834-5751-2 (hc)
ISBN: 978-1-4834-5752-9 (e)

Library of Congress Control Number: 2016905990

Lulu Publishing Services rev. date: 08/23/2016

Acknowledgements

Many thanks to great editors, Martine, Catharine and Chris.

To my mother, whom I miss every day.

Other books by L.L.Conrad:

My Time
Her First Loves, His Only

CHAPTER 1

A nudge from a fellow passenger alerted Tory Stanton that the flight attendant was trying to get her attention. She had been deep into the sex scene in the book she was reading. It was the kind of thing her mother called "smut," but it was what Tory used to escape her world. She felt a little dazed as she focused back on reality. The acute mental image of two men pleasuring a woman lingered in her head.

"Something to drink?" the flight attendant asked.

"Coffee. Black, please," Tory replied. She tried to pull the tray down and close her book facedown so her coworker, Joe, who was watching TV next to her, wouldn't see what she was reading. The cover wasn't that bad though. She took a quick sip of the lukewarm beverage. The coffee, however, was truly awful.

Tory wasn't sure why she troubled herself to care what other people thought about what she read. Perhaps a part of her realized it might not be healthy to devour erotic romances the way she did. *Fuck it!* She flipped the book back over. *What a rebel you are!* She gave herself a mental high-five.

Head back against the seat, she closed her eyes and tried to get as comfortable as she could. Her seat was between two guys with their knees spread open, and their overall bulk encroached on her space. She wondered if the airlines arranged passengers this way on purpose—wedged next to each other like puzzle pieces—so that everyone could fit into the short rows of seats.

She sighed. She really didn't want to start the trip in a bad mood.

Luckily, it was short flight. She would get back into her book as soon as she'd landed and gotten settled into her hotel room, and there, she could be assured of having no interruptions. Until then, she would let her mind wander.

Soaring in the air at thirty thousand feet—or something like that—she should be thinking about what she might get out of the Supply Chain Management Association's national conference. Instead, Tory was considering how she might vanish from her life. Running away would work, but the reality was that there were others who depended on her to be responsible. There was no escape, but over the four days of the conference, she'd enjoy getting away, learning something new, and having a bit of time to herself alone.

It was true that life had not turned out as planned. When she thought about it, she realized she was dissatisfied with her life. Whenever those thoughts surfaced, she couldn't help but dismiss them as silly. So what if she didn't have great sex anymore? So what if she'd given up on her dream of owning her own business? Or her marriage wasn't perfect? Or her kids were giving her attitude? Or money was tight? She knew none of that was the end of the world or different from what other people were going through, but she was still unhappy. It ate at her soul. The evidence stared back at her every time she peered at herself in the mirror. No matter how long she looked, she wouldn't see joy or happiness reflected back in her own blue eyes. *Maybe this is my midlife crisis?*

Taking another sip of tepid coffee, she tried shifting her thoughts in another direction, but she just couldn't do it. What was the point in obsessing about things that could not be changed when she had so much to be grateful for? She had always considered herself a practical, no-nonsense person who didn't indulge in ridiculous sentiments. However, she felt deprived, frustrated, and restless with strange cravings—and not for food. She couldn't comprehend it. What was happening to her? She felt, all of a sudden, suffocated by the idea of letting this status quo linger indefinitely. What if she bucked against everything and indulged in something selfish for once? She had no idea what, but the idea of doing something different or even forbidden—like having wild, passionate sex with a man who was not your husband, just once—was tantalizing. She had to admit that there was something wildly seductive about being reckless and not caring about anything other than her own pleasure.

A grin spread across her face until she was struck by a dose of reality. She had so many sessions to attend; the conference schedule was packed. The likelihood of anything interesting happening in San Antonio was very small. Her smile faded; it seemed juvenile to be so discontented with life, to want more. After all, she was not an idealistic adolescent anymore.

She realized that for a few seconds, she had been feeling a bit like her old self from a long time ago. Eighteen-year-old Tory had admittedly been a little wild, willing to experiment, daring with boys, and popular with her friends. Oh my, the fun they had enjoyed! Now, at the age of forty-two, those days were long gone. Where had that spirited person disappeared to? She closed her eyes again, wondering if there were any hope of ever again getting a glimpse of that carefree person. What she wouldn't give to get back some of that passion for living—even a little taste to counter how *alone* she felt.

And it wasn't just the loneliness. After all, she was married and had a busy life, surrounded by people who gnawed at her. Other feelings, some she had never experienced before, left her hungry. But those feelings and the way she was making so much of them? It just didn't make any sense. In fact, she was ashamed of her musings lately; they were so erotic and graphic. There was one—

No! Stop! Head out of the gutter, girl! Think about something else!

She had promised herself not to dwell on her life situation while she was on this mini-vacation, but here she was pondering it yet again. Avoiding the subject was like trying to leave a hangnail alone: Once you noticed it, your subconscious mind kept reminding you it was still there, urging you to remove the loose piece of tissue, even though it might hurt as you pulled it away. Leaving it untouched was never really a viable option. So it should have been no real surprise that this train of thought could not be stopped.

The fact was that some of the issues in her life simply could not be fixed—no matter how much she worried about them or wished otherwise. If she were to make a list of everything that bothered her, her husband would be at the top. John's illness and the way he treated her were never far from her thoughts. He had been diagnosed with prostate cancer three years earlier and was no longer in remission. Their lives revolved around him and his moods. Most days, it felt like she walked on eggshells every time he came back from a doctor's appointment. Nothing she did was right in his eyes.

He never missed an opportunity to point out her faults or deficiencies; he treated her like a child and not an equal. She was embarrassed whenever the kids witnessed one of his verbal tirades directed at her. These were usually triggered by an inconsequential event such as her buying the wrong brand of peanut butter. She had learned to recognize the warning signs that he was about to start, and she would invent errands for the kids to get them out of the house. They did not need to be exposed to their dad's bad behavior.

The pattern started with a sarcastic comment, which would lead to rehashing some past minor incident. If he were allowed to continue, it would escalate into a ridiculous argument. Sometimes she went outdoors to escape him. If redirecting the conversation did not work, she would grab the hose to water the plants, wash the car, or just clean something. If he followed her outside, he would retreat back inside as soon as he saw her wielding the spray nozzle because she had once soaked him with it. The soaking and her inability to stop laughing had ended the discussion that one time, and he knew her well enough to know that she wouldn't hesitate to drench him again.

Sure, as a couple, they had their problems. Being married for twenty years was probably reason enough for that. Not everyone got along like her parents, Alice and Al, did. She had always expected to have a close and loving relationship like theirs. Some days, she felt cheated. Her own marriage was an existence based more on *tolerance* than affection—on her side, at least.

In the past, because John worked in sales. Tory had accepted his long work hours and his frequent business trips, but there were other aspects of their life together that were more of a challenge for her to keep defending, even to herself. The easiness that used to exist between them had evaporated as their mutual respect dwindled like a flame going out. It had happened so gradually. She surmised that it was due to a number of things, but foremost among those had to be his jealousy over her successes.

She liked her job, was good at it, and had been promoted. She did meaningful work as a registered nurse. Now, as a manager of the purchasing department, she was in charge of buying products and equipment to be used on patients. She earned a higher wage than he did. He began criticizing her in private, but it progressed to doing it publicly. She had noticed that these episodes often followed someone complimenting her about her career. His snide remarks—both the ones she overheard and the ones he made directly at her—all reeked of envy. It had become difficult to laugh off.

Once, at a friend's wedding reception, he had been even nastier than usual. Afterward, he tried to blame it on the alcohol. Tory didn't buy it. He repeated the behavior in front of the neighbors and again in front of Alice. Now they behaved more like siblings than spouses; whenever he made a comment about her inflexibility or some other unflattering characteristic, she tried to ignore it and him.

She attempted to pretend that his words had little impact, but the opposite was true. He had never been that way—and he wasn't always like that now, she reminded herself—but she was aware that she was trying to paint the picture better than it was. She colored over the bad to create the illusion that everything was better that it was. Somehow, it was easier than accepting or placing blame. Along the way, though, she had begun to believe some of what he said. She began to question herself. Was she rigid, cold, inflexible, a control freak, and a dreamer? Was she all the unflattering things he had accused her of being during one of their more recent disputes?

And then there were his unexplained absences. Tory suspected he had cheated on her. She had no real evidence; it was just a feeling. She didn't confront him, though; she didn't want to know the truth. In all honesty, she was past the point of caring. When he was gone, the children seemed happier and the entire household felt calmer. Her whole demeanor became more relaxed when she didn't have to worry about what John might be upset about next.

To be honest, the whole family had to deal with John's moodiness and the reality that he would die. John had cut her out of his business.

He didn't want her to accompany him to the oncologist anymore, but she knew. So did the kids. She could see it in his eyes: he was angry at the world because he felt cheated by everything. Why hadn't science cured the disease yet? He resented being the victim of something that was beyond his control. She knew him and understood his frustration at the unfairness of it all.

Gradually his anger was directed at everyone around him. Jake had always been a sensitive child and wanted to spend time with his dad, but John seemed incapable of recognizing this need. Samantha, although the eldest, spent her time away from the family. It might have something to do with how her husband had become a different person altogether. His personality had begun changing in recent years, but it had become more abrasive since the reoccurrence of the cancer when the management of it became his primary concern. The family was a very distant second priority, and she sometimes wondered if he even realized it.

His recent birthday was a memory she wanted to forget. Sam and she had baked a cake, and Jake had helped her get the new barbeque put together in time for dinner. A meal that they had all helped create went uneaten since John didn't even show. The looks of disappointment on her children's faces when their father's absence could no longer be ignored were painful to recall. Even though she had reminded him that they had planned something special, he obviously had other plans.

His oncologic treatment had been quite aggressive, so he did have the right to complain. He had undergone a radical prostatectomy to remove the organ and surrounding tissue, and then he received radiation and chemotherapy. The man had been through the wringer before, and other than the surgery, he was going through it all over again. He had lost an incredible amount of weight due to constant diarrhea and chronic illness syndrome, so she understood the cause of some of his moodiness. But no matter how bad it was, nothing excused the way he was shutting them out by ignoring their very existence most days. Even if his treatments were slowly killing him, he could have handled it better. His attitude was affecting their children and Tory in ways she could have never imagined.

When John stopped looking after their home, that—and all his other duties—fell to her. Although Tory had known it would eventually happen, the reality was much worse than she'd imagined. The burden of shouldering the responsibilities for her family was hers and hers alone to carry; some mornings, she didn't want to get out of bed to face the day and wondered whether she had the fortitude to keep juggling all the balls.

There was no break from the constant weight of obligation. She paid their taxes and bills—what she could of them, anyway. She balanced the checking account, which took a great deal of effort. She made sure the kids were correctly registered for all their school programs. As the weeks flew by, she only knew to put out the garbage when she noticed her neighbors' trash on the curb. She managed the many appointments with the dentist, oncologists, dietician, and clinics, but she couldn't keep enough food in the house for her growing son and his friends. There was never any milk. Never mind the chores. The list of things that needed tending to was endless.

John had not so much as thanked her for being supportive or taking over for him. He hadn't kissed her or acknowledged her in more than six months. He practically ignored her. They had not had sex in more than a year, and it had been even longer since they'd last shared real intimacy. That part had always troubled Tory, and John could never explain it. At least, not well enough to be believable.

Tory's nursing education helped her appreciate the mental and physiological changes that an ill person might experience. But he ignored all of her attempts to initiate sex or any intimate act. When it became apparent that he could no longer perform, he had not even considered trying to accommodate her by using other techniques. It was as though she was invisible to him. Most days, she felt like an unpaid employee, and it was more and more demeaning.

She wanted to be a good wife and mother with a positive attitude who was supportive of everyone in her family. People in her community expected her to be that and more, and she had always thought she was well suited for that role. Her experience in dealing with the ill and dying should have made things easier for her, but it didn't. It wasn't an unknown patient who was dying, a stranger she could walk away from at the end of her shift, but someone who depended on her 24-7.

Other cracks threatened the foundation of her marriage and her family. Samantha wanted money to buy a car. Tory told her to get a job, save up, and prove she could take on the responsibilities of car ownership. John overruled her and wrote out a check. Just like that! The incident made her angry every time she thought about it. Understanding why he had done it hadn't made it any more palatable. He wanted his daughter to remember his generosity after he was gone. But since Tory handled the finances, she knew they couldn't afford it. The bills continued to accumulate. She had to be the bad guy and limit the family's spending because her husband was not behaving rationally.

It was going to get worse, and she knew it. John would require assistance in all the activities of daily life before he died. Because of her previous role as an RN, his parents and the parish assumed she would be his professional caregiver. But she had already decided that that wouldn't happen. She'd place him in a hospice when he needed more help than she could provide. It was not a callous decision; it was a practical and sustainable one. How could she keep her job if she needed to stay home to care for her husband? Besides, she didn't want him to die in their house. She and the kids would continue to live there, at least for a while, and the memory of her own father dying in his bed still bothered her. That was one of the reasons why she hardly went over to her childhood home any more.

Tory had stopped working as a registered nurse three years before—despite all the time it had taken her to get there—because her family had needed her at home. She had liked nursing, and the thought of leaving the profession didn't cross her mind until it became evident that spending nights away from home was taking a toll on her family. Her twelve-hour shifts, especially the all-nighters, and the weekends and holidays at work were causing problems that could no longer be ignored.

At sixteen, Samantha had begun to change for the worse. She was acting out, running wild, and looking for attention. Jake was just a year and a half younger than his sister, and he had been having difficulties at school. He was withdrawn and had very few friends. Both teenagers spent too much time unsupervised. Tory would call home from work after midnight to find out that Sam was out at some unknown location, Jake was alone watching TV, and John was who knows where. Meals she prepared before going to work were left uneaten. School assignments and chores didn't get done. The kids missed classes. She knew this because the attendance monitor notified her each time. At their ages, some kind of parental supervision was essential, despite what John thought. Tory was worried that her kids would get into serious trouble. Something had to change.

She packed it in. She had to get a day job, but there weren't any in nursing unless you had thirty years' seniority or a master's degree. After going back to school to take some courses, she'd made the switch to product, service, and equipment procurement in health care.

Now she worked nine to five at a hospital in southern Ontario. She could manage the household, at least on most days, and was present for her kids. This last year especially, she had become closer to them; it seemed they could openly discuss their troubles with her. It had all been worth it. Eventually, she came to find her new work very rewarding. It was not always so.

In the early months, there had been too much chaos and not enough resources in the purchasing department. Between union demands, the heavy workload, and missing nursing, Tory had often felt she was not making a meaningful contribution or being very productive. Others must not have seen it that way, though, because after a couple of years, she received a promotion. This allowed her the flexibility to make sweeping changes, and everything ran much more smoothly after that. The positive results of her modifications to procurement, including new legislation, brought her to the attention of the hospital leaders, and before she knew it, she had become the manager of the program.

One of the requirements of her designation as a public buyer was to attend events and continue to learn. This was why she was on a plane with two of her employees and a purchaser from another hospital. They had obtained a discount rate for the small group that worked together on projects. Their company should have made the journey less lonely, but still she felt isolated.

She placed high expectations on herself as the boss. It wasn't just that she didn't think she should fraternize with the staff; she had nothing in common with them or with her peers, acquaintances, and neighbors. Also, she felt it would be unwise to share too much of herself with them. It was strange how different things were from when she had worked on the ward as a nurse. Being able to complain to the other clinicians on her unit had given her an emotional release that she had taken for granted. Her coworkers, most of them female, had all faced similar issues and could relate to her. She missed them and promised herself to make time to call them when she got back.

The people she worked with these days didn't have almost-grown children and a husband who was dying in front of their eyes. Nor had they recently lost their own father. Outside of work, she didn't socialize much and rarely attended events that brought her in contact with other women. She recognized that it was her fault. Everyone managed hectic work and home schedules; her circumstances were not that special or unique. No, she had no one to blame but herself. Through a misguided attempt to behave how she thought a manager should, she barely knew her staff. And due to a degree of laziness about staying in touch with the nurses she had worked with, her circle of friends had disappeared.

These days, she only had her mother to confide in, and there was no way she would discuss the lack of activity between her sheets with Alice. Nor would she have raised the subject with her father, if he were still alive, despite how open-minded he had been when it came to one-on-ones with her about drugs, boys, and other topics that were difficult to talk about. She had always admired her dad's ability to bring logic and wisdom into any conversation by considering both sides.

His death had been the most traumatic loss in her life. He had passed away unexpectedly and left a huge void in her life.

Her parents had been married a long time and been very close. However, since Al's death, Alice had thrived, which didn't make sense to Tory. She had expected her mother to grieve for a long time, but that was not the case. Within a few months, Alice was back to her old self, and she looked better and seemed happier than ever. This was puzzling. Tory wondered if her mom was seeing someone, but she squashed that thought. Her mom was in her sixties. Surely she wouldn't get intimate with a man who wasn't her husband. Then Tory realized how ridiculous she was being. Everyone needed human contact, regardless of age.

Tory suspected that her parents had had their ups and downs, as all couples did. Who really knew what anyone's relationship was like? One aspect of their relationship that she envied was how much they had respected each other. It was evident in how they treated one another and all of the little things they did—even when they had no idea Tory was present.

Maybe her mom had moved on, met someone, and was getting some.

Okay, stop thinking about your mother and sex!

She took another sip of cool coffee in an attempt to veer away from the topic, but it didn't work.

Other than her family, sex was the subject that occupied her thoughts more and more. What was wrong with her? She'd be at a meeting and start to wonder how the man across from her made out with his wife. Did he go down on her regularly? Did he think of it as a chore—or was it something he liked? Sometimes she'd catch herself wondering how a stranger looked when he was nude or how good he was in bed. More than ever, she was convinced that a marriage could not flourish without touch and play.

She couldn't remember the last time John's hands had been on her body, but she didn't want to think about him and the part of her life that was lacking anymore. She sighed, shifting her thoughts back to her mother. It was her mom who had insisted that Tory go to the conference. In fact, Alice was staying at the house while Tory was away to look after the kids and, likely, the cleaning. Alice didn't like the way Tory kept house. She probably already had the vacuum cleaner out and was bossing everyone around. The thought of John having to deal with his strong-willed mother-in-law actually made Tory smile.

The flight attendant came by to offer another drink, which she declined, nudging Tory out of her worries. She didn't want them to taint her short time away. She needed these four days to gain some perspective, to remember how normal people lived, and maybe have a little fun.

She glanced around and considered making an attempt at being sociable, even though what she really wanted to do was take a nap. She was exhausted most of the time. Stress probably had a great deal to do with it.

Beside her, Joe was watching a movie, his headset in place. He seemed engrossed in what was happening on the screen, so she just waved at him. He was a senior buyer and worked across town in another hospital. She found him enthusiastic about his job and a good influence on her employees. Two of them were sitting one row in front of them. Deb and Kal were also fairly new to procurement and got along well. They worked in Tory's department and needed the education points, as she did. She leaned forward, engaged in casual conversation briefly, and then sat back to look out at the fluffy clouds.

Soon she was deep into the same erotic dream that she had been having nightly. Some of the scenes had familiar themes, clearly fueled by the graphic romance books she devoured. The explicit scenarios revolved around a large man who invited her to play through touch.

His big hands caressed her with care at times; at other times, he was rough. He aroused her as though he knew her intimately, switching it up and performing surprising acts, some of which—like shaving her legs or washing her underwear—should have made her uncomfortable, but didn't.

This lover was unconcerned about his own pleasure, and Tory basked in the novelty of being cared for and cherished. He made her remember what it was like to feel sexy. The way he looked at her body and expressed his desire made her warm all over. He pleasured her for a long time, making her toes curl and her breasts tingle.

The loudspeaker announcement awakened her. She found herself using the shoulder of the stranger next to her as a pillow and sat up, ignoring his slight smirk. Wiping the drool from her mouth, she noticed her erect nipples poking through her bra. She crossed her arms, hoping no one had noticed, and raised her seat in preparation for the descent. Joe teased her that she had been snoring. All she remembered was the dream.

They landed at the San Antonio International Airport and were whisked away to their lodgings. Tory's colleagues had opted for the high-priced Hilton on the River Walk; Tory had chosen a more modest La Quinta some distance from the San Antonio Convention Center. They all planned to meet for dinner at a restaurant.

She was not disappointed in her accommodations. The setting had a Mexican flavor, and the décor was rustic. There were two levels of rooms in four blocks, adjacent to each other. Hers was on the ground floor and faced the pool. A large, wide window let in the bright light, and she had a clear view of the entire resort even with the wrought-iron bars in place.

Tory checked out all the room's features, put on her running gear, and started off on a run. She eventually slowed her pace and explored the area. There were authentic eateries that provided ethnic foods, and she located a trail that led directly to several tourist attractions. A theater and a large museum that showcased artifacts from the Alamo. She stopped at the convention center, registered for the next day's opening activities in order to avoid the morning lineups, and followed the road back to her hotel at a more challenging pace.

In Tory's mind, the conference had officially started, and she was determined to enjoy it. It was great to get in this much-needed exercise without worrying about organizing dinner or any other mundane chore. It would be a good opportunity to live in the moment instead of rushing through activities like she normally did, and she gave herself permission to do so.

CHAPTER 2

Chris Enns had been checking out the pool from his room's window when a beautiful woman passed by and entered the room next to his. It looked like she had just returned from a run; she was wearing fitted jogging shorts, and her face was sleek with sweat. She didn't seem too concerned about her own appearance, which attracted him. Her trim, well-developed body didn't hurt either.

His own body began to heat up instantly, an instinctual response to his close proximity to a female. She was not just any female; she made him remember what it used to be like. It didn't matter that he didn't know her. She had the power to make his blood boil. His cock hardened painfully at the mental image of her, and his sudden urge to lick her made him close his eyes. Shame slammed into him like a freight train. What was he doing, thinking like that again?

For many months, he had been preoccupied with the idea of having a sexual liaison. A no-strings-attached, one-time occurrence with complete, non-negotiable confidentiality. No one could know. Finding a woman who would be willing to do that might help him keep his promise to abstain from women in general.

Later that night, he watched his new neighbor dining with a small group of people at a Mexican restaurant that had been recommended by the concierge. He recognized her immediately and was captivated by how little makeup she wore and by her feminine clothes, which were not too tight or revealing. Not the kind of thing worn to troll for men. She was classy.

He wondered about why she was there and who her friends were. He noticed that she seemed a little too serious. She rarely smiled. Was she sad?

Sitting alone, contemplating his life and the little joy he squeezed from it, he could relate to unhappiness. He lived on the fringe of other people's lives, trying to make a difference. Once in a while, he got to hold someone's child, as if this could make up for what he had to endure. Lately, his life of sacrifice was just not cutting it. He ached to be held and loved for himself rather than being treated with deference. He was only a man, after all.

Later on, back in his room, he heard noises from the next suite— and then there was quiet. Feeling like a voyeur, he moved to the door of his unit. Before he could talk himself out of being reckless, he left the suite and situated himself in the open patio area, hoping for a glimpse of her. Her drapes were closed, so he had to make do with imagining her in the throes of passion. What seemed like hours went by, but he stayed where he was, hoping to see something. He wasn't picky. Any little evidence of activity would be welcomed.

Finally, she emerged, wrapped in a towel, passing him on her way to the small outdoor pool. If she noticed him, she did not let on. Perhaps, he thought, she had been on the phone and was still be preoccupied. Normally, women noticed him. The thought of doing the pursuing was kind of nice though. If she was unattached and he could convince her, she would be perfect.

Chris followed, wanting to catch a glimpse of her body. He stood beyond the gate that opened up onto the pool and took in her graceful movements as she dropped the towel and dove into the deep water. He could make out her strong strokes cutting through the water, even in some of the dimmer areas. She swam laps, back and forth. He wondered about her restless energy. Was she angry? Did she have sleep issues as he did? Did she want a man to distract her?

Her one-piece bathing suit accentuated her form, and her fluid movements made her bottom sway with each stroke. He gazed at her, taking in everything about her: the long brown braid that went down her back, her striking facial features that showed a tenseness, the grace and effortlessness with which she propelled herself from one end of the pool to the other.

If there was no one else around to observe him, why was he so hesitant and uncertain? Why was he making this so difficult for himself? He could walk up to the edge and ask her if the water was warm. Break the ice. Make small talk. Give her an opportunity to notice him. Start something. It could be innocent. He could cough and just wave hello. She wouldn't feel threatened by a stranger who coughed and waved hello from this side of the fence. There were many things that he could have done, but he turned around and went back to his room.

Just as he was about to close his door, he heard someone yell to her that the pool was about to close for the night. He moved to the window to watch her pass by, feeling like an idiot standing there with a hard-on.

After doing several hundred sit-ups, he went to bed and dreamed of this woman. In his dream, he had no problem meeting her and getting her to play. What transpired between them in the water was mind-blowing. Like a nymph, she made him whole and treated him to her body in ways he'd only ever imagined.

The next morning, he was enjoying an early breakfast when he spotted her crossing the street. He left some money on the table and followed her at a distance to the convention center, admiring her long legs. Seated on a low bench in the foyer, she changed from runners to heels. When she stood up and resumed walking, he felt himself give in to temptation.

He had been a legs man before and noted that this had not changed. Her well-shaped legs drew his eyes, looking even better in the spiked heels, but the rounds of her ass were what got to him. Each step she took made one cheek jiggle at a time, and the sight mesmerized him.

He quickly looked around to see if anyone he knew had observed that his eyes had been glued to her buttocks and was relieved to find most of the other men had been checking her out as well. The women were busy talking or with other pursuits.

From the moment he decided to cross the line, he knew there would be no going back. He had to get her to give him what he needed. First, though, he had to find out a little about her. She was busy reading a sign on the communications board where delegates could post items of interest. He walked over and looked at the badge on the lanyard around her neck. They were attending the same conference, and this convinced him that he had been handed an opportunity. He couldn't imagine that fate would be so unkind as to put her in his path for the sole reason of testing his will. In any case, he was about to find out.

As one of the conference committee organizers, he was one of a small army that volunteered every year to help out. The whole business had begun a few years earlier when a friend asked him to lend a hand with stuffing tote bags for a thousand delegates. He had been hooked from that day on. This role gave him complete anonymity. No one knew him. They presumed that he was like them. However, he knew nothing about procurement or supply chain. What he did have thought was access to all the registrants' personal information.

Chris memorized the name on her badge and accessed the conference database on his phone to find out her full name, e-mail address, phone number, and which sessions she had signed up for. For the first time in a very long time, he was going to allow himself to do more than just be tempted. He ignored the niggling warning in his head that he was treading in dangerous territory, that he had invaded her privacy. He expected that he would do much more and much worse than that by the time they were through.

The opening ceremony went off without a hitch, and the morning progressed without a hiccup. When his duties were over for the day, he sat in on a breakout session he knew she would be in. Now that he had a name, Tory Stanton, and knew that she lived in Waterdown, Ontario, he wondered about her life and what kind of person she was.

The session was already in progress, and he sat in an empty chair behind her, positioning his body so the casual observer would think he was captivated by the speaker. Tory's thick brown hair was loose and slightly curled at the ends. He was tempted to grab handfuls of the shiny, rich hair to feel its softness or tug her head into position.

In such close proximity, he could smell her. It wasn't a strong, perfumed odor. Some women's bottled scents brought on instant headaches in him. Rather, it was a subtle mix of vanilla and rose. Taking in deep breaths, he focused only on her.

She wore a short black skirt, and her shapely legs were bare. This close to her, he could make out her hard and stunningly attractive calf muscles. At that moment, she crossed her legs letting one shoe dangle from her toes. Even her foot was sexy. Its deep arch and delicate form suggested that her femininity extended to all parts of her body. Chris couldn't see her chest from his angle, but he knew from his earlier perusal that she would suit him nicely.

He felt a deep longing to touch her, to make contact with any part of her. The urge was so strong that it took all of his will not to brush up against her. His right hand clenched with the effort of controlling his impulses. Gradually, he calmed himself and then sighed—out of relief as well as resignation. This woman was way out of his league, he figured. For one thing, she was married, and that bit of information bothered him a little. Well, more than a little, actually. She belonged to another. He was trying to come to terms with that while hoping that the absence of a band on her finger had some significance. The other worrisome factor was her obvious disinterest in men. She seemed to have no awareness of how she attracted their gaze and engaged every male's attention—with the exception of the younger man who had been part of her dinner group. Chris would have to find out more about him.

He was accustomed to women of all ages voluntarily disclosing all kinds of information to him, sometimes inappropriately coming on to him in not-so-subtle ways that required his finesse in gently fending them off. Over many years, he had learned to read the opposite sex quite well.

Tory was fidgeting a little, and he recognized her movement as boredom mixed with restlessness. A couple of times, she rubbed her neck. Like most people, she probably stored her tension there. The seats were a little uncomfortable; maybe that was part of it.

When she took out her phone and started fiddling with it, he knew what to do. Ignoring any personal ethics or morals, he decided on a course of action. Not wanting to give himself the opportunity to backpedal, he pulled out his own Android phone and typed in her mobile number before taking another full breath. He typed a message and pressed send without stopping to consider the ramifications. He felt the need to appease a side of himself that could no longer be denied. If he wanted her—and he did—then he had to make a move.

He waited.

And then waited some more, rethinking the contents of his text.

Hi, I'm in the same conference as you. Can we chat?

Should he have used other words to express his desire? Perhaps other guys came on to her like that all the time. He should have used a better line.

Then she responded.

Who are you? How'd you get my number?

He jumped. He had almost expected her to ignore his message.

I want to chat with you.

He adjusted his chair a little to get a view of her face so he could see her expressions as they communicated. Now he had every confidence that they would.

So you said. Why?

To get to know you better.

Why?

Why not?

Why me?

Because you're beautiful and sexy and look like you need some company.

She stiffened and looked up toward the speaker before responding.

Okay.

He took this as a good sign.

You look bored.

I am a little.

He's not very good, is he?

I'm smiling.

You call that a smile?

Are you in this room?

Yes.

You're right. It's more of a frown.
Tell me about yourself.
Not much to tell. Do I know you?
What are you doing later?
Tory looked around the room, likely searching for him.
Don't be scared. Just want to talk.
Yeah, well, I do need that.
I'm a good listener.
I meant I *don't* need that.
What do you need?
I'd tell you, but then I'd have to kill you.
He hesitated. Was she just deflecting—or was she really on the verge of sharing something?
LOL. I'll take that chance.
When time passed, he pushed.
Go ahead. Unburden yourself. What do you need?

***

Tory felt a little wicked telling him—at least she presumed it was a man—what she wanted, but she also felt pretty safe since she was only texting. She gave herself permission to step out of character and flirt.
Great sex—without it being anything more.
Anything more?
No repeat. No commitment.
Why not?
It can't happen again.
So this is a one-time offer?
Yes. No. I don't know. If she were going to do this—not that she had any intention of following through—but if she did, what would her answer be? *Yes, definitely.* If it were a one-time thing, she could convince herself that it was just a whim. She might even be able to forgive herself for the misjudgment, over time. After that, indulging in sex with anyone other than her husband would be out of the question. She had taken vows. She was committed to getting through the worst part with him even though there were times when she didn't

want to. That did not give her the right to cheat—at least for now. *Shit!* It was not logical, no matter what spin she put on it.

It would have to be.

What the hell had she just gone and done, texting like she was some kind of tramp? That wasn't who she was. She would never go through with something like that, no matter how badly she wanted to. Besides, the guy who was texting was probably ugly and had bad breath or some other disgusting turnoff. Otherwise, why wouldn't he just introduce himself like a normal person?

She continued to wonder about the guy texting her. *There must be something wrong with him. Maybe he needs dental work? The condition of a man's teeth tells the whole story about his health and his habits.* She shivered, imagining stained, yellow teeth and all of the bacteria in such a decaying oral cavity. Definitely a deal breaker.

Forget it. Sorry, bye.

Don't go!

Do you have your own teeth?

What does that have to do with anything?

Just answer the question.

I have my own teeth. Three are capped. Why do I feel like a horse at auction?

She grinned. She liked it that he wasn't put off by her direct question and that he had a sense of humor, but she hadn't meant to really share anything personal.

Sorry, just feeling stressed and needing to blow off steam. Not serious. This is embarrassing.

Well, I'm in.

Just like that? Who is this guy? Did it even matter though?

No.

No?

I don't know anything about you. How could I possibly? You know.

Have sex with a stranger?

She couldn't even call it what it was. What must he think of her?

You're probably not my type anyway. Probably bald, fat, and old.

Someone laughed nearby. Tory looked around. Most of the people around her were looking at their phones, so it was impossible to tell who was texting her. Her phone vibrated with another message. He wasn't going to be put off easily.

I am older than you, but I'm not bald or fat. How do you know I'm not your type?

Tory didn't know how to respond.

Why don't you ask me what I look like and what I like in bed?

Is this guy for real?

Why don't I just tell you? I'm a little taller than you, with brown eyes, gray-brown hair, a good body. I've been told I'm easy on the eyes.

She smiled. He did sound cute. But if he was attractive, then why was he hitting on her when there were so many other woman around?

As for what I like in bed … it's been so long for me. I'm trying to remember what I enjoy when I'm with a beautiful woman.

Oh, my! Still, she refrained from texting back.

I like it slow and fast. I like it gentle and hard. I like some edge to it.

She felt the urge to fan herself. *Is it getting hot in here?*

To explain that last part: I like it raw, when a woman hungers for the feel of my skin against hers and presses against me. Or she gets so close it's like we're fused together, knows what she likes and can get herself off, lets herself lose control, maybe scratching my skin in the process. She doesn't mind me pinching her skin, grabbing her ass with enough pressure to let her know I'm in control. She's not too shy to demand that I make it good for her.

Despite herself, Tory was turned on by his texts. How on earth had a (supposedly) good-looking guy with such a way with words ended up without a sex partner on speed dial? Maybe he was married to a woman who didn't find him interesting anymore. Maybe she had something in common with him.

Haven't had sex in a long time.

I can relate.

You want to know why?

Do I need to?

You're right, not important. The speaker is about to wrap up. So? Do you want to get together?

Not sure.

Everyone began clapping for the speaker, shaking Tory out of her conversation.

The next session she had signed up for was down the hall. Making a slight detour to get an iced drink in the main hall, she looked around and pondered who the mysterious texter might be while surreptitiously checking out the men who walked past her.

Someone touched her shoulder, making her jump. It was Joe. "How was the talk?" he asked.

"Not bad," she lied. "Where are you going next?"

Joe answered, but she didn't even hear it. At that moment, a very handsome man went by, nudging her slightly as he moved around her in the crowded hall. When they made eye contact, her pulse sped up. He was fantastic, lean, and tall. His dark eyes were gorgeous, and those lips would make a girl weep.

Stop ogling the men, Tory! she scolded herself.

"See you at dinner later?" Joe said.

"Hmm? Yes."

As Joe departed, Tory's cell phone vibrated. Another message. It was from *him*.

Hey, gorgeous! You looked so sexy standing in the hallway.

She felt a little uneasy. He'd never explained how he'd gotten her number in the first place. Was this his usual routine? But she was past the point of pretending to be scandalized.

Are you stalking me?

Yep.

WTF?

In a good way.

There's a good way?

;)

Have you done this before?

No.

She put away her phone and hurried toward the next session. She didn't really trust a word this guy wrote.

***

He could hardly believe his luck that he was communicating with Tory this way—and that he'd successfully slipped that envelope into the outside pocket of her bag without her noticing. It had been a risky move on his part but surprisingly easy to do. Anyone could have noticed, but luckily no one did.

He wondered what her voice sounded like as he watched her entering the room.

She found a round table and sat between two other women. Probably because she felt exposed and wanted to be cautious. She chatted for a while with the women, and Chris hoped she hadn't been completely creeped out by his admission that he'd been stalking her. Finally, though, she pulled her phone out of her pocket. He texted her immediately.

So are you interested?

Maybe.

How long will it take to decide?

Well, I know one thing about you.

What?

You're not patient.

I am right now.

Oh, really?

Instead of throwing you over my shoulder and carrying you to my room to strip you naked and kiss every inch of your body, I'm sitting here waiting.

She actually lifted her mass of hair and looked like she was uncomfortably warm. *She liked that, did she?* She started typing with one thumb, and Chris noticed that she took her time.

Waiting for what?

For you to be ready.

I might be getting there.

A wave of excitement washed over him, reminding him anew of how desperate he was for her. Was she really starting to be convinced?

He could hardly contain himself. It was like being a kid again on Christmas morning. The anticipation was beginning to make him feel giddy. When had he last felt this way? Hopeful and looking forward to something.

Are you married?

He already knew the answer from looking at her conference info, but the question was a good way to test the waters.

Yes. Are you?

He would have preferred an additional comment to ease his conscience like "We're estranged," or "We're separated," but he realized that he wasn't going to let her marriage vows stand in his way anyhow. It was selfish of him, but he didn't care.

She was watching her screen, waiting for his reply.

In a way.

I get the feeling there's more to that story, but let's not talk about personal stuff.

Works for me.

I have to listen to the presentation now.

When you're done here, check the outside pocket of your bag. Not until after the session!

Tory immediately picked up her satchel and searched the pocket. As she pulled out the envelope, he noticed she was left-handed. Learning about her was his new obsession.

You don't follow directions well!

He watched her face break into a wry smile as she read this. It was beautiful. She put the envelope back in her bag, looked at her phone, and started to tap something into the screen—but stopped and put the phone back down. She did this not once, but twice. He could tell that she'd thought about sending back a message, but decided against it, and he wondered what she was feeling right now.

Thinking about his plan for later made his heart race. He felt undeniably guilty about what he was about to do—but again, he knew there was no way he would let that guilt stop him from doing it.

CHAPTER 3

Tory waited until the session was over to open the envelope. Inside was an embossed card: a certificate for a whole-body massage at the spa of the Hyatt adjoining the conference center. A gift from her unknown admirer—a creepy gift. Still, Tory couldn't remember the last time she had indulged in a massage. And this weekend was supposed to be about taking time for herself, for once. Because of her hectic life, she never had time to do the things she enjoyed, like running. Swimming last night had been nice. But she had been alone. Now it looked like she could have company here, if she wanted it. This man was offering her what she wanted—at least, it looked that way. But something felt off. It all seemed too perfect, coming up at an ideal time, under the right circumstances, with a willing partner who agreed to her terms.

The card bore the spa's location, as well as an appointment date—today—and time. She debated whether to accept the gift or not. The idea of taking advantage of a free hour of relaxation therapy was so tempting. But everything had a price. She tapped the small rectangle of cardboard against her mouth. The fact that a specific appointment time was already booked was a bit worrying. That meant that her admirer knew when she would be at the spa—undressed and vulnerable. Was he planning to hide somewhere in the spa so he could spy on her? Or accost her when she came outside afterward?

Suddenly, the possible risks Tory was imagining didn't seem to matter. In her head, she was already half enjoying the luxury of the pampering, and admittedly, the idea of the man hiding to play peeping Tom—without being seen by anyone in the spa—was far-fetched. If he wanted to accost her, he could probably do it whenever he wanted. He'd clearly been following her all day and somehow knew a lot about her. That still made her uneasy, but not enough to forego the massage. She made a decision and started for the spa before she could talk herself out of it.

The spa was on the ground floor of the adjoining Hyatt, near the indoor pool, and also offered other indulgent services like pedicures and facials. She was led into a treatment room by the young man at the desk and then left alone to prepare. The room was dimly lit, a soft violin-and-harp melody was playing, and there was a scent of cloves mixed with something else. It was appealing, not too strong, and reminded her of Christmas cookies baking in the oven.

She undressed except for her panties and, as instructed, lay down on the table, covered herself with a white cotton sheet, and waited for the masseuse. Flat on her stomach, her face positioned in an open oval cushion, she sank into the padding of the table, willing herself to get into the right mood. To forget about everything and everyone else.

The door opened, and Tory heard the young man enter again.

"Okay, I'm going to give you this eye mask so you can totally relax," he said.

Tory lifted herself, accepted the mask, and slipped it on gratefully. The enforced blindness of the mask would likely help her to relax, she thought as she resettled herself.

"I'll just shut the door," the young man continued.

Tory waited and tried not to feel self-conscious. She was accustomed to having female masseuses and had been secretly hoping the young man wasn't going to be her masseuse. *But there's nothing to feel embarrassed about. These professionals see skin all the time*, she told herself.

"Do you like this music?" he asked, speaking very softly, now that he was in relaxing masseuse mode, she guessed.

"Yes, it's fine."

The masseuse gently moved her arms, which had been glued to her sides, away from her body. Tory felt the sheet shift, and she tucked the sides underneath her chest before replacing her arms.

"Leave your arms like that," he directed her quietly. "Are you comfortable?"

"Yes."

He began working on her neck, and then he worked down her shoulders and upper arms, where she harbored a lot of stiffness. The oil and heat of his hands transferred warmth and languid energy to her muscles. She gave in to the sensation, and her whole body appreciated the attention. Tension slid away from her body.

Folding the sheet down from her back, he moved along her spine, and she groaned—it felt that good. *Who cares what he sees?*

After a while, the masseuse asked her to roll over. Tory didn't want to seem like a prude, but she covered her breasts with her hands as she shifted onto her back.

The man knew his stuff. He gently moved her hair aside, cradled her head for a few moments, and then pulled on the base of her skull. Tory sighed as he rubbed circles under her jaw. She was getting sleepy. She'd had precious little the night before.

She awoke sometime later. His hands were on her right thigh, working the muscles deeply. Her legs were fully exposed; the blanket was no longer tucked into her underwear. Even though her panties were still on—of course!—it felt odd to feel his fingers so close to her groin. Her lower body tensed a little at the thought.

"Relax your leg," he said softly, almost in a whisper.

She tried to, she really did, but her body didn't cooperate. It was like the impossible task of trying to relax her tongue when she was in the dentist's chair. She became aware that moisture had gathered at her perineum and dampened the thin piece of fabric between her legs. How long had she been soaked?

He started working her calves, and then he cradled her foot and applied pressure to her instep. Tory moaned in gratitude. It was like he knew her body better than she did. She suddenly felt silly.

"Sorry! That feels great. You're really good at this. You must get that kind of reaction all the time."

"I'm glad you're enjoying it."

When he targeted certain areas on the balls of her feet, she felt a slow burn in her pelvic area. She was being turned on big time, and she worried that she might be reduced to propositioning the guy if he stopped. Or she might climax right here on the table. Her lower body began to squirm the way it did when she was aroused. It was embarrassing that even an innocent massage therapist was not safe from her selfishness and craving for male attention. She was glad to have the mask; it prevented the chance of any eye contact.

She didn't need to worry any longer though; time was up. Still speaking softly, barely above a whisper, the masseuse asked her to take a deep breath and then release it slowly. Before leaving the room, he cautioned her to take a few seconds before sitting up to avoid dizziness and then to drink some water.

Tory showered and got dressed, taking her time. Out front, she thanked the young man and started to reach into her bag so she could leave a tip, but he refused it. Perhaps her arousal had been too obvious and had embarrassed him. On the other hand, she figured, it might just be hotel policy to refuse tips.

She floated back to the La Quinta, feeling limber and relaxed. She would have to make time for this type of therapy when she got home. It was the next best thing to sex. And for the first time, she would request a male masseuse. She had really liked having such strong hands working on her. The pressure exerted by those long male fingers had covered more of her skin and applied the right type of force where required. It felt almost sinful to let a complete stranger manipulate and stretch her willing body. She grinned, feeling younger and more carefree than she had expected one massage to make her. It had been years since she'd felt so good!

Later on, she bought a bag of potato chips from the hotel's convenience store. It would be a while until dinner. On her way back to her room, she saw the best-looking male specimen she'd seen in a while exiting the pool area. He was some distance ahead, and she sped up a little to get a better view. He could have been anywhere between forty and sixty years old, but he looked amazing. It was really unfair how men could look so good as they got older.

She tried convincing herself that she was not really following this gorgeous man in bathing trunks since they were both taking the same route. However, her steps slowed as she got close enough to make out the muscles of his legs contracting as he walked. She perused his other attributes: wide shoulders, a tapered waist, big hands and feet.

Pure maleness oozed from him and made her tummy feel like she was famished.

Trying to appease her hunger, she imagined the novelty of being with him. She must be rapidly losing restraint; she was trailing a man and lusting after his body. The saliva in her mouth increased at the thought of licking him.

He turned slightly toward her. A baseball cap and sunglasses obscured his face, but she noticed the light peppering of dark hair on his chest. Her hands itched to feel its coarseness against her palms. Imagining the differences in their skin textures, his hardness, made her heart race.

She couldn't even properly see what he looked like, but Tory was half mad with desire. The hope of feeling him against her drew her like a magnet. She wanted to offer him free use of her body, to allow him liberties of the basest kind. The prospect of getting down and dirty with someone she didn't know and who knew nothing about her was both shameful and alluring.

What the hell was wrong with her? It must be the effects of her dry spell combined with the naughty texts from earlier and the wonderful massage, which reminded her to text her admirer and thank him.

The man she was following stopped at the door of his room. It was the one next to hers. What a coincidence. After he went inside, she had the urge to knock on his door and make an indecent proposal, the kind of daring act of a woman with nothing to lose. Her pride was crumbling in the face of her longing, all due to the fact that a man who could undoubtedly satiate her sexual appetite was so near.

It was not easy, but before she could do anything stupid, she struggled to get control of herself and nearly ran the short distance to her suite. She had been so close to abandoning all sense of dignity. She shook—not with relief, but fear. Her traitorous body and mind were conspiring against her.

Locking the door and leaning against it for support, she willed herself to regain some composure. It was insane, the way she was behaving around some random guy. She had to get a grip and stop letting her hormones lead her around like she was on the prowl. And that included sexting anonymous conference attendees. *Is this what happens to women of a certain age who don't have an outlet?*

Pushing away from the door, she turned on some music and crawled onto the bed. Picturing her neighbor's body, she pleasured herself, the bag of chips forgotten on the floor.

***

Tory picked up her phone and promptly put it back down again. There had not been any further text messages from her admirer or any messages from John. Not that she expected any. Gone were those simple gestures that reminded you that someone cared. She blamed herself for some of the discord between her and her husband. Unwilling to let him get away with the way he treated them anymore made her retreat into herself and ignore him most days or confront him, which usually resulted in a fight. It was easier sometimes to pretend he wasn't nearby. After a while, they just stopped talking to each other.

Heaven knew she and the kids didn't need any more drama in their lives, so it worked for them. Although you wouldn't know it by the way Samantha was behaving.

Her call home last evening had lasted longer than expected and left her feeling stressed to the extent that she had to go to the pool to swim away the tension. Tonight, she would take a few minutes to brace herself for the call.

Last night's conversation replayed in her head. It had started with Tory's mother reminding Tory to remember what it was like to be eighteen. As if that would soften the impact of the news she'd just delivered: Samantha had come home in a police cruiser. Her daughter had been part of a group that had gone skinny-dipping in a man-made lake that used to be a quarry, and they had been drinking alcohol. That wasn't such a big deal, but the fight that had broken out between some of her friends that led to the 911 call was.

Thinking back, Tory tried to gauge whether she had conveyed the right measure of fairness and compassion, along with authority, as was expected of a temporarily absent parental figure. She had known there was no way she could count on John to address it, so it was up to her to get more details, make sense of it all, and dole out whatever punishment was required. Her husband, when he was around, never wanted to be the bad guy, so the task always fell to her. He probably had no idea that Sam had been delivered home in a cruiser in the first place.

And so her mother had put Samantha on the phone.

"Mom?"

"Hi, honey. Are you okay?"

"Yeah …"

"Tell me what happened."

"Didn't Nana tell you?"

"She gave me a quick rundown, but it's important that you tell me." A big sigh. "We were just having fun."

She paused, so Tory had urged her on, careful to maintain a non-accusatory tone. "Doing what?"

"What do you mean?"

"I mean, how were you having fun? Were you swimming?"

"No. It was too cold to stay in for long. We built a little fire, and other people showed up."

Tory waited patiently for about thirty seconds before speaking again. "Were you drinking?"

"Everybody was."

"Okay, but you're underage, and you agreed you'd only ever drink alcohol in our home. Did you have a lot to drink?"

"No. Not like the others. I think that's why Officer Stein drove me home, instead of … well, whatever the other kids had to go through."

Officer Stein lived in their neighborhood. Samantha had babysat his daughter on a few occasions. Tory felt a little better hearing he had been there—and that her child had not been inebriated. However, they still had more to get through. Sam had been lucky not to get arrested, but that didn't mean that her activities were sanctioned. Something else had occurred; otherwise, Alice wouldn't have been so upset.

"Nana tells me that you were wearing a borrowed shirt and nothing else."

"I couldn't find my clothes. People started panicking and were running every which way. Pete gave me his T-shirt. It's so big that it almost reached my knees, so you don't have to worry that I scandalized Officer Stein."

"I'm not concerned about Officer Stein. I'm only looking out for you. There was a fight?"

"It started with two guys I know. Then it got out of control."

"Do you know why it started?"

Another sigh. "Yeah, but it's stupid."

"Tell me anyway."

"I went with a group because ... there's no one right now." Tory knew this about her daughter. Sam never dated the same guy for long. In fact, Tory never saw her daughter with the same boy more than once. In fact having a "reputation" was a nonissue for Sam because "everyone does it." This was not the time to bring that up though. "Anyway, Mike—he's at Queens now and wasn't happy about what Gabe was doing."

Tory had no idea who Gabe or Mike were, and that was not comforting. When had Sam stopped bringing her friends around? "Have I met him, them?"

"No."

"So what happened?"

"I'll need to go into my room now."

Tory closed her eyes. If her daughter needed privacy for this next part, it was going to be bad news. She worried that Sam was being reckless with herself. No matter how many times they discussed safe sex and the risks, Tory felt that the message still wasn't getting through. Kids that age felt immune to transmitted diseases and pregnancy.

"Mom?"

"I'm still here."

"Promise me you won't go off the deep end."

Tory grinned in spite of it all. "I promise."

"I was coming out of the water, and Gabe pulled me over to this outcrop with a couple of trees. It was kind of hidden, but Mike must have noticed where we were headed. And then he went ballistic when he found us."

"Why?"

"Uh ... so Gabe tied me to a tree with his belt ... it was kind of a joke ... and we were ... we were ..."

"Having sex?"

"Yes."

The pause had seemed to go on forever. Tory waited for her daughter to continue, wondering what was going on. They had been communicating better and the acting out had lessened. How had Alice managed not to lose her mind when Tory behaved badly?

Tory was worried about so many things, but Sam's wild side was incredibly difficult to address. It was like she intentionally went out of her way to make Tory upset by ignoring all the warning signs.

Finally, she continued. "Thanks for being okay about it. You always said that I could talk to you about anything."

This was true, although there was a lot Tory would want to discuss with Sam when she got home. She stayed silent, waiting for her daughter to continue.

"So ... we were going at it, until Mike threw a fit and pulled Gabe off me. They started fighting, and other people came to see what was going on. I was still tied to the tree, with nothing on, feeling dumb. A few of my friends came over to get me loose, and about then was when the police came. I don't know who called them."

It took a while to get all the facts. As a younger girl, you couldn't have kept Samantha quiet. Everyone around her knew her every thought and all the details of the lengthy stories she made up. John had never had the patience to just listen, so Tory had sat through all of Sam's descriptive narratives. She believed that listening was the most important part of communication, especially with her children.

Since Sam had turned eighteen, though, Tory had had to draw out every little bit of information she got from her daughter. Sam kept it all to herself unless she was prodded.

Tory had been a little worried to hear about Sam having been restrained during sex. Presuming it had been consensual, she still might have been upset by the rough treatment. Or had she done this before? In any case, the time for trying to open up that line of questioning was later, when they were face to face. Instead she asked, "So … you're really okay?"

"Aside from being a little embarrassed 'cause it took a while to get me off the tree, I'll live."

"No injuries or anything?"

"I don't think so. I didn't check yet. Nothing hurts. They wanted me to go get checked out at the hospital, but Nana let me decide not to. I'm pretty sure I'm fine, but I'll tell you if there's anything."

"Use some aloe if you've got any burns or scrapes."

"Okay."

"Honey?"

"Yeah?"

"I love you."

"I love you, too. So … am I in trouble?"

Tory tried hard to understand her daughter and keep their bond strong. She wanted them to have the kind of relationship that she shared with her own mother. It was important to always be honest.

"No. I was really worried that you might have gotten yourself into trouble. That's all. Look, we'll talk more about everything when I get back, but …" Alice's words when Tory had been a teenager came back to her, so she used them. "I know you're at a time in your life when you're experimenting with sex. Just please remember to take things slow and don't take too big a risk with anyone."

"I know all about protection—"

"I know you do, but that's not all I'm talking about. When I was your age, I dated a lot. Nana doesn't know the half of it. Well, maybe she does."

They both laughed because they both understood how smart Alice really was. Not much got past her.

"Seriously, sweetie, I know how it is. Most young guys don't know that much—they think they do, but they don't. Older men may have experience, but you need to be able to trust that they won't hurt you. And trust takes time to foster. Do you know what I mean?"

"Yeah, I do. You want me to be careful and make sure I'm comfortable with my partner. I will. I know I'm young, but I won't be stupid."

Tory spent the rest of the evening trying to come to terms with the fact that her daughter was so similar to herself at that age. It only made her worry more.

Tonight's call was to check in on the whole family and find out how Sam was doing. Alice answered after the third ring.

"Hi, Mom!"

"Hello, sweetheart!"

"Any new drama at the Stanton residence today?"

Her mother laughed, but neither of them was fooled by the lighthearted tone.

"Everything's fine. We're all good. Don't worry."

"It's my job to worry. Didn't you tell me that a long time ago?"

"I know. It's a mother's lot to fret about things. I did the same. But really, everything's fine. Hey, Sam got a job today. She starts tomorrow. I'll let her tell you about it."

For a while, Tory had been trying to persuade her eldest to find some part-time employment, but it had been met with resistance. What was with the change of attitude?

"What's John been up to?" If he was upset about Sam coming home in a cop car last night, he had yet to let her know. If she had to guess, she would say that no one had told him about the incident, and if they connected, it was only right that he know.

"I haven't seen him since early this morning. He said he was going fishing."

That didn't sound right. The man hated those kinds of activities. Besides, she couldn't imagine him expending that kind of energy. Ultimately, she didn't care what he did, and she let it go.

"If he comes home at a reasonable time, can you ask him to call me?"

"Sure, honey."

"And Jakie? What's he been up to?"

"He's out back, finishing up the lawns. He's such a good boy, that one."

"Yes, he is." Tory often wondered what she had done to deserve a son who could be counted on to complete his assigned chores. He was helping her keep the outside of the house maintained and doing most of the yard work, something she disliked anyway.

"Are you spoiling them with your cooking?"

Alice laughed. "Just making the kids' favorites. That husband of yours can fend for himself."

Alice had never been openly antagonistic toward John, but it was no big secret that they didn't like each other. And after so many years, there was no sense in Tory dredging up any of the defenses for him she had used to spout. Instead, she switched topics. "Does Sam still seem all right?"

"Yes. She's fine, honey. Some guy sent her flowers this morning, and it made her grin. Has she gotten any before?"

"At graduation, I think, or was it her formal? I can't recall. At least once, anyway."

"She said that she sent you an e-mail."

"Oh, I didn't see it. I'll check when we're done. How are things with you?"

"Just fine. I have a date to look forward to after you get back."

"You do? Anyone I know?"

"Not sure. Do you know the Forrester boys?"

"No."

"Well, they're twins. We're going to the movies."

Had she had heard her mother correctly? "You're going out with both of them?"

Alice's laughter was so loud Tory pulled the phone away from her ear.

Tory continued to smile for a long time after the call was over.

CHAPTER 4

Back from the pool, Chris still felt like a caged animal, restless and uncomfortable in his own skin. He was behaving like a lunatic. Risking a young man's job by convincing him that he knew Tory, invading a woman's privacy, and willing to go to extremes to get close to her was beyond nuts. This wasn't like him at all.

He couldn't understand what had come over him to pursue her like this. He didn't even jaywalk for heaven's sake. Yet in the space of a few hours, he was corrupting an innocent person. His behavior was inexcusable, yet he felt driven.

The part of him that wanted to taste a woman—not just any woman, but the one he'd had his hands on that very day—roared. He was so agitated that it was impossible even to sit down. He continued to prowl the confines of the room.

Television held no appeal. He found himself repeatedly walking over to look out the windows. Needing sexual release while he was alone had never bothered him before. He knew the intensity of his yearning now had to do with this particular woman. From the moment he'd first seen Tory, she had occupied his thoughts. Then, this afternoon, after he'd touched and smelled her body, she had affected him even more.

It was unhealthy, this attraction to a woman he had yet to properly meet. God, what he wanted to do to her. During their text exchange, he had sensed that she was pulling away. Suddenly panicked that she would slip through his grasp and he would never have her, he had thought up the massage idea. He had found the young man performing massages at the spa that day and offered him a ridiculous sum of money to let Chris step in. He made up a story about him and Tory already being lovers with a kinky side who often played out this massage scenario, and the young man agreed reluctantly. Chris couldn't be sure if the man had really believed it, but the story had at least encouraged him to accept the bribe. Even after it had been settled, Chris hadn't been sure Tory would even show up. She might be suspicious of the pre-booked appointment, after all. But no, she had miraculously shown up and unwittingly put her delectable body in his hands.

Remembering the massage was a mixture of arousal and self-disgust at what he'd done. It scared him that he had so thoroughly allowed this reckless side to overrule his morality. What had he been thinking, taking advantage of an unsuspecting female? He had never done anything like that before. No one he knew would ever believe that he could orchestrate and follow through on something so criminal. He could barely believe it himself. What had gotten into him? At the time, it had felt like he had no choice. What if he never got a chance to see her body? But that was no excuse. He was ashamed for having succumbed to his baser urges.

She was like a drug that he could not live without. Just looking at her made him want the things he had been denying himself for over two decades.

Massaging her limbs and perfect form for an hour had been sweet torture. Her skin had the softest texture. Her body responded to his touch. She welcomed him like a flower soaking up water. His senses had been fed by every sound she made, the feel of her skin, her smell, and her blush. She appealed to him at another level as well—one he'd almost forgotten could feed his desire. She was femininity and lushness personified.

He had also enjoyed the fact that she was feeling pleasure from the quiet whimpers and moans, her honest response to his manipulations. It took some effort not to groan along with her as he pressed his rigid penis against the massage table in self-punishment for his inappropriate seduction. At one point during the massage, she had dozed off, and the sheet had slipped away from her lower body. He could see that her panties had gotten moist at the crotch while he'd been rubbing her thighs and feet. The evidence of her desire made his mouth dry with longing to taste what was forbidden.

This captivating creature gave him much fodder for his dreams. He couldn't wait to go to bed, but it was too soon for that. Besides, he had obligations to fill that evening. He was expected to attend the conference's formal dinner and reception.

He wondered whether Tory would be attending. He hoped they might meet properly, like normal people. They would probably hit it off. He could tell she had not been immune to his looks from the way her eyes had flared when he'd passed her in the hallway earlier. But what could he say to her now—after he'd invaded her privacy and touched her like some kind of sexual predator? Would he be able to meet her eyes?

In the shower, he jerked off to images of Tory undulating under him, remembering her slight movements on the massage table. He tried to ignore his guilt and disappointment in himself. He would never do anything like that again. But, he decided, neither would he meekly retreat into the background anymore. The time for that had passed. Somehow, he would make things work with her.

***

Tory scanned the crowd, looking for anyone she recognized, and spotted Joe. She would have liked to stay alone in her cute room and read or take a walk in the neighborhood, but she felt compelled to attend the dinner. She wasn't on vacation, after all. She was supposedly learning and participating as part of her professional development. Besides, the organizers had put a great deal of effort and expense into staging this conference. She owed them a few hours at least.

As Tory made her way to Joe, a tall man caught her eye and smiled politely. He was the good-looking older guy she'd noticed between conference sessions today.

"Hi, I'm Chris." So she now had a name to attach to him.

"Tory. Nice to meet you," she said.

"I'm just networking a little. How are you liking the conference?"

"It's good so far."

"First time?"

"Yes. You?"

"I've been before."

"I should get going. Nice to meet you." She was attempting to move on, and he extended his hand. It would have been rude to refuse, so they shook hands, and a flash of something that felt like electricity skidded up her arm as they made contact. His eyes widened slightly, so she knew that he had felt it as well. It was weird, too much like a scene from a romance novel—exactly the kind she liked to consume— so she giggled.

"It must be static," she said. She attempted to disengage her hand, but he continued to hold on to it. She let him, imagining what it would feel like to be under this man's spell. He maintained eye contact, and the expression on his face was serious, but not troubling. His height and broad shoulders didn't intimidate her either. He was looking at her as though he wanted something.

Not the sort of person who shied from prolonged eye contact, she kept her eyes fixed on his. His pupils dilated, and the dark brown irises seemed to darken, making her breath catch.

She suddenly remembered what it felt like to be the object of a man's interest. It drew out welcomed, almost forgotten feelings of being simultaneously warm and cold. Her arm got goose bumps, and she flushed under his gaze. She hadn't experienced that kind of reaction since she was a teenager. It didn't seem right at her age.

Shivering involuntarily, she pulled away again, this time with more force. His intense heat unnerved her. Something about his presence made her uncomfortable. Well, maybe not uncomfortable, but it challenged her. It was almost as though he were looking inside her head at her secrets and desires. Just the thought of this made the crotch of her panties moisten.

Get a grip! All she'd done since arriving at this conference was lust after strange men! The anonymous texter, the masseuse, the random guy at her hotel, and now this man—for the second time today.

He broke contact just as Kal and Deb approached.

The intensity of that moment had made her feel oddly guilty. She shook it off and introduced her colleagues, amazed that her voice remained steady. Looking for something to say, she asked, "Where did Joe go off to?"

"He's around," Kal said.

Chris told them he was on the conference committee, and the conversation moved on from there. Deb was coming on a little too strong, in Tory's view, but that was none of her business. Chris seemed courteous, perhaps even too much so. But then that thought bothered her a little, and she had to shake her head, feeling like an idiot. She had no right to be possessive. She didn't even know the guy. And she was married.

"Who's Joe?" Chris asked at a pause in the conversation.

Kal explained that Joe was a colleague. Tory wondered briefly why Chris seemed so interested in a man he didn't know but promptly dismissed the thought. What did she care?

He said his good-byes shortly after, and Tory let out a sigh of relief. Spending any more time around that guy might have led to trouble. Years of not having been wanted by a man were making her nuts.

Her phone vibrated, and she took it out, thinking it might be her kids. Instead, it was another text from *him*. After her phone conversation with Alice, she'd told herself that she needed to smarten up and stop texting this stranger. It was time to end the immature flirtation. And it hadn't been the smartest idea to accept the gifted massage, nice though it had been. He was probably some kind of pervert anyway. He'd already admitted to stalking her. Now, though, with her blood racing again, she felt almost pleased that he'd contacted her again despite her text silence.

You look very pretty tonight.

So he was nearby and he was observing her again. Tory felt her cheeks immediately redden.

Thanks for the massage. How much was it? I should pay you back.

You could pay me back in kind. ;)

Did she even want to know what he had in mind? Before she could talk herself out of it, her thumbs typed.

How?

Interested in a little game?

Depends.

So much for not communicating with him anymore.

On what?

Is it naughty or nice?

Where was this coming from?

Both.

Her mouth suddenly became very dry. What the hell was wrong with her? Why was someone she had never met making her feel like this? Like she wanted to be daring and do something totally out there.

Still there?

Explain.

Naughty for you, nice for me. Well, maybe a little naughty for me as well.

Oh God! She couldn't believe it. His words were setting her on fire. She wanted so badly to be naughty. Just once. How did he know that? No! He couldn't possibly know that. What was she doing? It didn't even matter anymore. Her heart was racing, and her mind was a blur. Heaven help her, but she wanted to know what he had in mind.

No one would find out. It would be her secret. Well, hers and whoever was texting her. There was no way that she could pass up this opportunity, could she? There would never be another time—or a better time—to do something totally wicked. Oh, she hoped that it would be at least a little wicked.

This time away was supposed to be all about her. Leaving the pressures of her home life behind for just a few days. Be irresponsible and selfish. The massage had been great! This was just another unexpected bonus. Okay, this was it! She was going to through caution to the wind and have her thrill. Go for the ride on the roller coaster—no matter how nervous she felt.

Before she lost her nerve, she responded:

I'm game.

Go to the washroom. Take off your panties and throw them in the trash.

Tory looked around to see if she could spot who was texting her, but again, most of the people around her were looking at their cell phones.

Her whole body heated up. She was actually contemplating it! His request turned her on, along with the fact that doing things like this was totally out of character for her. What was the worst thing that could happen?

She walked down the main hall to the ladies' room. Inside, she entered a stall and followed his instruction. It was better than she imagined. Following through made her feel alive and so aware of herself as a sexual being. How had she lost that?

Afterward, back in the ballroom, she snatched a glass of wine off a circulating waiter's tray and drained it. The wine was cold and dry and settled her nerves a little. She had to get herself under control, or at least pretend to. The fact that a stranger in the room knew she wasn't wearing panties made her feel bad and excited at the same time!

She threw herself into the spirit of things, grinning widely at a random hot guy nearby. He gave her a double take, the kind of appraisal she'd get when she was closer to her daughter's age.

Ping! She fished her phone back out of her clutch.

Good girl!

How do you know I did it?

Because you're looking guilty and hot. Also, I have your panties in my pocket.

She goggled at her screen in shock.

I don't believe you.

About me having your panties or you looking fine?

Neither

They're black, sheer, and tiny. And the smile you just gave that guy was sensational. Did I mention how much I like the dress, btw?

Tory was wearing a black sheath dress that stopped just above her knees and fit her like a glove. It left a lot more to the imagination than did what some of the other women were wearing. It was elegant and classic—but surely not worthy of such praise.

You don't get out much, do you?

I love knowing you're bare, that we're the only ones in the room who know that, that your pussy is exposed. And you're right. I don't get out at all.

She swooned internally and headed for her assigned table. Maybe he was just weird and needed this as much as she did, but the truth was that nothing this exciting had ever happened to her before today. She decided that she would continue the game for as long as she could tonight.

When dinner was served, the handsome man, Chris, just happened to slip into the chair to her right. Her admirer's texts had already made her giddy, but having a man that sexy by her side was too much to handle.

She conversed with the people at the table whom she didn't know. She checked her phone intermittently for new texts. Anything to get her mind off Chris.

He was sitting so close, although not nearly close enough for what her libido urged her to do. He was way too distracting. His left hand rested on the table within mere centimeters of hers. Then it moved and almost touched her. She could actually feel his heat; he was positively sizzling.

Could he be as aware of me as I am of him? The energy that flowed between them—in her mind, at least—felt like he was caressing her. On the arm closest to him, her hair stood up straight, and her skin erupted in goose bumps; she was overly stimulated. It was ludicrous, this feeling of illicit attraction and expectancy.

She was just staring at his large hands—trying unsuccessfully to pull her gaze away from the long fingers and the broadness of his palms, wondering what they might feel like on her skin—when he bent to retrieve his napkin, which had fallen on the floor between them. His arm grazed her calf, and she jumped from that slight contact alone. The man was that potent. Well, it was that and the fact that she wasn't wearing any underwear.

Tory barely perceived what was served for dinner, how it tasted, or what her tablemates were discussing in the hour or more she sat in Chris's presence. She was hyperaware of him; he invaded her personal space and her thoughts. The worst of it was that probably none of this registered for him. No doubt the attraction was a one-way street; she was the only one affected.

He looked so cool and put together, like a man about town enjoying an evening out. He probably socialized all the time; he appeared so comfortable in the midst of a group of people he didn't know and was able to contribute to almost any topic. She felt inept and gauche, unable to think of anything intelligent to add to the conversation. He refilled her glass a couple of times—though he also treated others to that same attention over the course of the meal. Mr. Social conversed with everyone, oblivious to her desire.

She drank alcohol only rarely, especially since she'd had the kids. Between the pre-dinner wine and the wine with the meal, she became quite tipsy and not quite herself.

Chris leaned in after having ignored her for a good fifteen minutes. "Having fun?"

"What? Oh, yes."

"Drink some water," he commanded. When she ignored him, he repeated the directive. The way he spoke to her turned her on while also pissing her off. Where did he get off, telling her what to do? She pressed her side into him and whispered, "Chris, don't take this the wrong way—oh, fuck it, take it however you want! Did you just give me an order?"

His intoxicating cologne and the heat that radiated off him scrambled her thoughts—she was so close to him. She leaned away and watched his sexy lips as he said, "I know you can take direction well." *What does he mean by that?* Not missing a beat, he moved closer to her. "Be careful," he murmured. "You're playing with fire."

Looking into his eyes, she felt it then: he wanted her. She heard herself say, "What if I don't care?"

He placed his napkin on his plate and stood up. "Excuse us," he said to the others. Tory felt her chair being pulled back from the table and was mortified to see Deb's mouth open in shock. "Tory needs to get some air," he said, lifting her by the arm. Tory tried to resist, but his grip on her arm was firm.

When she rose unsteadily to her feet, the room swam before her. She was suddenly aware that she felt extremely hot. She couldn't help feeling grateful he had hold of her, although she was indignant at being treated like a drunken teenager. "The only reason I'm coming with you," she muttered as he ushered her away, "is because we have witnesses should anything happen."

"You can delude yourself all you want. You're leaving with me because I'm seeing to it. And nothing is going to happen."

So he doesn't have sex on his mind? His resolute comment confused her intoxicated mind. She could have sworn he was interested in her a moment ago, from the look in his eyes. "Why not? Am I not attractive enough?" What was coming out of her mouth?

He glanced at her with an incredulous look. "Don't be ridiculous. You're one of the most beautiful women I've ever met."

"But not enough to want to screw?"

He let go of her and stopped walking. Suddenly unsupported, she stumbled dizzily on her high heels, nearly falling. His strong arm gripped hers once more. The look on his face was fierce and unhappy. "I don't fool around with inebriated women."

"So where are we going then?"

"I'm taking you to your room."

"I'm not staying at the Hyatt."

"I know. I'm in the room next to yours at the La Quinta."

Her mind struggled to grasp what he was saying. Was Chris the same guy in the trunks with the great body? Maybe that was her other neighbor.

After that, all that registered in Tory's intoxicated state were glimpses of sensation and thought. His hand on her shoulder as he helped her into a cab, guided her into her room. The tingles running down her back as he slowly unzipped her dress. Longing for him to trail kisses along her spine. Wondering what he was thinking when he saw that she was mostly naked underneath—no panties or slip. Hoping that he liked what was revealed.

And all the while, there was a lot of talking—all by her, although she had almost no awareness of what she was saying. Chris said little, if anything, in reply. While she babbled on, he gently, yet firmly made her drink some water and swallow some Advil—taking medication from someone she didn't know? She should know better—and then put her to bed.

Before drifting off to sleep, she thought that she might have begged him to screw her. God, how could she speak that way to a total stranger? No matter how good he looked or smelled. Disjointed phrases circled in her head:

"Please … I need it!"

"Sorry. Not tonight."

"Can't you pretend that I'm not drunk?"

"No. You just rest."

"I haven't been properly fucked in a while."

"Again, I can't."

Was that a troubled look on his face that she caught as he ignored her request? Perhaps it was just her vivid imagination. She certainly relied heavily on it when she self-pleasured at night beside her slumbering husband. This had to be a personal low, she thought just before the world faded to black. Begging for it. Some women stood on street corners and charged for sex, but she couldn't give it away.

***

Incredibly, he managed to get her safely tucked into bed for the night and then lay down beside her, fully clothed, keeping his hands to himself. Tory had demanded that he help remove her clothes, and he had only complied when she started trying to unzip herself in the back, losing her balance so that he was afraid she'd fall over. She'd tried to remove his clothes too, though not successfully.

He remained awake while she softly snored. He was set on watching over her in case she got sick or had trouble breathing. She clearly wasn't a frequent drinker, and he felt responsible for having filled her wineglass so many times. And he was ashamed for having sent those texts, for making her do things she hadn't signed up for, for creating a scenario that had culminated with her drunk and needing sexual relief, exposing her vulnerable side to him, brazenly propositioning him. It had taken every last bit of his will not to give in.

Memories of his sister and how she had been taken advantage of as a young girl had helped him control his actions. But when Tory had said in slurred tones that she wanted to suck on his penis and that she gave good head, he had literally broken out in a sweat. It had been touch and go for a while as to whether he'd be able to maintain control of himself.

This had to be his penance, knowing he could look but not touch as he removed her dress and thigh-high stockings. Her breasts fell out of her bra as she removed it, and their pendulous shape beckoned him to taste her nipples, which were deep red and erect, evidence of her arousal. His hands itched to fondle her hips, her ass, and her shapely legs. They remembered how impossibly soft her skin had felt when he'd massaged her.

Everything about her appealed to him. For hours, he lay by her side, thinking about everything he had done and regretted, and about the fact that she was completely nude under the sheets. This made him stay hard for the entire night. He couldn't remember it ever being that bad—even when he was a teenager.

Abstaining from one of life's greatest pleasures, making love to a woman, was unnatural. He had denied himself that pleasure for so long that his desires had wreaked havoc on his common sense. And he had taken out that frustration on Tory.

When the sun came up eventually, he rubbed his face with both hands, tired and weary. His internal debate for the last few hours had made him determined to try to make things right. It was time to take responsibility for his actions and to stop wavering.

In the light of the day, she was so beautiful. Her eyelashes feathered over her creamy cheeks, and her plump lips were begging to be kissed. She had tossed around frequently during the night. Her preferred sleeping pose was on her back, but he'd kept rolling her onto her side so she wouldn't have any breathing problems. Several times, her movements had dislodged the bedspread, and he'd had to cover up her exposed breasts or other tantalizing bits.

He was glad that he had stayed with her, despite the toll on him, but it was time to go. She appeared to be fine. He made sure she was firmly on her side before leaving. He had to get away from her, even if only for a few minutes, to get his head clear for what was to come.

He knew that he had to come clean about everything he'd done, and he was afraid it would ruin everything. It was a gamble, knowing he might lose his chance with Tory, but he had no other option that was right. Now, all he had to do was figure out how to break it to her.

CHAPTER 5

Tory awakened to the sound of ringing. Groaning, she opened one eye and briefly struggled to sit up. A pillow wedged under her back made this a more difficult task. She reached for the in-room phone, picked up the receiver, and croaked, "Hello?"

"Geez, Tory, it's about time you answered! Kal's been texting you ever since you left, and Deb wants to talk to you. Are you okay? You really tied one on last night."

Tory's head was splitting, and she struggled to remember any of the night before. Memories of the dinner surfaced. Chris had been sitting next to her, and then ... he had been here with her, in this room! She remembered talking a lot. And getting undressed. His hands on her back, shoulders, and legs. Pulling down the zipper on the back of her dress, slipping it off, drawing her closer to the bed.

No, she must have dreamt it. She would never do anything like that, like letting a complete stranger come into her room and handle her that way. None of that had happened. It couldn't have.

"Tory?"

"Yeah, Joe?"

"When you didn't join us for breakfast at our motel like we talked about, I figured I'd try again to check on you."

She looked around the room, recalling a little more of the dream: the moonlight highlighting the planes of his face, the firm yet gentle pressure of his hands. God, his hands! The light on her room phone blinked, which meant that there was at least one missed call. "Um ... I guess I didn't hear the phone. I was sleeping."

"I've never seen you drink like that before," Joe said.

"Yeah, I don't usually." She wanted nothing more than to get back under the covers and ignore the world. When was the last time that she had overindulged like that? It seemed like forever.

"You sound awful."

She felt groggy and dehydrated, but it wasn't the worst hangover she'd ever had. "Yep."

"Well, take it easy. Okay … the first session is about to start. See you when you get here."

She hung up just as the door of her room opened. For a couple of seconds, she became a little panicked about some random guy gaining access. After she realized who it was, her mouth fell open—a gorgeous hunk was entering her room. It was the man himself, Chris, holding cups of coffee and a white paper bag. So it hadn't all been a dream. His dark hair was wet, and he smelled like soap. He was every woman's fantasy, but then he had to ruin it by speaking.

"You're awake, I see. Stay in bed." There was that forceful tone again. It grated on her nerves, and his voice sounded too loud. That kind of arrogance rubbed her the wrong way. Last night—whatever happened—had all started with him ordering her around like that. Who did he think he was?

"Stop telling me what to do. You're not my father," she muttered, pulling the covers up and closing her eyes in misery. More was coming back to her. The interminable meal pretending she wasn't affected by his physical presence, all the wine, leaving with this man—and in front of her colleagues! "How did you get in here?"

"I used your key."

Just what she feared. Her face heated up. "So you brought me back here."

"You don't remember anything?"

"Some. You were in here, right?"

"Don't be ashamed."

She took a deep breath, thinking that she probably had a great deal to be ashamed about.

"Come and eat something," he said, putting the coffee and bag down on the small table.

"I'm not hungry."

"How about some juice?"

"I'm not dressed."

"Believe me, I know. But that doesn't have anything to do with juice. Do you ever just do as you're asked?"

Arrogant bastard! Strutting into her room like he had a right to be there. Maybe they'd had sex, which made him feel like he could tell her what to do. She sat up angrily, for a moment forgetting that she was naked. But she grabbed the blanket before her breasts were entirely exposed. "Look, what exactly—"

"I undressed you."

"I gathered that. But did we? Did you?"

"If you're asking whether I stayed the night, yes, I did. Just to make sure you were okay. If you're asking whether we indulged in anything more, the answer is no."

"Thank God," she said. She was flooded with such a strong sense of relief over both not having forgotten about a sexual liaison and not having cheated on her husband that she fell back against the pillows. Who was she to give advice to her own daughter when this was how she behaved? Her gut began to make a gurgling noise, which she attributed to a combination of things. Guilt, alcohol, and anxiety.

"God had very little to do with it," he retorted.

"Did I embarrass myself?" A memory of something tugged at her. Had she propositioned him?

He tilted his head, thinking. "You were hard to resist—and not just because of your words."

His cryptic response didn't make her feel any better. And the memory surfaced: she had actually unfastened his belt and offered him a blowjob. What else had she done?

"I'm sorry," she said. "This year has been tough. Honestly—"

"Yes?"

"Ever since I hit forty, my hormones have been in control. It's like sex is all I crave these days." Maybe it was the hangover that was making her so candid. She had to get up. Suddenly, nausea and the general feeling like she was about to vomit propelled her to the bathroom. She tucked the sheet around her as she went.

In the relative privacy of the small room, she emptied the contents of her stomach, which made her head hurt about ten times worse. When she was done and came out, he was still sitting by the small table.

"Tell me about it," he said, nodding.

"What?"

"You were telling me about your cravings."

"Oh. I'm not sure why I said all that. Look, please … don't feel you have to stay. If I'm keeping you from anything —"

"Nothing that's more important than this."

Tory wasn't sure what he meant by that. She didn't have the energy, at present, to analyze his personality, but he did seem to be understanding. It was nice to feel listened to, considering everything that was going on in her life.

As though he'd picked up on her thoughts, he added, "If you need to unload, you should know I'm a good listener."

She got back into bed and closed her eyes. "So what did I say last night?"

"A lot of things."

"Do I have to guess?"

"You told me your teenage daughter is messing around with boys you're not keen on or haven't even met. Something about being tied to a tree, but I couldn't make out much of that. Also, your husband is sick and can't perform his … marital duties. Your son constantly washes his sheets, and for some reason, that makes you wonder if he's gay. Your girlfriends are all divorced and telling you about their dates and escapades. And you're having *vivid* sex dreams. You actually shared a couple of them."

She groaned. "Kill me now!"

"So I thought we'd spend time together today."

"What?"

He got some mugs from the sideboard and started to pour out the coffee.

"To get to know each other. We'll just hang together, like the kids say."

"I don't think so."

"Why not? I'm good company."

"I ... don't want company."

"I don't believe that. I'm pretty sure you want it."

Is he talking about sex? What did it say about her that, despite having dodged a bullet last night, she was sort of open to the idea? "One question."

"Shoot."

"If I had been sober last night, would you have wanted to?"

He stilled from pouring, and his eyes got very black. She could see them clearly as he approached and handed her a mug. "To play? Yes, I would have."

Her face suffused with heat, and he grinned.

"If you knew me, then you'd know that admission is momentous," he said as he poured himself a mug of coffee. "I don't share intimacies with women."

"Men, then?"

"No."

Tory sipped the hot beverage, and Chris sat down by the table as though he had all the time in the world.

"So what's in this for you? Why are you here?" she asked. She needed to know where it all was heading.

"I'm not sure. I know that's a vague answer, but it's the best I can do. There's something about you. I mean, you're cute and everything— even with morning breath. But there's something more than that."

She had to grin.

"I haven't been with a woman for a very long time, and you appeal to me in so many ways."

"Even though I'm a lush?"

"You're clearly not a lush. No, you're sweet, sexy, and too good to be true. And ... I need to tell you something."

"Why don't I like the sound of that?" She was trying to be coy, but the truth was his grave demeanor made her truly concerned about what was coming. She braced herself mentally.

"I ... I'm the guy who's been texting you. And I'm also the one who gave you that massage yesterday. I want to apologize—"

Tory's hand jerked, and hot coffee sloshed from the mug onto her, though she didn't even feel it. So much for bracing herself. Her husband's cancer diagnosis had been less of a shock.

"Tory!" Chris jumped up in alarm and dashed over. "Did you burn yourself?" He yanked away the bedspread, leaving her exposed to his gaze.

She had no idea what to make of his confession. At first, she was stunned, and her stomach felt like it wanted to rebel again. The sheer impact of his statement seemed to take forever to process. Then she knew only one feeling. From incredulity to anger in thirty seconds flat. Words tumbled over each other as she tried to speak. "You? You ... you bastard! How could you?"

"I'm sorry. I'm not proud of myself ..."

He looked down at her breasts, distracted, it seemed, since his eyes fixed there. He stopped talking. Tory's nipples stiffened just from his blatant stare. They were practically begging to be fondled, but she curbed that impulse quickly and pulled the bedspread toward herself.

The horrifying picture fell into place. Not only was Chris the man she had walked behind, admiring in his trunks ... he was also the man who had somehow gotten her number and texted her, told her to remove her panties, *and* given her a massage unbeknownst to her. She shuddered at all the lines that had been crossed. All the same, part of her noted that she hadn't been going nuts and lusting after every man she saw, but in fact, had been lusting after the same man every time. A man who was some kind of sicko stalker. But why was he doing it to her when there were so many other women at the conference to pick from?

"Why did you target me?" she whispered. When he said nothing, she raised her voice. "Chris, whatever your name is, answer me!"

"My name is Chris. I noticed you checking in here two days ago. Later, when I saw you at the conference, I looked up your registration information."

"I can't believe you." Her mind was reeling. He was a manipulator and obviously had a lot of resources for his deception, given how he had masterminded that massage session. And after feeling up her nearly naked body, he'd proceeded to convince her to lose her panties.

And yet, despite knowing what he'd done, she still kind of wanted him. How sick was that?

"I've never done anything like this before. The texting and watching you and—"

"Why?" She hated the fact that part of her was turned on by the subterfuge. "I don't understand why you did all this. Why lie to me? You're not shy. You're comfortable with people."

"But I had no idea how to approach you nonprofessionally. I haven't picked up a woman in a very long time. I'm a mess. I don't normally do this kind of thing."

"What kind of thing?"

"Take your pick. Following you. Lusting after your body. Trying to get closer to you. To see if you might be interested in me, at least for a little while. I'm so out of practice, and you're making me do things … no, that's not accurate. You aren't responsible for any of it. I am. This is all me.

"I haven't got a clue what's right or wrong anymore. At first, it was about getting to know if you liked men or might the interested in a one-night stand. Then, it became more about touching you. I just had to put my hands on you. I can't explain because frankly I don't understand it. This has never happened to me before.

"I don't know why I didn't just knock on your door and ask you out. Well, maybe I do. You intimidate me. Your self-assurance and the way that you are. I've never seen anyone who was less affected by others. I didn't think that you'd be interested, so I decided to try another approach. To get you a little intrigued first, I guess.

"I know that this must sound bizarre. I mean, I'm saying the words, and I can hardly believe them myself. Who does this kind of thing? I just don't want you to be frightened."

"I'm not." And she wasn't really. After all, he'd had plenty of opportunity the previous night to take what he wanted. She might be little confused and angry. A part of her was having difficulty believing him. "You have my panties?"

"I do."

"You actually went into a ladies room and looked in the trash?"

"I wanted something with your scent—"

"Stop! Stop right there, you freak!" What else had he done? "Get out!"

His steely eyes challenged her. "Listen to me, Tory."

She lunged for the bedside phone, intending on calling security.

Chris grabbed her arms and crossed them over her head against the headboard, not hurting her, but not relinquishing his grasp either. A low moan vibrated in his throat as he looked down at her breasts.

Tory should have been frightened, but more than that, she was disgusted by her own mixed reaction to his sudden demonstration of power and passion. She closed her eyes and turned her head away, savoring the moment, but hating it at the same time.

"Please give me another minute."

"I don't want to. Who does things like that?" She wasn't only referring to him, and it was sobering.

"I know you probably think that I'm bent. A pervert. But I'm not. Open your eyes and look at me," he said. "I'm not going to hurt you. You need to know that. Whatever happens, I will walk out that door, if that's what you want."

Although she was a little upset and didn't want him to see her attraction to him, she complied. His dark brown eyes bore into hers, and the heat made her whimper. She soaked up the sight like a parched plant. Here was a man who wanted her. She was pretty certain about that since she could feel his erection through his pants.

The truth of the matter was that she didn't really know what she wanted.

She wasn't being ignored now, was she? This man was nothing like her husband. This was undoubtedly refreshing, but it was not normal or right. Dreams never became reality. Did they? Chris had chosen her and wanted her—just the way she fantasized about being wanted. She should fear him because he had stalked her. She should hate him because he'd violated her trust. Instead, her pulse raced with excitement. She shook her head to dispel that thought and began to review recent events.

Reminding herself again of last night. He could have taken advantage of her at any time throughout their time together. He hadn't. During the massage, he had touched almost all of her body—but not done anything outside the realm of accepted technique. The truth was that she wanted him to cross that line now. Was she not allowed another selfish act?

"I'm so sorry. I hope to make you believe that."

She wondered why he hadn't kept this from her to begin with. He stood to gain more by remaining silent. Surely he was aware of the fact that she would likely not appreciate full disclosure, and he risked ending this right here and right now. However, because he had done some things, he wanted her to know about them. Why?

"Why did you tell me all this? What game are you playing?"

"No games. My conscience wouldn't let me—that's all."

She read only sincerity in his eyes, and all of a sudden, she believed him. This could be the dumbest thing that she had ever done, but he seemed sincere. That didn't mean that she had forgiven him though.

"You need to go."

"Okay." But he didn't budge. Instead, his cheeks grew ruddier, and his soft, sexy lips beckoned her, like a red flag taunting a bull. This man was in his prime, and he wanted her. She would be insane not to take advantage of that. Wouldn't she?

What's the worst that could happen?

He could ravish her and make her deliriously happy. He could find her wanting and leave off before she was satisfied. After all, he might not need this as much as she did, and she was not young and firm anymore. He could be aggressive, abusive, or just bad at sex. He could be insane and end up murdering her. That wasn't likely, but her mind continued to plague her with doubts.

Finally she sighed. What did it matter? Did she even care that he had gone to such extremes? Should she be flattered by all his efforts? No, she wasn't at that point yet. She had calmed down a great deal and tried to look at it logically. If she passed up this chance to find out what would happen, she would regret it for the rest of her life.

And who would know?

"I won't hurt you," he said again. He didn't know her at all and was probably trying to gauge her behavior. Since she wasn't screaming or blindly accepting his story, he could only offer her what he thought she needed to hear.

A sudden, uncontrolled laugh burst out of Tory. She did not believe that for a second, but it didn't seem to matter anymore. Nothing else mattered but the moment. Was she about to let passion rule her head and deal with the rest of it another day? It was pure insanity.

She gave in and kissed him, putting aside all of her insecurities and doubts, showing him, without words, that she wanted whatever he had to give her. He reciprocated, and she lost herself in the moment. His lips fit hers perfectly, as though they had done this before.

***

He tried to take it slowly, be gentle, and give her time to know him. He saw the vulnerability in her eyes and wanted to assuage her doubt. Somehow he had known that they would click, that their joining would be like two puzzle pieces sliding in place, meshing perfectly.

There was no awkwardness. Being with her felt natural and predetermined, part of some bigger plan. Her lips were welcoming and familiar—and even better than he'd imagined. She moaned when he nipped at her upper lip and licked her to remedy some of the sting. He explored her open mouth with his tongue, and she gave as good as he did. Her hunger matched his own as a little more force came into play. God, how he had missed this!

What would intercourse feel like if the pleasure of kissing her was this incredible? The thought made him shake with anticipation. She was not shy, and they participated equally in feasting on each other's mouths. Their tongues circled each other, and heat built as he sucked her tongue into his mouth. He could spend all day locked to her lips without tiring or getting his fill.

When she sucked at his tongue, his heart hammered in his chest. He longed for her to take his cock into her mouth and give it the same treatment. He tested her limits again by gently biting her lower lip, and she moaned into his mouth. Her lips were swollen, and his own felt like plump pillows. Passion enveloped them both. He knew she was his now. There was no way that she would end this. He was overwhelmed by an intense need to connect even more closely to her body.

He was still holding her arms above her head, but he let go of them and plunged his hands into her tousled hair, clenching his fists. It was wonderfully soft, just as he'd known it would be. Her scent surrounded them, and he could not get enough. He understood how animals could identify each other by smell alone. Tory's smell was distinct and raw, and with it, there was a hint of sex in the air. The heat generated by their bodies made it stronger every minute.

He felt her pull him against her pelvis, and hunger screamed in his veins.

***

With her hands now free to roam, she instinctively grabbed his buttocks. Her arousal quickly escalated to ravenous hunger. Within seconds, they were kissing as if their survival depended on it. A switch had been flipped; her body was revving up like an engine ready to surge forward, and nothing could stop it. It felt so good that she actually hummed against his mouth.

He pressed himself along her torso, and the friction of his clothes rubbing against her bare skin was perfectly satisfying. It was like an itch being scratched. Even the small area on her abdomen that had been scalded by the coffee felt tingly.

When they came up for air, he took a deep breath and said, "I've had all night to think about this. Hear me out. I'm going to tell you what I'd like to do."

She took a breath. What would he say? If she were going to send him away, this would be her last opportunity.

He must have sensed her hesitation because he tried a different tack. "If you tell me no, if you want me to find a younger man for you, I'll do it and watch you both. I'll do anything to hear you climax, knowing that I had a hand in it."

Her head was spinning. The reality of what her body and mind needed him to do was at war with her conscience. She hated needing sex so badly that yearning was overtaking her will, her morals.

His hold on her hair slackened. Tory realized that if Chris walked out of the room, he'd take with him her only opportunity to have uncomplicated sex, to know the touch of a real lover and not just a figment of her imagination.

And without warning, as rational thought pushed through again like the shock of being doused with cold water, she came to her senses all at once. What was she doing? *This is not who I am.* She was warring with herself, but she had to take a stand and end this now, no matter how much she needed to be with a man. "Please, stop," she gasped.

Several emotions crossed his face. Regret and pain mostly. But to his credit, he simply rose and stood by the bed.

"I'm sorry." She was trying to get some control back, and she felt the need to make some sort of apology for cutting things off so abruptly.

"No, I'm the one who should say that."

She recognized the look of discouragement on his face and felt a little sick. "This ... is not me. I don't do this kind of thing. I don't jump into bed with men. I mean, not since I was very young, not since my husband. I'm sorry I started kissing you. It scares me how much I want—" She stopped short. "I'm really sorry."

"Was I too rough?"

"God, no!" Just thinking about the amount of force he'd used tuned her on. It was just right.

They both started to speak at the same time.

"You go first," he said.

"I want to be with you so badly, but I can't. I know that it would be so good, and that's part of the problem."

"I don't get that."

"I like it a little rough. At least, I think I do. It's been so long. I'm sorry, I don't know what I'm saying."

"You don't need to apologize. Help me understand, if you can. Tell me, what's the real problem? Is it your husband?"

"It's more than that. It's so many things." So much of it had to do with her own mixed-up feelings about how profoundly he affected her. She had no one in her experience to compare him with. "I feel like I'll lose all control of myself, who I am, how I should behave. And then how will I stop? Where will it end? Since the first time you texted, I've been acting like someone else. The woman in my own fantasies knows no restraint. It's almost like you epitomize the perfect man in my fantasies. But you can't be him, so I'm delusional to even think that. None of this is real. So ... I can't do this."

His broad shoulders slumped as her words sank in and he saw that she was not going to talk herself back into having a good time. Watching him, she felt even worse. She hoped that he understood it had nothing to do with how attracted she was to him—that was unquestionable—but she had no idea how to reassure him without sounding like a flake.

Watching him leave was one of the saddest moments in her life. It felt like she was letting both of them down, and her regret was instantaneous. She almost called him back, but she managed to remain silent until the door closed behind him. Even then, not trusting her voice to sound anything more than a moan of frustration and lust, she covered her mouth as tears began to trickle down her cheeks.

For a long time, she did not move from the bed, replaying the scene over and over in her head, wondering how she could have handled it better. Finally, though, she resigned herself to accepting that she had behaved as a responsible adult should. Still, it was small comfort knowing that. She had done the right thing, but it had felt wrong somehow.

She made it to the afternoon breakout sessions. Avoiding Chris proved to be quite easy, since he didn't seem to be around.

After the sessions, she met up with her colleagues for a quick bite to eat, and they all went their separate ways.

CHAPTER 6

Later that evening, Tory responded to e-mails from the office, returned John's call, which went straight to voice mail, and called home since she had run out of reasons to stall that activity. After she spoke to her mother for a while, she got into an argument with Sam over the new tattoo she wanted—despite Tory's warnings about motivations, health risks, and long-term consequences. Now that Sam was about to start earning her own money, the subject had come up again.

"I thought we talked about this," Tory started, using a reasonable tone.

"Mom, come on! It's just tiny."

So, it was already a done deal. She should have known. "Did you go to a reputable place?"

"Ah, geez. Yes." Which actually meant no. "What do you expect me to say?"

"The truth would be nice."

"I don't know, Mom."

"You think that I'm on your case because I want to be? I worry about you and the choices you are making."

"Don't make this a big issue. It's really not a big deal."

Tory hated when Sam made it seem like it was something that only bothered Tory and wasn't what normal mothers needed to concern themselves with. It was a constant tug-of-war, trying to highlight the truly significant issues from what her daughter wanted to consider inconsequential. However, tonight, they were not going to revert back to old patterns where Tory got all bent out of shape and the screaming started. What good would it do anyway? The deed was done, and it was about keeping the situation contained instead of making things worse.

It was often that way between them. Though Tory struggled to keep their conversations from veering off onto contentious subjects, they still did all too often, inadvertently sparking flames that grew into full-blown arguments that never burned out or got fully extinguished. There was no resolution to these arguments, especially when strong emotions were involved. Harsh words spoken in the past could not be recalled, and they made it difficult for Tory and Sam to achieve anything positive. Tory knew that if she didn't do something different soon, their relationship would suffer.

After they had both cooled down, Tory dialed Sam's cell number. If she wanted them to enjoy the same kind of friendship that she had with her own mother, it was up to her to make it happen.

Sam finally picked up after several rings.

"Listen, honey. I'm sorry. I have no right to say anything. You're an adult, as you're constantly reminding me, and I need to remember that." Tory managed to get all the words out. "I don't want us to fight."

"I get that. It's not much fun getting ragged on."

Tory was determined to keep the conversation flowing smoothly. "You didn't say what you were up to tonight. Are you going out?"

"I might."

"I'm not giving you the third degree, but are you going out with anyone I know?"

"No, Mom. He's someone new."

"You know what I'd like?"

"Yeah?"

"For you to be able to tell me anything, knowing I won't judge. My dad was good at that, and I've come to really rely on Nana. I'd like us to be that way too. You know what I mean?"

"Yeah, I think so."

"So have fun tonight."

"I will. Do you want to talk to Dad? Jake's out."

"Sure." Tory had no inclination to speak to John, but she waited for him to pick up anyway.

Her daughter came back on instead. "He said to tell you that he'll call you later. Okay, Mum. Gotta go, love ya!"

"Love you too, baby." She sighed and smiled.

Not tired enough to sleep, Tory went out for a run. It wasn't the smartest thing to do in a strange city when the sun was already setting, but it was necessary. Her mind wouldn't quiet down, no matter how many yoga and deep breathing exercises she did. The sobering fact was that it was not just her family she was concerned about. Thoughts of Chris continued to plague her, causing a deep restlessness, and making her second-guess sending him away. She could have had a man's hands on her body, and her preoccupation with the idea grew stronger as the day wore on, frustrating her no end.

She could get her head into a better, safer place. Losing herself in running would do the trick for a while. Besides, she had promised herself to spend time enjoying this trip. Determined to take advantage of the unique setting of San Antonio, she stretched before heading to the area where lots of people were gathered on illuminated paths. Tory felt safe and tried to set her pace while freeing her mind of all thoughts.

She was running over a bridge that spanned the River Walk when, just before she'd reached the other side, someone ran up behind her—she heard the pounding footsteps—and grabbed her. She tensed, ready to scream and lash out, and then her attacker's words stopped her cold. "It's me."

It was Chris! Did he want some kind of payback for her pushing him away? No, he wasn't the type—and he didn't sound upset. And what the hell did she know about types, anyway? Chris was definitely the type to have stalked her, touched her body, and made her do things that were indecent.

He pulled her toward the footing of the bridge, his arms still around her.

Tory realized that her sudden jolt of anxiety had been replaced by something else. Part of her wanted to slap his face for scaring her like that, but a bigger part wanted to wrap her legs around his waist and let him take her, not hidden by the shadow of this structure, but in full view of anyone who might pass by. His erection pushed at her back. He was as aroused as she was, if not more so. Would he take it further if she asked?

She willed herself to see things more rationally. Nothing had changed since the morning. Why was she having second thoughts? It was this man. He did it for her.

He relaxed his arms, spurring her into action. She twisted within the circle of his arms and then pulled him by the shirt to bring his lips close to her own. Any willpower she'd had abandoned her.

His face was cast in shadows, but she could see that he looked ill, perhaps even tormented. Maybe he was just as upset with himself and what he had done. "What are you doing? What are you doing to me?" she asked.

He sighed and brought his forehead down to touch hers. "I don't know what the hell I'm doing, but I can't seem to stop."

She could understand that feeling as well. They had chemistry; it was futile to ignore it. For so many reasons, Tory was tired of fighting. She gave herself permission to live in the moment, to embrace this, and to see where it led. She had tried to do the right thing, but the mental torture of not knowing what she was missing had driven her to distraction. There would be time for second-guessing and recrimination later. Tonight was about sharing herself with a man. The truth was that she couldn't fight it any longer. Once she realized that, it all seemed so simple.

"I think that you owe me a kiss for that stunt," she whispered, hoping that he could read between the lines.

"Whatever the sexy lady wants." His lips pressed against hers, and within seconds, he had her up against the curved stone wall and was devouring her mouth. Some passerby whistled at them, but it didn't stop them. It was like nothing she had ever experienced before, yet it felt so familiar. They were wildly abandoning propriety and behaving like young lovers in the throes of passion. Maybe that was why it felt familiar. It didn't really matter why. Nothing mattered. Gluttony pushed them to get closer together and to devour each other like they were starving.

It was everything she wanted, but she felt compelled to rein him in. Otherwise, she wouldn't be able to keep her hands off him. Short, raspy breaths escaped her as she pushed against his chest. "Okay, we have to stop, or else—"

He released her immediately. She couldn't read his expression, but she sensed his frustration.

"I get it," he said. "Let's walk,"

She nodded, and they stood slightly apart until their breathing somewhat returned to normal. Then he took her hand and led her off the bridge. It was so civilized and the complete opposite of what had just happened; she hardly knew what to make of it. She had expected him to cart her off to one of their rooms, but he had thrown her for another loop.

They hardly spoke as they walked the sidewalks and roads. She wondered what he was thinking, but she said nothing, not wanting to risk breaking the temporary, fragile calm. If he was even a fraction as unnerved by their attraction as she was, he might also be feeling that his world had shifted from reality to fantasy. She had a feeling that it wouldn't take much to lose herself in him and any control of the situation.

They spent the rest of the evening strolling through the tourist area. At midnight, they headed back to the hotel. The closer they got, the more nervous she began to feel. Only one scenario would slake the thirst within her, but she had no idea what to say or how to approach getting what she wanted.

He seemed to sense her uneasiness as he followed her into her suite.

"Are you certain?" he asked.

He was probably worried she might back out again before it got too difficult to apply the brakes, Tory thought. She wanted to reassure him that she had her head on straight this time, to ease into the next phase of whatever this was with complete honesty.

"More than you know," she whispered, looking into his eyes. She would not run from intimacy this time. They were going to do the nasty if he still wanted to.

"This is probably going to be very fast," he said, like it was a bad thing.

"Just one question. No, two."

He nodded.

"Have you done anything else I should know about, like … I don't know … planting a bug in my room?"

"No. Second question."

"Do you think once will be enough?" She grinned.

He smiled, and her breath caught in her chest at this rare expression. The man was seriously gorgeous when his dimples came out.

Chris took the lead. "Don't move."

"Hold on," she said, scooting away. "I'm not stalling, but I do feel sweaty. I need to use the bathroom. Just give me five minutes."

"I don't mind. I like sweaty. I plan to get you very sweaty. Okay … you have exactly five minutes. I'll break down the door if you're not back in this bed by then."

She ran into the bathroom, turned on the water so it would warm up while she brushed her teeth, used the toilet, and jumped into the shower. She didn't bother looking into the mirror because she knew what she would see: a look of anticipation and a smile. There was a hot man on the other side of the door who wanted to touch her, and that was going to happen. After the shower, she considered blow-drying her hair, but in the end, she simply wrapped a fluffy white towel around herself. This man had already seen her wet from swimming, drunk, and nude, so dry hair wasn't going to make any difference.

She took a deep breath and opened the bathroom door. All she saw was an empty room. The only sound was her own breathing. Was he hiding? Had he gotten tired of waiting?

Then her room door opened, and Chris entered. He was wearing a terry robe. From the look of his wet hair, he had also taken a shower. Without so much as a word, he shrugged out of the robe and, naked, went over to the bed.

Happiness bloomed from within. He hadn't abandoned her and was committed to being with her like this.

He had no trouble being naked in front of her. She wondered where that kind of confidence came from. Were most men able to walk around undressed in front of someone else without any hesitation? He made himself comfortable on the bed. Nothing could keep Tory from taking in her fill. She refused to rush her visual examination.

As a nurse, she had seen many male bodies. Bodybuilders, police officers, athletes, young men in their prime—but nothing like this. The woman in her appreciated the better-looking ones, but no matter their age, shape, or ethnicity, those men had just been patients. None of them had ever had such a strong effect on her psyche, the way Chris did.

This perfect specimen of a man was displaying all of his assets to her. It was intoxicating to see him this way: on the bed, aroused, and open to her perusal. So she took it all in. His physique was something else. Broad pectoral muscles defined his chest. Light brown chest hair with some hints of gray concentrated between his nipples and then formed into a V shape as it tapered toward his navel. His legs were well formed, with thick thighs, and she wanted to taste every inch of him. His skin was a healthy, flushed tone. His erection jutted out proudly, as it should. His maleness was breathtaking. So different from her husband. *Stop! No thinking about that!*

She envied him the self-assurance to remain so exposed to her greedy gaze.

"What are you thinking?" he asked. She sensed vulnerability in his voice, a subtle hint of concern. Perhaps he was not as confident as he appeared.

"I'm ogling your body." She pointed to a design near his groin. "You've got a tattoo? I bet all the women love that."

"What women?"

"The women you sleep with."

"I haven't had sex of any kind in several years."

It seemed impossible for such an attractive man not to be sexually active. "Are you for real?" she said.

He didn't answer, and he looked a little lost or even sad. For some reason, she believed him. Why would he lie? He had nothing to lose. After the next couple of days, they would never see each other again.

"I'm sure there's a story there," she said.

"No."

"That makes my situation seem not so bad."

"What's your situation?"

"I haven't been with anyone other than my husband for longer than you've gone without, probably, and I'm starving for this. Do we need condoms?"

He seemed startled by her question. More reason to believe he hadn't had sex in a while.

"I didn't think of that. I can get some."

"No, I want us skin to skin, if that's okay." She was on the pill, although in her case, it was more for the purpose of regulating her monthly cycle than for contraception.

"It's more than okay." His eyes skimmed over her. "Drop the towel, Tory. This may be the only time I ever get to experience you. And I don't want to miss a second of it."

Clearing her throat, she opened the loosely wrapped towel and let it fall to the floor. Then she walked toward him on surprisingly steady legs, considering he was looking at her body as though she belonged to him now.

She needed to have him inside her, but all of a sudden, she felt like a virgin, not knowing how to proceed.

"It's going to be okay, you and me," he said.

"I know."

"No, you don't. But I'm going to help you."

"I haven't even touched you at all yet—"

He grabbed her hand and placed it over his heart. "We have time for it. We have the rest of the night. But, please, can we …"

She understood his urgent haste because she felt the same way. So she touched his lips with her finger and straddled him. He slid down in the bed, and she rocked against him before taking hold of his penis and placing the tip against her folds, rubbing herself a little.

"Do you like this?" she asked.

"Yes!"

"More?"

"So much more! But you set the pace."

She sensed that these were not empty words and that he needed her to follow through. She eased the tip of his penis into her and paused. Her thighs shook with the strain of holding her body in position above him. Painfully slowly, one centimeter at a time, she sheathed his stiff penis with her vagina so she could savor every detail. It was a test of her will not to rush.

His face was a mask of constraint and tension. A ruddy flush covered his cheekbones as he watched her with those eyes that saw everything.

When her vaginal muscles clenched at the intrusion of his penis, her eyes closed, and she heard him gasp. The sensation of being breached was the most gratifying feeling, perfect—and when he was fully seated in her, they moved together in unhurried synchronization.

This is really happening! This is really happening. Oh. My. God!

***

Chris pulled out, wanting to take her from behind. That had been his fantasy ever since he had seen her walking in those heels. She clawed at him, objecting to the interruption, until she understood that he wanted to change positions. Her body was so primed for him that he was back inside her warmth within seconds. He curbed his primal urge to pump into her like a stallion to savor this sweet moment that was perfect in its simplicity and totally arousing. He could feel her insides clenching around him, tight and welcoming. Her wetness and her heat made the sensation around his penis so rich that he wanted to cry with relief and gratitude. He had no notion of what she might want from the intercourse, so he followed his gut and went with what felt natural.

The curve of her back and roundness of her ass beckoned his touch, but he could not let himself get distracted by her physical beauty. Next time, he would savor every appealing part of her. Now, he took a firm hold on her hips so he could moderate the pace, despite her struggles to go faster. When she gave up control, he wanted to worship her body for that alone.

One moment he was cresting a wave, and the next, his heart was racing, losing all awareness of who he was. In one corner of his mind, he heard her cry out, and then he reaped the reward of her channel clamping him like a wonderful vise. He collapsed over her. He wanted to feel bad about crushing her like this, but he rather enjoyed it. His claiming of her was complete. Sex with her was so much better than he had imagined and remembered. It used to feel good, being so intimate with another body. However, it had been missing the fire of need. Of taking over his whole being.

"Am I too heavy?" he asked.

Her hand came around his back to hold him in place. "No."

He raised his head and saw tears rolling down her cheeks. He was choked with alarm and regret. Had he been too rough? What had he done? "Are you hurt? Did I—"

"It was incredible!" she said, smiling through her tears. "I never knew it could be that way."

He laughed in relief—and in complete agreement. "It was shattering."

"Mmm-hmm."

"It was too quick."

"Yes, that too. Well, what can you expect with two people who haven't gotten any in a long time? I think we did pretty well, considering."

"Oh, yes?"

"Personally, I didn't think I would last as long as I did. I was already halfway there as soon as I saw you on the bed. You have the sexiest body. And then there's the fact this was our first time together, and we didn't even discuss what gets each of us off. You don't know what I like, and I don't know your tastes."

"You're my taste," he said, rolling off her so they were chest to chest, skin to skin. He sucked on her tongue and heard her moan.

"I want to devour you. Inch by inch," he said. "This might be our only time together, and I want to do everything."

"We don't have time for everything," she said.

"Yes, we do. I'm going to have you on every surface of this room. I'm going to lose myself inside every one of your orifices. You're going to demand for me to pleasure you until you can't stand anymore. I'm going to try everything I've ever thought about doing, and we're going to chase orgasms until we're wasted."

"I don't know what to say, except … I can't wait."

"Oh, baby. I'm so grateful."

She grinned. "You say that now, but in a few hours, it'll be a different story."

"Why?"

"Because I'm going to gorge myself on you and make you burn for me. I want these memories to last me a long time. I'll get under your skin and in your head. I want you to give me all you've got. The rough stuff. The kink. The tender. And the best of you. I'll wear you out. You'll be begging me to stop. But I won't. I'll wring everything from you. I need this for me. You won't be the same person when I'm through with you. You might—"

"You've already changed me," he said with sincerity.

CHAPTER 7

Chris put his leg between hers, and she began to hump him like a bitch in heat. It was as if they had known each other forever. Tory found this new, wild version of herself frightening, but she grabbed hold of it anyway. She tasted him, moving along his body, hungry for him in an elemental way that she could not understand. Never had she experienced such ferocious desire. Her aggressive sexuality was a side of her she'd had no idea existed. It was exhilarating!

Chris's penis was flaccid from his ejaculation just moments before, but this didn't dissuade her. Nuzzling his groin, she touched him with reverence.

His hands reached toward her hair, and he grabbed it in bunches. Because it was still wet, the pull of the tangled strands between his fingers was just the edge she needed to shut off her thinking mind.

They fought over who would do what to whom, and he won. Even though his cock liked her touch—that much was evident—he had other ideas.

"I want to taste you," he said, holding her still.

"Your hands have roamed all over me already. I want a turn," she said.

"You will. I promise. Give me this, and then you can have your way."

"My way? Why don't I quite believe that?"

He grinned, and she immediately wanted to give him whatever he desired. He licked her right nipple, and she felt an instant rush of awareness throughout her body.

He plumped both breasts in his hands and treated them equally to his undivided ministration. Gentle teasing progressed to sucking and biting of the hard nubs of her nipples and every part of the surface of her breasts. He nipped them with his teeth and then blew on the sensitive tissue: shock followed by warmth.

She yearned greedily for more. John had never treated her like a rare dish to be savored, and he never paid attention to what she responded to or what made her hot. She wanted to reciprocate and show her affection and approval. She moved her arm, which felt heavy in her sex-intoxicated state, to cup his head and travel to the hairline of his neck. She ran her fingers through his short, soft waves, trying to convey in her touch that everything he was doing felt wonderful.

"I could do this all day," he said, "but I need to move on. I have a promise to keep."

She laughed and then felt suddenly grave, realizing that she couldn't recall the last time she had felt so happy.

"You okay?" he asked. He was so attuned to her. It warmed her heart that he was considering her feelings.

"I'm so okay that it's not even funny."

Chris moved lower and spread her legs wide open. Her entire body began to shake with anticipation. If she was near an orgasm just from having his mouth on her breasts, she couldn't even imagine the glorious pleasure that awaited.

He began by kissing her thighs. "So soft," he murmured. "I love your skin."

His lips moved agonizingly slowly and still far from where she needed them to be. She moved her pelvis as an invitation, but he held her more firmly, intent on following his own agenda. He did not need to voice any commands, and she had no choice but to let him take the lead.

She sighed, resigned to the fact that he was going to take his time. Her patience was tested as she watched him blow on her perineum and gaze at her body. *What could possibly be that fascinating?*

She knew what he was doing—delayed gratification—but to keep from giving him the satisfaction of knowing how much she needed his touch, she schooled her reactions as much as she could. There would be payback for his delay tactic, she promised herself. Then all thoughts vanished as his fingers explored her folds, parting them.

"You're so wet for me. Later, after I bring you to climax, or maybe to more than one, I'm going to give you a massage inside and out, after I shave you. Have you ever had that done to you?"

The idea immediately set her on fire. Her mind instantly returned to the dream she'd had on the plane: male hands on her body, intimate attention with touch, learning and experimenting with sex play. This was her fantasy come to life!

"How do you know so much about massages?"

"Don't know. I just go with what feels good. You didn't answer my question."

His tongue traveled down her middle and made her back arch. Her entire perineum was paying attention now.

"No!" she screamed at the extreme pleasure of his teeth scraping against her sensitive clitoris.

"So sweet. I knew it would be. So pretty and swollen. All for me."

She groaned with pleasure. Just watching and listening to him was enough to make her feel good, but his mouth was something else. So this was how other people enjoyed sex? This could be addictive. But was it the sex—or was it him? Was it his talent or something else? *Get your head on straight, Tory! He's a flash in the pan. This is a one-time thing and nothing more. This isn't something to get used to or something to require beyond this one time. It is important not to get burned by this experience.*

"I've imagined this, being with you like this, but this is so much better than my fantasy," he said, bringing her back to the moment.

The intensity of pleasure became too much for her. "Please!"

"What do you want, Tory?"

"I want … I want you to fuck me with your tongue."

"Just my tongue? Or can I use other parts of my mouth?"

"Anything! I don't care!"

"One question."

Oh, my God! "Chris—"

"Do you squirt when you come? I was too far gone to notice before. I really hope you do."

She moaned. The man was trying to kill her.

He didn't wait for her to respond; the fantastic assault began. Within seconds, she was incapable of uttering a word. His mouth was made for this. He teased her clit with the tip of his tongue, using just the right amount of pressure, and then he changed it up when he sensed that she needed more.

He invaded her vagina like he owned it. No beating around the bush there. His commanding tongue rimmed the opening and then plunged inside as he attached himself to her, palming her buttocks and raising her to him. She felt like an offering about to be consumed.

His strong tongue moved in and out of her. This was not just obligatory cunnilingus; it excited Chris to go down on her. His moans were almost as loud as hers. She didn't feel rushed to take her pleasure. He seemed thrilled to continue for as long as it took to coax an orgasm out of her.

It was strange how well he knew what she needed. When she was writhing and ready to explode, he said, "Touch yourself and make us both happy."

Licking two of her fingers, she lowered them to her clitoris and began to rub the sensitive bud. The swell of mounting pleasure made her whimper incoherently.

"Oh, God!" she yelled as she reached her peak within seconds. It was so satisfying that she never wanted it to end. The way he sucked and drank from her as though she were a fountain made her orgasm last and last.

"Nice and juicy. Perfect," he said. He lowered her bottom to the bed and pulled her legs over his shoulders. "One more, baby."

It took her a second for her to realize what he meant. He wasn't ready for it to end just yet.

Several fingers filled her. Other fingers tapped, arousing her clitoris. He made sure that she was thoroughly wet, and it did not take long for her to reach another pinnacle so strong her vaginal walls contracted with incredible force. They were not the only muscles to engage, and she proceeded to leak urine.

Undaunted, he placed his stiff penis inside her. She registered his look of desire.

"I'm so turned on by your noises and the feel of you. The slick, squishy sound of our juices is incredible. The wetness of the bed, the way you let go all over me. Now with my dick inside you, you're milking me like you'll die if I don't give it to you hard."

Her moisture coated the lower part of his face, and he made no attempt to wipe himself off before seeking her mouth. She tasted herself on him and in him. Once, she might have thought it depraved, but instead, it was so raw that her toes curled.

"Is it hard enough?" he asked. When she didn't respond, his penetrations went even deeper. He used such force that she was pushed higher up the bed each time he entered her.

"Answer me!" he said.

She could hardly breathe. Her body was on fire again—even though she'd been through the wringer and had wanted time to recover only moments earlier.

He bent over and pinched her nipples, hard. Just when she thought she might not be able to take anymore, he moved his hands to spread her buttocks. She jumped when she felt his finger tickling her anus. Then he moved, and before she knew it, he had pushed his digit into her rectum.

"Oh, God!"

No one had ever invaded that channel before. She felt just like the inexperienced person she was. The missionary position was her husband's favorite. She could count on one hand the number of times that they had managed really good oral sex. Having intercourse with John was like brushing her teeth: routine and necessary, but not satisfying. This was what she had been missing: sex that didn't resemble anything in her repertoire. A nourished libido. Under Chris's influence, she could learn things about herself she hadn't known before. Submitting to the sexual prowess of an expert appealed to her.

"It's just my thumb, baby. Relax now."

Relax? Fuck that! "I don't want to relax," she groaned.

"Bad choice of words. How does it feel?"

"I can't talk. Please don't make me!"

He laughed, rotated his thumb in her anus, and stretched her.

She jerked, totally alert and aware of his slightest movements.

"You're so tight. You like this, huh?"

"You know what I don't like?"

"Tell me."

"Men who talk too much."

He chuckled and redoubled his efforts. What she was feeling was too stunning to be called punishment. Her body and mind began to shut down. Nothing existed but this moment.

This time, when she erupted, he did as well—and for one second, everything went black.

***

Chris couldn't find the words to express what he was experiencing. His emotions and sensations overrode all reason. He suspected that it wasn't his long-time abstinence that made him want her in every possible way and want to consume her like he was dying of thirst; it had something to do with this particular woman who was underneath him. The way she looked when letting go, over and over again, made his heart sing. She was so giving and sexy.

His head gradually cleared, and he knew they needed to rest and recover. He rolled off of her, went to bathroom, and ran a bath. Then he took her hand, lifted it to his lips, and pulled her up from the bed. Wordlessly, he brought her to the bathroom, and they sank into the hot water.

She sat behind him in the bathtub, and he soaked up her attention as she sponged water onto his shoulders, letting it run down his chest. This domestic intimacy soothed his soul. His solitary lifestyle was not one conducive to females lovingly cleansing him.

"You haven't said anything in a while," she noted.

He understood that she needed to know what he was thinking, but he had no idea how to express what was on his mind. He felt underserving of what this woman was giving him.

"I'm reliving everything," he said. Which was not a lie. "It was … I don't have the words."

She giggled. "I know! Who knew? My whole life, I've never had anything like this with anyone."

"It's too bad we don't have more time."

"Yeah."

"Are you sore?"

"No. I don't think so. You?"

He laughed. "No."

"Why are you laughing? Don't penises get irritated from too much sex?"

"I don't really know, but I'm thinking not so much. We're kind of rough with ourselves when we jerk off."

"I've always wondered about anal sex. Have you ever done that before?"

He considered how best to answer. "I've tried." It had not gone well. He had been young and foolish. The girl had told him to stop, and it had taken him years to try again. When that time came, it was another failure because the woman refused. He'd never attempted it again.

"Will you try with me?"

Her generous offer unmanned him. Well, since he was going to hell anyway, he may as well go whole hog. "I'd like to, but you're very tight there."

"You could stretch me with a lubricant. Just give me some warning. Take it slow and easy. I've never done it that way before, and I'd like to try it with you."

"Why?"

"I'm not sure why. I guess it's because I might never have another opportunity like this to be so open and free with another person. It's not like I can hold it against you if it doesn't work out. The odds of us ever meeting again are slim to none. And at my age, there might never be another time."

"You're hung up on your age."

"Not really."

"How old are you?"

"Forty-two."

"Not over the hill yet."

She laughed. "No, not quite."

They relaxed against each other for a time without needing to speak. Companionship, intimacy, and sharing had never been things he'd placed any importance on.

"I'm ready to shave you," he finally said.

She was silent for a moment. "Then I get to do the same to you."

He had to think about it for a second. It wasn't something he'd ever contemplated. "That seems fair. I won't have to explain it to anyone. How about you?"

"Uh, no. I doubt he'll even notice."

"Good."

He was grateful she didn't prod, because he didn't want to lie. He wanted to tell her what he did for a living, but it didn't seem like the right time. The more he thought about it, the more it seemed wiser to keep his profession to himself. Things could get complicated, and he really didn't need the additional stress.

After a quick trip to his room to pick up a few items, he found himself back in her room, once again fixated on her groin. After they trimmed their pubic hair with scissors, they started in with the razor. The angles were tricky, and neither of them wanted to nick the other's skin. At one point, they were laughing so hard that the hotel manager phoned with a request that they keep it down.

They were no longer laughing when they were both finally bare.

"It took a lot more time than I thought it would," she said.

"There was so much hair to shave. I'll need a new razor in the morning." He threw the one they had used into the garbage, and his words hung in the air. Their time together would be ending all too soon. It wasn't something he wanted to dwell on.

"We'll go to the evening closing ceremony?" she asked. This told him that she'd made the same observation. The conference would be ending soon, and so would their liaison.

"Yes, I'm expected. It won't take long. We still have all night when we get back."

Tory made no comment. She simply picked up the towel from the bed. The mood had changed from playful to serious, and Chris didn't like it.

"Come here," he said, and she complied, which pleased him.

He sat at the foot of the bed, and she stood beside him. He rubbed her hips and nuzzled the juncture of her legs, then kissed her pubic mound, enjoying the feel of her skin on his lips.

"I thought you were soft before we shaved, but this is even smoother."

"Like a baby's butt?"

"Only sexier."

"I feel so exposed, like a plucked chicken."

"You don't look like any chicken I've ever seen."

She laughed. He tongued her labia. "You don't taste like one either."

"I think one of my favorite memories of this week will be the look on your face when I started shaving your scrotum. That and getting to see your entire tattoo. The mouth of the snake and its tongue."

"I don't know what I was thinking when I did that."

"How old were you?"

"Young. Sixteen, maybe. My parents never knew."

"The tattoo artist must have shaved you."

He thought about what it had cost him to pay for that tat. He'd been a different person then: rebellious, cocky, and popular. When he got the tattoo, he had been stoned halfway out of his mind. He must have been, to do something like that. To save a little money, he had let the artist fuck him. That was after the artist taught him how to swallow a man's penis while others looked on. The design idea of the serpent had come from someone in the audience who had first suggested a narrow tongue inked along the length of Chris's cock. That would have meant being restrained. Luckily, since Chris had been too wasted to make any smart decisions, the shop owner had intervened.

"Hello? Where did you go?" she asked, waving her hand in front of his face.

"Remembering my misspent youth. But yes, to answer your question."

"It must have hurt, having needles so close to the base of your penis."

"It must have. I was too high to really notice until almost two days later. I woke up at a friend's house, went to the washroom, and found a dressing on my groin. In the mirror, I could see the bandage went all around my waist, so I freaked out at first. I remember jumping around like a lunatic and tearing the bandage. My skin was a red and scabby.

"At first, I had no memory of what happened. I thought someone had played a joke on me with a Sharpie and then cut me to make it look authentic until someone barged into the washroom to see what the commotion was all about. Everyone told that story for a long time. They laughed about it, and I tried to forget about it. I can't tell you for sure whether it hurt, but it must have. I was such an idiot in those days. Some of the stuff I did ..."

"Tell me."

"No, it's not worth telling. Let's talk about you."

"I live a boring life. Two kids, a job you know about, a mortgage. Nothing to say, really."

Her skin was unblemished and so white. He could not get enough of her. He wanted to spend all his time looking, feeling, and tasting her.

"You don't have any marks on your body. How is that even possible?" he asked.

"I never liked lying out in the sun, and I never got the big deal about tattoos. All my deliveries were vaginal, and the stretch marks were minimal, so no scars. I breezed through my childhood without any major injuries, and it's probably good genes that take the credit for my skin."

He ran a finger down her arm. Her smooth, silky skin erupted in goose bumps as it responded to his touch. "So responsive and soft. Do you use anything?"

"If you mean lotions or waxes or any treatments, then no. I try to remember to apply moisturizer after a shower. It's hit or miss, though."

"I like that about you. You're not caught up in all of the hype about beauty stuff."

"I'm not sure I follow."

"In the bathroom last night, I saw your toiletries on the counter. There was only one small bag. I peeked inside, and there are only a few things. A little makeup and one bottle of something."

"Oh, that's sunscreen mixed with a cream for when I'm outdoors. It's more about preventing skin cancer than wrinkles."

He expected her to chastise him for snooping instead of explaining what the product was.

"See, that's what I mean. You're comfortable in your body. You're not looking to be glamorous and forever youthful. Instead, you have a natural classiness, which I find extremely attractive. You really have no idea how beautiful you are. The way you are. How you walk, how you carry yourself, how you wear clothes. It's so refreshing and ... I don't know ... sexy."

They were quiet for a few minutes, each lost in their own thoughts. He wondered what was going on in her head and whether his observation had insulted her somehow. "Are we okay?" he asked. The silence was not yet uncomfortable, but in his experience, females normally disclosed their every thought. Tory was obviously not like that.

She looked at him. He had no idea what her response might be. Usually, he was able to read people, but Tory was a puzzle.

"I think so. Don't look so serious. I'm not accustomed to compliments. That was a compliment, right?"

Relieved at her answer, he grinned. "Definitely!"

"Chris? Tell me, have you always been nosy?"

He laughed. "I was hoping that you'd miss that part."

"You mean the part about you looking through my things?"

"Just one little bag."

"Right. Stay out of my stuff."

"Deal."

"You still haven't answered my question."

"Yes. We're okay. It's all because of you. You make me do things I would never ordinarily do."

"Like shaving your crotch?"

"Yeah. I enjoyed shaving you. Your whole bottom is soft and white now," she said.

"Hey! It was supposed to be only my pubes in front, not my balls, and certainly not my crack!"

"I wanted to be sure there wasn't anything else hiding. Like a two-headed serpent."

"When it starts to grow back, it's going to be itchy as hell."

"Same here, but you don't hear me whining. You'll think of me then."

He nodded. "I'll be thinking of you long after it grows back."

Chapter 8

He nudged Tory's legs wider apart and fondled her sexy bits to let her know it was time for further sexual exploration. They had held off for long enough, and she was more than ready.

It looked like he was getting ready to fuck her with his mouth again, but for this round, she had plans of her own.

"You said I could have my way with you," she teased.

He flopped back on the bed with his head against his interlocked fingers. He exuded such confidence that she wanted to shake him up a little.

She hadn't decided where to start, but she knew talking dirty would be part of it. Since his words had a strong effect on her, maybe hers would have a similar effect on him.

"When I first saw you, I thought you were handsome. Then I thought you were sexy."

She crawled up until her mouth captured his flat nipple. She spent a lot of time sucking and nibbling the tight nub and then the other one. She slowly kissed down the center of his abdomen, making him inhale sharply. His penis nudged her chest. She barely recognized herself in this sex-driven woman who knew her way around a willing male, and she luxuriated in the power and self-discovery. She was not about to let him rush her; she wanted to linger for no other reason than because she could.

"You're going to make me suffer, aren't you?"

"Yes," she hissed. "I'm going to suck you dry, eventually. But not yet."

He groaned as the tip of his cock received a gentle kiss.

"Move up and turn over." When he complied, she added, "Hips up a little." As he got into position, she murmured her approval. "Yes, just like that."

Chris was on his knees with his buttocks up in the air and his penis dangling down.

"I'm going to tell you what I'm going to do every step of the way." She moved behind him so that her abdomen touched his bottom. "You're going to feel me against you. I'm going to rub your back."

He remained quiet.

"Now I'm going to slap you to get the blood circulating."

She could tell that he was a little surprised because he turned his head in her direction.

"Easy, big fella. I'm only going to use my hands."

She made chopping motions on his back with the sides of her hands, which made him relax. She stepped it up with smacks to his back and buttocks, and his muscles tensed. Every few moments, she tugged on his penis or his scrotum, and with each tug, he got harder.

"I'm going to taste you now. Let me know if it hurts."

She began to bite the taut muscles of his buttocks. He was firm and so appealing. "That tight ass is yummy." She could tell he really liked it, especially as she got closer to his anus. "I'm going to fuck this—just like you want to do to me."

Even a kiss to his anus made him jumpy. Judging by his reaction, he was as untried as she was in this department.

Moving on to his smooth scrotum, she fondled him and applied pressure to the base of his penis while her tongue laved him. His moans emboldened her.

She captured his balls in her mouth, making him squirm. Gently tugging them turned him on in a big way.

"Get onto your back again. I want to rock your world."

His cock was so stiff that the skin was stretched tightly over its red-purple tip.

"I'm going to pretend you're my favorite kind of Popsicle." She licked the whole length of his penis, following a large vein that ran the length. "Oh, it's dripping. I need to suck it up." Her lips captured the drops of pre-come on the crown. "Mmm, circumcised. Nothing in the way, and it looks so needy. It's searching for my mouth, but I have to finish my treat."

She ran the flat of her tongue along the underside of the shaft, following a straight path, and felt his tremors. "I'm going to blow you and then swallow you whole—all the way up to your balls. Then I'm going to suck until you come down my throat."

"Tory, stop talking!"

She giggled and got down to business. She began to suck him hard, and his hips bucked. When she inserted a finger into his anus and gently pressed his prostate, he swore and emptied into her. On her way back up, she placed dozens of kisses onto his heaving body as his breath calmed down.

He made her keep moving forward until she was kneeling over him and his face was buried into her groin. His nose, chin, and wonderful mouth tormented her in a good way. She ground into him shamelessly, wanting to be devoured. Without pubic hair, everything was much more sensitive.

Chris stopped for a moment, and Tory wondered if he was having trouble breathing and wanted to pull away.

"Baby, use your hands to spread your folds wide apart," he ordered. She complied.

"Yeah, that's it," he said. "Your clit was trying to hide."

"It's overstimulated."

"Really? Let's address that." He began to tap on her clit with one finger while he invaded her other two holes with his fingers. Even though she was wet, his thrusting was too much for her. Her mind went blank, and he took advantage of her disorientation to bite her thigh.

She reached out for the headboard to keep herself upright and screamed as she rode her climax.

He was not done with her, though, and he would not give her a moment to recover. His tongue played with her clitoris, and more fingers found their way inside her openings. She was stretched to capacity.

"My baby likes that. You're so hot right now that I could get burned."

Tory groaned, incapable of doing much else.

"Once you go off again, I'm going to fuck this ass."

By saying that, he lit her fuse, and she convulsed with a release that was so intense it robbed her of her breath. Before she could get her bearings, he had moved her onto her hands and knees on the bed and was pushing his fingers into her rectum. She tried to relax.

"Two fingers, baby. You're getting looser."

"But we need a lubricant."

"Let's try your juices. If it's too much, we'll stop." When she didn't respond, he asked, "Are you okay with that?"

"I think so."

"Promise you'll let me know if it hurts."

He was asking her to stay in control of what he was doing even though he was desperate to take her that way.

"I promise."

It felt strange at first when he removed his digits and placed the head of his penis at her opening. He seemed to be struggling against the barrier. She wanted to make this a successful event for both of them and thought of a possible solution. She bore down, helping him gain access, and then she relaxed her body, letting him penetrate further. It was such a foreign experience to finally have sex that way. Nothing could adequately describe how it felt to be taken like that. She had always wondered.

"I'm in!" he said with glee. "It feels like nothing I've ever felt before. You're so tight here. I won't be able to move."

The pressure was intense. Her body was having some difficulty adjusting; it was much more girth than just a couple of fingers.

"Relax, baby."

"I'm trying. But it's so much!"

"Does it hurt?"

"No ..."

"You'd tell me, right? I don't want it to hurt."

"It doesn't really."

"What does feel like?"

"There's a burn where you've entered me. Like you're searing me from inside ... the heat ... actually, my mind can't decide if this feels good or not. It's so weird you're in there to begin with. My other organs … it's like they're trying to move out of the way. Can you stay still for a little while longer? I'm still trying to adjust."

"Anything for you."

Several seconds passed, and a drop of moisture tickled down her back. His sweat. She realized that it was costing him. He was forcing himself to refrain from what he wanted, which was to move in and out. "Does it still feel good?" she asked.

"You have no idea. I don't think I've ever been this hard. Just feeling the soft ridges and the spasms …"

"It's called peristaltic movement."

"I can't wait until you come and the muscles tighten around me even more."

"Yeah, well don't hold your breath on that. I'm not sure that I can."

"Oh, you will, baby."

"Right," she said as her body slumped a little. She was too uncomfortable to stay in position.

"Oh, no, you don't. You don't get to quit. We have more playing to do."

"Knock yourself out. I'm done!"

He couldn't accept that. He began to tease and pull at her nipples. Unbelievably, they became hard again, and not long after, she felt the slow rise of renewed arousal.

"You say you're done, but look how your body wants me."

"You've taken control over it, that's why."

"If that's true, then let me do this." He licked and bit her neck.

"Not too hard or you'll leave marks."

"I'll buy you a scarf."

"And that won't look weird," she scoffed.

Chris soon made her forget about that and everything else as he began to move inside her. It didn't feel good at first. It felt too tight, and she had the urge to pull away. She was briefly concerned that the stimulation would make her want to evacuate her bowels. Before too long, he either got larger or she shrank. The pressure became unbelievably intense, and her discomfort bordered on painful. It felt like he was splitting her in two.

"Try to relax."

"I can't," she said through clenched teeth, disappointed with herself for finding it so difficult.

He moved her upright so that his thighs supported her.

"Look at us in the mirror," he said.

When she did, she saw herself on display. He touched her pubic area with his fingertips. "There's no more hair, so I guess we can't call this a pussy anymore."

"Some cats are hairless," she said, grateful for the distraction from her discomfort.

"Yeah, but they're ugly, and you're not."

"Sweet talker."

"We'll call it a pretty cunt."

"So what do I call you without your bush?"

"I don't need a name."

"I'll think of one."

Looking at their reflection, she met his eyes. She knew nothing about this man, yet she had never felt closer to anyone. The intimacy they were sharing quenched her long-time drought for affection. And something even deeper was brewing, something that assuaged a basic need she'd never known she had, for acceptance of some kind.

He made her feel safe and reassured that whatever she wanted sexually required no explanation. Even though she was uncomfortable and starting to question her own determination to achieve anal penetration, she did not feel judged by him.

Then, in an instant, everything changed. Basking in their silent communication, she felt very warm. Feeling empowered, she made the first move to direct them in their mutual experiment.

She lowered her hands and began to stimulate her clit with the fingers of her left hand while entering her vagina with the fingers of her right hand.

Chris brought her right hand to his mouth and sucked on the lubricated fingers, closing his eyes. He brought his own fingers into his mouth too for a moment, and then he inserted them into her vagina.

Tory angled her body so she could kiss his mouth. Their tongues dueled, and he sucked her tongue into his warm mouth. The thrum of their mutual arousal started from within and surrounded them like a bubble.

She undulated her hips, feeling his cock swell and lengthen. Her fluids ran, and her temperature increased—along with her pulse. With his free hand, he pinched one of her nipples, and then he moved his hand down to press on her lower abdomen. He began to pump in and out of her ass—slowly at first and then faster.

She felt herself climbing to the edge where the only thing that mattered was getting to that precise point where the fall was guaranteed. The pace of her fingers rubbing against her clit increased, but she worried she might not be able to keep it up. The fear that one of them would stop worried her in the back of her mind. But she knew where she needed to be, and she was certain he would not question it.

Muscles inside her that she had never before paid much attention to, began to contract and release. He groaned, and his lips moved away as he jerked, spilling into her. She was still shaking when her head fell back on his shoulder and his chin rested on hers.

Minutes passed, and they remained still.

"Open your eyes and look at us," he said.

She did and saw someone she barely recognized. Who was the woman she saw in the mirror? A porn star?

"Do you feel me still?" he asked.

She nodded.

"If that had been on video, I'd want to watch it again. It was that good."

"I need a rest," she said.

"You know what I like the most?"

"What?"

"How you get what I want. How you squirted all over me."

The intensity of what they had just done, although it was fantastic, also made her just a little uncomfortable. It was almost too much of a good thing. She needed some time to get herself under control. She was at serious risk of begging to see him after the conference ended.

"I need a shower. And we need to get out of this room."

"Five more minutes. I don't want to slip out of you yet."

He did not have to explain. It had nothing to do with the semen and other fluids in her rectum oozing out and making a mess on the sheets. It was the closeness, the rightness of their joining, which might never be experienced again. She would treasure it and file it away in a memory bank to bring to light whenever times were tough, whenever loneliness threatened to engulf her.

She wondered what his life was like. Was he in a loveless marriage too? Did they have that in common? Did he have children? And as for his job, did he find joy in it? She shook herself mentally to remind herself that none of those questions needed answering. It was a one-time affair, and she had to stop wanting to make it into anything more. *After tomorrow, we will never see each other again.*

"Where do you want to go?" he asked, jolting her back into the present.

"A walk or a run. Maybe some dinner."

Chris pulled out, stood up, and carried her into the bathroom. He plunked her on the toilet while he got into the shower. She watched him wash himself, the suds rolling off his shoulders and sliding down his back. The way he lathered soap around his penis and scrotum with brisk efficiency was so erotic. The flex of his gluteal muscles as he parted his legs to reach areas she wanted to taste again.

"Stop looking at me like that—or we'll be here for another hour," he said.

She laughed and joined him in the shower, closing her eyes. She always appreciated the first few seconds: the hot water making contact with her skin, the delicious washing away of sleepiness, and getting ready for the day ahead.

Her mind wandered. She was getting rid of the physical evidence of sex, but removing the mental stain of her infidelity would not be as easy. Before she returned home, she would need to some take time to come to terms with what she had done. But not now. Not yet.

He shampooed her hair. It felt wonderful to have his broad fingertips massaging her scalp. She applied some conditioner, and he cleaned her lower torso and legs.

It took a great deal of will for her to get dressed instead of going at it again. As she combed her hair, he called to her from the bed.

"Come and sit. I want to braid your hair."

"Seriously?"

"I used to braid my sister's hair. I'm pretty good at it. Or at least I was."

Sitting cross-legged on the bed with his legs on either side of her made her feel so safe and happy. The bristles of the hairbrush pulled a little at her scalp. His tender ministrations almost undid her. He followed the strokes of the brush with his hands, cherishing the task.

"I'm not fussy. Don't stress it," she said.

"I'm not. I want to get it right though."

When he was done, she looked at the complex braid he had woven. It was a fishbone design with uniform, exacting detail.

"Wow! You weren't kidding. You are good."

He grinned shyly, and she had the urge to get on her knees in front of him. He tried to still her head and her hands, but she was determined.

Once his penis was down her throat, she wrapped her lips around her teeth and sucked while pulling. It took him seconds to lose his load. She stood up, licking her lips like a cat that had just been served cream.

Before he could recover, she ran out the door and down the hall. She could hear him following behind. They ran out of the hotel and onto the street. Eventually she slowed her pace, and he caught up. Chis pushed her against the rough stone wall of an underpass and melted her with a scorching kiss. He then swatted her bottom to get her to resume their run.

After a short time, though, his energy depleted, he began to lag behind.

She slowed to a walk. "Tired, old man?"

"You wore me out," he said.

She laughed.

***

They wandered the streets, looking at hundred-year-old homes that were quaint and full of historical significance. Between her phone going off every ten minutes and short conversations or text messages, they still managed to browse a couple of knickknack shops before it was time to go back to get ready for the closing ceremony.

At one point, she said, "Sorry. People are wondering where I am and work beckons. I noticed you hardly use your phone?"

"I know. Can't stand the thing. I decided to leave it in my room. I don't need to be at anyone's beck and call."

"Oh," she said, but he read more into that one word. He could tell that she wondered about him and what he did for a living. She wouldn't understand. How could she when he didn't himself? How could someone in his position disregard everything that he was supposed to believe in for time spent with a woman?

It was strange to go to separate rooms to dress. It was even stranger to attend an event where they were forced to pretend they barely knew each other. Regardless, their eyes met several times that night. It was unavoidable. What he saw in her eyes was warmth, desire, and happiness.

After the closing ceremony, they went to an authentic Mexican restaurant and sat on the outdoor patio.

Chris watched her eat, feeling an ache in his chest at the thought that he might never see her again.

He poured her some wine from the carafe, but she stilled his hand.

"Not too much, honey. You know how I get."

Her simple statements almost brought him to his knees. His hand shook as he lowered it back to the table. He had never before been the recipient of that term of endearment, *honey*, which had so casually slipped from her lips. For the first time in his life, he felt loved, really loved, for who he was—and not for what he was or how he might help someone else.

Tory was an insatiable sex partner; when he was in her arms, he felt like he was in another dimension. She hadn't shied away from anything because she thought it obscene or perverted. Tory had used her mouth on his ass and actually liked sucking his cock. She had no inhibitions, which made everything they did okay. He might never again see a beautiful woman on her knees with the sole motive of pleasing him. And, oh, how she had pleased him!

The memory of his dick being swallowed up to his balls, rubbing against her throat, her dedication to sucking him dry, how he had pumped into her sweet mouth was unlike anything he'd previously known. That erotic, decadent act was the stuff of youthful fantasies.

He thought that he'd experienced everything as a young man, but that belief had been stripped away. He had had a girl's mouth on his dick before, playing with the tip or kissing it, but not doing what Tory had done. Her swallowing him whole had blown his mind.

As they ate in companionable silence, he was already mourning the loss of her. He had no words to express the crushing agony of knowing it was their last night. He felt like he would be losing the best part of himself. The irony was not lost on him as they lingered over coffee.

Then an idea emerged. What if they made it an annual event? He wondered how she might react to the suggestion. He shook his head, realizing it would never work. Tory had too many obligations. Still, the lure of this possibility tugged at him as they walked back to the hotel.

That night, their coupling was almost too poignant for words. He sensed her sadness, though, and hated that only a few hours remained for them to enjoy each other. Determined to make the most of the time left, he decided to show her what being with her meant to him.

CHAPTER 9

The next day, they attended some final breakout sessions. Neither of them had any interest in the subjects anymore, but it would have been odd if they hadn't shown up.

Although they wanted to remain naked and in each other's arms, they went back to the conference, sat at the same tables, and tried not to look at each other. It was damned hard to pretend they hardly knew one another when he had been up to his balls inside her body more than once.

Chris had to attend to some of his responsibilities and assist the conference volunteers. He tried to remain focused on his tasks, but his mind frequently wandered back to her. He couldn't get the feel of her skin out of his head. It was so soft and alluring as it changed from its usual pale tone to a blush when she was aroused by him. The disturbing thing was knowing he might never see it again. It was clear that Tory wasn't looking for anything beyond these few days, and that bothered him like an achy tooth.

In such a short time, she had become like an addictive drug to him. Was it even possible for an attraction to develop into something more in virtually no time at all? When had it all changed from a fling, a little sex, into a craving for her smell and her warm body? There had been no transition or easing into this—whatever it was. What would he do when his supply was cut off?

He was tied in knots over the situation. Tory had been willing to indulge in a few days of togetherness, but she was putting out signals that she had no intention of making anything more out of it. She seemed to be adjusting to the play sessions much better than he was.

In many ways, he had trouble accepting it for what it was. Each time they climaxed, she got under his skin and into his head a little more.

In addition, his lack of mental control made him a little nuts. He had just wanted some sex after such a long period of abstinence; now he wanted something else. He had started off enjoying the idea of this little interlude and changed his tune to wishing there were some way to prolong their relationship. Now that he had enjoyed a taste, he could not accept that he might never have it again.

As the day wore on, he craved her with a hunger that scared him. He tried to think of a new experience they could share that would tempt her to return to him the next year. An idea came to mind.

That night, back at the hotel, he steered her toward the deserted pool area. It was almost dark. There were only two underwater lights illuminating the whole space, and they were near a man-made waterfall.

"What are we doing?" she asked.

He was grinning like a kid. "We're going skinny-dipping!"

"What?"

"Don't be a chicken shit!"

"I'm not a chicken anything. What if we get caught? The pool's closed for the night. Besides, we might know someone—or someone might recognize us."

He pulled her close and growled into her ear. "Forget about everyone else. I am. I'm going to get you out of your clothes and in the water. And then I'm going to fuck you in front of God—and anyone else who wants to watch!"

Her instantaneous grin made him even more urgent. The first hurdle was the locked gate, but that was easily overcome by placing an overturned garbage can at the lowest point of the barrier. He tried to coax her into climbing onto it, but she appeared nervous. Instead, he picked her up and plunked her down on top of the garbage can, joined her, awkwardly jumped over the decorative metal fence, and assisted her down from the other side.

He lifted her and carried her to the pool. "You want to go in with or without your clothes?"

"You wouldn't!" She wiggled, trying to get free of his hold, but he held her aloft. "Okay, okay!"

They stripped and dove into the cool water, surfacing close to the deep end. He noticed her hardening nipples and warmed them with his mouth. Once she arched into him, the game was on. Her legs circled his hips as he sucked and bit her erect nipples, liking how they felt against the upper palate of his mouth.

He looked into her eyes and said, "I'm really going to miss you." He could tell from her suddenly grave expression that the sincerity of his statement was not lost on her. He wished he hadn't uttered those words. Her sadness mirrored his own, replacing the arousal that had been on her face moments earlier.

She placed a finger on his lips. "Please don't, or I'll—"

"I know. I didn't mean to. It just came out."

She brought her mouth to his, and they communicated through actions instead of words, which suited him just fine.

He made her cry out once and started working toward a second time. This time, he had her pushed against the side of the pool, his tongue in her mouth and his cock filling her cunt. She tapped his shoulder.

"What?" he whispered. The night was quiet, and the only noise to be heard was the movement of the water as he drove into her and their moans of pleasure.

"Someone's watching us."

"Where?"

"Up and to the right."

"How do you know?" She groaned as he adjusted the angle slightly.

"The light ... it's a cigarette tip ... how it flares when you draw on it."

"Good."

"Good?"

"Yeah, I bet we're turning them on."

"What if he calls someone?"

"He? You can tell?"

"No, just a hunch."

"We'll deal with it."

"You think he likes what he sees?"

"Yes, quite a lot. If the other guy on the balcony up there is any indication," Chris said, nodding his head behind her. "I'm pretty sure he's jerking off."

"What?" Tory pushed him back in alarm, but he held her firmly. "We can't—"

"We can, and we will finish."

"You know what bugs me about you is how bossy you get. And that tone of voice."

"It'll grow on you. Come on. You kind of like this, don't you? Admit it."

"I don't know."

"I know you're getting turned on by how you're squeezing my cock. Soon you'll be milking me when I make you scream."

"I won't be able to come."

He pulled out, dove under the water, and licked and sucked on her folds. She writhed under his attention until he came back up. "What do you want?"

"I want him to see your cock in my mouth."

He pulled himself out of the water to sit at the pool's edge and let her have her wish, allowing himself to relax and be submissive.

She stopped after a moment. "It's so hot watching him watch us. His fist is going fast. What's the guy upstairs doing?" she asked before resuming her work.

"He's at the edge of the balcony. I can't see what he's doing, but he's moving." She groaned around his dick, and he pushed into her. "My guy's jerking off, too," he continued. "You need to come, baby. Or should I invite him to join us? Would you like that? Huh?"

She released Chris and climbed out of the pool, going down on her hands and knees on the deck. He mounted her like a stallion, and that invited no further discussion. He sank into her core and felt the last of her hesitation dissipate. Their first voyeur on the balcony threw back his head, and a stream of ejaculate flowed. Chris's balls drew up. He was so close to losing his load that he knew she had to be ready to go soon too.

"You have to come now, baby. If you saw what I just did. Our guy must be young because so much come just flew out."

He pinched her tits and rubbed her clit like crazy. She screamed and squeezed him so hard inside her that he caved, groaning out his release. He fought to stay inside her as the intense pressure of her contracting vagina tried to push him out. He gripped her hips with brute force to stay in place.

At the same time, he felt a now-familiar twinge of regret: fucking Tory always ended way too soon. That perfect moment of climax he always wanted to reach so badly was also one he wanted to hold on to longer. He missed it as soon as it was over. Nothing in his life had ever come this close to bringing him to his knees. How would he survive without her?

***

Their last night was comprised of touching moments mixed with extraordinary ones. After they'd finished at the pool, they pulled their clothes back on. One of their voyeurs clapped for them, and they waved up at him before climbing back over the fence.

They ran back to Tory's room, laughing like children. She felt like a naughty adolescent, but had loved every moment of it.

He threw down her on the bed almost immediately after closing the door. Not knowing what to expect thrilled her the most.

"You were fabulous out there," he said, grinning.

"So were you. I never thought I'd like being watched."

"You'd probably like watching then—maybe even being enjoyed by others."

She shrugged, not comfortable admitting that she was, in fact, turned on by voyeurism, and that she had fantasized about having more than one person touch her and make love to her.

"Next time," he said.

Next time? What does that mean? There won't be another time.

"There are still a few things I want to do."

"Yeah?"

"Lie back and relax."

She laughed. "You won't be able to get anything more out of me for a while."

He ignored her words, instead taking her foot in his hand. "When you were on the massage table, and I had your foot in my hand, I wanted to do something."

She felt greedy for more, despite being exhausted. "Show me."

He flexed her toes forward, and she felt the stretch and pull all the way up her leg and to her lower abdomen. Then he placed his fingers between her toes, bent down, enveloped her big toe with his mouth, and sucked on it. It was an incredible sensation. Warmth and energy ran up her leg.

He removed her toe and nipped at the side of her foot. She closed her eyes in absolute delight as he moved to her other foot. She'd never realized how enjoyable it could be to have parts of her feet teased and sucked. All too soon, he was done and prowling up the bed. They kissed for a while.

She wondered if he might like having his toes sucked as much as she had. "Let me do it to you."

"You don't have to."

"I know, but I want to." When he said nothing, she licked his lower lip. "I'm going to give you a whole body massage. By my count, I owe you one."

His grin spurred her on.

She scooted out of bed, got her makeup case, and located a small bottle of baby oil. She turned the television to an easy listening station and began with his feet. She tasted them first, and his reaction to her sucking his big toe was rewarding. He was ticklish at first, but he settled down to let the novel experience take him to a restful place. It seemed to surprise him that this could feel so good. The man really was adorable.

Then, taking her time, she oiled her hands and started to rub him, concentrating on key muscle groups, working up and down the length of his body. He had rough areas on his knees, and she wondered where he'd gotten them as her hands glided over his skin. She liked the feeling of his thick chest hair against her palms. Chris seemed to enjoy that part as well. When she proceeded to run her hands up the entire length of his legs, he groaned quietly.

Sex as a young woman had never been like that. The learning curve from the mechanics of how to kiss to getting to first base had been exciting—but unfulfilling. She remembered with a grin how her breasts had gotten all tingly when they were touched softy by inexperienced hands. She had felt quite daring, letting a guy touch her anywhere below the waist, stripping for him, or being adventurous and actually touching his penis. Those days of fumbling copulation had eventually morphed into a desire to experiment. Feeling wicked and inventive, she had challenged some men too much up front, and they had never asked her out again.

Maybe that was what Sam was going through. Most guys weren't interested in testing limits or in taking or giving up control. They just wanted the release and didn't care about anything else. A man had once told Tory that she was selfish. Well, she had no regrets. *Youth is the time to learn what you like and ensure that your partner knows it too.* She had been self-assured enough to know that this intimidated some men. John had been the exception—or so she had thought. He had pushed her sexual boundaries a couple of times while they dated, and she had hoped that it would continue.

What am I doing thinking about the past?

Right in front of her was a man who seemed to understand that she needed to be in charge of the play once in a while. At the moment, he was very compliant. "Roll over," she said.

She straddled his waist so she could reach his neck and shoulders. Using all her strength, she teased out the stiffness, applying pressure with the base of her hands where they joined her wrists.

"I like your cunt on my ass. Your lips on my crack feel like flower petals touching my backside, soft and dewy," he said.

After a while, his knots loosened. When his shoulders relaxed, she moved on to his spine and his lower back, which eventually led her to his buttocks. Her slippery fingers played with his anus. When he grunted, she formed an idea.

"Up on your knees. Chest flat on the bed," she commanded.

He complied.

She lubricated one hand and grasped his semi-hard penis in it, pumping it slowly. She ran the index finger of her other hand down the seam of his buttocks and drew it around the rim of his puckered opening before inserting it.

He jerked, but it seemed a natural reaction.

When he didn't object, she continued. Her index finger was firmly ensconced in him. Now she pulled it out and pushed two fingers inside. She made a scissoring motion inside his rectum, pulling her fingers apart and bringing them back together again. He was instantly aroused. As she repeated the movement, he clamped his hand around hers over his penis and pumped it harder. His grip was so strong that she worried she'd inadvertently injure him. However, he continued, even more frenzied.

She wondered how he felt with her inside him—if it was at all like the way she felt when he was inside her. She bit and kissed the taut tissue of his buttocks along his tattoo.

Together, they worked to make him erupt. She concentrated on his rectum and located the prostate gland. He began ramping up and tensing for his release. She watched him spill his seed, keeping her fingers in place as he fell forward.

It took him a long time to recover. She waited, giving him whatever he needed with no intention of moving until he was ready.

When he eventually rolled to his side, she felt his grip loosen, and she gently extricated herself to wipe him off.

***

They did not speak when she returned from the bathroom. He thought it best to keep his feelings private until he could even understand them himself. Besides, he needed time to digest it all. He had never felt that way before. It was too unexpected to deal with.

He cautioned himself about becoming infatuated with a married woman; it was supposed to be about guiltless sex and nothing more. The lady had made it abundantly clear that she was not looking for anything else. That should have been a relief, given that he was in no position to continue the affair.

There was no doubt in his mind that he would miss their time together—and his access to her body. She had taken him to places that he had almost forgotten existed. This recent gift had almost been too much.

He pulled her close. They slept for a while until a dream awakened him.

It was dark outside. He had very little time left to fit in what he still wanted to accomplish. He felt selfish, but he refused to let that stop him.

He took advantage of Tory's being asleep to position her before getting the baby oil. Time was too precious to waste. He would wake her up by getting started.

***

Tory opened her eyes, wondering briefly where she was and what was going on. She slowly began to register what Chris was up to. He was kneeling back on his feet before her, and he had her legs spread open on either side of him. She felt his soothing touch on her skin as he rubbed her inner thighs. Only this man could make her feel so wicked. He was obviously intent on getting in as much playing as possible. Tory became instantly alert.

Chris must have noticed that she was awake. "Hands behind your head," he said.

"Why?"

"So I can remember you this way. Warm. Soft. Obedient. Even though that's not your nature. So fucking sexy you take my breath away."

She rolled her eyes. "What are you doing?"

"I told you I was going to give you an internal and external massage. While you were on the massage table—"

"Back to that, are we? I think you enjoyed that more than I did."

"Yes, I did. When you lay down for me with your eyes covered, thinking I was some massage therapist with no ulterior motive. You dozed off at one point, and I breathed you in. Your panties were wet, and I wanted to lick you through them. Some of your curlies were peeking out of the lace. I wanted to taste you. Your scent was exquisite."

She looked down and saw that he had dressed her in her underwear while she slept.

"You're not wet enough yet, but you will be."

He rubbed the flesh where her legs met her groin and ran his fingers along the elastic edge of her panties. He played with her through the cloth barrier. Somehow, it made her hotter than touching her directly. She could hardly believe the lust she felt for him every time he used his hands on her body.

"Ah, yes. Here we go." He leaned forward and licked her, just as he said he would. The heat and moisture from his saliva made his touch so erotic. When he'd had enough of that, he yanked away her panties, shredding the fabric as though it were paper.

He spread her folds open so she felt totally exposed. His fingernails gently scratched at her vulva. She wasn't sure what he was doing, but it felt amazing. He made her taut and tingly as he touched various parts of her perineum. She wanted him inside her.

His fingers slid into her vagina, and his other hand kept rubbing.

She raised her pelvis to hint that he should massage her clitoris, but she need not have bothered. The man was bent on doing as he pleased. She told herself firmly not to beg. She would not be reduced to that. It was nearly time to return to reality anyway.

Back home, there would be no Chris to play with. There would be laundry to do and a new week to prepare for. Her son had missed a dentist appointment, and she would have to reschedule it.

"Stop thinking," he said.

She grinned and was about to say that he could read her too well, but then his fingers located a certain spot inside her that made her back arch.

"You like? Don't think about anything but how good my hands feel as they fuck you."

She closed her eyes and let reality fall away so he could deliver on his promise. Her climax crested slowly and then rocked her with shattering intensity as he eased her through wave after wave of aftershocks.

His hands cupping her breasts as he spooned her from behind was the last thing she remembered before being pulled into slumber.

CHAPTER 10

The phone rang, and Tory jumped. On the other end of the line was a robotic-sounding voice: her wake-up call. She couldn't remember requesting one, so she flopped back on the bed. Something was off, and it took her a few seconds to figure out what it was. Chris was gone.

What had she expected? To wake up beside him? No, he had been right to leave without a word. It was better that way. A clean break.

She looked around her room to confirm he wasn't here, rolled out of bed, and started to pack for checkout. Thirty minutes later, after one last glance around the room, she closed the door on a part of her life that already seemed like a dream. If not for some marks on her skin and her shaved pubic area, she would have questioned whether or not she had really had an affair with a man she just met. It hardly seemed possible. Not in her world anyway, and it was something never to be repeated.

Unwilling to stay at the hotel a minute longer, she took an early shuttle to the airport and texted Joe, Kal, and Deb to let them know where she was before finding a place to wait for them. She tried to read a magazine, checking her cell frequently in case Chris texted. She was acting silly. What had she expected? That he would want to say good-bye? That wasn't how people behaved in real life.

The time dragged on. Thirty minutes before boarding time for their flight, Joe appeared and sat down beside her. "Hi, stranger!"

"Well, hello!" she said, trying for cheeriness. "I was afraid you guys would miss your flight."

"That guy we met a couple of days ago, Chris, insisted he drive us. He said had to return his rental at the airport anyway. Here come the others," Joe said.

Tory looked up, hoping to see Chris with them, but he wasn't. She forced a smile and welcomed her colleagues.

Then her phone buzzed. She looked at the screen and froze.

Come to the family washroom. Ahead of you and to the right.

"I'm going to use the restroom," she said. "Can you guys watch my stuff?"

She hurried to the private restroom to see him one last time. Her heart was beating so fast that she worried she might pass out from the excitement.

At the door, she swallowed and tried to compose herself. Once she went in and saw Chris, though, she fell apart, despite her best efforts. "I thought I'd never see you again!" she said, perilously close to crying.

"Hush now."

"I thought you left without—"

"Without this?"

His lips found her trembling smile, and he kissed her with such passion that her legs wobbled.

"I went to my room to shower and pack. When I knocked on your door, you didn't answer. The desk clerk told me you'd checked out already. Why didn't you wait to say good-bye?"

"You were gone when I woke up. I thought you wanted it that way."

"I should have left you a note. I would never—not without this."

He kissed her again, this time licking the tears that ran down her cheeks.

She felt ridiculous letting her emotions show. "Sorry. I'm not usually like this."

"I had to track down your friends so I could—" He kissed her again. "We can't be in touch at all after today. I don't know how I'm going to do it. How I'm going to face a day, a week, a month, a year without you in it," he said.

She sighed, knowing she would feel the same way. "I'm going to miss you so much, Chris."

"I know, baby. But we haven't talked about next year yet."

"Next year?"

"Yes. We'll meet again."

She couldn't get her head around that idea. Their affair was to be a one-time thing; it was unthinkable to continue it, no matter the appeal. Guilt had nothing to do with it. Even if John weren't in the picture, she didn't want to need a man this way or deal with all the emotional baggage. No, they would never see each other again. It was too risky. It would be too easy to lose herself in him. All they had shared these past few days was incredible, but it was not enough to tempt her into repeating them.

But looking into his eyes, she knew she couldn't tell him that.

Placing the flat of her hand against his chest, she inhaled deeply, turned around, and walked outside without another word. It was one of the most difficult things she had ever done. She was leaving a lover who seemed as essential to her as air to breathe.

She went into the women's restroom to wipe her tears and put on a brave face. There'd be time for grief later that night, when she was alone.

***

The thing about returning home after a trip is that everyone wanted your attention, and it didn't seem to matter how tired you were. She addressed work issues while she waited for her luggage at the airport, but her phone continued to chirp and beep as soon as she entered the door. Taking a page out of Chris's book, she ignored it and went in search of her family.

She didn't want to be alone with her thoughts anyway. Not yet. A diversion was required, and as expected, she could count on Sam for that. When she approached the kitchen, she could tell that something had occurred because her kids were sitting at the table while Alice looked at them with her hands on her hips. Her mother only ever did that when she was really pissed.

"What's going on?"

Everyone began to talk at once—and then just as suddenly stopped when she raised her hand. "Mom?"

"Hi, honey! These two got into a fight."

When she didn't elaborate, unease ran up her spine. "What about?"

"He called me a *skank*!" Sam said. Tory could tell that her daughter was struggling not to show how offended she was about the term.

"Jakie," she admonished.

"Well, she deserved it, Mom. I'm sick of the way she dresses and acts around guys. My friends don't want to come over anymore because of the way she is."

"You're so full of it!" Sam yelled.

"Okay, okay. Settle down, you two!" Remembering that her mother had a date, she said, "Before we go on, Mom, do you need to leave?"

Alice nodded and left soon after. Then it was time for a long talk. When her kids were little, she used to make them hold hands after they had a skirmish and work through the details of what had set off the argument. Now, she reached across the table and took each one's hand in hers before restarting the conversation. After about thirty minutes, they seemed to have worked it out a little. At least enough to revert back to their normal sullen behavior.

She listened more than she talked and gave them her undivided attention. It seemed like the best course of action. While she made dinner, they stayed nearby, telling her about events that had occurred while she was away. Something about a raccoon into the neighbor's garbage last night and other benign topics. Her mind was only half engaged. Her emotions were all messed up. Although she was glad to be home, a part of her resented her life, but she couldn't imagine a different one.

They ate together, and then Sam went out.

Tory lugged her suitcase to her room, sat on the edge to the bed, and thought about San Antonio and what she could be doing instead of sorting through clothes. Felling a little sorry for herself, she took a shower and settled on the bed to read a book.

She heard John come home sometime around midnight. She could have turned the light on and made it easier for him to find his way to the bed. She could have at least acknowledged him. But she did neither of those things. Instead, she pretended to sleep while feeling a little melancholy. Part of it was guilt at having betrayed her husband with another man, but the other piece was that her life held little appeal at the moment.

They remained apart in the queen-sized bed, like strangers. She remembered how it used to be. When she worked shifts and he would join her, no matter what time of the day, and snuggle in behind her. Why hadn't she cherished those times more? When everything seemed so easy and better. Those days were long gone. Tonight was a perfect example of that. He stayed on his side, and not a body part touched hers.

As she replayed her evening with the kids, she realized that not once did they mention John. It was like he didn't matter anymore. Like he was already gone from them. His body might still be present, but the rest of him had checked out a while ago. She wasn't certain when or why it started to feel that way. It just happened.

Perhaps she could have done something, she thought, but she couldn't come up with a single thing to say or do. It would be even worse now, she realized. Time with another man had taught her what a relationship could be like with someone who wanted you. There was no going back.

She had no desire to even try anymore to be what John needed. No matter how she felt about betraying him, she couldn't bring herself to care about him anymore. It should have made her feel worse, and in some ways it did, yet in a fundamental way it did not. She had come to a decision to emotionally distance herself from the man she had made promises to so long ago because he didn't want her or their family. They deserved better.

When morning came, she got ready for work. Her new attitude from peacekeeper to ignoring him didn't sit well with her husband.

"I said that I want to go on a trip," he said. "Don't walk away from me!"

"We can't afford it, John, and I have to dress."

"I'm talking to you!"

"So talk." She kept her tone even, determined not to let it escalate into a fight. *I would have to care to do that anyway.*

Before she knew what was happening, he grabbed her arm and threw her against the dresser. They both stood frozen for a second before he realized what he had done. She had no idea how to react because she was in shock, she guessed. In her head, she couldn't get over the fact that it had come to this. How had the man she knew become a different person? Could brain metastases account for the disintegration of the person?

Jake came to the door and knocked. "Mom? Everything okay in there?"

"Leave us the fuck alone! Take your queer ass to school!" John bellowed.

Her heart broke. She had always known that her husband lacked any tact, but she couldn't stand the way he spoke to and treated Jake. Her son, bless him, came into the room anyway, looked at her then at his father, and said, "Take your hand off her."

There was no inflection in his voice to betray his anxiety that he must be experiencing; it was just a straightforward command that left no room to misunderstand the intent. She was so proud of her son, but she worried that John might try something. Instead, she was surprised when John released her and stepped away.

Even if she had not yet decided that they were officially done, that would have tipped the scales. She couldn't forgive him for that. And she didn't want to.

***

The nausea began five weeks later. At first, she convinced herself it was the flu. Deep down, though, she knew it was something else. No matter how much she wanted it to be otherwise, three home pregnancy tests and one doctor's appointment confirmed it no matter how much she wanted it to be otherwise. She had been on the pill when she had been with Chris, but the fact was no method of contraception was 100 percent effective, and they had increased her odds of getting pregnant with the sheer number of times they'd fooled around.

What the hell am I going to do? Tory lost weight and looked dreadful. Her mother and coworkers mentioned it tactfully, but they presumed it was due to John's illness. In reality, she was suffering from a combination of morning sickness and guilt. Plagued by the consequence of what she'd done, she couldn't keep down solid food.

For the whole first trimester, she stayed in a state of denial and paralysis, not telling anyone her secret.

And then, without warning, John collapsed one evening and was admitted to the hospital. He had been getting steadily worse for the past few months, but his sudden decline took Tory by surprise. He was moved into palliative care hours after his arrival.

Over the few days John spent in hospital with Tory and kids by his side, she kept her secret, despite her internal anguish.

The day that John passed away in his sleep, she was almost four months pregnant.

The kids were coping surprisingly well—they had been preparing for John's death for a long time and had made their peace with him a while back. They both settled back into their respective schools. Alice seemed to be worried about her though, likely believing Tory had taken her husband's passing harder than expected. Finally, unable to keep it secret anymore, she told her mother she was pregnant.

Naturally, Alice assumed that John was the father and that Tory's anguish was due to having to raise this child all be herself. She felt guilty but not enough to correct her mom's impression. Her mom had several questions though, which made Tory wonder if her mother bought the whole story.

She didn't have the energy to address it with anyone. It seemed like the easiest road to take, so she kept up the lie. That was what everyone thought anyway. Tory could read the pity in her neighbors' eyes. She felt like a fraud, but she let the lie stand. What choice did she have?

Tory's work had suffered during John's last weeks; she had been forced to take a leave of absence. Now she no longer had a sick spouse to care for, things were back on track, and her priorities were shifting. Being pregnant did that to you.

The last thing she'd expected was having another child at forty-three. It had been almost seventeen years since her youngest was born, and all of his baby stuff had been given away to others long ago. With Alice's help, Tory went shopping and filled up her home with baby necessities. Considering all the sickness and loneliness she'd had to contend with for so long, in some ways, getting ready for this new baby was the best time of her life. Everything was not rosy, though.

She had difficulty settling in most nights. For weeks before John had died, she'd cried herself to sleep, thinking about Chris, battling her longing for the man she hardly even knew and the guilt of having betrayed her dying husband. She knew it was stupid and unnecessary to be experiencing this internal struggle—with their failing marriage and the advanced stage of his disease—but it didn't even matter.

Since John's death, Tory's ability to fall asleep had only slightly improved. Most nights, she prowled the house or watched TV.

If her kids caught her wandering around, she blamed her insomnia on heartburn, making sure to have a glass of milk in her hand as a prop. It was simpler to pretend that everything was normal and fine. That she was a responsible parent instead of being accidentally pregnant and living a lie.

Sam teased Tory about getting fat, but she was looking forward to having a new sister. Jake acted cool and uninterested, but Tory knew better. He had volunteered to clear up the spare room and set up the crib. Sam and Jake seemed to have grown up a lot in the few months since John's passing. Tory observed signs of maturity in them almost daily, and she hoped that all the time she'd spent with them in the past three years had been some impetus for that. The two of them hardly fought with each other anymore or give her attitude.

Years ago, when Tory had taken the procurement job and tried to address her son's difficulties at school, she had started out just sitting in front of the TV with him, watching sports and other mindless shows at night. At first, very few words were exchanged between them, but gradually, he'd begun to relax enough to talk to her. John had called her son a mama's boy, but she and Jake had ignored it.

One time, for a treat, she'd gotten Jake tickets to a hockey game and encouraged him to invite some friends, maybe a girl. It was then that he'd shared with her his confusion over how he felt about sex and girls. She realized that he might be gay, but knew she would accept him, no matter what, so she didn't push him to talk about it more than he wanted to. Since then, the two of them had been close.

She was less successful in trying to be what Sam needed her to be. Even before John had become ill, Sam had looked for attention. She was always coming home with a new piercing or tattoo or outrageous haircut. Her choice of attire was also interesting. She experimented with colors and texture and never wore the same thing twice, except for some pairs of jeans. In contrast, Tory had never believed clothing mattered—unless it was too revealing.

But since switching schools, Sam's personality had changed yet again. It had settled a little, as though she had discovered something about herself and accepted it. Tory could see it in the way Sam smiled more and didn't try as often to antagonize Tory, which had always stressed their relationship. In fact, they had stopped being so adversarial with each other. Regardless of how well they were relating to each other, though, Tory would not share her secret with her daughter or anyone else.

After her ultrasound revealed the baby was a girl, she texted Chris, asking him to contact her. She owed it to him to tell him, and it didn't feel right telling the man he was about to be a father in writing. The least she could do was break the news over the phone. She was desperate to unload her secret with the only other person she could tell, and she really wanted to hear his voice again. She was entirely aware that he might not want anything to do with her and the baby, but then again he might. She wasn't completely sure she wanted him around, but if he wanted to be, they could probably figure things out somehow.

He never acknowledged her messages, however. After a second and third attempt went unanswered, she gave up.

At first, she was angry about his being incommunicado. Yes, the rules had been set, but if he had reached out to her multiple times, she would have responded, wouldn't she? She would have liked to think so, but a small part of her wondered. She could imagine myriad reasons why he hadn't responded, and they were not all unreasonable. It was probably better for him to remain in her past. He was, after all, little more than a stranger. Why should he care to raise a child with a woman he barely knew? And why would she want a man in her life again telling her what to do while she swallowed her resentment? So her baby's fatherhood would remain a secret, and a nonissue.

Being free to make all of the decisions was liberating in so many ways. She realized that she'd never need a man in her life again. She had her career and her kids to provide what she really needed. If she required help, her mother was nearby. That would have to be enough.

Because of her age, Tory had to rest quite a bit in the last trimester. She spent most of the last month in bed, being catered to by her kids and mother. Zoey was born two weeks early, but she was healthy, and that was all that mattered. Sam and Alice seemed overjoyed, and Jake took it all in stride. The newborn spent her first weeks in someone's arms, and for the first time in a long while, Tory felt whole again.

Tory knew Zoey was special from the moment she opened her eyes, which she'd gotten from Chris; they were dark brown and soulful. They stared back at Tory, and tears of bittersweet joy, as well as sadness, leaked from her own eyes.

They spent every moment together. Tory carried this precious infant in a sling against her chest for most of the day so she could get tasks done, but often she found herself just sitting and gazing at Zoey for long periods of time, not accomplishing much else. Nothing seemed to matter but looking after this tiny person. She had softest skin, the cutest lips, and the best disposition.

The bond she shared with Zoey was more intense than her bonds with Sam or Jake. She felt a little guilty, but it made sense. She was a mature mother this time, with experience in child-rearing. Sam had had to endure the mistakes of rookie parenting, and by the time Jake came had along, she had confidence, but less patience. This time around, she would get it right.

Between day care and Alice's help, Tory returned to work after a month. She was reluctant to leave Zoey, but at the same time, she was glad to be back at work. She was someone who needed to stay busy and stimulated beyond her mothering.

When the notice about the Supply Chain Management Association's annual conference in Texas came across her desk, she dismissed it at first. It was too soon to be leaving Zoey—and she wasn't sure she wanted to face the memories—but there was a chance

Chris might show up. While she was pretty set on keeping him out of Zoey's upbringing, she did like the idea of seeing him again. When Joe asked if she planned to attend, she said she was giving it some thought. When she mentioned it to her mom, Alice convinced her not to miss the opportunity; she could take care of Zoey.

She struggled with the decision for days. At one point, she believed she was just fooling herself about what she really wanted. If nothing else, she could get some closure that was long overdue. Pushing ahead before she could change her mind, she registered, booked the room and flight, and started counting down the weeks until she would be back in Texas. There was always the option of backing out. If the odds were slim that Chris would show up, why was she going?

It took many more days to refrain from canceling the trip altogether, and right up until the night before she was scheduled to leave, she still had her doubts. It took a little soul-searching to come up with a valid reason to return to a place that held such good memories. It wasn't really to recapture the past or even expect to resume a similar experience; it was simply to appease something within her that had to be done. Revisiting the location might bring her a sense of peace because she still held on too much to what had transpired there to move on. At least that was what she finally told herself.

***

She arrived safely in the same San Antonio hotel room that she'd occupied the previous year. Nothing had changed since her last visit. She touched the familiar pattern on the duvet cover and glanced at the headboard, remembering too many moments.

At the window, she looked out at the pool and smiled. Whether or not she saw Chris, she had a few days off from her duties at work and home to make the most of.

Tory changed into running gear and tucked her room key, ID, and money into a zippered pocket. She walked around downtown for a while, reacquainting herself with the streets, getting her bearings, and then she ran a little, ending up at the convention center to register early, just like last time.

She picked up the small tote bag that was a gift to registrants, stopped at the market for some fruit, and started back to the hotel, intending to call her mother. She was already missing Zoey and wanted an update.

As she turned the corner to get to her block of rooms that led to her door—she saw him.

Time stood still. He had a goatee, but she would recognize him anywhere, anytime, regardless of how he looked. He had yet to notice her, which gave her a few moments to observe him and figure out a plan. She had promised herself that even if Chris were at the conference and they decided to be together, she wouldn't dive into marathon sex sessions again. It had nothing to do with the fact that John had passed; it just had to be that way. She didn't like the way Chris affected her. And she didn't want to trust any man ever again. She didn't like the person she became around him. And then there were all the feelings that came along with what they'd had together. All that shit afterward, missing him and hating herself, had been too much to endure, no matter how good the sex was.

And then he raised his head and looked directly at her.

She had been holding her breath, and it came out in a whoosh. He was handsome and virile in jeans and a blazer—much too handsome, even better than she remembered. And he was looking at her intensely, like she was his.

"Hi," he said as though they had seen each other only yesterday.

She tried hard not to give away how affected she was to see him. "Hello! Fancy meeting you here!"

"I took a chance that you'd come."

"Huh?"

He took a step toward her, but she raised her hand so he'd keep his distance.

She wanted to be honest, to let him to know how she was feeling, but she also had no intention of telling him certain things. Especially about Zoey or about how much she thought about him, especially when she looked at her child. Then there were other things she had thought she'd come to terms with. Such as what had transpired last year and how she would just indulge in sex this time, holding everything else at bay. Ignoring the closeness they'd shared in those physical intimacies. But now he was here, she clearly understood more than ever that he had a great power over her, and it was too unsettling.

"I'm not ready for this. For you. I thought I could act all cool, but you're too much," she said, feeling slightly sick to her stomach.

He frowned, and she tried not to let this emotional temperature bother her. Her goal was to make it into her room and to call her mom. She walked past him to her door and went inside.

While she was talking to Alice, there was a knock on the door. She checked the peephole and groaned.

"What's wrong, dear?" her mother asked.

"Oh, one of my colleagues is here. Can you hold for a sec?"

She opened the door, raised her index finger at Chris, and let him in. "I'm almost done," she said to him before continuing her conversation with her mother. "There's more milk in the freezer. You know how to thaw it, right? Okay. Give Zoey a kiss for me. Love you too, Mom. I'll call tomorrow. Bye."

She hung up the phone and looked at him. "Did you want something?"

"Why do I get the feeling you're not happy to see me?"

"It's not that."

"You're not upset?"

"No."

"Something's not right."

"Why do you say that?"

"You're different. You look different."

She laughed. "I have put on some weight."

"You look good. But it's something else."

"You know that, do you? You've spent at best a few minutes with me."

"Are you going to tell me?"

She looked him in the eye. If she were going to do it, this would be the moment, but she held back.

"Forget it," he said when she didn't respond. "I don't care. Can I hold you at least? I just need that."

Tory hated that she also wanted that. "No funny stuff."

119

"No funny stuff."

He came closer.

She'd expected that there might be some awkwardness between them, given how long they'd been apart, but the embrace felt right. Still, she would not read anything into it or let her urges rule her head. She closed her eyes. Chris smelled so good, and she had missed sharing intimacy with a man. The ease of closeness. Strong arms around her.

She pulled back, and he asked, "Now what?"

"I don't know." It was an honest answer. She was torn between wanting him and still being miffed that he hadn't answered her texts and e-mails. *Perhaps he has a girl in every port.*

"Have you eaten?"

"No." She was not often hungry these days, even at the best of times. Add a little stress to the mix, and her appetite was nonexistent.

He grinned, as though her distant tone wasn't having a negative impact on him. "How about you just keep me company then?"

"I'm sorry, can you just … tell me what you want?"

Chris moved toward her quickly and pushed her against the wall, taking her breath away with his mouth on hers. All the loneliness of the past year left her body.

She pushed against him while also dragging in some air. Then they broke apart.

"Okay, that answered part of my question." Even her nipples were tingling.

"If you don't come with me, then I'll have you the way I want to, against the wall, in two seconds."

"Maybe. But you're leaving my room now."

"Why?"

Her breasts were beginning to leak milk. She fought the urge to cross her arms. "So I can change. I'll meet you in the lobby in fifteen minutes."

He looked at her as if to judge the sincerity of her response. "What if I don't want to leave?"

Tory had done a great deal of thinking while they were apart. She was not going to make this easy for him. "That's not your decision."

"Tory—"

"Let go of me, Chris." Proud of herself for being firm, she did not break eye contact. But she could tell he wasn't quite convinced. *Smart man.* "Look, you can't expect to start up again as though we saw each other yesterday. Too much has happened."

"What do you mean?"

She sighed.

"Okay, I'll see you in a few," he said. He gave her one last look and left the room.

Tory leaned against the closed door, touched her lips, and shut her eyes. The way his eyes seemed to pin her in place, the man was lethal.

Who was she kidding? He had to know that the only reason she was there was the hope of hooking up with Chris. The sexy lingerie and added birth control she'd packed, the manicure she'd gotten before leaving, and the wetness of her crotch were all evidence of her intent.

Scoffing at herself, Tory went to the mirror to make herself presentable. She wanted sex, but she would need to be careful not to completely lose herself in him again. Furthermore, they had already made a daughter together, and she had to keep that from him at least a while longer. Tory had no idea who he really was or even where he lived. But the majority of conference attendees were likely American, since she could pick up the different dialects and those who were in the various forces, like the navy, wore a crest somewhere on their clothing identifying them as such. She wouldn't risk having her precious child uprooted regularly to another country just because Chris demanded access or visitation. No, she would get what she needed out of their liaison and return home.

Staring at herself in the mirror, she cringed, allowed herself one second of guilt, and walked out the door with a spring in her step.

CHAPTER 11

Chris knew she was hiding something, and he sensed that it was big. Tory had changed. She had admitted that. So it had to be something significant.

If she tried to barricade herself inside her room, he would camp outside her door. If she pretended to be distant, the way she had earlier, he would find a way of warming her up. Somehow, he would get her to open up to him. He was finished waiting. It had been an agonizing year of missing her. He wasn't entirely sure why she was acting so reserved since she must have come to the conference to see him. Perhaps she was shaken by actually seeing him again.

When she walked out of her room—looking sophisticated and put together in a beige suit and sandals—she took his breath away. She was even more beautiful than he remembered. Seeing her earlier had brought it all back—her gorgeous and giving body, her soft skin. The idea of never again sampling that was out of the question.

She met his gaze. *I'm so screwed*, he thought. If Tory was looking for a pound of flesh, he would give it to her, and anything else she might ask of him.

"Ready?" she asked.

"Yep. What's in the bag?"

"Running shoes, just in case."

"In case?"

"In case I have to ditch you fast," she said, deadpan.

He wanted to remain serious, but broke out into a laugh.

She grinned. Thank God! He took her hand and led her to a nearby eatery.

They made small talk until the wine was served.

"How's your family?" she asked. "Oh, right, I don't know if you have one. Maybe you were hatched from an egg."

"Very funny. My parents are dead. I had a younger sister. Not married before she died. She hated men."

Tory laughed. "I get that."

"I never talk about my family," he said.

"Why not? No, never mind. How about the weather? That's a safe topic."

"Your husband was ill last year. How is he?"

The color drained from her face, and she looked ill. He worried she might make a dash for it. "I'm sorry. I didn't mean to pry."

She let out a long exhale. "He died."

He took hold of her hand. "Oh, Tory, I'm so sorry. I didn't—"

"Didn't know? Is that what you were going to say? And why would you, Chris? How would you have known?" she said. She tried pulling her hand away, but he had a firm grip.

"Was that why you tried to contact me? Please. Why are you angry?"

She closed her eyes, and a tear escaped.

He felt like shit, making her miserable in a public place. "Do you want to leave?" he asked.

She shook her head. "It doesn't matter."

"Of course it matters. Your husband passed away, and you're angry with me."

"Never mind."

"We have to talk about this."

"No, we don't."

Perhaps he should just keep his mouth shut, but he needed to make this right. "Okay, let me guess what's bothering you."

"Chris—"

"Number one—"

"You want to do this now? Here?"

"Yes. If we don't get past this right now, we'll lose precious time getting to where we need to be."

"And where is that?"

"Like you don't know? In my bed with me inside you."

"Shh!" She looked around to see if anyone had overheard them, but he continued, undaunted.

"One: I didn't do what you expected, right? You thought I'd call you."

"No."

"Even though we'd agreed not to, you didn't appreciate the fact that I made no attempt to contact you."

Her eyes flared, so he knew he was close.

"Two: You tried to contact me, and I didn't respond."

A pained expression flashed across her face. *Bingo!*

"Three: You tried to Google me, but you came up dry. My name's very common. Last time I checked, there were at least thirty Chris Enns, most of them without an online mug shot to distinguish them from each other. Four—"

"You're going to go on and on, aren't you?" she said. "Would you shut up?"

He didn't like her being upset with him.

Luckily, the appetizers arrived. They ate—or he did, at least.

She took a few bites and then put down her fork. "I had to deal with a lot before and after John died," she said more calmly. "And I had some things I wanted to tell you. I texted. And e-mailed. More than once. You never responded. I was disappointed."

He flinched inside but remained silent. When he'd received her messages, he'd had no idea she was trying to contact him about something as devastating as her husband's death. It had been difficult to pretend that she hadn't reached out to him. He'd decided at the time that he had to be strong enough for the both of them and not respond to her. And in truth, he couldn't risk doing so; if she had wanted to meet somewhere or something like that, it wouldn't have taken much for her to convince him. She was his biggest weakness. He was still convinced he'd taken the right course of action, but that made him no less troubled to hear that she had been grieving. His silence had made her feel worse.

"But it doesn't matter," she continued. "I knew the rules. I should have known better. I got over it."

"No, don't lie. You didn't."

She stood up and left. He had messed up already. He scrambled for some bills to pay for the meal and rushed out after her.

She was nowhere in sight.

All of a sudden, he was so angry that he wanted to punch something. It was such a strange urge coming from someone like him. When he reached the hotel, he saw the light on in her room. He stared at her door for a long time. What should he do? He felt uneasy about his next move. Mostly because he had no clue how to proceed.

Finally, the door opened and she came out in a bathing suit. She didn't look at him as she passed on her way to the pool.

Then it came to him what might work. He hadn't gotten anywhere trying to talk to her; it wasn't what she needed. He had to communicate in the only way she couldn't resist.

He changed into trunks and joined her in the pool. Again, she didn't acknowledge his arrival, but she didn't object when he swam laps alongside her, matching her strokes. He glanced at her every once in a while, noticing that she was gradually becoming more relaxed, but he knew she needed some space. Sooner or later, she would either stop to take a rest or make the first move. Then he would gather her in his arms to remind her about what she needed.

He had spent the whole year thinking about her, so he was more than ready for the challenge. It was difficult to deal with the emotional distance when they were so physically close. He had been expecting her to throw herself at him as soon as they reunited, which he realized had been a strategic mistake. Grief and guilt were likely part of what was holding her back. She also seemed to be quite bothered by his not answering her messages.

At the time, he remembered thinking that he couldn't afford to respond. Any indication from her that she wanted him would have led to a struggle to deny her anything. That part worried him the most. Even if it was only a shoulder to cry on because her husband had died, he couldn't do it. In the end, it was a conscious decision to ignore her messages. It was safer for all to keep his distance.

He wondered if she had needed more than emotional comfort for her grief. If there had been anything urgent or crucial, surely she would have said so in her messages, wouldn't she? But the truth was that he didn't know her well enough to answer that.

He thought about their conversation earlier.

I don't know if you have a family. Maybe you were hatched from an egg.

Didn't know? Is that what you were going to say? And why would you, Chris? How would you have known?

It doesn't matter. I knew the rules. I should have known better. I got over it.

He had to find a way to make it up to her. He had screwed up big time.

Over the past year, he had revisited their time together over and over again. He felt a great deal of guilt at having sampled something he had no right to, and it had eaten at him for a long time—although not enough to dissuade him from returning this year in the hopes she'd be here, wanting to pick up where they had left off. But he was such an idiot.

She began to slow down, and he did as well. When she climbed out of the pool, he followed her, picked her up, grabbed her bag, and carried her to his room. What he had planned was not for anyone's eyes but his own. It was not lost on him that she placidly allowed this to happen. The pressure to make the hurt go away and get them back on even footing weighed on him heavily.

Her body trembled, as did his hands, as he laid her on his bed and removed her one-piece suit. This took much longer than he would have liked; the fabric clung to her wet skin and his frayed nerves made the task more difficult than it should have been, but he persevered. When he was finished, he dropped his trunks and crawled over her, suffusing heat into her chilled skin where they made contact.

Propped up on his elbows, he gazed at her beautiful face, searching for something, anything, to make the hard lump of anxiety in his gut go away. He looked into her liquid-blue eyes, getting lost in them. She was not easy to read, but she seemed more resigned than welcoming.

He took his time to reacquaint himself with her mouth, savoring her whimpers as his tongue danced with hers. Unable to resist any longer, she wrapped around him, and he sighed in relief. She had begun to thaw.

He spread her moist folds to check that she was ready. Her legs parted in invitation as he sunk in two fingers and then stimulated her clit. His whole body shook with desire and longing. He impaled her suddenly, unable to control himself any longer. The overwhelming need to be inside her overrode all other thoughts. They groaned in unison at the perfection of the moment. The way she drew him in and clenched tightly around his dick brought back their adventures from the previous year.

He saw a tear track from her eye to her hairline, and he licked it away instinctively. Although he didn't understand why she was upset, he wouldn't pretend her emotion wasn't real. It would be a mistake to ignore signs of her distress, and he had made too many blunders already. He could not afford another.

"Don't cry, beautiful lady. This is us at our best."

"It's not because I'm sad."

"I know that. It's everything, isn't it?"

She nodded.

"Can we call this *conference time*—when nothing or no one matters but us?" he asked.

"No."

"Why not? Sorry, you don't have to tell me."

"I have responsibilities."

"I get that. You need to check in. But the rest of your time is mine."

She sighed and clenched him from inside. His cock, semi-rigid already, became hard as stone.

"Are we good?"

"I'm sorry for the way I acted. My period is due, and I get this way."

"How do you get?"

"Bitchy."

He had to grin at the look on her face as she struggled not to smile. God, she was fucking gorgeous.

"Can we still do this when you get it?" He had always wondered whether couples generally abstained from intercourse during that time of the month.

She looked at him. Did she think it an odd request—or was she wondering why he didn't seem to have experience with this? "You mean can we have sex during my period?"

He nodded.

"No reason not to. As long as you don't mind things getting messy."

"Not if you aren't bothered."

"No. Now stop talking."

He sealed her mouth with his, and their bodies danced as if they had never parted. He knew what she liked, and she obviously knew what he did as well. Her body felt a bit different, though he didn't pay much mind. She was soft and searing hot, just like he remembered. He was so grateful that this wasn't all one-sided. She seemed to need it as much as he did. To be touched and to share this intimacy was so comforting.

Wanting to savor the feeling, he made his strokes slow, feeling the walls of her vagina clench at him, sucking him in deeper when he altered his angle by raising her right hip. So much better than his own hands.

"Faster!" she begged.

He complied, and they rushed to the finish line within seconds. When his breathing normalized, he realized that his chest was wet. He rolled to his side and saw liquid trickling from her nipples.

She met his gaze evenly. "I had a baby recently."

He jumped, uncertain why, but alarmed all the same. His eyes went to her abdomen and then to her face. Placing a hand on her stomach where the skin was a little flabby, he asked, "Should we be having sex?"

"Yes. It's fine. It's been over six weeks. Actually, she's three months old."

He thought for a moment. "The Zoey you mentioned on the phone?"

"Yes. She's a wonder. So good."

"Did your husband—"

"No, he died before meeting her."

"I'm sorry."

Tory became very quiet, which made him feel a little uneasy; they had been making great progress. She began to rise from the bed, but he couldn't let that happen. Besides, he'd never dreamed he'd have the opportunity to do what he was about to. He licked one her of nipples and then latched on, as though what he was doing was normal, and not a little fucked up. He stopped to ask, "Do you mind?"

Tory moaned in response.

He was glad, and he whispered, "This is fantastic." He sought out her other breast. If she did think his behavior bizarre, she gave no indication. Instead, she rubbed his head to let him know she was enjoying it as well.

Assessing the taste of her milk, he sucked harder.

She groaned louder.

"Am I hurting you?"

"No, it feels good. I was getting engorged."

"What were you going to do about it?"

"I have a breast pump with me. I can also use my hands, but a machine is quicker."

"Can I watch you do it?"

"Sure." She looked into his eyes. "You've never done this with your wife?"

He had no choice but to be honest and give her what she wanted: some information about himself. "No, I've never been married."

"No children, then?"

"No." It wasn't as difficult as he'd thought it might be, sharing these tidbits of information with her. She seemed to accept them without question. He felt lighter than he had a moment ago as she closed her eyes and continued to fondle his head.

"I can't believe I'm doing this," he said before latching on again. He couldn't get enough of what she was giving.

For a while, they simply lay together in silence. He craved more personal details of her life and expected she would want the same of him, but she said nothing. He wanted to know if her husband had ever fed off her that way; instead, he asked, "I won't get diarrhea, will I?"

She laughed, and the beautiful sound made his internal ache ease away. His cock instantly hardened.

They played all night. When morning came, so did her period. They shared the bathtub, and he tried to be attentive and read her nonverbal signals. She still seemed moody. He had to choose his topics carefully.

"Lean back, and I'll wash you," he said, taking the opportunity to soothe her with his actions. The water covered them both up to their waists; her breasts were exposed. Wetting a sponge, he squeezed water directly onto her nipples and watched them pucker. Enjoying the feeling of her back against his chest, he whispered, "You are fucking gorgeous. You make my mouth water to taste you. You have no idea how hot you are."

One of his legs was draped over the edge of the tub, and she absently trailed her fingers over his kneecap.

"Don't you have to go to the conference?" she asked after some time.

"I'm not involved like I was last year. I didn't even register for it. I'm here only to be with you. The committee posted the attendee list on the website, and your name was on it."

"What if I'd changed my mind? I almost backed out a couple of times."

"Because of Zoey?"

"Yes. She's not the only reason though. I've been extremely busy. I only just came back from maternity leave. Between bereavement leave and mat leave, I need to make up for lost time at work. And I've had to sort through things at the house, since my husband … but yes, she's the main reason. I've never left her for this long before."

"Your mom is watching her?"

"I wouldn't trust her to anyone else."

"Why don't you call your mom?" He felt certain that would help her mood. "Then we can go out for breakfast. And after that, back here for a nap."

"Just a nap, huh? Maybe I'll go to the conference."

He laughed. "Are any of your colleagues here?"

"No. Just me. No one else wanted to attend."

That worked out well for him since he had plans for her—for them both.

He pulled her out of the bathwater, dried her off, and dressed her in his T-shirt and boxer shorts, which she had to hold up as she returned to her room.

"Next time, we'll get adjoining rooms," he said.

"Next time, huh?"

***

It was so amazing, even better than last time. Part of her wanted to do a happy dance. The other part of her, where wisdom was housed, was beginning to feel some concern about how she would handle their imminent separation.

Later, while she pumped her breasts and her eyes feasted on him as he lounged beside her, she was already anticipating how it would feel when they parted. It was important for her to keep this time with him separate from her real life in southern Ontario. That was what really mattered, and the last few months had taught her to value what she had: the freedom to manage her life as she wished, without any male influence. Yes, these four days were all that she wanted from him.

It didn't matter that a whole year had passed or that he hadn't been around when she needed him. A pattern was developing. Again, she capitulated to him as though it were a forgone conclusion, and he continued to share very little about himself. He knew more about her life and her body than she had ever disclosed to another person. And yet, he was a nonentity, closed off, offering nothing. Why wouldn't he share even small, insignificant details of his own life? It seemed like he was deliberately hiding his identity, and that worried her. He dressed well and seemed to have money. How did he earn a living? Why all the secrecy? He was so unlike other men who bragged about themselves or talked about topics she barely related to, like sports and cars.

So much mystery surrounded him, and it made her a little uncomfortable. She had no idea who she was dealing with. What if he had wealth and influence and resources and an inclination to threaten her happiness? Directly asking him questions was not her style, and there was little likelihood of his disclosing any worthwhile details without being prompted, so she really had no hope of learning anything more. Besides knowing him in the biblical sense, knowing that he was a good lover, and knowing that he was easy to be around (most of the time), she had no idea who he was or where he came from. It shouldn't matter, given their arrangement, but it did. Part of her wanted a little more.

No. She was better off on her own, using him for her own pleasure and nothing more. It would never do for him to spill into her home life. He would take over, and she knew it.

"Does it pinch? It looks like it's pulling," he asked, rousing her from her thoughts and back to her current task.

"At first. But you get used to it, and eventually it feels good. I have to pump to keep up the supply."

"It's not as thick as I thought it would be," he said.

She grinned.

"Is it weird that I'm into this?"

"Not really. It's a novelty. No one has seen me do this, you know."

"Not your husband or your mom?"

"No."

"Your breasts are quite something. They look like they're right off a marble statue. There are tiny blue veins. They look heavy." He plumped one.

"They are."

"Sit between my legs, and I'll rub your shoulder and where the pump is pulling your skin."

She moved where he wanted and succumbed to his attention. His hands on her body always felt good. The hum of the pump motor lulled her to sleep.

She awakened, briefly, to find him trying to remove the pump shield, and she showed him how. The last thing she remembered before falling into a deep sleep was his mouth firmly attached to her nipple, suckling.

So different from what it's like with Zoey. That thought felt kind of strange, but in a good way.

CHAPTER 12

The next day, she gave up the pretense of attending any of the conference. Instead, they took a tour of San Antonio. Chris called a taxi and paid the driver to act as their guide. He drove them slowly past many beautiful homes. They visited a few museums and art galleries. Since they weren't interested in visiting the tourist traps, they walked along the man-made river, looked into shop windows, and stopped for the occasional drink.

Eventually, they relaxed on an outdoor patio.

"I'm enjoying the wine," she confessed.

"So what do you want to do tonight?"

"Besides the obvious?" She grinned.

"How about dancing?" he suggested.

"Can you dance?"

"Not really. Slow dancing, kind of. Hopefully there's dancing where I'd like to go. There's a show tonight at a place near here. The taxi driver told me about it. I understand it's a little risqué. It's like a sex show or sex theater."

Her eyebrows rose.

"Yeah, I know. But why not? Let's see how the other half lives."

"What do you mean?"

"It's formal. We have to dress up."

She had brought along a new dress and some nice undergarments to go with it. "Okay."

"Let's go back for a rest and then get ready."

"A rest, huh?"

"I noticed that you aren't shaved, and I brought some equipment that might make it easier than last time, if you're game."

"You aren't shaved, either," she said.

"It ... I didn't want anyone but you to do it."

Her chest tightened. *That was how I felt about it as well.*

Walking back, they held hands, and Tory realized for the first time that she was now free of the guilt of cheating on her spouse. She was single again and could handle whatever came along. The past year had proven that.

Over the course of John's slow death, she had lived through many days whose physical and mental toll she hadn't thought she could withstand. And then there was giving birth to Zoey alone because her mother and coach was recovering from cataract surgery, and caring for her new daughter without a partner. She wasn't going to waste the short time she had with Chris thinking about her life up north.

Chris went to his room to collect his shaving things while she showered in her own room and called her mother, who reassured her that Zoey was fine. It was such a comfort to have Alice looking after her. Sam was at university, but Jake was at home, helping around the house, so she spoke briefly with him as well. It seemed he had become a man all of a sudden, and she worried about him.

Jake rarely went out and stayed close to home as though he felt the need to be there for her. Tory tried to make him go out more, assuring him that she could manage and he didn't have to share her load, although she was grateful, of course. He was too young to be so responsible and so serious all of the time. He was already talking about applying to local colleges so he wouldn't have to move out. Between now and next fall, she would have to convince him otherwise.

Chris came in just as she was finishing up on the phone.

"Everything okay at home?"

She smiled. "Yes, it's all good. Did you check in with anyone at home?"

"No."

"Okay."

"I know you want to know more about me. I feel the same way about you. But you already know what's important: what's in my heart." He pulled her hand toward him and rested it on the left side of his chest. "I'm asking you to let it go."

He was right. What did it matter? There had to be a reason why he remained so secretive, and she would respect his decision even though it went against her natural inquisitiveness.

She shaved him first, taunting him and leading him into a wrestling match and much laughter. When it was her turn to be shaved, he was gentle and focused.

He left her to get ready. She pumped her breasts so she'd be fine for at least four hours and donned her fancy black dress. She hadn't gotten dressed up since last year.

She greeted him at the door. "I'll just be a minute," she said, putting on her heels. Her old insecurities and doubts started to resurface. She should have brought something different, a dress that would better hide her midriff. She was nervous about being seen with such a handsome man who could have anyone he wanted; it was affecting her ability to buckle the straps of her heels.

Chris knelt beside her. The look of desire in his eyes made everything better as he took over fastening her shoes. She felt lighter and happier than she had in a while.

***

When Tory opened her door, Chris saw a vision. Her hair was piled high, leaving her neck exposed. The top of her thigh-high stocking showed through the side slit of her dress, and he wanted to run his finger along the upper edge when she sat down.

Not knowing what to say, he cradled her foot and bent to kiss it before helping her fasten her shoes.

"Thank you," she said.

"You look amazing!"

She grinned. "So do you."

"You seem ... uncertain. What's going on?"

"I don't know. No, that's not true. I do know, but it's stupid. Forget about it."

"Tell me."

"Not tonight."

Perhaps she could be persuaded to share her thoughts later. He searched for something romantic to say.

"I wanted to bring you a bouquet, but the florist downstairs was closed."

"I don't want any flowers."

She was in a mood that he had no idea how to manage. He pulled her to stand, and they faced each other. "Okay, here's what's going to happen. When you get into the car, you'll be blindfolded. Don't worry, so will I. This place we're going is supposed to be top secret." He let her digest the information before continuing. "You can't take your phone. Picture taking isn't permitted. I'm told it's to protect everyone's privacy. Oh, I almost forgot. There's going to be a quick body search."

"For hidden cameras?"

"I think so. I didn't ask. But it could also be for weapons. So … you still want to go?"

"I still do."

**

The large black vehicle waiting out front surprised her. She wanted to ask what make it was, but she didn't wish to come across as unworldly. That was exactly how she felt, however, as she gazed at it.

"It's a Bentley," Chris said, guessing her question. "An old one."

The smell and feel of the buttery leather of the high-backed seats made her feel decadent. In the dim lighting, she could not quite tell whether the interior was dark beige or light gray. There was a surprising amount of headroom. When the chauffeur closed the door, she felt very safe, as though she were sitting in an armored car. She spent a few moments admiring the detail of the precise stitching, shiny knobs, and other decorative aspects of the interior. She might never again sit inside such a luxurious car and wanted to preserve the memory.

She and Chris secured their own blindfolds. She sat back and tried to relax, telling herself it was just a ride in a very expensive car. They were on their way to a secluded destination and wouldn't be able to contact anyone outside. Nothing to worry about.

They didn't speak, but soft music surrounded them. Chris located her hand and held it, which settled her nerves—until they finally stopped about twenty minutes later. The car door was opened, and they were instructed to remove their blindfolds. It took a minute for her eyes to adjust to the light. They were standing in front of a large, plain-looking building

A man in a tux was waiting with his hand out to assist her from the car.

"What's this place called?" she asked.

"The George, madam," the man said in a French accent. He escorted them to the entrance at the side of the building. Just inside the door, he searched her purse, made Chris take off his jacket, and confiscated Chris's watch and lighter.

The man placed the items in an envelope with their names written on the front. He gave them each a waiver and a confidentiality agreement to sign. When all that was completed, he directed them to a passageway that led to the actual entrance of the club.

Chris took Tory's elbow as they entered the foyer and climbed the stairs. They joined several other guests in a theater with wide seats and were served champagne. A violinist was playing alone on the stage.

Tory tried to take it all in: the art, the glamour, and the well-heeled patrons in sparkling jewelry. The room was stunning with bright chandeliers and plush seating that was deep burgundy with purple accents. It was a mixture of Old World and modern conveniences. The room was full of people, but no one was engaged in chatter.

She looked at Chris and grinned.

"How some play!" he whispered into her ear.

They sipped their drinks, listened to the music, and tried to fit in.

A soft tinkle of chimes announced that the show would soon begin.

The lights dimmed, a long moment passed, and the curtain began to rise. When Tory's eyes registered what she was seeing, her jaw dropped.

Chris took her hand and rubbed it, more to comfort her than in a sensual way, as though he needed comforting as well. She wondered what he was thinking.

Women of all races and sizes were being fucked by men—and that was just the backdrop. A young, nubile girl—at least, she seemed very youthful—was dragged by a man into the middle of the group by a rope fastened around her neck. She was struggling, begging to be released, and pleading for mercy, but there were no real tears.

Tory reminded herself that the girl was a performer, an actor, despite how real the scene appeared. The orgy grew more intense. Nothing was left to the imagination.

The man on stage, who was fully dressed, was having difficulty subduing his young captive. Others joined in to help him strip the girl of her clothing. Her limbs were secured to an X-shaped device so that her back faced the audience.

The restrained girl raised her head and began to sing, releasing her voice up to the ceiling. Her operatic melody trembled with feeling, and Tory got caught up in the moment.

The first whiplash made many in the audience flinch as four men began whipping the girl. A red welt marked her pure white skin. Her voice cracked and then she resumed singing. The men continued to apply the whip until her buttocks were red, peppered with welts.

The singer begged to be taken however they desired. She was released, and the men carried her, each raising one limb, to a table. They bent her over it and took turns fucking her. What should have been obscene seemed inevitable, almost welcome. Her loud groans and cries of release resonated through the domed room.

By then, Tory was simmering with desire, feeling similar emotions to the actress. She felt Chris's fingers on her leg, sliding the slit of her dress aside. Her breath hitched when he ran his finger along the top of her nylon. Then he leaned into her. "Touch me," he said into her ear.

"Where?" she whispered, still transfixed by what was happening on the stage.

He guided her hand across, and it touched his exposed and aroused penis. She jerked at first, shocked that he had exposed himself in full view of anyone who might glance their way. But then, looking around, she saw other woman and men fondling each other the same way without the slightest concern.

The only sound in the cavernous room was the moans of performers and the audience. The music stopped. The open display on the stage had given everyone permission to exhibit their own expressions of sexual fulfillment.

Tory turned slightly to take a firm hold of Chris's erect penis. She glanced up at him. The look on his face made her want to do more. She bent at the waist and took him into her mouth.

The play went on. Tory, giving herself fully over to Chris, couldn't see what was happening on the stage, but she felt the room's atmosphere becoming even more charged. Chris controlled her pace with his right hand on her head, making her take him in deeper.

Suddenly, she felt the people around them begin to shift. Chris pulled out of her mouth as she brought her face up to meet his, noticing that the people nearby were looking at them. Chris looked at her questioningly, and she knew what he wanted: to let others see her as he did, to give herself to him while others watched or participated. His eyes assured her he would protect her.

"Stand," he said.

She complied without hesitation. There was no one there that she recognized, and she refused to cower. It was a chance to explore a side of herself that Chris had awakened. It was what she had been looking for as a young woman—but had never really understood. She'd always had an urge to test limits, find boundaries of sexual pleasure, and discover what heights of sensual exploration were possible.

Slowly, Chris began to remove her dress.

Raising her arms, she let him. She didn't know what he had planned, but she understood that she would have to let go of any inhibitions to get through it. In all likelihood, people would see her nude and watch Chris make her climax.

In one swift jerk, Chris lowered her panties and removed her tampon. He turned her so he could enter her as they both sat back on his chair. Her back to his chest, both facing forward. The rest of the audience had begun to watch them as well. Someone blindfolded her, and she lay back against Chris. His hands raised her arms and brought them around his head. She felt his fingers at her back, working the clasp of her bra, and then the bra was removed.

Her nipples hardened instantly in the cold. His hands moved lower, spreading her folds. It was freeing and exhilarating not caring about anything besides being in the moment with Chris—open and exposed for everyone to see.

Her breasts were squeezed—by Chris or by someone else?—and her milk squirted. She heard murmurs of approval.

Many hands—strangers—began touching her body. Mouths and hands tasted her. Men's beards abraded her skin while Chris grew inside her. Her skin felt hot and tender. The welcome attention continued for some time. Both women and men sucked on her nipples; she could somehow tell the difference from their technique and approach. She could feel the longer fingernails of women grazing her skin as they held her breasts; they tasted her with their smooth tongues and fastened their mouths to her nipples. The men never hesitated. They squeezed the plumpness of her globes before latching on like starving feeders; their approach was rougher, although not painful.

She'd thought it might feel like an invasion, but the strangers were mostly gentle, probably more interested in getting a taste of breast milk than in doing anything else.

Things changed, though, when her clitoris became involved. Fingers rubbed and stimulated her, bringing her to another level. Then they stilled just as she was at the edge of the precipice and about to plunge.

"More!" she screamed, whenever her tiny bundle of nerves was ignored.

Chris bit on her earlobe. "You're so hot. They love you."

Now two mouths sucked her nipples with more force, and the pull of their suckling went right to her groin. Her legs were held by several rough hands, and she was moved up and down on Chris's stiff penis.

Cold liquid was poured over her freshly shaven crotch and dripped down her perineum. She recognized the sting of alcohol as it made contact. Chris must have nicked her with the razor, she thought as a hot tongue licked her center and bit her clitoris. Soon after, everything was one big blur as she careened toward the most intense climax of her life.

Listless from so much pleasure, she fell into half consciousness, unable to fully open her eyes. She was vaguely aware of being carried out of the club and thought she heard someone calling Chris by name. *Who would know his name?* She didn't know or care if she was being transported naked through the streets. Nothing mattered.

She didn't awaken until they were in the shower in her hotel room. She was so gelatinous that Chris had to prop her against the wall while he washed every inch of her. As he was drying her, she noticed a troubled expression on his face.

"What's wrong?" she asked.

"You're bleeding."

"Don't worry."

"But it's so much."

"This is my heavy day. It's normal."

"Okay, if you're sure."

"Just put a towel on the bed. At least I hope we're going to bed."

"Yes, baby."

CHAPTER 13

He held her as she slept. She barely moved all night. They had yet to talk about what had happened at The George. He hadn't been able to revive her for a long time after the group sex, and that had made him almost lose his mind. His depravity knew no bounds. He couldn't blame her for being exhausted, considering what had been done to her. This was all his fault.

She groaned and shifted. Her eyes opened, and she smiled. His heart began to relax a little. He pushed a lock of her hair behind her ear. "How are you feeling?"

"Hungry."

"Just hungry?"

"Well, I could use some loving from you, but I can tell that's not on the menu at the moment. You're looking kind of ... I don't know ... scared?"

"I thought last night might have been too much for you."

"Oh, it was!"

His gut clenched with regret. "I knew it."

Her fingers touched his face affectionately. "But I thoroughly enjoyed it. Didn't you?"

Flooded with relief, he squeezed her.

"Chris? Are you okay?"

"I am now."

"You didn't like it?

"I did until you passed out."

"I remember a few things. I was falling in and out of consciousness, not totally incapacitated. Big difference. Why was I blindfolded when everyone was fucking me?"

"I saw this man gesturing to an attendant to cover your eyes and then mine. I thought maybe he was a politician or something who didn't want to chance being recognized. Maybe it was to protect us as well."

"Not sure that makes sense. I thought it might have something to do with enhancing our pleasure."

"Possibly," he said.

"I don't want to go back," she said. "I mean, I loved the experience, but it was one of those things you do only once."

"I'm of a similar opinion."

"Cross that off the bucket list."

"Uh-huh."

"I can't believe what we did!"

"I hope you weren't scared?"

"Not once. I was with you. Actually, I was more concerned about disappointing you."

He sighed, wondering for the thousandth time what he had done to deserve her. "You could never do that. We should talk about all the things that happened."

"Can I go to the bathroom first?"

"Of course."

He was still worried about her, but she seemed to be steady on her feet. He called for room service and opened a bottle of water. She needed nourishment and hydration.

She joined him in bed and drank some water before placing it on the bedside table. She took his hand and snuggled it between her breasts.

He was uncertain how to begin. So much had happened, and he could barely come to terms with it. How had she known what he wanted before even he did? Why had she let him and the others do what they did?

"Okay, big guy, let's talk. You've got something on your mind."

"I'm still trying to sort it all out."

"Last night?"

"Yeah."

"I could hardly believe it myself at first. How much I wanted to please you. To take you in front of everyone. I liked the fact that people would see us—and see me pleasuring you that way. And then, having so many people touching me like that, letting loose on me was mind-blowing, incredible. It all became about giving myself to you and to them. Letting them take their pleasure because it fed ours. Does that make any sense?"

"It does."

"Were you pleased?"

"Very much. You don't know how much."

"Why do I sense a *but*?"

He wasn't sure how to put it.

"Be honest," she said, turning to look into his eyes.

"I … I was worried about you, how you collapsed at the end. I thought maybe we'd gone too far."

"I'm not sure what that was about. That's never happened before. It was like when I let go, the orgasms just kept on coming, over and over, like waves, and there was no end in sight. I think my body shut down as a way of stopping them."

"It didn't bother you to have so many people touching you like that?"

"At the time, not really. They were like props. Now it feels a bit strange. Did it disturb you?"

"I guess that I feel a little like you. It was a turn-on to see so many people into us. You were so free and giving. I got caught up in the moment. But now it seems surreal, doesn't it?"

"Yeah."

"How did you know?" he asked.

"How did I know what?"

"What I wanted to do in front of everyone—when I didn't even know it? I mean, from the little I knew about this place, I guessed that group play might happen, but I didn't have anything concrete in mind. But you did."

She sighed. "I didn't. Okay, I sort of knew what you wanted me to do. It was in your eyes. Like a dream or fantasy. What you needed. Was I wrong?"

"No. You nailed it. I ..."

"Are you worried that this makes you a freak? That what we did makes us abnormal?"

She reads me perfectly, he thought.

"That because you enjoyed something others would consider perverse, you must be an unstable, unfit human being?" she continued.

"Possibly."

"Well, was anyone harmed or offended?"

"I don't know."

"No. If I'm okay with it, then so should you." When he remained silent, she kissed his lips. "Stop obsessing about it. What happened changes nothing. Not who you are."

But it did. It had brought back memories of his youthful past, when nothing was too outrageous for him to undertake—the darker, the better. He was always up for trying something new. It always seemed like he needed to prove to the world that he could do anything. As one of six kids, he'd often felt invisible. But that wasn't who he was anymore. He'd changed when his sister died. It bothered him how easily he could revert back into his old persona.

"Did I hear someone call you by name?"

He stilled, reminded of that close call as they were leaving. While an attendant had been helping to get Tory inside the car, Chris had been waylaid by an old acquaintance, Serge Mandez. Chris had struggled to keep a flash of panic under control, deflected with the excuse of needing to leave, and promised to catch up later with his childhood friend. Not that they would. That man was involved in some shady businesses these days, if the rumors were true, and he should be avoided at all costs. He didn't want the man anywhere near Tory. They hadn't seen each other in years, didn't live in the same city, and Serge didn't know what Chris did for a living; the chances of another accidental meeting were slim. But what were the odds of them both having been at that place, on that night, in San Antonio? And what should he tell Tory?

"No, you must have been dreamed it. Running into an acquaintance there would have been embarrassing!"

A knock on the door ended the discussion, but Chris was still experiencing that moment of panic and was unable to move.

Tory glanced at him, pulled on a robe, and let in room service. After they set up the tray on a small table by the window, Tory poured the coffee.

Tired, worried, and unsure of himself, Chris's feet felt heavy as he slowly made his way over to her.

"Sit. Eat. Then you're going to tell me what's going on in that head of yours, and then it's back to bed for you, mister."

He liked this bossy side of her. "Yes, ma'am!"

She cuffed his head lightly, which was the right thing to do to get him out of this funk.

After they had eaten, she made him shower while she pumped and then they cuddled in bed. He finally let her coax some personal information out of him. He told her about his tendency to be selfish and overthink everything because he was afraid of reverting back to adolescent behavior, his fundamental belief that he was flawed even though he had changed his life completely, and devoting himself to others.

"I think that you're the nicest man I know," she declared at one point in their conversation.

He had to absorb that for a little while. To her thinking, it was a compliment—and he might agree if he didn't know better. That was how most people saw him because that was how he wanted them to, but for her to say that after what she had obviously gone through was momentous. It was the exact moment that he realized that she forgave him for being incommunicado and that his feelings for her were more powerful than anything he had ever experienced.

"I'm glad you think so." It was a stupid response, he knew, but he felt too numb to say anything more. The impact of the realization was almost too much to come to terms with. Never in his wildest dreams would he have thought himself capable of loving another person so much.

She nudged him. "Now you're supposed to say something about me."

"Why?" He was truly baffled. Was this a simple reciprocal kind of expectation—or did she need him to say something profound? He really wanted to understand that before possibly ruining the bubble of intimacy they were sharing. Besides, he still needed a few seconds to grasp the meaning of what he had just discovered about himself.

Laughing, she hugged him. "Don't be scared."

"I'm not."

"You're such a liar. You should see your face right now. It's a mix of being taken aback and uncertainty, I think. I'm not sure why such an innocent comment should have that kind of effect."

How and when had she learned to read him so well? It wasn't as though they had weeks or any real time under their belts to grow to understand each other this way. Sure, they could both read each other's body language or moods fairly accurately, but for her to pick up on his expression was telling. "I'm not always nice."

"I would agree, but I actually think you don't believe it yourself. I mean, that you're generally a nice person and just not pretending to be. It's a genuine part of you that you're completely oblivious to."

It was time to change the subject. "No. I'm actually trying not to screw this up and thinking of what I could possibly say to you."

"Oh?" She laughed. "So, you can't come up with one single compliment or observation?"

"No. I didn't say that. Here, give me a sec … okay. Here goes. You make me see myself as I never have before. You're the only person I know who could make me want to face things that I never thought I could. You're the strongest, most generous, and most spirited women I know. You're also one of the most influential people in my life. How am I doing?"

"Pretty good."

They grinned at each other, and it was special having the time with her. He couldn't tell her that he had been responsible for the death of a loved one, which had shaped his future and the decision to give himself to a higher calling, but he longed to unburden himself to her. The thought of sharing more of himself was enough to make him question so many things. It wouldn't be right though. It wasn't the right time or place for that.

In time, they both dozed off. Later, they got up and spent some time swimming and lounging by the pool. It felt like a real holiday, and it was one of the best days he'd ever had with her.

***

"Because of our time together, I'll be able to make it through another year without letting them get to me," he said.

She had no idea what he meant by that, but she didn't question him. They spent a great deal of time together in bed, sharing meals and taking walks or runs for the remainder of the conference days.

They said their good-byes in his rental car. Tory knew she'd be returning to meet him in twelve months. They agreed on that, and it felt right.

This time, it was easier to get back into the routine of her life. Her vacation with Chris was just an escape from everyday life, nothing more. She enjoyed being with him, but she didn't need to be in a full-time relationship.

Firmly established in her career and managing her family better than ever, she was happy with how things turned out. She made her own decisions. And she looked forward to the yearly indulgence of spending time with her stranger.

***

Tory continued to meet Chris every year. Sometimes they barely greeted each other before he had her in their shared suite, against the wall, or on the floor. She learned a little more about him each time. Basically little things that didn't amount to much. Likes and dislikes about music, movies and such. They rarely discussed deeper feelings or beliefs or even insights into their daily lives when they were apart. She imagined that this was intentional on his part. It's what kept her from not going on about her kids and work.

The fifth year was different, though. She'd had breast cancer that year. She was recovering, but her body had changed a lot. How would he react to seeing her like this? And was she prepared for him to be repelled? She had lost a great deal of weight. Her face was too thin. This and other worries kept her up all night before she was due to leave for San Antonio. Sometimes she felt that surviving cancer had been a small consolation, considering the damage done. She hoped above all that he wouldn't pity her. She got enough of that from her mother.

Normally Chris was the first to arrive at the hotel. This time, Tory made certain that she would be in the suite before him so she could try to talk to him before his usual uncontrolled passion took over. They never took it slow the first time; the demanding hunger had to be satiated.

She dreaded the possibility that he wouldn't be able to accept her the way she was now. But if, once he saw her, he didn't want to have sex, she would accept it. At least, she tried to convince herself that she would.

Their usual hotel was booked due to an unexpected number of conferences in town, and they'd had to book a suite in a different hotel. The unfamiliar suite she was waiting in added to her discomfort and unsettled feeling. Chris had made the hotel arrangements and e-mailed them to her as usual, not saying anything more. Nothing had changed in that regard. They still kept so much from each other.

This time, though, something felt off, wrong. The time he was due to arrive came and went. Hours later, there was still no word from him. There were many reasons why he could be running late. The weather, traffic, or something equally non-catastrophic. However, what if he changed his mind? Surely, he would call.

If for some reason, he'd decided not to come this year, how would she feel? Maybe he met someone, and it was over between them. A man like him had to have other women in his life. Perhaps it was some kind of sign? Part of her was relieved that she might not have to face him, but still, she sat there waiting.

Finally, the room phone rang, making her jump. She grabbed the handset and listened.

"Tory?"

"Chris, where are you?"

"I missed a connection. I won't get to you until early tomorrow."

She closed her eyes. He was still planning to come. "You don't have to come," she said, trying to let him off the hook.

"What do you mean?"

"I understand. Things happen. There's always next year."

"How do you know we'll have next year? We might only have this time!" He sounded almost frantic, and the desperation in his voice made her sit up. Something was going on.

"Why are you so upset?" she asked.

"Why are you doing this?"

"Doing what?"

"Don't be obtuse. I can tell by your voice. You're giving up on us. If we don't connect this week, there'll never be another time, will there?"

"You know how much I hate it when you speak to me that way. I have half a mind to end this call."

The man knew her so well. He was right. She never would be able to face him again. She began to cry. The last time she'd been that broken was when John died. Before that, it was at her father's funeral.

She wasn't a pretty sight when she cried, all red-eyed and snotty, and she was grateful he couldn't see her.

"Baby, please don't," he said.

She could not deal with his compassion. When he was angry, obstinate, curt, and controlling, he was a piece of cake to manage, but when he got all nice, she had no defense. She hung up the phone.

Three seconds later, the phone rang again. She looked at it for a couple of rings before picking up the receiver.

"Don't hang up on me!"

That actually made her smile. She wiped the moisture off her cheeks and nose with the back of her hand.

"Talk to me," he said in a more controlled voice.

"Chris, I can't."

"Try. Please. For me?"

She cleared her throat and went on. "This was a mistake. I'm going home. I won't be here when—if—you arrive, so—"

"I'm coming, and you're staying where you are! You're going to sit tight and wait for me!"

"No!"

"Listen to me. There's nothing you can say that will keep me from coming."

"Okay, fine! This'll be easier over the phone anyway," she paused, gathering her courage. "I've had breast cancer this year. I had a radical mastectomy and some other treatments. I'm scheduled for reconstructive surgery in a couple of weeks, but my iron stores are low, so it might be postponed again. I have nasty scars. I've lost all my hair and a good deal of weight. I don't look or feel like myself anymore. I don't want you to see me this way. I don't know what I was thinking when I came here. I'm an idiot!"

There was absolute silence on the phone. Tory had no idea whether Chris was still on the line or they'd been disconnected. Perhaps she had just opened up her heart to dead space. "Chris?"

"I'm here."

"Did you hear me?"

"I heard you. Is that all?"

Is that all? She held the phone away from her ear and looked at it. Was the man nuts? *Was that all?* As though what she'd been through was nothing? The nerve of him! "Yes, that's all!"

"Do you want to hear what's been going on with me?"

Was he actually going to tell her something about himself? Despite the fact that they'd continued meeting for years, he had never shared with her the way he had the day after they'd gone to The George. "Yes, sure."

"Are you sitting down?"

Geez! Why is he being so melodramatic? Tory sat on the bed and reached for the box of tissues on the bedside table. "I'm sitting." The box was empty, so she made her way to the bathroom to get some toilet paper.

"The reason I'm late is that I checked out of the hospital against medical advice. And I ran into a problem."

She stumbled on her way back to the bed. "What kind of problem? Why were you in the hospital?"

"My heart. It turns out I'm not supposed to fly so soon after surgery. And I still had these metal clip things on my chest."

"You had bypass surgery? When?"

"A month ago. I'm fine, just an infection, but I had to be readmitted."

"You shouldn't be traveling. Tell me you're not driving."

"I'm on a train."

She closed her eyes. "You should not be under any stress."

"Well, if a certain woman would listen to me and stay put, then I wouldn't be."

"I'll stay," she said. She needed to see him for herself, to make certain he was recovering. "But no fooling around."

He actually laughed. "Both the physical therapist and the wellness instructor said that very thing, although not in those words. So what are we going to do then?"

"Compare wounds, eat healthy food, and watch porn."

"Okay. But no porn. I can't watch porn, knowing we can't fuck."

"God, I hope you're somewhere private."

"The lady in the seat next to me is asleep, and the teenager in front of me has a pair of giant earphones on. I don't think he can hear me. I've missed you. I've spent most of the past month dying to see you. The thought of seeing you is what I've been living for. I picked up the phone to call you so many times, just to hear your voice, to know someone cares about me."

"Why didn't you?"

"I thought … I don't know what I thought really. Maybe that you might have another man in your life."

"If there were someone else, do you really think that I'd be here waiting for you?"

There had a few occasions when she'd thought they might take things to the next level, considering how well they got along. It hadn't happened, though, and it wasn't likely to. Her husband had been gone for a few years, and she really didn't see herself tied permanently to Chris. Besides, being a widow gave her certain freedoms that she wouldn't give up for any man. The sole right to make all decisions was a perk not to be ignored.

Just because she didn't need one around all the time, however, did not mean that she ignored all other men. She had tried going out on dates, but they'd never panned out—despite how much she wanted them to. The problem was that she was constantly comparing them to Chris. Some of them did make the cut and wanted to get serious, but she always pulled the plug. The fact was that men were not necessary to her existence; it had taken her a long time to figure that out.

Chris didn't respond. "Take your time. I'll be here," she said, no longer concerned about how he might take her changed appearance. Nothing mattered but seeing him and reassuring herself that he was on the path to recovery.

CHAPTER 14

Early the next morning, he dragged himself into their room, shed his clothes, and joined her in bed. He enveloped her body with his, though she was fully clothed. Not caring if he was too rough, he held on to her until he could breathe again. *She smells the same she always has*, he thought before falling asleep.

When he roused, she was looking at him tenderly. He thought he saw love and acceptance in her eyes, even though he knew she fought against those feelings. Everything else might have changed—but not what he saw in those eyes. When she asked to examine him, he let her raise his undershirt. She didn't say anything at first as she looked over his scar. It was still red and looked like he had been gutted with fish knife and stitched back together. Small holes where bands of metal had once been anchored still looked raw. She didn't seem too disgusted though.

Finally, she asked a battery of medical questions that sounded so clinical he wondered how she knew so much about surgery. When she was satisfied, she sighed in something like relief.

He didn't know how to broach the subject of her cancer. What was the right way to ask someone about having lost a breast? He glanced at her chest and saw the outline of a bra. *Which one had been amputated?*

"The right one," she said as though reading his mind. "You can ask me anything," she added.

"Can I see?"

"I'd be more comfortable with questions first."

"I know, but I'd like to see it with my own eyes, not let my imagination take over. Then I'll have all the answers I need." He knew she was the same that way, trusting only what she saw to allay any fears.

"I'm not ready for that."

"Why not?" She gave him a sharp look, and he quickly rephrased the question. "When?"

"I don't know." She started to cry again.

He pulled her to him and gently rubbed her arm. "Shush. It's okay, baby."

But she was not okay, and he knew it. He was lying just to comfort her.

In his head, he knew the woman he was looking at was Tory, but this new version of her was so strange, with cropped hair and a thin face. He didn't want to spend their precious time together discussing their health issues. Instead, he wanted to think of them as they had been the year before.

He sighed. Wishful thinking did not make it so. What was the best way to handle the situation?

"I'm going to tell you a story," he finally said.

"Chris ..."

"Hear me out. It won't take long. When I'm done, you're going to take off your clothes—or let me do it. Either way, I'm going to worship your body."

She looked at him as if he were delusional.

"So, a long time ago, there was a girl. She followed a boy everywhere and tried to do whatever he did. She was teased a lot. They both were, actually. Every dumb-ass thing the boy did, she copied. She looked up to him, even though he was only a couple of years older than her. As time went on, they became inseparable.

"The boy never understood what the fuss was about. He treated her like a guy, so it seemed only natural for her to join his circle of friends. As time passed, her breasts developed. He noticed, and so did other people. They made nasty comments, and though he did nothing when he heard them, he would have liked to have punched some of the guys who made them. The girl and the boy never discussed it with each other. The boy sensed that she was more uncomfortable with the changes in her body than she was with being the subject of taunts. She wore layers to disguise her shape, no matter how hot it was outside or what sport they were playing. She even wore a T-shirt over her bathing suit. She got razzed about that more than about her figure, come to think of it.

"Anyway, one day, the boy decided to go swimming. He chucked off his clothes, and so did she, after he dared her. It was the first time he had ever seen a naked girl, and she was beautiful, the way young girls are. But when she dove into the water, he briefly glimpsed all these marks on her, welts marring her perfect skin. They seemed a sin against nature, and the boy became enraged.

"When the girl came up for air, he was in her face, wanting to know who had hurt her. She wouldn't say, and they never discussed it again. Nor did they swim together after that. He eventually found out the marks were from her father's belt, but something in their friendship broke that day. He understood that she was fearful, but he was hurt that she didn't trust him enough to confide in him or to let him share her burden. Every time he saw her after that, he imagined worse things being done to her. Open wounds. Skin that wouldn't heal. Scars. It was so much worse not knowing."

Tory placed a finger on his lips and rolled out of bed. "Did you make up that story?" She came around to his side of the bed, undoing the buttons of her top.

He was about to defend his story when he noticed how awkwardly she shrugged out of her sleeve.

"I had a small piece of muscle removed," she said, answering the question he hadn't asked out loud. "I can't lift my arm like I used to. PT isn't helping much."

She stood before him in a white bra, and he noticed that it was specially made to house an artificial breast. From his vantage point, she looked normal.

"I feel like I should prepare you for what you're going to see," she said as she undid the clasp.

He nodded and sat up, swinging his legs off the bed and facing her.

"It's not pretty. There's been a lot of healing by second intention," she said.

"What does that mean?" He wondered again at her technical terminology.

"Malformed or wide scars. The skin is discolored, puckered in one spot, and rough in another."

"Okay." And it would be.

He watched her sliding her bra straps off her shoulders. Holding his breath and mentally bracing, he watched the garment fall to the floor, and then he looked at her troubled expression. She needed him not to react negatively, and that was what he intended to do. He thought of the ugliest wound imaginable: pus and blood oozing out of mangled skin. Then he moved his gaze to her chest. He exhaled and touched her.

"Not too bad?" She was looking at his face.

She must be able to tell I'm not disgusted or anything. "No. Not at all." It was the truth. He had expected much worse. The skin was mostly smooth, unlike his own, and only faint pink raised areas provided any clues to what she had endured. It wasn't ugly at all. In fact, it made her more attractive to him somehow. The slight imperfection on an otherwise unblemished body made her more real.

His thoughts shifted to what the alternative might have been had she refused surgery and treatment. She might be dead, and they would never have their conference times again. He realized that it was insensitive and selfish to think that way. It was more about her, as it should be, but he couldn't see it any other way. The thought of never seeing her again was too painful to think about.

When several minutes had passed and he knew that she was expecting him to further comment, he struggled with what to say or do to make her feel better. "Does it hurt?"

"No."

"You must miss your breast? Sorry, that's a stupid thing to say."

"No, it's not, actually. I do miss it, which seems shallow, I know."

"It's not. You had beautiful breasts. Now you have only one. It's only natural to miss a part of yourself that's no longer there."

"It's not like it's an arm or anything important."

He touched her, and she stopped talking. "Is it okay if I touch your scars?"

She nodded, and he could tell she was trying not to cry.

"What's wrong?" he asked.

"I didn't think you'd want to."

"Why would you think that?"

"It's ugly." She had obviously spent a great deal of time looking at her scars in the mirror.

"Silly woman, did you look at the mess on *my* chest?" He pulled her closer and kissed every part of the scar tissue. She didn't pull away.

When he felt her begin to shake, he nudged her to sit on his lap, wrapped her up in his arms, and cradled her body for a long time. He felt her loss. He decided it was best not to offer any platitudes or words of encouragement. He didn't want to minimize her pain. All he did was hold her against him, showing her that he would provide the warmth, acceptance, and empathy she was missing. He guessed that no one else had provided her with that kind of comfort.

Were her tears of relief? He hoped so. He was too much of a coward to bring himself to ask; instead, he said nothing and trusted that he was all she needed at the moment.

***

Emotionally spent, Tory fell asleep in Chris's arms.

She jerked awake to find him trying to lift her. The man had just undergone surgery; he shouldn't be carrying her. "Chris, don't try to lift me."

"My arm's asleep. I was just moving you. Take it easy."

She kissed his lips. It was their first moment of shared happiness that year, she realized. She made him get under the covers. "Thank you for handling this so perfectly." She kissed him again and lingered against his mouth. "Let's rest a little more, and then we can decide what to do next."

He nodded. "Only if you're naked beside me."

She grinned. "I can do that."

She took his pulse as he slept and considered who he was under his ashen skin. He needed to rest before they did anything more strenuous than watching television. An idea struck her. She made a quick call while she was in the bathroom, and the arrangements were in place.

When he woke up and saw the wheelchair by the bed, he was not impressed. It took some convincing to get him to sit in it so they could go to the hotel spa. Once there, he admitted that it would have been a long walk unassisted, and he grumbled something about getting old as the attendant helped him onto the massage table.

Tory had to step in and veto the hot tub. Chris couldn't take it yet. As it was, the masseuse used some interesting techniques. He placed flat, heated rocks on their lower lumbar regions, which was extremely soothing. He also dipped their hands and feet in melted wax and let them steam.

Back in their room, room service had delivered a cart laden with healthy food. She handed Chris the remote so he could choose a movie. They spent hours watching comedies, laughing and holding each other, completely at ease. To think that she had almost called off their yearly meeting!

The next day and the one after that, they lounged by the pool, reading under the shade of an umbrella, drinking smoothies, and enjoying each other's company. Every once in a while, they would look at each other and smile. The gentleness of Chris's expression made her think of Zoey and how much she looked like him. For a moment, she was tempted to divulge everything, but then she thought about how the news might affect him. Stress, even the good kind, could tax his heart, and that was a risk that she wasn't willing to take.

He teased her when it came time to take his medications, saying that she acted like his private nurse. When he discovered that she actually had been a nurse before getting into procurement, he looked a little impressed. He made a bit of a fuss when she took charge of ordering all their meals, choosing only the heart-healthy items on the menus, but he gave in good-naturedly and ate whatever was delivered to the room or the pool.

On their last full day, they looked for something new to do together. They took a taxi to a mall, had lunch, people watched, and talked.

"I find it odd that you're in procurement, but you don't like to shop," he said, grinning. The conversation had moved on to her dislike of trends, and she had casually mentioned that she wasn't big on spending her free time looking at shoes or clothes.

"I'm always shopping for kid things, groceries, gifts, and such. I hate waiting in line or wandering around aimlessly and thinking about what to buy."

"Speaking of which, how about souvenirs? You didn't buy anything today." He knew she always bought a little souvenir for each of her kids.

"Oh, I'll pick up something small at the airport. They don't expect much. You sound almost disappointed that I'm not like other women."

"No. Not at all. It's just one more thing to like about you."

What she really wanted was to turn the questions back around on him, but she was long past trying to prod information out of him. If he wanted her to know anything about himself, he'd have to divulge it himself.

That evening they ate dinner in the hotel restaurant and went to bed early.

On their final morning, they ate breakfast and talked. They were all packed and would be checking out in a little while.

"Thank you for being here with me," he said. "I worried that you'd be disappointed because I wasn't 100 percent. I'd say it worked out in my favor. Something good came from our being together when neither of us were well."

She smiled. He was correct. "Maybe it was fate?" she said flippantly, though the idea was growing roots in the back of her mind.

"Maybe. I prefer destiny. You're my destiny."

"How can I be your destiny?"

"I don't have all the answers. I just know that you're meant to be with me. Even though it's not full-time, I'm so much better after we've been together. You make me see who I am—not what everyone wants me to be. With you, I get back my true sense of self."

She pondered his words. Was it the same for her? A little. He made her see everything through a different lens. He forced her to face her fears. All except the biggest one: telling him about their daughter.

The risks were too great. Now she feared telling him because so much time had passed, and it might be too difficult for him to deal with. The shock of the news and its possible impact on his heart weren't her only concerns though. She wouldn't risk any chance that Zoey would be taken from her, not even for short periods of time under shared custody. She would never allow her relationship with her own child to exist on a part-time basis. If he knew about Zoey, it would change everything. He would insinuate himself into their lives, and there would be nothing she could do to prevent that. No, silence was still the best strategy.

He said, "You're the yin to my yang."

She laughed. Who said only women were sentimental? She wondered if he read romance novels as well. *Sappy nut!* "I don't know about that. You're good for a girl's ego though. I'll give you that."

He wiggled his eyebrows. "Maybe by this time next year, we'll both be healthy enough to play. I'll show you what I can do with your ego."

Grinning, she said, "You need to follow the doctor's orders from now on. No flying. No discharging yourself from hospitals. Do you hear me?"

"I love it when you boss me around. Have I ever told you that?"

"No."

"Then I guess I've never told you I love you either."

Her fork slipped from her fingers and clattered on the plate.

"I wanted to tell you that," he continued. "When I thought I might die, it was the one thing I regretted not doing."

She had no idea what to say. He had taken her by complete surprise. Of course, they cared for each other. She liked him—at least, she liked what little she knew about him. But what kind of love was he suggesting? The way you might love a new car or a dress? Or the real kind, the type that lasted? A few days a year was not a relationship. She asked herself how she could truly love a man she didn't trust enough to tell was the father of her four-year-old child.

He said, "Hey, you don't have to say anything. I know you don't feel like I do, and it's okay."

A few tense minutes passed.

"I've got some news," he said between bites of toast.

"Yes?"

"I'm being transferred."

"Is that a good thing?"

"I think so. I've been in the same place for more than ten years, which is unusual in my field."

She was tempted to ask what that was exactly, but she held back. She had come to appreciate not knowing much about him. It helped her keep her distance, which she wanted and needed. He knew she worked in procurement and that she had been a nurse. He knew that she had three children. Meanwhile, she didn't know what he did for living or even where he lived. *But if he took a train there, he must at least reside on this continent,* she thought.

She tried to consider their arrangement from his side and was continually stumped by his evasiveness. Why did he remain so closed off as far as personal disclosure went? Was he embarrassed by what he did? Maybe he was a salesman? He was certainly good-looking and charismatic enough to be one.

"Then congratulations are in order," she said. She could tell her tone was insincere, but she didn't care. It seemed to roll off him anyway.

"I sure hope so. Since my surgery, I think they're worried I can't manage the responsibilities or workload anymore. I tried telling them I'd be fine, but you know how it is. People don't see reason. Anyway, I'm looking forward to it."

Why was he telling her this? There was no real context for her to take it in. Who were *they*? What kind of responsibilities or work did he have that would cause his bosses—if that's who he meant—to be concerned? She had no idea what any of it meant, but she refused to question him. After all, she did have *some* pride. He could choose to expand on his cryptic remarks or not, but she would not be the one to make him.

They parted like always, saying their good-byes privately in the cab. The only difference was that she got dropped off first, at the airport, and he headed to the train station.

CHAPTER 15

That year, she sold the house and moved into a smaller one closer to her mother. It made her feel better to move from the address Chris presumably knew from her registration information. Ever since his admission that he loved her, she'd felt even more concerned about keeping him out of Zoey's life. There were other reasons for her move. Her older kids had basically moved out; Jake was at university spending the occasional night at home, and Samantha was working and had her own apartment. Besides, there were too many memories of John in the old place.

Since Tory was new to the area, one of her neighbors suggested church as a way to get to know some people. She considered it important to make an effort to meet people in the area since Zoey had had to change schools just as the year was ending.

Apparently, a new priest had taken over the parish the previous month. Some big-shot bishop who had stepped down in position to come to their part of the world. Although Tory had been raised Roman Catholic, she hadn't exactly been a regular churchgoer over the past few years. Her mother had had stopped attending mass some time ago.

Since Sam was visiting that weekend, the three of them went to church together. Zoey chatted about school the whole way there, but Tory ignored most of it, still thinking about her conversation with Sam the previous evening. It had started off innocently enough, with Sam talking about how she was fitting in at work and about some of her love interests. Tory was glad Sam had no trouble sharing about her disastrous dates and laughing about it. It only reinforced how times had changed between them. She was proud of the fact that Sam could disclose such aspects of her personal life without fear of censure or nagging.

Sound bites replayed in Tory's mind: "Mom, why don't you join a gym? You might meet someone. Daddy's been gone a long time now. Why aren't you dating more?" Sam didn't accept any of Tory's excuses as valid. In her eyes, a total of five dates over the past year didn't count as a real effort to troll for men. But Sam was only twenty-four and had her life ahead of her. She didn't know that the one man Tory cared about was unavailable—or that Tory didn't want a full-time man in her life anyway. It was all so much easier and simpler this way.

Tory felt a little odd as the church service began; she hadn't been at a service for about twenty years. Everyone stood up, and the altar boys and girls entered before the priest. Zoey was yanking on her sleeve when the priest entered, and Tory asked Zoey to be quiet. When she looked up again, the priest had turned around.

Tory's throat constricted and, for a moment, she forgot to breathe. Her eyes were telling her one thing, but her mind was refusing to believe it. Spots danced in front of her face, and she felt dizzy.

In front of the congregation stood a man she had not been prepared to see again until later in the year. Chris. The priest. It all started to fall into place as her brain processed the information: why Chris had been so secretive about his life, how adept he was at evading questions, why he was so well spoken. Some of the things he said now made sense: his transfer, the reason he hadn't been intimate with a woman for so long, his rough, calloused knees. That was from all of the kneeling while he prayed. God, what an idiot she had been!

Her body was instinctively eager to be close to him as she checked him out. Then she wondered, with a shock, whether he had planned all this. Did he already know where she lived—and about Zoey? Before panic could overtake her completely, she let some of her simmering anger bring her mind into focus.

No, he would have come to her if he'd known he would be working in her neighborhood. Otherwise, he'd be risking a scene when she found out. Just like she was finding out now. It was conceivable that this was a coincidence; he might not have any idea that she was present in the congregation. If that were the case, she intended to keep it that way. She sat down on the wooden seat, hiding behind the other standing bodies.

Samantha gave her a look, probably wondering why her mother was sitting down. Tory was a mess inside, but she held it together. What choice did she have?

Well, this must have been the transfer he mentioned: a demotion from bishop to priest. Though she'd already talked some sense into herself, she wondered again if he had come to her parish intentionally. Had she accidentally disclosed something about wanting to move or where her mother lived? Not knowing what was going on was driving her nuts. Did he somehow suspect Zoey was his?

Zoey was leaning into her. She wanted to take her in her arms and run. Instead, she made herself focus on Chris. It appeared that he had regained his vitality. His coloring was a lot better, and he looked agile. And really handsome. She shook her head in self-disgust.

When everyone else sat down, Tory slumped down lower in the pew, hoping he wouldn't see her in the sea of faces. When the time came for Communion, she leaned over to Sam and said she was taking Zoey to wait in the car because she was so fidgety. It was a believable excuse; Zoey was often restless and disruptive when she was bored.

From the doorway as they left, she glimpsed Chris handing Sam the host, frowning slightly, and looking about the room. Sam was a clone of Tory at twenty-four. It was only a matter of time before he put things together.

For now, she would stay away from him and keep Zoey out of sight. Her little one had his eyes and his coloring. With one look at her, he would know.

A week later, Chris knocked on her front door. With a review of the parish books or the Catholic school directory, he would have found out all about her. And it wasn't exactly a secret where she lived. She had known it was only a matter of time before he located her and came round. She had been both expecting and dreading his arrival.

What was less clear was what he wanted. To confront her about Zoey? To make sure she didn't blow the whistle on him? To find out whether she wanted to play? Weren't all men were the same?

She looked through the closed screen door. He was wearing the white and black collar that advertised his profession. He'd obviously left it behind when they were in San Antonio. "Well, if it isn't the new priest come to call."

"Knock off the sarcasm and let me in," he said.

"I don't think so."

"We have to talk."

"About what exactly?"

"Are you alone?"

"No."

He sighed. "She looks just like you."

"Who? Sam? Yes, so I'm told."

"The family registry says you're single."

"Yeah, too bad that conference program didn't list you as a priest."

"I'm not going to stand out here and have this conversation," he said.

"I'm not asking you to."

"You look tired."

"It's not one of my best days. I have a sick child, and I'm not 100 percent myself."

"Which one's ill?"

"Not that it's any of your business, but Zoey. Look, I'm busy. What do you really want? And don't say you just want to talk."

He sighed again. "Fine. Have it your way, but I'll be back. You know you can't avoid me forever."

She watched him walk down the drive, away from her.

***

He knew Tory wouldn't willingly welcome him into her home, so he found another card to play. He was just walking away from the house when he noticed that striking young woman, to whom he'd given Communion the week before, walking up the block. She was so clearly related to Tory that he'd done some investigating into the parish books. He'd discovered the name Tory Stanton in the registry and been stunned to learn he'd just been transferred to Tory's hometown.

He made a point of lingering on the sidewalk until the girl approached and recognized him. He explained that he'd come to the house to introduce himself but had gotten no response to his knock. She insisted that her mother was home and that he come in to meet her after they formally introduced themselves.

"Mom?" she yelled as she opened the front door.

"I'm in here!" Tory called.

"Maybe this isn't a good time?" he offered, feeling a twinge of guilt.

"Father Chris, please don't give it another thought. My mom wants to meet you. She probably didn't hear the door. Zoey, my little sister, is sick, and Mom's busy looking after her. I came home this weekend to help out. Lucky you happened to run into me."

"Yes, it is," he murmured. Lies after lies. Where would they end? "I'll wait here," he said, stepping into the living room.

Samantha shrugged. "Suit yourself. It's not like you'll catch her doing anything ... wicked." She grinned, and he did as well.

If she only knew, he thought.

She left the room. After a moment, Chris heard some muffled conversation—half of which sounded angry. When the young woman returned, her face was red.

"Everything okay?"

"Sorry. My mom's angry I let you in because she's worried you'll get sick too."

"I should go then." He rose, intending to do that very thing. This gamble hadn't played out. Then he heard a crash, and all thoughts fled as he and Samantha raced toward the back of the house.

The sight that greeted him was not what he expected. Tory was bent over on the floor in front of a bedroom door, mopping up liquid. She was wearing only skimpy underwear. He had a perfect view of her ass, and it did things to him—things that he welcomed. He wanted to touch her, but he settled for taking in the skin that was revealed.

Samantha looked at him as if to apologize for the sight and caught him smiling.

Tory turned to look at him. "What are you doing here?" she demanded.

"Mother!"

"Everything's fine. I dropped the bowl and made a mess is all."

"I was just leaving when the noise—"

"I'm fine. We're fine," Tory repeated. She gathered an armful of soaking wet towels and threw them into a metal bowl.

"Let me help you," he offered. He bent to assist her with wiping the floor.

He could tell that she really wanted to tell him to go to hell. They were at eye level, and she glared at him before standing up and walking away.

"Mom, don't you think you should put something on?"

"Look, I didn't like being covered in vomit—even if it was watered down—and I took my soiled clothes off. If you'll both go into the other room, I can change. Didn't I tell you to stay away, Sam?"

"I was worried about you and Zoey."

"The flu?" he asked, trying to defuse the situation between mother and daughter.

"Yes," Tory responded without elaboration. She stood in front of the doorway to the bedroom, presumably Zoey's room. Chris tried to get a glimpse of the child, but his view was obstructed. "Sam," Tory said, still glaring at him, "bring me some ginger ale from the fridge." It was a command, not a request.

When Samantha left for the kitchen, Tory whispered, "Go into the living room. I'll be with you in a few minutes."

He nodded and returned to the living room. He sat down for a while, then, feeling a little nervous, got up to examine some of the portraits. *Nice-looking family.* He was replacing one of the photos on the mantel when Tory cried, "What do you think you're doing? Put it back!"

He was alarmed by her distress, but he was also distracted by how good she looked. *Perhaps she's sleep deprived or … premenstrual?* She was wearing a loose top and capri pants. Her feet were bare, and her toenails were painted a bright red. It was a new look. She usually used lighter shades of polish. He had never seen her look so casual. She looked really good. He wanted to lick her all over.

"Don't look at me like I'm a psycho," she snapped.

How had she read him so wrong? What was wrong? "Then stop acting like one," he said.

She took a breath, obviously not having expected him to say something like that. She pulled her hair back from her face. It had grown back in and was thicker than he remembered. The gesture was utterly feminine, and he enjoyed it. "Do you speak to all your parishioners this way?"

"Only those I've had sex with. And you're the only one—"

"My kids are here!" she hissed.

"Both your girls are down the hall."

"Yes, and what about my son?"

He jumped, having completely forgotten that she had a son. He looked around foolishly, as though he'd find the boy standing in the corner.

"Relax. He's not here," she said. She looked weary and flushed.

"Geez, Tory."

"Look, I am not getting into this with you." She sat down abruptly and started to slide to the floor.

He lunged for her. Her skin was burning hot. *Shit!*

He called out for Samantha, and they hustled her into bed. Samantha phoned Tory's mother to come over, and then she went back to see to Zoey, leaving Chris to wait with Tory.

Tory spoke to him only once. "Have you had your flu shot this year?"

"No." He stroked her cheek and bathed it with a cool washcloth. She had gained some weight, and her face was less narrow than it had been after her mastectomy. He glanced down at her body, wondering whether she'd had the breast reconstruction. He smiled to himself. He'd ask her the next time they talked.

He immediately felt bad for having put her under additional stress while she was ill. Stubborn woman! Why hadn't she told him she was this unwell?

He took her hand and held it the way he did when they slept together.

That was how Tory's mother found them. One look at the old girl, and Chris knew she was one shrewd lady. The jig was up. Samantha might not pick up on their relationship, but Alice would, he felt certain of that. Disengaging himself from Tory, he stood to greet her mother. Alice introduced herself in turn.

"So, you're the new priest everyone's talking about."

"Yes."

"You don't look like any priest I've ever seen."

"I haven't seen you at church—"

"I gave that up long ago, so don't think you'll get anywhere with me."

He grinned, liking her instantly. He could see where Tory had gotten her spunk.

"Chris? May I call you Chris?"

He nodded.

"You might think I'm a foolish old woman—"

He tried to contradict her, but she waved off his interjections.

She continued, "But I'm not. I'll say this only once: I don't know how it happened and frankly, I don't care, but I can tell by the look in your eye when I came in just now and by the way you touch her that you two have a thing, and it's not new. I understand from Sam that you didn't blink when you saw her in her underwear. And you actually smiled."

He blushed. So he'd been wrong about Samantha's level of shrewdness too.

"So here it is: Stay away. She's been through a lot. She's strong, but even the strongest of people can be broken. And on top of that, what does it look like? You, a man of the cloth, with my daughter?"

"I know."

"I figured you did. But you're not going to stay away, are you?"

"No, I'm not going anywhere. She won't like the fact that you know and that I'm here to stay."

"Maybe I won't tell her—and I'll just let the two of you work it out. It's none of my business, really, but I'm making it my business.

In a town this size, you won't keep this a secret for long. I'll bet you half the neighborhood knows you came by today."

"One visit won't hurt, especially when they learn that she's sick."

She continued as if he hadn't spoken. "And if you hurt her, all bets are off. Are we clear on that?"

"Crystal."

"I'm curious, though. How long?"

"Just over five years."

"Ah," she said.

He wondered about that the whole way home.

He spent the next day struggling against his urge to return to Tory's house. It was important for her not to feel that he was crowding her and making his presence felt. Although that was exactly what he wanted to do. To give her no opportunity to believe that he would take a back seat. She had to know that he wanted her and if the kids were part of the package then he would take the deal. Somehow he would have to make that clear to her.

A couple of days later, he was also struggling with a slight fever and was not able to do much of anything since he couldn't risk passing whatever he had to others. By the end of the week, he was in bed with the flu and felt as though he were at death's door. His housekeeper, Ms. Stratt, had orders not to let the parish women in to see him. But they were relentless, trying to visit, bringing him casseroles and flowers—anything to get in his good graces. And the one woman he did want to see was nowhere to be found.

One night, after a feverish day spent semiconscious, he had a vivid dream that made him ache for Tory. He called out her name. "Please lie down with me!" he begged, and she did.

Not until the next morning did he learn from Ms. Stratt that Ms. Stanton had spent most of the previous day watching over him. Feeling happy, he tried to get up, got dizzy, and promptly lay back down again.

When Alice waltzed into his room, he felt a twinge of dismay. What was Alice's last name? He had no idea if Tory used her maiden name or not. Was Alice the Ms. Stanton who had cared for him? Had he propositioned Tory's mother during the night?

"Were you here yesterday?"

"Off and on. Tory was here last night."

He exhaled in relief.

Alice continued, "I hear the ladies really like you. Ronnie was having quite a time taking care of you, doing the laundry, and protecting you from the ladies."

"Who's Ronnie?"

"Veronica Stratt. Your housekeeper."

How had he not known the woman's first name? "Those ladies mean well, but they're kind of a pain."

"That they are. One of the reasons I left the church was because of the way they offered themselves and their kids to men like you. Tory tells me you're different though. I'm not talking about the sex thing either. She told me you don't take advantage of people. And Ronnie says you don't like it when the parish women throw themselves at you. We go way back, so I'm inclined to believe her. Frankly, I'm impressed. So that's why I'm here. That and to spell Tory."

"She's well?"

"Yes."

"Zoey too?"

"Uh-huh."

She gave him the impression that she knew something more, and he wasn't sure he liked that. What did she know?

CHAPTER 16

Once Chris had recovered from the flu, he resumed his duties. One of them was to attend the pre-K and kindergarten graduation ceremony. His role was purely peripheral; he would offer up a prayer at the start of the event and say a few words at the end. Otherwise, he was prepared to be bored. He always had to be sociable at those types of events; as the mothers prattled on about their gifted children, he pretended to listen.

Out of the corner of his eye, he spotted a little girl in a pink sweater. She had dark hair and was fighting with a boy a little bigger than her in the coatroom. The teacher had her hands full trying to get the graduating class to don their caps and gowns and stand in single file; she hadn't noticed the two wrestling children. No one else was doing anything to break up the fight, so Chris intervened.

He pulled the children apart. The little girl rubbed a smear of blood across her face.

"Did you hit her?" Chris asked the boy.

"No, sir."

"It's Father, you dummy. Don't you see his collar?" the little girl spat.

"Okay, settle down, you two. Does anyone want to tell me who started this?"

The girl pointed to the boy. "He did."

"I did not!" the boy snarled.

"You said I had to kiss you!"

The boy's face turned red. *They're starting younger and younger,* Chris thought.

"I didn't mean it. I don't kiss ugly girls!"

Before Chris could do anything about it, the little girl got loose, kicked the boy, and ran off.

The little boy began to cry. *Now what?* Chris regretted not having minded his own business. Still, he was impressed with the little girl. He'd thought initially that she needed his help to defend herself against the little boy, but she'd held her own and even let the boy have it. It made Chris think about how tough it must be to raise female children. He wished the girl's father good luck, whoever he was. He was in awe of all parents with young children.

"Let's go find your mother," he said, bringing the boy out of the coatroom. His steps faltered when he saw Tory. She was comforting the little girl he'd just been speaking to. This must be Zoey. He paused to watch their interaction.

Tory lovingly calmed Zoey down while efficiently cleaning her face with a tissue.

Zoey's name was called to get in line. She turned toward him, and his heart seized.

At first, he thought his eyes were deceiving him. Zoey was a duplicate of his own sister. His eyes followed her, drinking in her image as she stood in line. Only then did he search out Tory, who had moved to sit with the other parents and guests. For long seconds, they stared at each other. He couldn't read her serious expression, and he was aware of the sudden paleness of her face. And then, it didn't matter anymore. It didn't matter that Tory might be upset. All that mattered was to get through one second at a time.

He had no idea how to deal with this sudden emotion of joy mixed with anger when the truth began bloom inside him. The seconds ticked by, and he tried to keep it all contained. So many things made sense now. How had he not picked up on it before? The second time they were together, she had been leaking breast milk. He had been too self-absorbed to question anything, and for some reason, she remained close-mouthed. Oh, right! She had tried to get in contact with him that year, but he'd ignored her messages. Only it hadn't been about her husband dying; it had been about Zoey.

He and Tory had conceived a child five years ago, and all this time, he'd had no idea.

Luckily, he was sitting down. A sudden and intense weakness overcame him as the shock dissipated. His mind continued questioning the obvious. The impossible had happened. He had a child. Tory had kept it from him, which hurt, but he had a child. He placed a hand over his mouth to hide his quivering upper lip and watched his daughter laugh with her classmates and skip away.

He had no idea how he made it through the prayer and sat still for almost an hour without needing fresh air. When the ceremony was finally finished, he sat down again because his legs felt weak. At some point, Alice sat down beside him. "Good afternoon, Father."

"Please call me Chris."

"How are you holding up?"

"You knew?"

"I suspected. And your reaction kind of confirmed it."

"I'm in shock, I think."

"I'm not surprised. It's not every day something like this happens to you, I gather. I suggest you get up and walk out the door. People are looking at you."

"Tory and—"

"They left a few minutes ago. I'm taking Zoey for the night. Take my advice and give yourself a few hours to calm down before you go to her."

She was worried about her daughter's well-being, he could tell. She needed some reassurance that he would not go off half-cocked.

"I will," he said. He needed to have a drink and pray—in that order. He didn't care what anyone thought as he managed to get up and walk out the door.

***

She waited on the back patio with a bottle of wine. It was getting dark, though the sun had yet to fully set. The birds were still chirping. Zoey was likely asleep at her mom's, oblivious to the knowledge that a secret had been exposed and would change everything. All she knew was that she was grounded for fighting.

Chris's look of realization, the way the color had drained from his face, made Tory flinch each time she thought about it. She asked herself how she would feel if their situations were reversed.

She knew he would come by her house and that they would have to deal with it. She wasn't sure how to defend her actions. The choice she'd made had seemed logical at the time. At least, it had been the less disruptive course for everyone. The truth would have devastated her husband while he was alive. Her mother would have been disappointed in her, and the kids might have resented her. She couldn't guess what they might think about their mother having an affair, but betrayed was a good guess.

Then there was Chris, who'd had a right to know. She felt such guilt about never having told him. At first, it had all made sense. She'd had her reasons. Now, none of them seemed good enough—even knowing he had lied about being a priest. Would she have told him sooner if she'd known this about him from the start? Probably not.

She wondered how angry he was at her. Would his feelings change toward her permanently? Would he fight her for custody? God, she hoped not. And if he did, wouldn't he have to leave the church?

She closed her eyes, unable to deal with the worst-case scenario: that he would be willing to do anything to spend time with Zoey.

She heard her backyard gate open and sensed him approaching before she opened her eyes. He surprised her by picking up the bottle of wine and swigging from it before sitting down beside her. He took her hand in his as if nothing abnormal had occurred. They sat like that for a long time.

She had no idea what to say to the father of her child as the seconds ticked by and the minutes passed agonizingly slowly. She wished he would say something—anything. What was going on in his head? He must think she was a terrible person. All kinds of adjectives to describe her came to mind, none of them flattering. She ached for him. Tears began to leak from her eyes. Still, he said nothing, and she couldn't think of what to offer up that wouldn't sound trite.

At long last, he said, "I know why you did it. Or, I think I do. I can respect that you did what you thought was right. I'm confused about something though." When she remained silent, he continued.

"When you found out I'd moved here and the odds were good that I'd find out, why didn't you just tell me? Why did you let me find out the way I did?"

"I'm sorry about—"

"I don't want to hear *sorry*. It's just a word."

"What do you want then?"

"I've been thinking about it for hours. I always thought if you cared for someone, you wouldn't deliberately hurt them."

"I wasn't trying to hurt you. I was scared."

"Of what?"

"So many things. I didn't know anything about you, and in my head, I was convinced that you'd try to take her from me."

"You don't think very highly of me, do you?"

"I don't know you."

"Yes, you do."

She snorted. "When I had my ultrasound, I tried to get a hold of you, but you didn't respond."

He lowered his forehead to his hands.

"Another time, I sat there, alone in the doctor's office, waiting for the amnio results and praying for a healthy child. I was bitter. When I went into labor for days, alone, I accepted it as punishment for my sins. Zoey was breech, and I can still remember it like it was yesterday." She took a deep breath.

"Is there more?" he asked.

"Yes, there's more!" she snapped. Then she sighed, consciously moderating her tone, wanting to get this right and not antagonize him. "Okay. This is the conversation we should have had a long time ago. Do you remember how awful I was to you the second time we were together?"

"Yes."

"I was tempted to tell you then. I still hadn't gotten over the fact that you'd never returned my messages. I was still angry about that—and then you led me to believe we only had days together, that there was nothing more for us, no future. How could we raise a child together if we had no future?"

"If you'd told me back then, things might have changed."

"You're telling me you would have left the priesthood? For Zoey and not for me?"

"Maybe."

"Why? After John died, I had hopes for a little while that we might get together. But you never gave me the slightest indication that you wanted anything more than our conference time. So no, I don't think so. Besides, I came to terms with that, and I decided that I was fine with the situation just as it was. Better than fine, actually."

"I might have … maybe changed teams."

"Yeah, well, we'll never know, will we? There were times I lived in fear that Zoey might have inherited some health issues. I knew your name and a few details about your childhood—but not one other goddamn fact about who you were! You never even mentioned that you were Canadian. I thought you were American all this time. You knew so much about me and my family, and what did you share about yourself? A big fat zero.

"I worried that because you knew my address and other things about me, you might try to find me someday. I even thought, once or twice, that you might have a mental condition. Sometimes you said the weirdest things. How time with me made you able to make it through a year without thinking or letting *them* get to you. Now it makes more sense, but back then, I knew there had to be a good reason why you were so secretive. I imagined every scenario. For a while, I had you pegged as a politician and then a criminal and then a con artist. Even someone in a witness protection program. Nothing made sense. Why would I risk exposing Zoey to a person like that? Our sexual escapades were exciting, but there was no way I was going to let you slide into my family life."

He interrupted. "But when you found out I was a priest, couldn't you trust me then, for Christ's sake?"

"No."

"No?"

"Why would I? When I saw you that day in church, I almost lost it. I couldn't reconcile the fact that you were a priest with the man I knew. I never imagined you were a priest. Actually, strike that. You were a bishop when we were together, right? Then I began to think of the things we did together. I worried you would call me immoral and take her from me. I brought her into this world, nursed her, treated her colic, dealt with her moods when she was cutting teeth, and spent nights with little sleep or no sleep at all. I did everything. All by myself."

She stopped talking for a few seconds to regroup. Was this what she really wanted to tell him? Wasn't it time for the truth?

She sighed. "All the same, I knew I had to tell you someday."

"Why?"

"Because, despite what I feared, it was the right thing to do. I struggled with the timing of telling you. I was so worried you'd want to share custody. And then, the day that you came to see me, I wanted to tell you, but Zoey and I were ill. I thought for sure that you'd made the connection on your own. In the living room, you were holding her picture in your hand, for heaven's sake. Then you got sick, and I took it as a sign that it wasn't the right time. I guess I thought that since so much time had passed, what would a few more days matter?"

He looked at her then. "You really thought I could walk away?"

She nodded, tired from her confession. It wasn't the same thing, but each year, separating after the conference never seemed to cause him any negative effects. It was not a great leap to assume he'd want very little to do with Zoey.

Chris said, "Today at school, I broke up the fight between Zoey and that little boy. I saw how you held her, not caring whether she got blood on your shirt when you hugged her little body. And when she left your arms, she was smiling. That smile, my sister's smile, showed me the truth. That she's mine. She looks exactly like my sister, Jean. It was just a little glimpse of what it means to be a parent. I won't lie and tell you I'm not scared. I am. I don't know how to do any of it.

"The times we spent together—I believe they made me a better person. I thought I had us figured out before, but now I know I didn't. I actually believed you were content with our arrangement, and that Zoey was your husband's child. When I learned you lived in this parish, I thought that was all I had to deal with. I thought—"

The phone rang, and Tory stood up to get it.

Chris put his hand on her arm. "Let it ring."

"I have to get it."

"We have more to talk about."

"No kidding, we've just scratched the surface. But I have to—"

"Hey, get your hands off her!" a male voice rang out.

It was Jake. Tory wasn't quite ready to deal with this yet. "It's okay, honey!"

Chris released her arm as Jake approached them. He was taller than Tory and still growing.

"Jake, this is Chris." Luckily, Chris wasn't wearing his clerical collar, so she could leave the *Father* part out of the introductions for now. "Chris, this is Jake. I'm going inside. It's getting chilly out here."

She checked to see who called. Alice. She needed a break from Chris, anyway, and she was done talking for a while. A tension headache was building.

She returned the call and answered Alice's questions without sarcasm.

"Yes, he's still here. Jake just got in, so he'll probably leave now. Was he angry? No, I never felt threatened. We'll have to wait and see. We'll work it out, Mom. Please don't worry. Love you. Bye."

She turned around to see Jake and Chris: the men who meant so much to her. Jake was looking confused, and Chris was smiling. What did he have to be happy about? Oh, her side of the conversation.

"We're going to work it out?" he asked. She nodded, and he looked pleased.

"Mom, what's going on?" Jake asked.

Oddly enough, Tory didn't feel any shame or a need to defend herself. Maybe the passage of time and the closeness she enjoyed with her two older children had something to do with that. "Jakie, I need to tell you and Sam something. It has to do with me and Zoey and Chris. It's important, but it'll keep until she's here. Okay?"

Jake nodded and looked at Chris.

"Chris is going now," she said. It wasn't what Chris probably wanted to hear, but the man knew better than to argue.

She left Jake in the kitchen and walked Chris to the front door.

"Tomorrow's Saturday. Can we talk then?" he asked.

"I'll let you know."

"You know that postponing the conversation won't solve anything, right?"

"Yes, I know. That's all I've been thinking about since this morning. I'm not looking forward to it, but I know it needs to happen. I just can't at the moment."

"Why not?"

Her headache prompted her to take a detour to the washroom cupboard for an aspirin, ignoring his question. She wished she could close her eyes, make him disappear, and turn back the clock to before she'd decided to move here and have a do-over. She swallowed two pills.

"You okay?"

"Brain ache."

"I'm not surprised."

Perhaps it was all the stress of the day and the weeks leading up to it. It didn't matter. All that mattered was that she rest before a migraine developed. She hadn't had one in a long time, but she knew the signs. "Chris, you need to go. I have to lie down in a quiet, dark place—or it'll only get worse."

"All right. But first I need to do something for you. Can you humor me for fifteen more minutes?"

"If you don't talk or expect sex."

"Deal! Although I heard that sex can help a headache."

He took her arm and led her to the couch. Why did he look so pleased that she was allowing him to touch her at all? Other than when she collapsed due to illness, he had yet to show her that he cared.

Once she was settled, he turned off the lights, placed a footstool beside her, and sat down. She closed her eyes when he took hold of her hand. He began to rub the space between her thumb and index finger. The gentle, soothing, circular pressure soon lulled her to sleep.

Sometime in the middle of the night, she awakened to find herself under a blanket, headache-free, but also alone, with only her thoughts for company.

Aware that there had been a major shift in how they dealt with each other, she wondered if he wanted to continue their sexual relationship. Did he have other plans? It was too difficult to sort out what she felt for him at the moment.

She got up to check the doors and her kids—all asleep—before making some weak tea. Unable to sit still, she prowled the house like she did when she was pregnant with Zoey.

Her thoughts kept her unsettled for hours, picking up threads of their conversation earlier.

If you'd told me back then, things might have changed.

But when you found out I was a priest, couldn't you trust me then?

You really thought I could walk away?

You know that postponing the conversation won't solve anything, right?

She tried not to worry about what Chris might do. Instead, she considered her options. Short of leaving everything and everyone in her life and running away with Zoey, there weren't any. Now she knew for sure that he wanted to be part of Zoey's life.

Since they lived in the same town, her fear about Zoey being uprooted wouldn't come to pass. Was she worried he'd be a bad influence on her child? If she really thought about it, part of her was a little scared he'd be so good at parenting that Zoey would prefer him to her. She wasn't used to having to share her youngest with anyone. Having admitted this to herself, she felt silly and selfish, but it also felt a little easier to handle.

She tried thinking about the situation as a problem for which she had to discover the best approach for managing it. How could she look at things more objectively? They would have to reach a compromise that was reasonable and cooperative. Chris would surely agree to that.

Her thoughts were becoming more positive. She realized that the ball wasn't in his court. She could—and would—change her approach to the way she and Chris handled each other. She would try to be more giving and supportive of his needs. It was all about having the right attitude and not making it worse with a negative outlook. She could do this.

Having come to terms with that last bit of wisdom and with her resolve to handle the whole business more positively, she showered and got into bed. Sleep came easily. She managed to get in another couple of hours of rest.

CHAPTER 17

The morning lit up the room, but he had yet to sleep. So much had happened over the past twenty-four hours that he could not rest easy. He was off balance. Everything was off balance. His world had shifted when he learned that he was a father.

Out of the blue, he'd been given a child. He'd felt disbelief at first, and then he slowly started to accept his good fortune. *This must be what winning the lottery feels like.*

His experience with children had been limited to very short interactions and perfunctory obligations. He had never changed a diaper or cleaned up vomit, and he could not fathom the responsibility of shaping a young mind. Nevertheless, although daunting, the rearing aspect of parenthood did not disturb him. His worry came from another source: Tory.

She was not happy with him. In fact, she gave off strong vibes that intimidated him. She wanted him to keep his distance, but if he had any say in the matter, that was not going to happen. As far as he was concerned, he and Tory had a bond that the presence of a child only strengthened. He still couldn't get a clear picture of what Tory felt for him. It might have something to do with him being in her home territory, but he suspected it was more than that.

Not once since he'd arrived in her parish had she treated him the way she had during their conference time. There were no heartwarming smiles and intimate glances. He was not the center of her world. It wasn't completely surprising, given the situation, but part of him had hoped she'd have been glad to learn they were now living in the same town. He was. He admitted that finding out he was a priest was probably a huge shock, but she behaved as though he were a stranger. She said she didn't know him at all. Well, he felt the same way. He didn't even recognize this version of Tory.

She had many obligations; her life was full without him in it. He understood that now. Their annual encounters were something she enjoyed—not something she needed. That was not how it was for him. He counted down the months, weeks and days until they would be together. He lived for the moments when they enjoyed each other. Her touch calmed his soul.

As a young priest, he had given himself freely to the mission and his vocation. He believed he was making a difference in the lives of others. Perhaps that was true. He wasn't convinced even though tears had been shed when he announced his transfer at his last parish, where he'd resided for ten years.

Oddly, Chris hadn't been upset to be pushed out and demoted due to his medical condition. He had expected it, having heard of the same happening to another bishop. In some ways, he welcomed the change; it meant less responsibility. The demotion had not affected him the way Tory's pushing him away had. He had to consider what he would do about his future.

He had told Tory that he would have left his vocation if he had known about Zoey's existence, but she hadn't believed him.

You're telling me you would have left the priesthood? For Zoey and not for me?

After John died, I had hopes for a little while that we might get together. But you never gave me the slightest indication that you wanted anything more than our conference time. So, no, I don't think so.

He felt ashamed and ill, thinking about her words again. She had been right on the money. Making this right was going to require a great deal of introspection and some tough decisions. Starting immediately, he would address everything in his life. He would have to be honest with Tory if he hoped to make any headway with her and Zoey. First, he would have to look within and come to terms with who he had become and what he wanted.

When he decided to become a priest, it had seemed to be the right path. He was young and had lofty aspirations. For a long time, it had been enough. But not anymore. His disillusionment with the Roman Catholic Church had begun before he met Tory. Seeing the same people every day, following the same routine, and living the same boring existence had chipped away at the foundation of his belief that he was making a difference, but it never altered his faith.

Perhaps he was being drawn to another calling. There had to be a reason for this sudden upheaval that could not be explained away as a test of his convictions.

He thought about Tory and how their lives had converged despite their attempts to maintain distance. He regretted not sharing with her about who he was; this mistake had made him become, in her eyes, someone she wouldn't share her child with. He had no idea how to make up for that.

Tory's life had purpose. If he died tomorrow, no one would mourn his passing. He was fairly certain of that. Even his own child did not know him. If something ever happened to Tory, though, many would miss her, perhaps no one more than he.

After a second cup of coffee—something his doctor had advised against after his heart surgery—he showered. Dressed in clean, non-clerical clothing, he prayed for wisdom and guidance and drove over to the Stanton residence.

He had to get his head on straight and come up with a plan. He would start by getting to know Zoey and letting Tory see the real him, the kind of man and father he wanted to be. It was a challenging agenda, but he needed to integrate himself into their lives if he was to gain any ground. His goal was to ensure that Tory no longer considered his presence a threat to her family unit. He would ingratiate himself with all of her children if that's what it took. Then he would share more of his past so that Tory could understand him better.

He arrived at her house and rang the bell, telling himself to calm down. *You can do this.* He gathered his courage, remembering what it had felt like the first time he'd faced a congregation of several hundred people and the time Tory had told him not to meet her after his surgery. He had persevered, and it had paid off. He just had to hold it together for a little while longer.

185

Zoey opened the door. Her lovely face grinned at him. "Hi!"

Her simple greeting warmed his rapidly beating heart, and he returned the smile without any hesitation. Suddenly, he felt better. "Hello, sweetheart. May I speak to your mother?"

The little girl turned and bellowed. "Mom! There's somebody here!"

Tory came around the corner, drying her hands on a towel. She stopped when she saw him standing there like an idiot.

She is so damn beautiful, he thought.

"Zoey, please don't yell like that, and what did I tell you about opening the door to strangers?"

"He was at school yesterday," Zoey answered before running off.

"Sorry. I didn't mean that you were a stranger," Tory said to Chris. "I'm trying to teach her—"

"Don't worry about it," he said, smiling. Her expression was serious, and he wondered what she was thinking. "Good morning! Feeling better?" he asked.

"Yes, much better, thank you."

"I said I'd be back."

She shook her head as if suddenly deciding something. "Did you get any rest? You look pale." Her interest in his well-being was the balm he needed.

"A little." She gave him a look. Why did he ever bother not telling her the truth to begin with? "Strike that. I haven't been able to sleep."

They stood awkwardly in the foyer until Zoey returned and tugged at Tory's arm. God, would he ever get used to the idea of having his own flesh and blood? His eyes drank her in, and he noticed her cute sundress.

"Are we going shopping soon?" she asked.

He watched his lover bend down over their child and caress her hair. "Yes, honey. Give me ten minutes. Go brush your teeth and get your hairbrush. While you're waiting, Father Chris will braid your hair. He's a whiz at that."

Tory looked up at him for confirmation, he supposed, and he loved her more in that minute than he'd thought possible. She was extending the proverbial olive branch, and he would grab it with both hands.

"Your mom's right. I am."

By some silent agreement, they'd decided to ease into this, whatever *this* was. He was so grateful and humbled that it made him all the more determined not to mess it up.

He followed Tory into the kitchen. Jake was sitting at the table, inhaling cereal.

"Morning, Jake," Chris said.

The boy was too well mannered to ignore the greeting, despite how much he may have wanted to, and especially not with Tory standing there, tidying up the counter. "Morning," he replied.

Just as the moment stretched out and became awkward, Tory asked, "Have you had breakfast?"

He was about to lie and then thought better of it. "No. But I'm not hungry. I had coffee."

"I'm going to make toast and peanut butter, and you're going to eat it." She opened the cupboard without waiting for a response.

"Yes, ma'am," he said to bug her. She didn't have a comeback, which meant he had a ways to go before she felt easy with him.

Zoey returned, and Chris helped her up into the chair beside his. She sat quietly without fidgeting, and the room felt too quiet.

Chris began to brush and braid her hair. "When I was a little younger than your brother is now, my little sister would give me her brush and expect me to drop everything so I could fix her hair. Her hair was beautiful, just like yours."

"You did her hair?"

"Yes."

"Why?"

"Because it was our thing. No one else was allowed to touch her hair."

"What's her name?" Zoey asked.

"Ginette. I called her Jean."

"Why?"

"Because she didn't like her name, and she wanted to be called Jean."

187

"Do you still brush her hair?"

"No."

"Why?"

Tory came over to deposit a glass of milk in front of her daughter. "Zoey, stop pestering him. Finish your milk."

"It's okay," he said. "She died a long time ago."

The room got quiet again. He hadn't stopped to think about the impact his words would have on this family—who had dealt with the passing of one of its members—and he expounded a little more so that Zoey might comprehend. "Jean was sick. Now she's in heaven and not around to talk to me."

"Do you miss her?" she asked.

"Every day," he answered. "She and I were very close."

A plate of toast appeared beside his elbow just as he applied an elastic to the end of Zoey's braid.

"All done!" he said.

Zoey was about to get down from her chair, but Tory said, "Drink your milk! And what do we say?"

"Thank you," Zoey said with an impish grin.

He returned the smile. "You're welcome."

Zoey guzzled the liquid and ran off.

"Is she always like this?" he asked. "I mean, rushing about."

"Yep, she has so much energy and enthusiasm for everything. She wears me out sometimes."

While he ate his toast, the phone rang, a door slammed, and a toilet flushed—the expression of family activity. He sat quietly, soaking in the benign household sounds. He was looking in rather than being a part of it, but he knew he'd made some progress.

Jake sauntered out of the kitchen, leaving them alone.

"Is Samantha around?" Chris asked.

"No, she's away at a friend's. She has her own place anyway. She just likes to visit on the weekends."

"Can I come shopping with you?"

Tory considered his request. "It's not going to be fun, you know. I have to get Zoey some new shoes, and then there's groceries."

"I've never been grocery shopping."

One eyebrow rose. "You've never shopped for food and household items?"

"I must have, but I can't remember when. It's part of the duties my housekeepers always cover."

"Well, if you're sure."

"I am."

"Okay, then. I'll fetch Zoey." Just as she left the kitchen, she turned back to look at him. "Nice job with the hair and answering Zoey's questions."

"I know."

She gave him a smirk, which he considered a step in the right direction. She was giving him more than he expected, more than he deserved.

***

She watched Chris trying to keep his eyes open as he listened to Zoey's nonstop chatter. Tory didn't want him driving home in that condition. The shopping excursion had been more of an ordeal than he had expected, she would wager. Or maybe he was exhausted from sleep deprivation. She'd just put away all their purchases, and now it was time for downtime.

"Zoey, honey, can you go into the family room and choose a movie? Father Chris and I will be there in a couple of minutes."

He looked at her, probably worried she was going to ask him to leave. "There's a lounger in the family room," she said. "I want you to tilt it back and have a nap. No debate, you understand?"

He nodded, probably too tired to argue.

In the family room, he dutifully sat back in the lounger. Within minutes, he was asleep. She covered him with a blanket, stopping to admire his face as Zoey giggled at something on the screen. Tory forced herself to leave Chris's side without running her fingertips over his jaw, and she joined her daughter on the couch.

Tory was hyperaware of Chris. She gazed at him, so striking and handsome with his graying temples and strong face. His beautifully sculpted lips made her mouth water, knowing what they were capable of.

He had been so patient with Zoey at the shoe store. He'd showed a side of himself that Tory found captivating. She'd liked the way he interacted with their daughter; he was honest and forthright yet still able to express himself so that Zoey would understand him. She could tell that he was trying to get to know their daughter without rocking the boat.

He had deferred to Tory for the final decision. Perhaps it was no more than a tactical ploy to appease her while they worked through things, but she wanted to believe otherwise. He was finally giving her the opportunity to see a side of himself.

As they shopped for groceries, she had discovered things about him. His favorite foods, for example. He liked the strangest things, and they had laughed about that. He had no trouble with pickled sardines, but he balked at beets. She had known he had a sense of humor—but not the extent of his ability to find joy in the mundane. She was so susceptible to being swept up in his cheerful mood, and nothing could protect her from his charm. He was so good with people that she couldn't imagine him leaving his calling. She was preparing herself to accept whatever parts of himself he would share with them.

She thought of how different he was during their conference time. The self-assurance was replaced by something more real. After examining her own behavior, she realized the same could be said about her; she was more down-to-earth in her own home. It was like they were getting to know each other in a whole other plane of existence.

***

It was dark outside the windows when he opened his eyes and found himself on the leather lounger. He checked his watch, sat up, and scanned the room. It was empty, but the television was still on. Otherwise, the house was relatively quiet. He caught murmurs coming from the kitchen and headed that way.

The family, including Alice, was gathered around the table, having dinner. They stopped talking when they saw him.

"Alice," he said.

"Chris," she responded with a twinkle in her eye. The fact that she did not say more made him feel good.

"Don't let me intrude," he said. "I should be on my way."

"Please stay," Tory said. "At least have something to eat. I promise I don't have a casserole."

He laughed and accepted her invitation to sit. Earlier, he'd confessed that he loathed casseroles, which parishioners always brought him in abundance. He also felt Jake's suspicious eyes on him. Another piece of information shared earlier today, by Tory, was the fact that Jake was working part-time at a hardware store.

"How was work?" Chris asked.

"Fine," Jake said.

Chris accepted the response with a nod. He hadn't expected a long conversation.

"I can't get over how much work shopping is. No wonder you don't enjoy it," he said as Tory handed him a plate. She blinked. It must have taken her a second to remember that she had once mentioned her dislike of spending time at the malls.

"I try to make it a weekly task instead of having to go out every day. It seems to work most of the time, but I still end up stopping for milk and such before Saturday rolls around."

"Mom, don't forget Cassie's birthday party!" Zoey called out.

"Yes, honey." Tory grinned at him. "Like I said. It works most of the time. Not this time though." She mouthed the words *I forgot.*

Alice laughed, and Zoey wanted to know what was so funny.

"Your mom made us laugh, honey," said Chris. "I didn't know she wasn't perfect." This made everyone except Zoey stop and stare at him. *Oops!* He had been trying to tease her, but it obviously hadn't come across that way. "I mean, she's so efficient and organized. It was a lame joke because she does seem perfect—"

"I'm not, but it's nice to know that you think that." She grinned at his discomfiture.

Zoey, bless her, started telling a story about how awful some of the meals had been, diverting attention away from him. Tory took the teasing in stride. He admired her ability not to take things too seriously.

It was all very homey, and Chris was content to sit there and let the conversation flow around him.

CHAPTER 18

After dinner, with Jake out for the evening, Alice gone home, and Zoey tucked up in bed, Tory showed Chris albums of baby pictures. Then she pulled up more photos on her laptop. So many photos, of every stage in Zoey's life. She told him about all the milestone events of the last four years: birthdays, holidays, vacations, first steps, first teeth, first everything. She talked until it was very late.

"Enough," he said with a grin. "My head is reeling."

She smiled along with him until he lifted a strand of her hair and twirled it. His eyes became very serious, and she braced herself for whatever came next.

"So soft. Are you going to let it grow out?"

"Probably. I'm not worried about keeping up with trends."

"I know. It's one of the things I like about you."

She could tell that he wanted to kiss her. She wasn't against the idea, but they had more unfinished business to address first.

"We've been avoiding the big questions," she said. Discussing his intentions was a bit premature, but she couldn't help herself. Not knowing what he was thinking was killing her.

"What questions? Strike that. That was a stupid thing to say. I know there are things to decide, but I want you to tell me which questions we should be asking or talking about."

"Oh … I don't know."

"Sure you do."

He took her hand and rubbed it. She felt his warmth and encouragement.

"What will we do about Zoey?"

"Why do we have to do anything right now?"

"We don't … at least, I don't."

"But you want me to give you something. A hint of my intentions. I only know that I want Zoey in my life, Tory, but I don't know how I'm going to make that work. I know it sounds dumb."

"It's not dumb."

"It's not that I don't want to commit to anything; it's that I can't yet."

She could see that this level of honesty was difficult for him. Could he be as frank about other aspects of their relationship? "What about me? Where do I fit in now?"

He sighed. "I could ask you the same thing."

"Okay. You want me to go first?"

"Why not?"

"Being with you today, like this, was great. But I know that even if I wanted something more from you, it wouldn't be possible. You'll never give up what you do." It was the truth, and her own certainty about it scared her.

"You seem so sure."

"I'm not ready for more change either."

"I've been doing a lot of thinking. I might be due for a change in my life. When I'm in your home, I see you and your kids as one. I can't separate them from you. And I envy you that. What you have."

She nodded.

"Do you think that they—and you, of course—could accept me for me?"

"I—"

"I'm not finished. Could they accept me as a part of their life, your life?"

"We might. But it's a little too soon, I think." She needed to be honest with him—no matter how it might sound. She had no idea how anything would work out in the end or what risks she was prepared to take.

"Are you unsure because of our sexual past? Or because of what I did? Or, more accurately, what I haven't done? Sharing my past with you."

"We all have baggage."

"I'm not talking about baggage. You're still perturbed by something. I can't address it if you don't tell me what it is." She sensed that he was becoming frustrated.

"Don't you think I know that? I'm trying to handle this the best way I can. It's not easy for any of us. I get that. But putting Zoey aside for a moment, I have issues with you, and what you bring to our relationship. There are parts of your past that clearly haunt you, parts of you that are closed off, and this has nothing to do with you being a man of the cloth."

"I can tell that things have changed between us. The woman I thought I knew would have wanted to check out my chest to see how my bypass scars healed."

He had a point. She had been treating him as though he weren't the man who shared conference time with her. They wouldn't get anywhere in their new relationship until they discussed the past.

"Do you have any questions for me?" she asked.

"I have only two. Did you get the breast reconstruction?"

"That's one of your questions? Really?"

"I just wondered if you did and it made you feel more like yourself again. That's all. It's not about how it looks or what I think. Although if this were our conference time, I'd already know by now. And you'd know that."

"I did have the breast reconstruction. Second question?"

Chris regarded her wearily. Of course, Tory knew her pat answer hadn't addressed what he was really asking. He wanted the details of what had happened and how she felt about it, but she couldn't bring herself to discuss that experience yet.

"Do you care for me?" he asked. "I mean, do you still feel it? The way we click?"

She leaned in closer to him and brought her hand to his cheek. "Yes. Today, more than ever before. My feelings for you are so different from anything I've felt for anyone else."

He grabbed her so tightly she thought her arms might bruise. "I need to be with you, skin to skin. It's all I can think about."

She understood and nodded.

"Can I take you against the wall by the front door?"

"No, you goof!"

She felt his body sag. "Jake could come home—or Zoey could wake up. You'll need to come to my bed."

He jumped up, picked her up, and carried her down the hall. She was full of anxiety and excitement about experiencing lovemaking with him again. There was a little bit of trepidation about her chest. The new breast matched the other one fairly well, but there was still scar tissue, and the color wasn't quite right.

Her concerns fell away, though, when he slowly removed her clothing, touching her with such gentle reverence that tears ran down her cheeks. His eyes devoured her. He stepped back to hastily remove his own clothes, and when she moved to dim the lights, he put his hand out, stopping her.

"I've been thinking about you and us like this for weeks—no, months. I want to see all of you, clearly. Please indulge me."

She acquiesced.

"I'll be gentle," he said.

"You don't need to be."

His hand came to her face and cupped her cheek. "Yes, I do. This is our first time here. It has to be special. I can't believe I said I wanted to fuck you against the wall. It's always been fast and intense the first time. We hardly even wait to make it to the room. But this is here and now. It's different, isn't it?"

She nodded. It was so strange having him in her room, knowing what they were about to do. She'd never dreamed of having him—or any other man—in her own bed, with her kids down the hall. She felt a bit out of sorts.

Chris had a knack for knowing what she required. He looked deeply into her eyes. "It's going to be okay. We're going to be okay. Let me show you. Stop thinking and worrying about everything. I think you're worse than I am."

He knelt before her and kissed her abdomen. She closed her eyes, accepting this joyous gift of two people committing to a moment of shared intimacy. There were no rules, and they were in complete sync.

Rubbing her lower back, buttocks, and thighs, he continued to press his lips to her belly. His touch was unhurried, tender, pure bliss.

Cradling his head with her hands, she played with his hair, trying to convey her love for him in her haze of contentment.

He stood, his lips came to hers, and he took control, which made her legs tremble.

"I love you," he whispered, and she was lost.

They found their way to the bed. She was giggling in pure delight. The man she cared for was in her room, and they were about to have sex!

He grasped her leg, pulled it over his hip, and used his fingers to make her more than ready to complete their mating dance. Their mouths fused as his weight crushed her. Penetration was swift, and it made them both groan with satisfaction.

"You feel so good," she said during a brief moment when her tongue was not otherwise occupied. Her legs circled his, never wanting to let him go.

"Ditto, baby!"

They smiled at each other, the way they had before. Then, within seconds, all rational thought vanished. He dragged his hard length against the walls of her vagina, making contact that satisfied her inner itch and stimulated her. It was heaven, how he fit her completely. That combined with the push and pull of his stiffness at her vulva made her sigh and moan in sweet torment. How had she managed to survive without this for so long?

"Harder!" She arched up into him, and he gave it to her and more. Reaching deeper. Penetrating her core. Changing angles so that her G-spot was being titillated, causing her toes to curl in approval.

"Yes! Yes! That's it!"

The pace was frantic now. Breathing was difficult. His pounding pushed her up the bed.

"Hold … the headboard," he said through clenched teeth.

She followed his order and immediately began to spiral out of control. "Oh, *God!* I'm coming! Please come with me!"

Within seconds, they crested, and he released into her as she continued to ride out the climax. He fell on her until he caught his breath, and then he rolled them to their sides, still inside her, as she preferred. She always recovered from their coitus by holding on, not breaking their hold for even an instant.

"I'm not going anywhere," he said, always attuned to her.

Eventually they eased apart to snuggle, and she traced the line of healed tissue down his chest.

"Any shortness of breath?" she asked.

"Only when I'm with you. You take my breath away."

She grinned at the cheesy comment. "No swelling?"

"Stop worrying. I'm fine."

"What are you thinking about?"

"How irresponsible we were just now. And five years ago, I never even asked if you were on the pill or anything. Are you ... on it now? Should we be concerned?"

"I'm on the pill, like I was before. Mind you, I still managed to get pregnant. Another pregnancy is possible, but it's not likely if we skip the sex marathon. It's the wrong time of the month anyway. And you're the only other man I've slept with since my husband died. Have you been with anyone else?"

He repositioned them so he could look directly into her eyes. "There hadn't been anyone for twenty years before we met—and no one but you since then. I hope you believe me."

"I do."

"Now go to sleep."

"We need to talk."

"Not now, honey. You need rest, and we always have tomorrow."

He left sometime in the night. Her reaction, when she woke and noticed him gone, was disappointment. But then she put things into perspective. Chris had Sunday services to conduct, and it wouldn't be a good idea to have him turn up at her breakfast table just yet. She jumped out of bed, showered, and began her day, feeling lighter than she had in a long time.

It was more than the sex, which would never be a problem for them. They were becoming closer, almost united in their understanding of the challenges ahead and how well he knew her body and mind.

He paid attention to the little things. He seemed to want what she wanted.

She felt happy and that allowed her to bask in the good stuff of life today rather than dwell on serious thoughts: how her future might change if she and Chris openly became a couple, how others might react, and all the unknowns of a relationship. Her elevated mood could have to do with the novelty of having a man she cared for back in the picture, but she suspected it had more to do with how she felt about the whole situation. More relaxed. More open to possibilities.

When Tory found her way to the kitchen, four sets of eyes greeted her. All three of her kids and Alice were waiting for her.

"Sam? I thought that you were out of town for the weekend."

"Yeah, but Jake said I should come over."

"I told her you had something you wanted to talk to us about," Jake explained. "I didn't mean for her to show up at the crack of dawn and wake me up."

"And I just came by to see how you fared last night," Alice said with a grin.

Tory got out the griddle and began making pancakes while her mom cooked some sausages and the kids set the table. No one spoke except for Zoey, who chattered on as usual. The adults all let her fill the silence as they ate without speaking to each other. When the meal was over, Tory asked what everyone had planned for the day. No one answered. Zoey got up to take her dirty dishes to the sink.

Samantha leaned over. "Mom, what's going on?"

Tory shook her head to indicate that she wouldn't respond while Zoey was present. She needed to come clean to Jake and Sam. It was the mature thing to do—no matter how awkward it was.

"Mom, can you keep Zoey busy for a few minutes?" she said to Alice.

They went out to the family room to watch a video.

"Jakie, Sam, I need to tell you something."

She told them about meeting Chris at a conference years ago, right when her marriage with their father had been at an all-time low. She admitted that her liaison with Chris had resulted in Zoey's conception. She also told them that Chris had only just found out he had a daughter.

Tory waited for their questions, but neither said a word for several minutes. What were they thinking? When she couldn't stand the silent treatment any longer, she said, "Do you have any questions?"

Sam said, "He just spent the night, didn't he?"

"He left during the night."

"Did you have sex?"

Jake groaned, embarrassed by his sister's question. It was uncomfortable for them all, but possibly more uncomfortable for him since he typically shied away from any discussion about anything remotely related to sexual behavior. Thinking about his mother that way was probably killing him, but she owed Sam her honesty.

"Yes."

"And what would Dad say about this?" Samantha asked.

"If he'd known before he died, he would have been upset. But I think he would have understood. We hadn't been intimate, physically or emotionally, for a long time before he died. And now, after all this time, I think he would want me to move on." At least she hoped that he might feel that way.

"Did you know he was a priest?" Samantha asked.

"No. I only found out when we went to church that day."

"Is he moving in? Is he leaving the church?"

"Nothing's been decided. I don't know what's going to happen. Right now, we'll just take one day at a time."

"I don't know how to feel about this," Jake said.

Tory reached across the table to grab his hand. "I can't even pretend to know the shock and confusion you must be feeling," she said.

"This is so hard to believe," Samantha said.

Tory knew her children were struggling. With no more words to offer, she tried to provide silent encouragement for them to speak their minds. How could she explain careless indulgence anyway? Taking a leap with no thought of the consequences? How could she defend irresponsible behavior? She could see the desolation and disillusionment in their eyes. She was supposed to be the stable, mature parent. Had they lost respect for her? Had she damaged her relationships with them?

"Did you love Dad?" Jake asked.

"Yes, I did, but our feelings changed over time. As the years passed, we spent less and less time together. We tolerated each other, like married couples do. When you're in a relationship for that long, you try to make it work. And we couldn't. For a long time before he died, I wasn't happy. If he hadn't gotten ill, I probably would have left him. I know that it's difficult to comprehend—"

"Mom, this is so weird for us! You've had a whole other life with this priest. You've been living a lie!" Samantha stood up.

"*It's my life.* Someone once told me that when she quit university."

Sam started to protest, but Tory held up her hand.

"I know this isn't the same, but please pay me the courtesy of remembering that I am your mother. I don't have to defend my actions to you. Because you're adults. I want you to know that my *real* life has always been here with you. I spent only four days a year with a lovely man, and those were some of the most joyful moments in my life."

"Will he expect things to change?" Jake asked. "I mean, with you and Zoey?"

Tory shrugged. "I don't know. It's too soon to tell. He's struggling with what to do. But it's not just Zoey and me. The four of us are a package deal, and he knows that, I think."

"But he's a priest," Sam stated.

It was true; the situation was strange enough with that added fact. "I really don't know what's going to happen with that. He told me he's been thinking of a change, but I don't see him giving up that. All I know is we're very attracted to each other. We still have feelings for each other."

Jake nodded and stood up. "Okay, Mom. I'm going to go buy some gas for the mower, and then I'll cut the lawn."

Just like that, her son seemed to take it all in stride. Her eldest was clearly feeling conflicted. Not wanting to risk saying anything that might make things worse, Tory went to Sam and held her for a long time. It helped them both, once the tears were spent.

This is the impact of my actions. What she had done affected her adult children as well. Doubts began to resurface. Was she doing the right thing by letting Chris in? She was doing fine on her own—and she had no doubt that she would continue to do so—but she'd thrown a monkey wrench into their lives. A stranger was invading their home and making them uncomfortable. Perhaps she was rushing things too much. Expecting too much. She had such blind trust that everything would work out. *What if it didn't?*

Later, her own mother gave her hand in folding the laundry.

"How are you doing, honey?" Alice asked.

"I'm fine. Samantha's struggling." It had to be a shock to go from thinking your mother was avoiding men to discovering your mother had been having an affair for five years. "I guess she's dealing with it in her own way. She's more upset about this than she was about my breast cancer or her father's death. Jake seems okay."

"She'll come around. Give it time. When are you telling Zoey?"

"Oh, Mom. I can't even think about it. I guess Chris should be with me when that happens. I'm going to hold off for a while, I think."

"Why?"

"Because Chris needs some time. He has some decisions to make."

"He told you that?"

"No, but our lives aren't going to change too much. He's the one whose whole world has been turned upside down."

"Well, don't put it off for too long, honey. Word will get around, and you don't want her finding out the hard way by hearing about it at school."

"Mom, there's no easy way around this."

"Maybe, but you're raising a smart girl. She's self-assured enough to cope, and kids are resilient when they're given the facts to digest in their own time."

"I'm hoping the right opportunity will present itself."

Her mom was right. Zoey should know, but she had no idea how to share the story. Tory had to find a way of explaining it the right way—and at the right time.

CHAPTER 19

Two days later, Chris leafed through his mail and found an envelope marked "confidential." No return address. In it, there was a business card for a local Anglican minister and a Post-it note attached to the back of the card: "from Alice."

The day before, Alice had come to see him. She had asked him what he was planning to do. He'd put it all out on the table, sharing his thoughts more openly than he had yet to do with Tory. Alice's only interest was protecting her family; he could run his ideas past her and know she'd give him her honest opinion.

They had discussed his alternatives to leaving the priesthood, and she had suggested talking to clergy in other denominations of Christianity that didn't require clerical celibacy. If he were willing to convert, he could continue to preach and minister to people. Perhaps ministering in a different denomination would fit the bill, but after pondering that for a while, he wasn't sure it was what he needed long-term.

He had overcome his original internal struggle to break his own vow of celibacy, but he still felt pressured to lose his current safety net, to learn who he was and what was expected of him, given his current state of ambivalence, in his role within the Roman Catholic Church. It was all tied together. It was more than a little daunting to think about leaving the church. It was all he'd known for most of his life. Contemplating a dramatic change made him feel frightened and raw, but he was considering it.

He told Alice that if he decided to no longer be a priest, that he possessed no real skills for earning a living. She asked him about his education and had suggested various options, but he found the idea of learning to be a teacher or a business consultant at his age less appealing.

She had not hesitated to probe him about his savings, investments, and retirement benefits. Clearly she was worried Chris might become a financial burden to her already financially stressed daughter. Chris put her concerns to rest.

He grinned at the notion that if he became a family unit with Tory and Zoey, he'd be joining Sam, Jake, and Alice as well. Some of them had yet to accept him, but the idea of being part of a loving family was nice. It was something he'd never believed he could have. For years, he'd avoided becoming close to any of his parishioners out of paranoia. Accusations were as good as a guilty verdict, and they resulted in the swift death of any clergyman's career.

Over the past twenty-plus years of listening to and talking to others about their issues, eating bad food, and going to bed alone, being a priest had started to feel like hard labor that was part of a prison sentence. Recently, while counseling parishioners, he felt hypocritical and had started to modify the way he provided advice. There was no longer one way of addressing issues. He brought other elements into the pictures, such as humor and practical viewpoints, to aid them in self-discovery. Enjoying the entertainment side of his presentations and seeing the results of his efforts were satisfying.

He realized that many doors still remained open to him. Was it time to think about doing something different? Could he leave it behind and trust that God had better plans for him?

He was musing on all of this when Tory walked into his office like she had a right to be there.

"Hi!" she said.

"Well, hello to you! What's this visit about?" he asked.

"I've come to either take you away or have lunch with you here." She was carrying a picnic basket.

He thought briefly about his work responsibilities and decided to put all of it aside to spend time with her. "Let me make a call, and then I'm all yours."

"I like the sound of that. We should go to this spot I just discovered by the lake. I have a blanket in the car."

He liked her this way: interested in him and happy.

***

The sun was bright as they drove. Tory couldn't see Chris's eyes behind his sunglasses, but he looked relaxed in the passenger seat. Although they'd known each other for nearly six years, the real time they'd spent together only amounted to just over a month. It felt like much longer. There was a familiar ease between them.

As she drove, she teased him that it was his first time in a car with her behind the wheel, which gave her exclusive rights to control the music. He laughed and went along with her. She could tell that he was contemplating something, possibly whatever he'd been thinking about when she interrupted him for lunch. The look of deep concentration that had been painted on his expression returned and she wondered if it was about them or about work.

At the lake, she led him to a rock that was perfect for lounging. She handed him things from the picnic basket while trying to lighten the mood. "I love picnics," she said.

"Church picnics always involve large crowds, games, and baking."

"Well, not this one. This is the real deal. Two people enjoying time away from it all. And if you play your cards right, there's a little nooky for dessert."

He laughed. "That's not something you see on a menu every day."

They ate in silence until he said, "I know this is about more than just lunch and afternoon delight."

She put down her food. She suddenly wanted to be naughty before the moment was possibly ruined by talk. Feeling his eyes on her, she rested her head on his lap. Slowly, she undid his belt, button, and zipper, and then she located his semi-aroused penis, which soon became very happy to see her. She took it slow, letting him watch her put her mouth all over him. It was such a turn-on that they were both groaning in no time.

Chris wasn't content to feel her body through the barrier of clothes. He pulled at them until she was bare from the waist up.

Then, in a frenzied rush, they lost the rest of their clothes before he covered her mouth with his.

She luxuriated in letting him do whatever he wanted, and he did not disappoint. He meandered to her neck and the sensitive place under her ear. Each time, though, he came back for more. When he moved to mount her from behind, it was insanely erotic. Being outdoors was freeing, and the risk of being seen by anyone passing by made her scream as waves of pleasure racked her body.

They cuddled afterward. She used his dress shirt to cover their tender bits from sun exposure. It seemed to get better and better every time they were together. "I knew that ants might show up at our picnic, but not this," she said as she fondled his genitalia.

"I don't think I'll ever forget this picnic."

"Well, you can think about this when you're at those boring church events."

"That brings me to something we should talk about."

He was right. They had been stalling the inevitable, which was discussion about their future.

"I believe I'm going to leave the clergy. And not only because I've just learned I'm a father."

"What will you do?"

"Not sure. Maybe I'll be a stay-at-home dad, and you can be the breadwinner." He smiled at Tory, and she grinned.

"I like that idea."

"I'm sure you do."

So it was decided: They would be together. She was thrilled, even if a tiny part of her wondered whether she really wanted that.

"Of course, we'll have to move," he continued. "It's too bad. I know you've only been in that house for less than a year."

In that small community, everyone knew everyone else's business. Their family would be subjected to malicious gossip once the news got out.

"And you're okay with leaving your calling, your life, all behind?" she asked.

"You're my life now. I've denied that for years. I could no more walk away from us than end my life."

She had to know why he was willing to do it. Was he just trying to do his duty—or was it because of his love for her? It had been on her mind for days. "So it's really not just because of Zoey? Not because you think this is what you *should* do?"

He pulled up her chin with his index finger. "You're the one who means the world to me. I'll do anything to help look after Zoey—she's my flesh and blood—but I know that one day she'll grow up and leave. You and I will always be there for each other. Always."

"Are you thinking of getting married?" Tory wasn't even sure whether she wanted to get married to anyone again, but she wondered what his position was.

"If you want to. I'm open to anything. If you're worried about living together in sin, then we can get married as soon as I resign."

She hugged him fiercely, happy tears leaking from her eyes, and felt relief mixed with a bit of fear. She was glad he was telling her what she wanted to hear, but she worried that it might still be too soon. Neither of them was ready for living together yet. There was still a lot they didn't know about each other, and cohabitating wasn't always easy. She was annoyed that these thoughts were dimming her happy mood.

He continued. "You're probably interested in timelines, This does happen—priests leave the faith—but not often enough that it gets handled expeditiously or without hiccups." Was he worried about being excommunicated? What if they needed to stay apart for a while? "It's not a simple thing to give notice. A replacement will have to be found. And as soon as what I'm doing gets out, it won't be easy for us to see each other. So we should think about this carefully." The concern in his voice was real.

"We have time. People get uprooted all the time. But I would prefer to have Zoey start in a new place by September of next year, if possible. This school year's almost over, so we have a whole year. It'll take me some time to get the house ready to go on the market anyway. I bought it thinking I had years to fix it up. Depending on the market, it might not be a good time to sell."

"You're right. We don't have to rush. But a year?"

"I think we need to take our time to plan things. I don't care what people say about me, but I don't want to risk the kids being hurt by this." Her real worry was about Sam, but she didn't share that. It was difficult to forget her daughter's reaction. "I may have to move before you do. Or we can sit on this for a while and see how it goes. Or we can cut down how much time we spend together."

"The last one is not an option for me. I've finally connected with you, and I want to get to know you and Zoey better. You're right. It could get ugly. So we'll need to work out a plan A and a plan B."

She liked the way he was talking, letting her know that she mattered and her opinion counted. That was something John hadn't ever done. "Thank you for understanding."

He gave her a look she couldn't read and shook his head as if he needed to clear his mind. "Okay. I think some tongues are already wagging. I overheard something the other day."

"What?"

"Some talk between two women who volunteer at Zoey's school and are also involved on the parish council made reference to me and how I was taking an interest in a certain family where there was no father figure in the picture. We have a more pressing task ahead of us."

She nodded. "I told my mother and Sam and Jake about our relationship. I skipped over a great deal. They know how we met, that I had an affair with you, and that you're Zoey's father."

He sighed. "How did that go?"

"Mom has been my rock. Jake seems okay with it for the most part. With time, he'll come around all the way. Samantha's not taking it well. She'll be the biggest challenge."

"Did you tell them I wanted to be a part of your lives?"

"I had no idea what to tell them about that. Some days I'm still conflicted about us. And I didn't know for sure whether you'd leave the priesthood. I said that we're still very attracted to each other, that we have feelings. That's enough for now." She didn't want to commit to the kids about their relationship in case things didn't work out.

"Oh, baby, what am I going to do with you?"

She thought it was a mature and pragmatic approach, but she could tell by his expression that he did not like her vague choice of words. Or that she hadn't told the kids she loved him.

"We'll tell Zoey together?" he asked.

She nodded.

"And then we'll work on Samantha. I can see that I need to work on you as well."

They would face Zoey and Sam as a united front while working on their relationship. It should have warmed her to the core, but she couldn't help but worry. At the same time, he'd be making some big decisions on his own.

***

It turned out that explaining it to Zoey was less complicated than either of them could have imagined.

Later that week, they went to McDonald's for fries and pop.

Zoey said, "Father Chris?"

"Yes?"

"Do you like my mommy?"

"I do. And I like you too."

"Why?"

"Why do I like your mom? Or you?"

She shrugged. "Both."

"I've known your mother a long time, and I love her—and now I want us to be together. You don't know me, but I want to get to know you."

The little girl thought about that. "Do you like us because we're pretty?"

Tory laughed, and he grinned.

"No, it's because of nice feelings I have and want to keep having. I'm your biological father. Do you know what that means?"

She shifted in her seat and said, "Mom says that the mommy has an egg and the daddy makes it grow. Then the baby comes out of there."

"Good job, Zoey!" Tory said. She had tried to explain a kid-level version of conception to Zoey that morning.

Zoey smiled at him, looking for confirmation. How was it even possible that this enchanting little being was his?

"Smart cookie!"

"I'm not a cookie!"

"It's a nickname. Do you understand what I'm saying? I would like to be part of your life."

"Are you going to call me cookie all the time?"

"No, I'll call you sweetheart sometimes. Maybe munchkin. How about Miss Thing? Is that okay with you?"

She giggled. "I like some of those names. Can I call you Daddy? I don't have a daddy right now," Zoey said.

"I know. And I would like to be your daddy, if you don't mind."

"What about Sam and Jakie? Will you be their dad too?"

He hadn't thought about it really, but he could not refuse. "If they want that, yes."

She nodded solemnly before asking for permission to go in the playroom.

Tory said, "Be careful."

Zoey kissed her mother and Chris on the cheek before rushing off.

Choked with emotion, Chris had nothing more to say. *Leave it to a child to put it all into perspective,* he thought.

A smile spread across his face. His daughter had accepted him without any fuss. He was slightly dazed with relief now that the hard part was over, and glanced at Tory to gauge her reaction. On her face, he saw an expression of love. She had been at his side, supporting him. She took his hand under the table and squeezed it. Looking into her eyes, Chris was grateful she'd let him do most of the talking and had trusted him to find the right words.

***

Tory was proud of her daughter and of how Chris had dealt with the sensitive situation. It was interesting how her daughter seemed to accept that John was not her father and that Chris should want to parent her other two children as well. It wasn't something they had discussed, and she kind of like the idea that Sam and Jake would have a better role model.

A slight worry surfaced about what Zoey might disclose at school or when she was with friends. In an attempt to be pragmatic about the whole situation, she decided not to caution her daughter against talking about it. It would only complicate matters.

Chris continued to grin at her. She could tell that he had appreciated how it had all turned out. Inside, she was busting with joy—until she saw Joyce Summers staring at them. She dropped Chris's hand and nodded at the woman approaching with her son.

Mrs. Summers was one of the town's biggest gossips. Chris didn't seem to realize that if his reluctance to release her hand was any indication. He finally did, and Tory busied herself gathering the food wrappers on the table.

"Good afternoon, Joyce!" she said. "Is that Brent with you? My, he's grown. Hi, Brent! Father Chris, this is Mrs. Summers. Have you met? Oh, I see Zoey's getting into something. See you later," she said in a rush, leaving the table. She was too tense to stick around and pretend it had been a platonic lunch. They'd just provided enough fodder to feed the rumor mill for weeks. She fetched Zoey from the playroom, and they slipped out the side door.

By the time they got home, she'd already received a text from a neighbor about Father Chris. She had no intention of answering it. What other recourse did she have? Deny everything like the movie stars did? Claim to have no idea what they were talking about? Would that only legitimize the story? No, there was no good approach other than ignoring those types of queries.

It was all so complicated and confusing. Chris had professed to love her, but for some reason, she had a little trouble with that. It wasn't that she didn't believe him, but she had trouble convincing herself it was real. What was love anyway? A deep emotion that could fade with time, if she and John was this incredible? She could not deal with her doubts or let them taint the memory of their lunch. Seeing Zoey interact with Chris had been a special memory.

Tory decided to clean the house, which always helped her get her thoughts in order. Starting in the main bathroom and moving from room to room, she began sorting through items they rarely used and making piles: one for things to toss out and the other for things that should be packed away when they eventually moved.

Her youngest was busy in her room. As if sensing that her mother was going through something, she came to check on Tory frequently, showing her drawings she'd made and asking random questions. Tory reassured her that everything was fine, commented on the pictures, answered questions, and stopped to make Zoey a snack or give her a hug.

Eventually, her child seemed to regain some balance.

Within a few hours, Tory was her normal, pragmatic self, and her house and mind were less cluttered with things that didn't really matter.

CHAPTER 20

Chris phoned a couple of hours later. "You bailed on me."

"I thought it best."

"What are you doing now?"

"Cleaning. Packing."

"Really? That's what I'm doing. Can I put some boxes in your garage?"

"We're really doing this, aren't we?"

"We're really doing this. Is that a yes?"

"Yes! Can you stay for dinner?"

"Depends. What's on the menu?"

"Crock-Pot chicken and dessert, like we had a couple days ago."

"I'll be there in thirty minutes."

Tory hung up and turned to see Sam standing in the kitchen. "Hey, honey!"

"Hi, Mom. What's going on?"

"You mean the mess? Well, I've—we've—decided to move at some point over the next year. I'm starting to put away stuff we don't use."

"You're moving away, just like that?"

"No, not just like that. Of course we'll talk about it before then. It's going to take time, anyway. I'm just getting a head start."

"But you've only just moved."

"I know, I've barely settled in—"

"Are you moving somewhere with Father Chris?"

"I'll be moving with or without Chris. I am attracted to him, obviously, but we have a great deal to work out first." Why couldn't she admit to Sam that they *were* planning to move in together eventually?

Did part of her still worry something would go wrong, that he wouldn't leave the priesthood? "If the gossip gets out of hand, I want to be ready. I don't want you guys to end up bearing the brunt of it."

"So it's not to be with the priest, but it could be. You're just getting prepared for anything."

"Yes. Just like you, I have things to work through."

Sam had been distant ever since Tory's confession. Tory had expected her daughter to come to her with some more questions or even accusations before now. "So … what's going on with you?"

"Like you care," Sam muttered.

Tory took a deep breath and counted to ten, biting back the urge to say, *Sit down and stop acting like an adolescent.* Instead, she walked over to Sam and hugged her before guiding her to a chair. "Sit. I'll make us some iced tea." Tory was determined to get to the bottom of Sam's anger. "How's Shaun?"

"We broke up last month."

"He moved out?"

"I kicked him out after we had a big fight. He called me terrible things." Sam began to cry.

Tory closed the fridge door, sat beside Sam, and held her as the tears flowed. "What happened?"

"He was cheating on me."

"Oh."

"I found him in my bed with a friend. You remember Jenna?"

"Jenna Paterson?"

"Yeah."

"Oh, honey."

"Men are all scum!"

"No. Not all men."

"Why would you say that? Daddy cheated on you."

The shock of her daughter's comment struck her with the force of a slap. Sam knew? "No, that's—how did you—"

"Mom, I know about them. So does Jake. He saw it once."

Them? Good God, there had been more than one? And how had Jake seen it? Had John brought a woman to the house? She had never dreamed her children knew about their father's infidelity. Hell, even she hadn't been 100 percent sure. She had assumed that he'd cheated on her, true, but she'd hoped to protect her kids from that ugliness. She was suddenly furious at John, furious that Sam and Jake had had to live with knowing.

But this conversation was not about her marriage. Tory would digest this revelation later. She really didn't want to know for certain that John was having affairs. It didn't matter now anyway. However, she needed to understand what it meant to her kids.

"How did you feel about that? Knowing what you did?"

Sam sighed. "I don't know, Mom. It shouldn't affect me, but it did. I hated that he was doing that to you. I hated not telling you. I hated everything about it. I couldn't understand why you did nothing. I presumed that you knew and tried to hide it from us. It felt like he was betraying all of us."

"And how about now? Do you still feel the same?"

"I was younger then, and everything got to me. I'm a little surprised you didn't know about his wandering eye. It wasn't just the fact that he cheated on you. After a while, it became more about how he didn't seem to see us either. I stopped thinking of him as someone to respect."

Tory understood that she was partly to blame and likely making things worse with her own actions. "Now that you know about Chris and me, do you feel the same way about us?"

"I don't know how to feel about it. That's the problem. I see how happy you are, so I have to be okay with it, don't I?"

"So because of your dad and Shaun's behavior, you've come to the conclusion that all men are like that? You're too young to be so jaded, honey. Is anything else going on?"

"My life sucks! I hate my job. I'm getting fat. Seeing Shaun with Jenna just about made me go nuts. I'm eating constantly. Nothing is working out like I planned. I hate men! And now you're leaving me."

My little drama queen, Tory thought tenderly.

"I'm not leaving you, silly. I will always be here for you. You know that."

Sam nodded.

"So what else is bothering you?"

Sam rubbed the moisture under her nose with her hand and then her sleeve. Tory grabbed the paper napkins from the middle of the table and handed her one. It was not the time to chastise her daughter about the spread of bacteria or hand hygiene. It was time to delve deeper into what was bothering Sam.

"You know you can tell me anything, don't you?"

Samantha nodded, yet remained silent.

Drawing out information from her adult child when she was in a state was always difficult. "I'm missing something. Can you give me a hint?"

That her daughter still didn't answer was, in itself, telling.

"I want to help you if I can," Tory continued. "But you have to give me something."

"I'm not sure, Mom. It's all a mess."

"This can't all be about Shaun. He was just a guy, right? Someone you wanted to have fun with … and then it just became convenient to move in together."

Her daughter smiled. They were making progress.

"When I was younger than you," Tory said, "your grandmother sat me down and gave me a heart-to-heart. She told me about her own experiences with men."

"Nana did?"

"Imagine it, in her old house, sitting at the kitchen table—the wooden one that she still has. You know the one I mean?"

"Yes."

"Just like we're doing right now, she tried to counsel me, I guess. She was adamant that I not repeat her mistakes. Except she had real difficulty discussing sex and sexual preferences, that kind of thing."

"Oh, Mom."

"I know."

"What were her mistakes?"

"She felt that she had settled for your grandfather too young and too fast. It's not that they had a bad marriage, but I think she believed that she'd missed out on getting to know herself better before settling down. I gather this kind of thing runs in our family."

"Why do you say that?"

"Well, she told me it was the same for her own mother."

Alice came around the corner then, having let herself into the house.

Tory opened her mouth to speak, but her mother held up a hand as she sat down at the kitchen table. "It's okay. I heard. I was going to walk back out, but then I figured you two could use my help. It's all true, except that they weren't mistakes. They were regrets."

"I didn't—"

"I'm okay, Nana."

"Bullshit!" Alice said.

They all laughed.

"Okay, Mom. We both have some problems to share with you. Sam says hers are a mess. Mine are pretty messy, too. We were talking about infidelity and men. Then we moved on to regrets. I was telling Sam about you."

Alice nodded, and Sam looked away.

"I think women always have similar problems, no matter what generation or class," Tory continued. "We have issues with trust and understanding what makes us happy, understanding men. Do you agree, Mom?"

"Yes, I do. Take what they call the seven-year itch, for example. They make up expressions like that to legitimize what so many couples go through. I'll bet you learned in women's studies that because we live longer, having one mate for life is no longer a reasonable expectation."

"Yes, that's true," Sam said, smiling.

"In my mother's time," Alice said, "fornicating with your neighbor and coveting another man's wife were mortal sins, but that didn't stop anyone from doing it. In those days, a woman tolerated her husband having the odd indiscretion. But not my mother. Every time he messed around, she found someone too. She liked male companionship and attracted lots of interest, well into her eighties. My parents probably needed a change. Eating mashed potatoes every day of the week gets old."

Sam kept grinning.

Tory got up to make the iced tea. "Continue, Mom."

"I didn't have to be courageous or anything to get what I wanted when I was a young woman—younger than you, Samantha. It was all around us. It was a time of anything goes. Remember, I'm from the Woodstock era. Hippies, drugs, sexual awareness, the advent of the pill, rock and roll. And God, were we opinionated about everything. We gave ourselves permission to be irresponsible, bad, creative. My mother had no idea how to manage me, but she tried. She wanted to be able to help me and not put a damper on my personality. So she wanted to understand, I think.

"She used to say, 'Living life should be about having no regrets.' I suppose she's right. I have a few regrets. The first one is that I married too young. These days, you won't get pressured like I was to settle down with one man, not even if you get pregnant. Society is more indulgent nowadays. And I decided to take a page out of my mother's book and have the occasional affair."

Tory felt herself gasp, making Sam laugh.

"It's more like I needed to experience everything," Alice went on. "I hadn't quite finished with that when I met Al, your papa. He was older than me, and he seemed so worldly and sophisticated. I was so naïve to think that my tastes would never change. That I could be happy with one man my whole life. Don't get me wrong—I loved that man—but sometimes I wanted something else. I settled because I didn't know how to deal with how much I enjoyed change and experimentation. So I'm addressing that now."

"You are?" Sam asked. "Do tell."

"Mom? Please!"

"Okay, okay! It's nothing too out there. I'm just dating men again, mostly for sex. We've been watching porn for ideas. I don't mind being tied up, but I draw the line at spanking."

"Oh my God!" Tory placed a hand over her mouth to stop any other comments from escaping. Despite the conversation, it was difficult to imagine her mother having sex, let alone being so honest about it.

Samantha was doubled over in hysterical laughter. Between that and the twinkle in her mother's eyes, it became impossible not to join in.

"Mom, you're shameless. But I love it!" Tory confessed.

Alice looked at both of them. "Okay, now which one of you wants to spill first?"

"Let's keep going in order of age," Sam said. Tory stuck her tongue out at Sam, which made them all laugh again.

It took Tory a second to find the right words. "It's … it's not been the same for me. You gain some wisdom along the way. Mom, remember how wild I was as a teenager?"

Alice nodded. "You were a handful, but I knew you were just trying to find your way. One day, you'd come home with a boy your age. The next day, a man ten or more years your senior would be waiting for you in his car. Your dad got a little upset, but I'd smooth it over. You were eighteen, an adult really, so what could we have done? Secretly, I was hoping you were having fun and pushing your boundaries. It's what I would have done."

"I really did change over the years though. By twenty, I toned it down a little. I met John and got my degree in nursing. I was happy most of the time, but I married too young. But you couldn't tell me anything, could you?" Tory grinned at her mom before turning to Sam.

"After you kids came along, my life revolved around you and my work. To be honest, John took third place, and I don't think he liked it. Just around the time I hit forty, or maybe it was a couple of years before that, it was like a switch went off. I never knew how much I needed to be touched. Needed sex. That was the biggest piece of it. But John wasn't attracted to me anymore, it seemed."

Sam gave Tory a significant look. Obviously, she knew about John's affairs and that his infidelity factored into the equation too, but Tory's answering look communicated that they wouldn't discuss it now. She wasn't sure if Alice had any idea about it.

"For years, I survived the drought. I worried too much about what other people would think to do anything about it, I guess. Then he got diagnosed with cancer. Not much point in making it worse, so I stuck it out. I don't regret it, but I do regret not being honest with him and maybe discussing an open marriage or even divorce long before he got so sick. Obviously, we weren't meeting each other's needs.

"Then, as you know, I met Chris. I wasn't looking for anything, but then again, I wasn't not looking, if you know what I mean. So much came from that affair, not just Zoey. I got myself back. I know now that I like a different type of sex ... that's not for everyone."

She glanced at Sam to see if any of this was resonating with her. Sam's thoughtful expression told her it was.

"My problem now is what to do. Too much is happening all of a sudden. Most of it's good, but I don't want to screw it up by overthinking things or not trusting that what we have will last. Obviously things turned out a bit more complicated than they seemed at first. I never knew he was a priest, for example." Tory ran out of words then. What more was there to say?

Alice touched her arm. "Honey, no one can know whether something good will last, but if you find it, you have to grab onto it—even if it's for a short while. Otherwise, you may miss the opportunity of a lifetime. And time is too precious to waste. Go with what your gut tells you. You always have me to help, should the worst happen."

Tory covered her mother's hand with her own. "I know, Mom. Thank you for always being there."

There was a quiet moment. Tory refilled Alice's tea and sipped her own. "So ... my turn?" Sam said. She took a breath. "I've been hitting the sex club scene pretty hard since Shaun left. To help me get over some things."

Wow, Tory thought. *There are sex clubs in this part of the world?* She fought the little hint of concern that bubbled up. Sam was an adult and could handle herself and her limits. Besides, she'd had her own experience with a sex club and couldn't judge.

"Shaun said that I'm too needy and don't know what the hell I want. I'm trying to find out if he's right, so the club scene is working out for me. I don't know if you guys know much about it."

Tory raised her hand like a student in a classroom. "Chris and I went to one. It was like a club and theater combined. And we sort of ... participated."

Alice grinned, and Sam looked shocked.

"What? It's true. Don't look at me like that!"

"Um ... what did you think?" Sam asked.

"I was blown away actually. It was almost too much, but I lived. And it was a memory neither of us will ever forget."

"It's so hard to think of you and a priest going at it," Sam giggled.

"Tell me about it. I still have trouble getting my head around it sometimes. Go on."

"That's pretty much it. I'm being introduced to new experiences and people. There's this whole dominance-submission thing that I can take or leave. I don't want to be labeled one thing or the other. I guess I'll find my way."

"You certainly will," Alice stated. "Hold out for someone who you're really compatible with. It takes time. I know that young people are always in such a rush. Most times, like with your mom, it happens when you aren't looking."

"I just get depressed sometimes. It's hard being single."

Tory tried to offer some comfort to her daughter. "You'll find somebody else, honey. You can't tell me you were hoping to marry Shaun, right? Let him go and move on."

"I guess you're right."

"And wherever it is we end up moving, we won't be far away. You can still come stay on the weekends. I'd love that. I hardly get to see you anymore. I know! Why don't we schedule a regular night together? A girls' night out. Nana can join us if she wants."

"I'm in!" Alice said.

"Okay," Sam replied with less enthusiasm.

Chris and Jake joined them for dinner that evening. Chris sat at the end of the dining table, which had been moved from the old house. He had no idea that it had been John's spot, but if anyone was upset by it, they didn't say anything. Tory decided she'd get rid of the table when they moved. *This dining set is outdated anyway.*

The meal progressed at a steady pace. Zoey made everyone laugh with stories about her friends at school. Tory let the talk flow around her as she pondered the day's events. She was already coming to terms with her newfound knowledge about John; after all, she'd long suspected it anyway. She tried not to be too bothered by the fact that her children had known about his infidelities and never confided in her. They had likely been trying to protect her in their own ways.

Samantha said very little during dinner. Tory hoped their conversation had helped. Sam did seem to look at Chris with new interest (and luckily he was oblivious as to why). Chris managed to get a conversation going with Jake and made a few attempts to include Sam.

Jake was quiet when he wasn't talking to Chris. Tory asked him to help wash the dishes when everyone was finished so she could have a private moment with him. He tended to act like nothing was troubling him, even when it was, and she wanted to draw it out of him. They normally communicated well.

She asked about his feelings surrounding John's affairs but not much was said. He assured her that he was fine, not sharing anything else. Perhaps she would approach him again when there were fewer people around.

Once the kitchen was tidy, Tory invited Sam to have some mother-daughter time—just the two of them on the deck. They sat in lawn chairs with their backs to the house, gazing over the backyard garden. They didn't talk much, but the atmosphere was comfortable.

CHAPTER 21

When Zoey was tucked in bed and Samantha and Alice had gone home, Tory, Chris, and Jake watched television in the family room.

Chris was not certain of the protocol, so he let Jake choose the programs.

As the hour grew late, Tory yawned.

"I should be going," Chris said.

She nodded, which made him uncomfortable. Normally, she wanted him to stick around. He wondered about the unexpected shift. Perhaps she was still uncertain about how Jake felt about everything.

Tory walked him to the door. He pulled her outside, enveloped her in his arms, and kissed her.

"I've wanted to do that all evening. Actually, since I first got here and saw you with that apron on."

She grinned for the first time in hours. "Are we doing the right thing?" she asked. "I mean, is it too soon?"

"Tell me what's going on. Is it Sam?"

"Partly."

Tory told him about the revelations she'd received about Sam's ex-boyfriend and her late husband's indiscretions. Chris could tell that Tory was bothered more by the fact that her kids had known about the latter than by the actual news.

"And Jake's having a problem too, I think, but he won't discuss it with me. He told me earlier that it was no big deal and I wouldn't understand. My imagination is running wild now."

"Want me to talk to him?"

"I don't know."

"If you and I are going to be together, I should try to clear the air with Jake anyway, don't you think? He'll either confide in me or tell me to take a hike."

She sighed. "For the first time, I don't know how to deal with him. Jake's never given me as much grief as Sam has. Compared to her, he's been a dream to raise, so responsible and levelheaded, but a few years ago, things were hard for him. That's when I switched jobs so I could be there for the kids more. He felt like he didn't fit in with his classmates, and maybe he didn't. I don't know. He's struggling with something now."

"You can share the burden, you know. You don't always have to carry the load by yourself."

"I know," she said.

She touched his face, and he closed his eyes, feeling peaceful for the first time in hours. If something was bothering her, it bothered him as well.

"I needed to know you as a mother, and I am now. You need to see me as a man, not just your escape from reality, your fantasy guy."

"Fantasy guy, huh?"

"You know what I mean. How do you feel about finding out that John was messing around?"

"I don't know. I should be angry, I guess, but I can't seem to get too worked up about it. I'd suspected it for years; I just didn't do anything to confirm it or confront him. And it explains why he became so distant way before the cancer. It makes you wonder if you ever really know someone, even the man you're married to for twenty years. I'm not sure why Sam and Jake didn't say anything before if they knew about it."

Is this her way of asking me to open up more? He didn't usually talk about his past. It was where bad memories should reside. If she was looking to know something about him that might explain what had driven him to become a priest, it might help to know about Jean. He had never told anyone what had happened with his sister, but maybe it was time.

"They must have had their reasons," he said, changing the subject. "Maybe that's what's upsetting Jake."

"I want to ask them about it, but I don't see how it's important now. And who am I to bring that up when we've—you and I ... you know."

"Speaking of that, I need you," he said, rubbing his groin into her. He felt like a randy kid when they were alone. It was pathetic. It was awesome!

"This is ridiculous. I'm a grown woman, and we're going to be living together soon. Get your sweet ass inside and meet me in my bedroom. I'll lock up."

"Let me," he offered.

He walked back in past Jake, who was still watching TV. If Jake thought anything about it, he kept it to himself.

He went up to Tory's room. He wanted to be near her almost as much as he wanted to be inside her. How had they managed being apart for a year at a time when now it seemed like a few hours apart were unbearable? Feeling antsy, he went back out to see what was keeping her.

Tory was coming out of Zoey's room.

"Everything all right?" he asked.

"Yes. Just my nightly check. Have you used the bathroom?"

"No, not yet."

She took his hand and led him down the hall.

***

It was so good to have his hands on her. He rubbed her back with slick, sudsy palms and reached for her front. No part of her skin was left untouched. When he'd rinsed all the soap away, he lathered her up again. His probing fingers gave her the sweetest torture, driving her to the brink. As she gave herself to the moment, he did not disappoint. He gave her body his complete attention, reading her signals, ensuring her needs were met.

This was going to take some getting used to, having a man who liked to go down on her and didn't rush the process. His cunnilingus was not cursory, no mere working up to the main event. When she was not able to control her thunderous moans, he placed a washcloth between her teeth and continued tonguing her into oblivion.

She collapsed to the floor of the tub, and he joined her. She licked along his happy trail to his pubic hair until his jutting cock touched her face. He was excited with her this close, and his cock wagged like a puppy's tail. She had to restrain it with her hand to get it to cooperate. She rubbed the shaft and sucked on the tip, moving constantly so he could feel her teeth and tongue.

His hips jutted up, looking for more, so she gave him more. Tory repositioned herself to get comfortable, and then she swallowed him whole, feeling his body quiver in delight. Water continued to pelt down on them as he held her head just so. His legs were soon bent and resting over her shoulders so she could touch other parts of him as well. Her hands went to his buttocks and then focused on the natural division, running her fingers along the seam, each time, passing along his tight anus. She breached it with one finger and felt his cock expand inside her mouth. She sucked him harder.

She was so turned on by his unabashed response to her ministrations that her act of pleasuring him became equally pleasurable for her.

He grunted his release in spurts, ending the lovely session all too soon—or so she thought.

***

Chris turned off the water, led her out of the tub, and positioned her with her palms planted on the tile floor, her knees cushioned by a towel. He wanted to hear her moan his name just once before they went to bed. She had given him an amazing orgasm, and he knew that she could come again. Her face still had a glazed look of arousal. Hoping that no one would hear, he brought her to climax with his hands, giving her what she needed.

He wrapped her in a dry towel and carried her limp form to her bedroom across the hall. He left her briefly to retrieve his shorts from the bathroom and to brush his teeth. When he returned, she was asleep. He thought about waking her but decided to let her nap.

He grabbed a book off the bedside table, propped himself up against the headboard, and began to read.

Not long after, she roused from slumber. "What are you doing?" she asked.

"I'm waiting for you to regain consciousness," he said, turning a page.

"I didn't know you liked romance novels."

"I didn't either, until I started one. Here, you sit between my legs, and I'll comb your hair. You can read to me."

"Are you sure?"

"Positive. Go on, start at the top of the page, the part where he's about to deflower her. I wish I'd known such good porn existed in book form. It's much safer than downloading it from the net."

She laughed and started to read aloud.

The room was quiet except for the crackling fire.

They stood immobilized by their mutual attraction as the earl raked his eyes over her body and she got her first full-on view of a man in all his nude glory. His member stood out proudly. She should have felt some trepidation. Any normal virgin would. But she did not worry about whether they would fit together. She had seen horses mate, so she felt assured that no matter how large he was, it would somehow work.

Carissa was a spinster at four and twenty, firmly on the shelf, but she was now about to experience what her married sisters did ... all in exchange for some intelligence.

She shivered with awareness, her anticipation making her nipples harden. Many thoughts vied for her attention, like the urge to have him suckle her like an infant would or touch her with his roughened fingers the way he had yesterday in the barn. Before then, she had never known her own proclivity for such shameful, unsanctioned behavior. He should not see that. She desired him too much. It wasn't healthy, this wanting to be with him, however he chose.

Their deal was to have this night. She had promised, and he would hold her accountable. It was degrading, the lengths that she would go to for a taste of what normal couples enjoyed.

Deep breaths, Car, she told herself. He's just a man. A dishonest, autocratic boor most of the time. But for some reason, none of that mattered now. She could ignore it all in favor of this wickedness.

Giving him control seemed like a small price to pay for what was to come.

She was trying to control her body's response to his simple gaze, but it overrode her attempts. She moved to cross her arms to shield her wantonness from him. He held enough power over her. She wanted to hide this physical evidence of how he affected her, even though they had yet to touch.

"Don't!" he said. He prowled toward her like a wild animal. His eyes were dark, and the look on his face was that of beast, intent. His cravat was in his hand. "I'm going to tie your hands."

Why? Why would he want to do that, unless it was to restrain her as he tortured her? Perhaps he already knew that she had lied. That there was nothing she could contribute. No information to be shared. It had all been part of the ruse to get him to agree to tonight. How had he found out?

"No," she uttered.

"Yes," he growled, coming closer. In a second, all would be lost. Her virginity, of which he was completely ignorant, her innocence, even perhaps her life.

She struggled to keep still and not flee. Dear God! What had she agreed to? Her mind scrambled, looking for escape, but the rational part of her knew it was too late.

"Please!"

"Please what?" He gave her a wicked grin that did nothing to assuage her guilt and nerves. If anything, she felt her pulse begin to race. "Please hurry up and take what is mine to take? Please fuck me?"

"Don't hurt me."

He laughed, and she tensed as he grabbed her wrists, held them together, and bound them with the thin fabric until he was satisfied. His eyes searched hers, and she was lost in their deep blackness. Everything she had learned about this man had been accurate. His aristocratic lording over mere women. His brutal approach to any circumstance, no matter what proprieties were breached.

He pushed her back toward the bed. She bumped into a solid part of the frame. His glorious chest was against hers now. She could feel the coarse hair rub against her bosom, and it was divine. He was so warm; heat radiated from his torso. His rigid member pushed against her as well, and she knew not what to make of her sudden inability to stay still.

"Like that, do you? Patience, sweetness. I'll give you what you need."

He pulled her arms above her head and began binding her wrists to the uppermost part of the bedpost. She pulled against the restraint, but that got her nowhere.

She should have been terrified, but for some reason, that was not the case. She realized that no matter what else, she could trust him to make this night pleasurable for the both of them. Deep down, she felt it. He wanted this just as much as she did.

***

Ensconced between Chris's legs, Tory leaned back against his chest as he ran the brush through her tresses. He enjoyed the sound of her voice.

"More?"

"No, that's fine. Although I'd like to tie you up right now. But we'll save that for tomorrow after you've read another chapter. I thought we might talk for a few minutes, if that's okay. I know you have to work in the morning, so we won't have time then."

"What's up?"

She looked content and cheerful, and he didn't want to ruin that, but he had to. "I overheard some ladies talking today. The rumors about us have started. I'm getting looks. You know the kind. Someone must have noticed my car parked in front of your house one night or have seen us together when we were out. They were comparing sightings like we were movie stars or Martians or … I don't know."

"Mrs. Summers?"

"Maybe. But it could have been anyone. I didn't see who it was."

"I get the picture."

"So we need to plan."

Tory moved closer and hugged him. "What are you thinking?"

"You put up the house for sale now and move before I give my notice."

"That's all you've got?"

He put down the brush and wrapped his arms around her. "So far."

"What are you worried about?" she asked.

"To tell the truth, a few things. That you and the kids will be hurt by the gossip, that you'll come to your senses and leave me, that the bishop will get wind of this, that the sky will fall … I know I'm not making sense." He felt her hand on his chin and instantly felt better. "I'm an idiot," he confessed.

"You're not an idiot. Maybe a little silly. I'm touched by your concern for us. Actually, I'm impressed by so much, including your stamina for such an old guy."

He tackled her and tickled her in several places. After they'd finished playing, they lay down side by side.

"Does this mean we'll have to part ways for a while?" she asked.

"A few months, I think. I really don't know."

"What if it's longer?"

"Then we'll meet at a motel or something. We'll figure it out."

She grinned and grew silent for a moment. Her next words made him tense. "Are you really okay with leaving the priesthood? We haven't talked about it much."

"To tell you the truth, I feel like a fraud most of the time when I'm performing services. For years, I've lobbied for priests to be allowed to marry. I've considered converting to another denomination. I even went to see an Anglican priest last week. Alice gave me the contact. I think I need a bigger change. This has been coming for a long time."

"Why is that?"

He could tell she needed him to put her mind at ease. He didn't want her to feel guilty about him deciding to leave the priesthood, so he offered the truth. "Everyone tells me their sins. Or what they think are sins. But rarely are the confessions so terrible. I try to counsel people, but they don't want to listen. I just listen to them and perform the same rituals over and over. Honestly, I'm bored to death and tired of not making a difference."

"Still, there've got to be some parts you like. Won't you miss it?"

He shrugged. "Who knows? I can always volunteer to counsel troubled youth or something like that. I do like presenting to small groups. The marriage counseling type of thing."

"Volunteer, huh?"

"Don't worry. I won't be just another mouth to feed. I'm dependent on you for many things—your generous spirit, your love, the great sex, and a few other essential qualities—but hopefully, I'll be more of a help than a hindrance. I have money. Some I inherited. Some I saved. We don't need to worry about that. By the way, we need to start looking at houses." He mustered up all his mental strength. "I have a quick story to tell you. I've wanted to share it with you for a while, and now seems as good a time as any."

"Okay."

"I told you that my sister died."

"Jean? Yes."

"What I didn't say was how she died. Or that I'm to blame."

"I'm sure that's not true."

"Let me finish. You need to know that Jean looked up to me and followed my example. Back then, I ran a little wild. My parents didn't care who we hung around with. Their only concern was that we *appeared* to be good, went to Sunday Mass, and behaved at church. I ended up being an altar boy from grade three to high school. Only boys performed those duties back then.

"Anyway, when I wasn't at church, I smoked cigarettes, took drugs, got this tattoo you're so fond of, drank a lot, hung around with a rough crowd, and had a lot of sex. One night, Jean came looking for me at this bar. She had put on makeup and heels to look older. She was only fourteen. My crowd knew who she was, but they—even I—didn't recognize her at first.

"I saw her arrive but lost track of her after that. I was high out of my mind on something. A couple of guys took her behind the bar and raped her. They were older than her. They claimed it was consensual. I asked her, but she wouldn't discuss it, so I convinced myself it was. I realize now that I didn't make the time or the right words or the correct approach. And I didn't pick up on the clues. At the time, I was messed up and figured she asked for it, dressed the way she was. She didn't look too broken up about it. I laughed at her, I think, at some point. Not my proudest moment. It wasn't until months later that a different story came out. It's one of the reasons I became a priest. To get better at helping people like Jean."

She hugged him, probably sensing that the worst was to some.

"She collapsed one day, and at the hospital, she found out she was pregnant. The baby wasn't in the right place. It was in her fallopian tube."

"Ectopic?"

"Yes, that's it. Jean had surgery to remove it. It became this shameful event that my parents didn't handle well. They hadn't known she was sexually active. Just like today, it was acceptable for boys to be boys, but girls were held to a greater standard.

"My sister was always very shy. She became even more closed off from the world. She didn't see friends or go to school. She stopped living, eating, taking care of herself. And then she literally starved herself to death, right before my eyes."

"Oh, Chris."

"It took a long time to accomplish her goal. She wouldn't talk to me about any of it. I couldn't stand looking at her after a while. I used drugs to distract myself, anything I could lose myself in. But in the end, nothing helped. Not my attempts to bury my feelings, not the violence I vented my anger with, nothing.

"For months, I watched her shrink until she was nothing more than a skeleton. She died before her fifteenth birthday. I blamed myself for not having protected her from my friends, for not being the brother I should have been, for not getting her to eat, for not forcing my parents to get her professional help.

"The guilt and anger drove me nuts. The church would not bury her because the death certificate identified her as a suicide. I never forgave my parents for not making a bigger deal about it. And I vowed to make certain that it would never happen to anyone else."

"So you decided to become a priest when she died?"

"Not quite then. It took me a while to get over their refusal to bury Jean. But later on, I did join the priesthood. I wanted to rise within the ranks, become a bishop, and lobby for change. I naïvely thought I could have a voice and truly make a difference.

"My parents took credit for my complete personality overhaul. I hadn't spoken to them or even acknowledged them for so long that when they passed, it didn't really phase me."

"Do you have other siblings?"

"Yes, four other brothers. Only two are still alive. We're not close, and I have no idea what they're up to. I think one lives in Australia, and the other went to Asia. No one has heard from either of them in a long time."

"How did your brothers die?"

"My oldest brother joined the army. He was killed while on leave, biking in the mountains, about fifteen years ago. What a waste. My youngest brother, Francis, was shot in a fight. I can't remember when exactly, but it was a few years after Jean died. I think he took it worse than I did. Anyway, he hooked up with a rough crowd, left school, and was always in trouble, or so I've been told."

"That must have been hard on your parents."

"I don't know. I had left home by then, and I haven't been back."

"Are you going to spend the rest of your life believing you could have prevented her death?"

"Good question. Some days, I don't even think of her at all. In some way, I must have forgiven myself."

She rubbed his head. "I think you've done your penance, don't you? It's time to let it go. I'm not saying you need to forgive your parents, but I do believe life is meant to be lived, and you weren't really living until we met. Give yourself absolution. Jean would likely want that, if she loved you."

He nodded, too emotional to speak.

Placing a kiss on his dry lips, she said, "Thank you for sharing this. It explains so much. Now let's go to sleep. I don't care who sees your car in my driveway."

CHAPTER 22

House hunting was always a painful process. Tory tried to approach it practically. Her top priorities were finding a place close to her work with a good school district for Zoey. She wasn't bothered about a house's charm, curb appeal, or whether it looked expensive enough. She cared about practicalities only—how easily the property could be cleaned and maintained and overall affordability when utilities and taxes were included in the cost of the mortgage.

Chris, on the other hand, had never purchased a place of his own. The ideal he had in mind didn't exist in that area. He wanted to live in a large house in a secluded area on the water. Although they were not on the same page, he managed to convince her to take a trip north to tour smaller communities. They saw many properties, all of them too pricey, although that didn't seem to bother him. She was also concerned about where Jake would live once they relocated.

When they found a beautiful four-season cottage that slept eight, with three bathrooms and an amazing kitchen, she let him persuade her to let him buy it. That was the moment she realized he had meant it when he said he had money. When he paid cash for the property— no mortgage needed—his financial situation truly became clear to her.

The topic of his affluence had never come up in their conversations, and she had no idea how to broach it.

Zoey had no problem talking about it. "Daddy, are you rich?" she asked as they drove home from the notary's office.

He laughed. "No, sweetheart. But my grandparents were, I guess, and because I was their favorite grandchild, they left me some money when they died. I've given most of it away over the years. I never thought I'd have someone to hand it down to."

Tory knew that there must be a story there. "What about your parents?"

"I wasn't the only one devastated by my sister's death. Both sides of my parents' families were too. Both sets of grandparents cut my parents out of their wills. Add to that the fact that I was the only relative who took an interest in them. That was why I became their sole beneficiary." He grinned. "You know, Alice was worried I'd be a financial leech! She confronted me about it and drilled me about my retirement fund."

"You're kidding," Tory said, mortified.

Chris turned his head to look at her. "It's okay. She cares about you, just like a mother should, even though her child's a grown woman. And when you sell your place, the money is yours, okay?"

"But what about—"

"You keep it, or it can go to the kids."

For years, Tory had managed the household finances. It felt a little odd for Chris to now have a say in that. "We haven't talked about who's going to pay for what."

"I know you, lady. You've been in charge of things for so long that you don't know how to let someone else handle things. I have no idea how to manage money or pay bills. Other people have taken care of that side of things for me my whole adult life. So rest assured, you'll stay in charge of that area. But as far as whose money is spent, we can sit down and go over it."

He was right that she didn't like to relinquish control. She'd just obtained the deed to their new home half an hour ago, and already she'd started worrying about a million different things. What should she do about her job? About Jake? Would he want to live with them? Should she look for different work closer their new home?

Chris must have picked up on how preoccupied she was. "Tell me what's on your mind."

"I've got lots to sort out yet."

He took her hand. "I know." And she felt that he just might. "I thought I'd be a stay-at-home dad and take care of Zoey." Raising his voice to reach the back seat, he said, "Hey, Zoey, would you like Daddy to be at home to look after you on days when you don't have school or when you're home sick? I could just be around whenever you need me."

His daughter giggled. "You're funny, Daddy. Only mommies do that."

"Well, we're going to be different. I'm going to volunteer at your school, accompany your class on field trips, and maybe supervise after-school activities. I'll learn to cook and do some other things I've always wanted to do."

"Like what?" Tory asked.

"Oh, I don't know yet. I was thinking about painting or writing."

"And you don't think you'll be bored?"

"I'm looking at this like a retirement run. We'll see how it goes."

She examined his handsome face. He seemed to be adjusting to the whole situation too well. She felt silly, but part of her thought, *If he could give up the priesthood so easily, might he one day walk out on me just as easily?*

Within a few weeks, they had established a routine. Things began to fall into place. Between spending some nights at her old house and working some days from her new home, Tory was managing to stay on top of her job, but she knew she'd have to quit soon and find a job closer to her new place. She had finally come to terms with that. Or at least she thought she had.

Jake had decided to get his own place and was actively searching for an apartment. That resolved one issue.

Tory and Sam and had become closer ever since their talk in the kitchen with Alice; some of the hurt and confusion had been stripped away by the honest dialogue about their pasts and current situations. No one had all of the answers, but verbalizing their concerns helped make them feel less intimidating. Everyone went through similar struggles to get what they needed out of life.

Hoping to continue the discussion and to ensure that Sam knew Tory was supporting her in whatever choices she made, she'd deliberately spent as much time with Sam as possible. They developed a Thursday-night ritual of meeting for dinner and just talking and sharing, no distractions, their phones switched off. After a few months, they had progressed to the point of being friends. Tory was thrilled. No subject was taboo. They discussed everything.

Despite their new closeness, Tory still worried about Sam. She often became too quiet and subdued. *What is going on in her life?* Tory wondered if Sam was having trouble with the self-discovery she'd admitted to embarking upon.

After dinner one night, Tory cleared the others out of the kitchen so she and Sam could have a heart-to-heart. At first, Sam wouldn't open up, which was frustrating. Tory was just about to give up on the conversation when Chris came in to drop off a couple of cups he had collected in the living room. She noticed Sam's mood shift when Chris kissed her cheek before leaving the kitchen. The small gesture had a remarkable effect on Sam.

"Mom, why does he always do that?"

Tory remembered that John had never touched her or expressed his love like that in front of their children.

"I guess he's comfortable around you now and wants to show me—and possibly you—that he cares about me."

"But, like, does he do it all the time? Is that normal?"

"Yes, he does. I think it is with some people. I like it. It makes me want to be affectionate with him too. It wasn't like this with your dad."

"Father Chris and you look happy together."

"We are. I've never felt this way about a man."

"Not even Daddy?"

Tory wanted to be honest, no matter what the cost. "Not even him."

"Is Father Chris always … gentle?"

Another direct question and one that called for frankness. "No. But that's because sometimes I like it rough. It depends on the mood. Why are you asking?"

"Is it normal for a guy to want to control a girl when they're having sex? You know what I mean?" Samantha did not blush, but she was struggling to choose the right words.

"I'm glad we're discussing this. It's not something I ever addressed with my mom. You can talk to me about anything. You already know that, right?"

Sam nodded.

"Sex between consenting adults can take various forms. And it's imperative to discuss what's going to happen with your partner. He can have control if you allow it; otherwise, he does not have that privilege."

Her daughter nodded again.

"Relationships need to develop, and trust has to be fostered. You need to feel comfortable when you're experimenting with boundaries. And you need to have trust in your partner's ability to respect that. Whatever you engage in has to be something you both want. Are you with me so far?"

"Yes. But is pain supposed to be part of it?"

Tory's mind flashed a warning reaction, but she focused on articulating her response. "It depends. It can be, if you're ready for it. I mean, if it's a planned part of the play session, then you should be worked up enough that it's not unbearable. It should enhance the experience. Some people need some pain to climax. They need to feel the edge that comes with being uncomfortable. There's nothing wrong with that. It can be quite arousing. But you've visited sex clubs, so I'm probably not telling you anything that you don't already know. Can you be more specific?"

"I ... Shaun ... used a whip on me. He hurt me. God, I'm so ashamed, telling my mother this. I wanted him back, so I let him do stuff to me."

Tory felt her chest tighten with fury, but that was not what her child needed. "Had you done other, similar types of play before? I mean, had you let him use other kinds of equipment on you in that way?"

"Yes. It started with his hand, which I really liked, and then a flogger."

Tory needed to be strong. Her daughter required compassion and empathy—not someone threatening to castrate her partner.

"He escalated it without your consent?"

"Yes."

"Was he too rough?"

"I guess. We were at a party, and he wanted to show off. He gets that way sometimes. Anyway, I was tied to a wall, which I normally like, but he'd been drinking, and I knew it would turn out bad. I told him to untie me, but he wouldn't."

Tory clenched her fists under the table. She outwardly tried to stay calm, but the idea of running out of the house to teach Shaun a lesson was uppermost in her mind. Her daughter was her priority. Sam needed to unburden herself of the details. "Go on, honey."

"He tore off my top, and some other guys in the room cheered. I started crying, and he laughed at me. But after two slashes with the whip, this guy came over and punched him. All I remember after that is being untied and brought home by the guy who got me out of there. We're sort of dating now, but he's afraid to get rough with me."

"I think I like this guy. Who is he?"

"Timothy Paterson. Tim."

"Why haven't you brought him around?"

"It may not work out."

"Why not?"

"He isn't into vanilla sex."

"And the episode at the party is still fresh in both your minds, and he doesn't think that you can handle him."

"Yeah, how'd you know?"

"Just a guess. You want some advice?"

"Yes. I really like him." ·

"You're going to have to convince him that you can handle it. And that's not going to happen overnight. You've had a bad experience with someone who didn't care about you—but you cared about him. Talking with Tim is the best way to get through this. Be as honest as you can with him. Let him know what you like and don't like. Take it slow.

"If the relationship's going to work long-term, he'll have to see that it's worth taking the time to help you relearn trust. That'll benefit him as much as it does you. Make him see that. It's not easy to find someone who's compatible with you, no matter what the sexual preference."

"He thinks I'm too young and that I don't know what I want."

"Maybe that's true, but that's okay too. Is he much older than you?"

"Six years. He's Jenna's older brother."

"That must be awkward."

"Tell me about it."

"You really like this Tim?"

Her daughter's face lit up, which was answer enough.

"I could have a talk with him, if you like," Tory offered. "Set him straight about a few things. Discussing sex is tough for many people, but I don't mind it. It might be easier for him to talk about it with me because he doesn't know me."

"Mom! You think he'll want to talk to my mother about sex with me? And you're dating a priest. He's not going to go for it."

"Well, first of all, Chris is leaving the priesthood—and you have no idea what we do when we're alone. You probably wouldn't believe me if I told you."

"Mom, I'd be lying if I said I wasn't curious, but it's still kind of icky to think about you two that way. I figure you must be hot together if he's giving everything up for you."

Sex was only a small piece of the reason Chris wanted to be with her, but Sam didn't need to hear all about that.

"It's true."

She had to grin at the expression on her daughter's face.

Samantha laughed, and Tory wondered if she had offered the right advice. Should she have taken a different approach? Should she have recommended some kind of therapy? At least Tory was feeling a little less enraged toward Shaun.

Before Sam went home, they hugged for a long time.

"Will you remember to come to me for anything? Honestly, I'm worried about what that bastard did to you. It might affect how you view sex, the type of sex that you might need."

"Mom, please don't worry. I can handle it. I'm strong, you know."

"I know, sweetheart, but even strong women need to lean on others at times."

"Tim's been good for that. And for other things as well," she said, grinning.

Tory worried nonetheless. Then she thought about her own mother and realized that a parent had no other option.

Three days later, the doorbell rang. Chris answered it. From the family room, Tory heard male voices and thought it might be some canvasser. It seemed a little late for that, she thought, returning to the TV.

Heavy steps approached. She looked up to see a large man entering with Chris.

"Tory, this is Tim."

So this is the famous Tim.

Zoey was in bed, and Jake was out. Tory turned off the TV, and the two men sat down. Chris offered Tim a drink, which was politely refused, and intuitively took a backseat to the discussion.

Tory got right to the point. "I gather you're here because of Sam?"

"Yes. She told me what you said."

"I'm glad you're here. It means that you care for my daughter and have the maturity and confidence to approach me about a topic that's difficult to discuss. This probably won't be an easy talk."

He grinned, and she immediately understood what her daughter saw in this man. He wasn't intimidated by being in their home, and he exuded raw masculinity. He was very attractive in a bad-boy way while also seeming to be sophisticated.

"How do you want to begin? Do you have questions?" she asked.

"I have a couple of questions."

"Okay, let's start with them."

"Samantha says she's okay with what happened to her, but I'm not convinced. What do you think? You know her."

"I do know her, but not always as well as I think I do. She constantly surprises me. People grow and change, which is part of it. She's learning about what she likes and doesn't like—in her sex life as well as other areas. I know from experience that it can be confusing when a middle-class girl explores her own sexuality, especially if none of her friends seem to be doing so. Willingness to break the mold and experiment takes courage. I've been very open with my kids about sex, but she still has to develop her own tastes.

"She's had a setback. She was abused and degraded by someone she wanted to trust. She knows it'll take work to get over the whole thing, but she's not put off by that. The whipping incident made her feel less confident about relinquishing control, which is a privilege that comes with time. You're going to have to be patient and earn her trust—if that's what you both want."

Tim nodded.

"I don't think she's afraid of any of it—experimentation, pushing limits, or setting hard limits—but she might need time and a slower pace going forward. Shaun didn't handle it well, as you know. Maybe because he was inexperienced—

"No, he was just an asshole."

"I'd tend to agree. So what I'm saying, in other words, is that she's been shaken but not bruised. My daughter is strong, and she likes you. She's looking for an experienced partner. If you're not interested, then you need to step away because she needs to continue her search and find someone. Determination runs in the family," Tory said, grinning. "Feel free to ask me anything. I'm not shy about talking about this. Do you live near here?"

"Yes. But I'm getting a promotion. I might be transferred."

Tory wondered if Samantha knew that.

"Sam says you're six years older than her. My husband was my age, but Chris is much older than I am."

She grinned at Chris, and he smiled back at her. He'd understand that she was trying to make Tim feel comfortable with the age difference. She teased Chris about being eight years older, but she believed he had no issue with it.

"Are you a dominant?" she asked Tim. "I know that's popular again, and lots of people have a tendency toward it."

"I'll take something to drink now," Tim said.

Chris got up to mix some drinks.

241

CHAPTER 23

"Sorry, I'm just curious," Tory said. "No pressure to answer."

"I do have other questions, and I'm interested in all things to do with sex, just so you know. I don't get to talk about it often. It's not something you bring up at a party, a sex club, or anywhere else. Not sure why, though. I guess you just get busy and do it rather than talking about it."

"So you two met at a sex club."

"That's right. You don't seem surprised."

"Not really. Chris and I went to a private club on vacation once."

"Where did we go, honey?" Chris asked, bringing over the drinks.

"That place we went to, you know, the sex theater. What was it called?"

"The George."

"Right! We were blindfolded. It was all top secret. The things we saw and did …" She laughed.

"Best sex ever!"

Without missing a beat, Chris started telling Tim about that night. Eventually, the conversation went back to Sam.

"It's hard to believe that I'm talking about this with a priest and my girlfriend's—or sort of girlfriend's—mother."

"Chris and I don't get much opportunity to discuss sex with others. We don't mind really. It should be a topic that people should be able to discuss, don't you think?"

"Maybe," he said.

Tory wondered why Tim wasn't comfortable labeling his relationship with Sam. "So, you don't know what you are yet? I get the impression from Sam that she wants to get to the next level."

"Well, I know she wants that, which is why I'm here. We've been hanging out, but we haven't really done it yet. I haven't been sure she was ready."

"Has she said anything to make you think she wasn't?"

"No. I just worry about pushing her too soon."

"Then you need to read her signals. You'll only get good at that by observing how she reacts to anything new. My advice is to plan a play session. Tell her up front everything that you'll be doing. Set her at ease from the start. See how it goes. Don't make it a big deal, and she won't think the fate of your relationship rests on this one time together. Some exploration will help you two get comfortable with each other. Make it fun! Above all, it should be fun."

When Tim left, she and Chris snuggled on the couch and discussed what had happened. He told her she'd handled the discussion well. Before long, they were kissing and making their way to bed.

Chris wanted to check on Zoey before they began to make love. Seeing how much he loved their daughter made her feel complete.

***

When Chris woke, it took him a moment to get his bearings. He was at Tory's place. He was just turning back into her soft body to go back to sleep when he heard something unusual—a man's cry, he thought at first. He slid his arm slowly out from under Tory's head, got out of bed, and put on a pair of jeans before leaving the room to investigate.

Chris looked in on Zoey first. She was sleeping peacefully, so he made his way down the hall. He checked in the spare bedroom where Alice or Sam slept when they stayed the night. The bed was neatly made, and the window was closed.

He approached Jake's bedroom. Light was visible under the door. Everything was quiet, and he knocked gently.

No answer. He put his ear to the door and listened before whispering, "Jake?"

Worried something was wrong, he pushed the door open a crack unsure what he'd find.

Jake had his head in his hands and was crying his heart out.

Chris felt immediate compassion for the young man; he wanted to go to him and offer comfort, but he held back. They hadn't established that kind of relationship yet. He stood perfectly still, waiting to be either told to leave or asked to stay.

Jake noticed him and jumped up. "You scared me. I didn't hear you."

"Sorry. I heard a noise and—"

"Did I wake you?"

"I was just checking. I didn't mean to intrude."

For a moment neither of them moved nor spoke. Chris sensed that Jake needed to talk. Having spent time with a youth group and the recent meeting with Tim made him aware that he would have to share something from his past that someone might be able to identify with. He used to feel embarrassed by his own past.

"How about we go outside and have a beer?"

Jake shrugged, wiped his face on his arm, and followed Chris downstairs.

On the patio, Chris waited for Jake to settle down on the lawn chair with his beer before starting to talk. "When I was your age—actually, I was a little younger. You're what, twenty-three, twenty-four?"

"I'll be twenty-three in a few months."

"Well, I was about twenty or so and thought I knew it all. A group of my buddies wanted to go see a stripper, so I went along. It would have looked weird if I'd chickened out. The guys I hung around already thought I was a mama's boy."

Jake seemed to be listening.

"I wasn't a mama's boy though. I didn't even like my mother, and I think she felt the same way about me. It was nothing like the way your mom feels about you or vice versa. I'd always been very close to my sister and treated girls with respect, so I was called names like pansy-ass and suck-up. I think they took their cues for how to treat others from their own parents. So anyway, that night, we went to the strip club. I had a fake ID even though I already looked older than twenty-one. I was stressed and embarrassed by the way my friends acted, shouting crude comments and insults at the women dancing and taking their clothes off. It was like they were trying to outdo each other. The cruder the better.

"I wasn't shy, but I hung back from what they were doing. My friends teased me and called me gay, stuff like that. They joked that I was gay from that time on. For a while, I thought I might be gay too. I experimented with boys, girls, part of a threesome, and groups. I tried it all, and all of it appealed to me. After a while, I needed it to be even more intense just to get off. To be honest, there were times I thought I might be more into guys than girls. I liked how uncomplicated it could be with another man. There wasn't all that drama and high maintenance. The sex was straightforward and satisfying—at least it was for me. I didn't feel like I was competing or being compared to anyone else or having to convince someone to have sex with me.

"My dad asked me about it once. He said I was too tidy and spent too much time on my appearance. I guess that was enough in those days to raise suspicion. But we all primped like that. We were into our looks. You had to dress the part to be cool. It's the same today.

"I developed a reputation for liking everything so that no one would pigeonhole me as preferring one sex over the other. Don't get me wrong—it definitely would have been a difficult road for me if I'd liked only men. People weren't very tolerant. They were small-minded, I think. It's not so much that I worried about being labeled. I was struggling to understand myself, and I didn't need the pressure to choose one over the other. Do you know what I mean?"

Jake nodded.

"When I went into the seminary, some men there wanted me to have sex with them. But I didn't. By that time, I was devoted to being who I wanted to be. If girls had been throwing themselves at me, I would have had a much more difficult time saying no. By then, I knew which way I swung." He laughed. He hoped Jake could see that he was just like any other man who struggled with conflicting views.

"Sex generally lost its mystery and excitement after a while. It was just something to do, a natural release, like any other bodily function. Nothing special—so I didn't miss it. Not until just before I met your mom. There was a while back then, after many years of abstinence, when suddenly, sex was all I thought about. But that's another story, and I'm sure you don't want details.

"I was cocky as a young man. I didn't realize what was missing. Sex is one thing. Intimacy and deep bonds are something else altogether. It took me a long time to figure that out. I envied people who forged long-lasting relationships. I never thought it would be in the cards for me.

"I know it's tough out there. And you don't know me well yet, but when you feel comfortable enough, please talk to me. I'm a good listener. I've heard it all. I've been where you are, I think, so you don't need to sugarcoat it. And I'll keep what you tell me in confidence. Do you believe me?"

"Yes."

Chris took a pull of his beer, trying to make Jake feel at ease.

"I don't even know how to start," Jake said.

"Start anywhere. Start with what you're feeling right now. Sometimes that's the best place."

"I've been having weird thoughts."

Chris waited, refraining from asking the obvious question. Jake had just heard him spill his own guts. Prodding was not necessary. Jake would disclose things when he was ready. Perhaps not right away, and there was nothing wrong with that. Chris was trying to build a rapport with Jake to make him feel less alone in whatever he was going through.

"I'm worried about disappointing my mom."

"Not possible."

"Maybe. She thinks I'm this good person, but I'm not. I've tried drugs and so much other shit it would make her ... well, let's just say if she knew, it would change everything."

Chris held his tongue, sensing that any defense of Tory's unwavering love and loyalty would only stall the conversation. Jake knew this already. It would take more than drugs and whatever else he was into to sever the bond they enjoyed. But he could appreciate that Jake didn't want to disappoint or hurt his mother.

"My mom's pretty straitlaced. She'd freak out if she knew half the stuff I've done."

Jake had no idea how wrong he was. *Why do kids always assume their parents have never jumped into anything wild and crazy?*

"Tell *me*, then," Chris said.

"Some of it disgusts even me. I can't believe what I've let myself get talked into or what I've come up with."

Jake was hesitant at first, but he started to open up the way that guys did.

Chris smiled inside.

Jake gave few actual details, but Chris got enough to build a fairly good picture. Jake was having a sexual-identity crisis. It could occur to anyone of any age.

From all his years of hearing confessions, Chris was prepared for worst-case scenarios: child pornography, sexual assault, murder, and a variety of other illegal and horrific misdeeds. What he heard from Jake, sensitive man that he was, was pretty run-of-the-mill. It was a relief to know that the kid was normal. They spent another hour talking and then went back inside.

Jake seemed less upset when they parted at the top of the stairs. Chris was glad to have been Jake's sounding board.

Tory was awake and waiting for him, as though she knew what had transpired. She hugged him fiercely when he came into the room. Perhaps she had overheard some of their conversation from the window, which overlooked the back patio.

"Thank you for doing what you did tonight," she said. Tears were pooling in her eyes.

"I was glad to do it." It was the truth. Sharing his own story had reminded him how he had felt when confronted with his own conflicts. He had tried to ensure that Jake understood he would be accepted, whichever path he took, that Tory and Chris would always support him.

As the days passed, Jake started to come to Chris regularly, sometimes asking for advice. Sometimes they sat together in companionable silence.

***

One weekend, Chris took the whole family camping in Algonquin Park. Tory complained about the food, but the kids loved it. Even Samantha seemed to like roughing it, and she teased her mother endlessly for being a city slicker.

It was telling how little the kids spoke about John. It was evident that Tory's husband had ignored all of them. They could only remember having taken a couple of family vacations. Chris was getting a clearer picture of what their lives had been like before John's death.

When Tory put her old house on the market and began to stage it, the family gathered to help move things into storage. Most of Tory's stuff wouldn't fit the new place since the style wasn't right. She was taking only what was necessary.

Jake and Chris teased the females about all the boxes that needed lugging to the garage. Chris had convinced Tory to use a service for all of the heavy lifting, and the moving van was coming the next day.

He could tell Tory was pleased with how he'd developed a relationship with Jake. Although she might be less pleased to learn that he'd advised Jake to see the world and take time to travel. Things would fall into place as Jake gained more life experiences away from his mother and the small community he'd grown up in. He'd reminded Jake that urban society viewed same-sex relationships with much more openness. If Jake were lucky, he would meet someone—or maybe more than one person—to spend his life with.

***

Their lives were about to change again. Jake was going off to tour Europe. Tory wasn't sure about him leaving her, but Chris made her see that exposure to other cultures would make Jake's life richer and help him grow and mature. Deep down, Tory knew her son was a grown man and would eventually have to leave her, but he still felt like her little boy.

Chris and Jake had spent weeks plotting out Jake's journey—obtaining foreign currency, poring over maps, discussing hostels, tourist traps, embassies, and so much more. When they dropped Jake off at the departure terminal, Tory saw the affectionate look that passed between her son and her lover. It made her realize how far they had both come. She didn't want Jake to see her upset, so as he went through the security gate, she smiled and waved, pretending she was fine. Just like she had on his first day of school.

But once he was gone, she couldn't help crying. Chris's strong arms encircled her body, giving her his silent support. She was angry with herself at how emotional she was over it. It wasn't as if Jake were going off to war, where he might die in action. He wasn't leaving her forever. He would be back in four months. He had promised her that.

She tried to stop her sniveling and not make it all about her, but in the parking garage, he held her hand as she got it out of her system in the relative privacy of the vehicle. He knew her so well.

"What if he finds a job and meets someone over there?" she said.

"Then he gets to live his life as it's meant to be. He does have a right to that. It doesn't mean he's abandoning you. Do you know he's wanted to do this ever since you took him to the Canadian War Museum in Ottawa when he was in grade ten?"

"No, I didn't. Why?"

"I think seeing the locations of the wars intrigued him. He was full of questions, he confessed to me about those faraway places that he couldn't relate to. The diverse cultures maybe?"

"I'm so glad that he's had you to talk to. He seems so much happier with himself. Have you noticed?"

"I have."

"It feels like he's suddenly so grown up."

"I think he has a ways to go yet. It takes boys longer to mature than girls. A smart lady once told me that."

Tory smiled for the first time in hours. She was the one who had told him that once while they were watching a movie on TV.

She finally stopped crying and gained some control. A last deep sigh and a swipe of her nose with a tissue alerted him to the fact that they could leave. Zoey was staying with Alice; Chris planned to take Tory out to dinner, and they'd stay overnight in Toronto.

He extracted his hand from hers, and they smiled at each other before fastening their seatbelts.

"You're so good to me." She didn't tell him that enough.

"We're good for each other."

"Yes."

They rode in silence after that. Chris located a soft rock station, and Tory leaned her head back and closed her eyes. Eventually, she fell asleep.

Chris's hand on her shoulder roused her when they arrived at the Royal York.

CHAPTER 24

Chris had gone all out for their date. The reservations, the planning, and the details showed that he'd taken so much effort to make this special for them.

Tory decided not to ruin it for him by worrying. She could do that later. Chris was right: Jake needed this trip, and it was selfish of her to want otherwise.

By the time they were dressed—he in a charcoal suit and she in a new black dress—she had pulled herself together. A car was waiting out in front of the hotel, and it took them to an Italian restaurant a few blocks away.

They were seated in a round booth, isolated from the other patrons. She soaked in the ambience. The entire place smelled like fresh cheese and pasta sauce. The décor was classic, and the lighting was subdued.

The food was wonderful, and as they ate, they talked about everything and nothing. Determined to be good company, Tory discussed some decorating ideas for the new house after all other safe topics had been exhausted.

Looking at him across the table, she wanted to remember the moment forever. People often took each other for granted; she didn't want to be like that. Holding on to wonderful times brought joy to life and fueled memories. Chris had brought so much to her life. He had fit right in, and she was amazed by how well he was adjusting to having a child.

"Thank you for everything you do. And all of the planning for tonight. It's lovely."

"I thought we would do it up right, pretend we're much farther away."

"Mini conference time?"

"Mini conference time." He laughed. "We won't have those times again. In so many ways, this is better—even though we're hardly ever alone anymore."

"Do you miss that? Being alone?"

"Not really. Being alone is lonely. Being with you and our family trumps anything. We'll find time again. All too soon, Zoey will want to be with her friends instead of us. We'll get it back."

"Maybe we'll be too old to want to fool around then," she teased.

"Maybe." He grinned. "But I doubt it. We need to prove that theory wrong, don't you think?"

"I'm game!"

"I thought you might be."

"Why?"

"Because you're my other half, the piece of me I didn't know was missing. It's as though we're one."

She sighed, feeling emotional again.

"I have something for you," he said.

His suddenly serious expression as he reached into his pocket made her tense. He took out a small box, and her breath hitched. She had no idea how to react. Should she be pleased or concerned? Perhaps the container held only earrings or a necklace. But what if it didn't? Did she want to marry him? Hopefully, he wouldn't go down on one knee. She didn't like grand gestures like that. Being the center of attention made her feel uncomfortable. She was too old for any of that, but she could sense that he was going to make it a big deal.

So many thoughts were running through her mind that she didn't focus on him until he took her hand in his. She was being silly. She wanted this, didn't she? He was the same man who suited her better than any other person she'd ever met. *Where are these weird thoughts coming from?*

He smiled at her and said, "I can see you're speechless. Doesn't happen very often. At the risk of stating the obvious, I love you. I want us to get married. It can be a conventional ceremony or whatever you decide. I know, from knowing you, that whatever we do will be simple."

She swallowed, her throat suddenly dry, and she hoped she wouldn't cry in public.

He leaned forward and flipped open the lid. Three rings were nestled inside the box, and he took one out. "This is a promise ring, the kind that was popular a long time ago. It's my version of an engagement ring. May I put it on your finger?"

Her hand trembled as he slid the ring on her finger. She held it up and gazed at the ring. She had never seen anything so beautiful. It suited her tastes perfectly: a small band impressed with the image of a heart. It was understated and elegant—with no precious stones to distract the eye.

"Do you like it?"

She nodded, not trusting her voice.

He rubbed her hand, which calmed her right down. "I want you to know that I asked Alice for permission."

What? "You didn't!" The fingers of her free hand went to her mouth. She was overwhelmed by the gesture.

"I did. I'm not usually this old-fashioned, but I thought it appropriate. This has been a long time coming. Ever since that Saturday morning when you let me braid Zoey's hair. The first time you accepted me into your home. Do you remember?"

"Yes."

"I knew I wanted more—to *be* more than your lover and Zoey's dad. I wanted to be your partner. I've loved you for so long—even when I tried to convince myself years ago that it was just sex. I started looking for the right rings for us long ago. Luckily, I've had more free time lately to devote to the search. The rings had to be special. They had to be us." He showed her the other two rings. "These are identical. They're our wedding bands."

"They look old."

"They are."

Chris pulled one out and handed it to her. "A friend of mine, the priest who's pretty much taken over my parish, has already blessed them. So whenever you're ready, I'll be ready. Look at the inscription."

She squinted at the engraving, trying to make out the words. As she read them, her eyes filled with tears: *My Other Half.*

Without warning, panic set in. *How have we gotten here so quickly?* The pressure to make the important decision was upon her, but she wasn't ready. "I don't know what to say," she said, knowing that it was not the answer he was expecting.

"What's going on, Tory?"

She hated hurting him, but he needed to know what had happened. Handing back the wedding band, she said, "I got an offer on the house, but I turned it down."

"You're waiting for a counteroffer?"

"No."

"No? Why? And what's that got to do with this?"

"I'm not ready to sell."

"I'm not following you."

"I don't think I can do this."

The look of confusion on Chris's face changed to one of distress, and she regretted saying anything.

"What do you mean, you *don't think?*"

"I mean … what I'm trying to say is I can't do this. Us. I've got the kids to think about," she lied.

"The kids? Are you seriously worried about them not accepting me—or us? You know that Jake and Zoey are fine. Even Sam's warming up to me. It's not them, is it?"

He knew her so well. Her children liked him. Jake had bonded with him, Zoey was thrilled to have a dad, and Sam seemed to be adjusting.

"Everything's happening too fast." That was not exactly a lie. They had been moving toward the marriage proposal for a while, but something felt not quite right. *How can I explain something I hardly understand myself?* She had married John in a whirlwind romance, and look how that had turned out. Then she'd given in to her need for sex, and that had resulted in Zoey. Not that it was a negative outcome, but there were always consequences.

She still felt ambivalent about selling her house—the only home she'd ever purchased on her own, which gave her a sense of accomplishment and independence. Wasn't that a red flag?

Worst of all was the fact that Chris still hadn't severed his ties with the church. Joking about being a househusband aside, he hadn't told her what he would do when he finally left the priesthood. He was still withholding key information about himself. It all made her worry, more than anything else. His words just a couple of minutes earlier had just seemed to confirm it: *the priest who's pretty much taken over my parish.* He claimed to be fine with leaving his calling, but she was terrified that he didn't really want to leave. Would he regret it? Would he eventually blame her for it? Where would they all be then?

She had to be smart. They both did. "I've made hasty decisions before and lived to regret them."

"Are you saying that you're worried about us?" he asked, his voice slightly raised.

She had to get him to calm down. His anxiety and her current state of mind were making her say things that were unclear.

"No. Nothing like that. There's just been so much change."

"Help me understand why that's a bad thing."

Tory heard the pain in his voice. With her next words, she was about to test them—what they had built together. "It's not bad. It's just too soon. Setting up house the way you want, I mean. Things have been a certain way for me for a long time. What the two of us had—our relationship—was outside of my home life, and that worked. It's more complicated now."

"Of course, I get that. It's not going to be easy on any of us. I'm getting an instant family, and you don't see me going nuts over it."

"Yes, you're right. But I have to think of them first."

"And you think I don't?"

"I didn't say that. Stop putting words in my mouth!"

"So, tell me what you're trying to say. Spit it out!"

She took a deep breath and went for it. "This is not going to work."

He actually jerked back. Tory felt instant regret. She really didn't want to have that discussion with the man she loved right now, especially not in public. Perhaps she could just convince him to postpone the whole thing. Perhaps they could agree to live together full-time instead of getting married and leaving the city.

"Let's talk about this tomorrow and just enjoy the meal now," she said. Tory felt she might unravel if Chris pushed too hard.

"It's too late for that. Tell me why. Can you do that? Tell me, please."

***

He couldn't come to terms with the bombshell she'd just dropped. Hadn't everything been going well? Hadn't they been planning for marriage all along? "What's happened to bring this on?" he asked.

"I've been thinking that … I just can't let you leave your calling for us. You would be giving up a part of yourself, disappointing a lot of people … and the church has too few priests these days."

He knew bullshit when he heard it. She was not into religion, and she would not be worried about whether the church could fill his spot. Yes, if he was being totally honest, there was a part of him that would miss it, but she couldn't possibly know that, or did she? Something else must have happened. Had Alice had a change of heart about him? Had those nasty gossips finally gotten to her?

"Did someone say something to you?"

"No. I just sense this is wrong."

"I think you're getting cold feet. You've decided this without me, and that's not fair. Is this about John? You know that if he hadn't gotten sick, you would have left him. But when he got sick, you felt obligated to stay, and that was hard on you. Now you're worried it might be the same with me. Since John died, you've been on your own, and you've liked that. Now I've shown up and put a wrinkle in your well-ordered life."

Her eyes widened. He knew he'd touched some kind of chord.

"Are you worried you'll end up having to take care of me?" he asked.

"You've got it all figured out, have you?"

"I'm right, aren't I?"

"Now look who's not being fair."

Chris modulated his tone before continuing, knowing that she disliked it when he got too domineering. "I think I know you pretty well. You've changed over the years, even more so recently. I get it. You're not the same person you were when we first met. You're more self-assured. You don't need a man in your life. Back then, you needed a man for sex—and you got me. But one man is as good as another when it comes to sex, so I can easily be replaced. And you have the resources to pull up stakes whenever you want.

"You need to know you have options. That's probably why you didn't accept the offer on your house—and why you're not thrilled about the place up north. You don't want to sell. I'm okay with that. So we'll have two homes."

"You don't understand," she said.

"Then please enlighten me." It was all going downhill fast, and he wasn't able to keep the sarcasm out of his voice. That wouldn't go over well.

"Don't get all sanctimonious on me. Don't act like everything I say is crazy."

He sighed. They had never really argued before. But didn't all couples fight from time to time? Perhaps this fight was long overdue, and that was the reason for her stubborn and irrational behavior.

He looked at Tory's angry face. *There is no way we can work things out tonight.* He had to get her to realize how irrational she was being. *But not tonight.* They had to stop arguing right away, or he would say stupid things that would only make it worse because he wouldn't be able to take them back.

It had obviously been an emotional day for her. Seeing Jake off had upset her more than he'd expected it would. It hadn't been the right time to propose. Perhaps he should have waited. Now it would be a struggle to salvage the evening.

He tried to see things from her point of view. What did she see when she looked at him? An aging man on the other side of fifty, closer the sixty? Besides the great sex, they got along pretty well. He tried not to rock the boat. He adapted to all the things that were unfamiliar to him and went along with whatever she suggested. He didn't always like it, but he did it. Did she not see that?

Perhaps that wasn't the issue. Maybe she felt he was just someone else to look after. Most of the time, he was helpful, wasn't he? Then recent memories surfaced: teasing him about not knowing how to launder clothes, buy groceries, or shop for household items and reprimanding him for forgetting to pay the utilities. Those were inconsequential things, nothing to get all bent out of shape about, weren't they?

He sighed and said, "Okay," making a T for time-out with his hands.

She laughed. *Good sign.*

"Can we cool it for now?" he asked.

"We can."

He had been granted a reprieve. She wouldn't meet his eyes though, which bothered him. She was pulling away and sending him adrift. Losing her was not an option.

"This conversation isn't over, just so you know," he said.

"I figured."

"Okay, then. So we'll continue with the meal and pretend that everything's fine."

"Oh, Chris—"

"I don't want to pretend, but I will for now." *You can be sure of that!*

"I thought you called time-out."

"Sorry."

Tory looked at him oddly, probably wondering why he was capitulating. Her silence was telling. She ordinarily never held her tongue and let him know where he stood with her at all times.

Chris would have to show her who he was with actions rather than words. He had to prove that they fit together in more ways than one—and that he knew her better than she knew herself. He drew encouragement from the fact that she was keeping the engagement ring on her finger, but he couldn't erase the look on her face when she'd handed over the wedding band.

***

Why couldn't he see that things were moving too fast? Why was he in a rush to get married? She thought of her meeting with the real estate agent. The woman had looked at her like she was nuts to turn down such a strong offer.

Some parts of having Chris integrated into her life would be fine. Having him involved with Zoey would be fine. The prospect of regular sex would be great. But the rest was too much. He was taking over her life. She still had to sit down with her older children and make sure they were okay with everything that was happening.

Chris had become closer to Jake, but it was still early. Tory needed to know firsthand how Jake would feel about Chris becoming part of their team. It couldn't happen while Jake was away. He was only starting to discover who he needed to be. And Sam? It would be irresponsible to leave Sam alone in the city so recently after her traumatic experience. Her relationship with Tim was just beginning. Tory wanted to be there for Sam—just like Alice had always been nearby when Tory needed her.

Tory wasn't concerned about Zoey; her little love child was full of confidence and self-assurance. Tory grinned, thinking of her.

"What are you smiling about?" Chris asked.

"I was thinking about Zoey."

He did not comment, probably absorbed in his own thoughts. He had clammed up, and she imagined he might be turning away from her already.

The jewelry box was open on the table between them. He made no further attempt to convince her of anything, but the tension had yet to dissipate. He began snapping an elastic band that was around his wrist, for some reason, under the cuff of his sleeve.

As Tory chewed her last piece of steak, her mind went back to how things had been before Chris found out he had a daughter. Tory had been both mother and father to Zoey. Clearly Chris wanted some of that, and she hoped to let him have it. What a contrast to her early days of being terrified that he'd try to take Zoey away. He had rights where their daughter was concerned, but Tory had such doubt about them together as one big, happy family.

If she sold the house and eventually gave up her job for a new one, probably at a lower salary, how would she manage if their relationship didn't work out? What if she turned her whole life upside down, and then Chris decided not to leave the church? How would she explain to Zoey why her new daddy had abandoned her?

Then there was Alice. Tory had always lived in close proximity to her mother. How would she manage without having Alice nearby to listen and help out? And as Alice grew older, how would she manage without Tory around to assist her?

Tory had told herself countless times that her fears were based on projections and fictional scenarios, but she still worried. The wedding ring had forced her to see that she wasn't ready. What if it took her years to be ready? Would he stick around and wait for her?

She struggled with wanting to keep wearing the engagement ring. It symbolized a future with Chris, but her practical side knew that lust faded, and with it, so did marriage. Allowing any man to stake his claim to her was tantamount to having a leash around her neck. She felt a lump in her throat.

"The steak was a little tough," he said, still playing with that damned elastic band around his wrist.

She wanted to agree; instead, she said, "Everything's lovely." She wanted to be positive about something.

"Not quite everything. But I have hopes for tonight."

She smiled, trying to regain some of the prior ease between them. "You've been quite secretive about your plans."

"I do have something in mind, but you might not be up for it."

"I'm open to anything ... besides finding my family gathered in a room, waiting for us to get married on the spot."

He laughed. "Yeah, wouldn't that be something? Having to face a room full of people to tell them the wedding's off? Anyway, I wouldn't surprise you that way. It wouldn't be fair to spring something like that on you. Don't worry. It's nothing like that."

"Not even a hint, huh?"

"You'll find out soon enough."

They ordered coffee and a dessert to share. Chris took his time. When the chocolate cake was positioned between them, he took her fork and placed it out of reach so he could feed her the best morsels himself. The cake was sinfully good. She groaned a little as the moist treat met her taste buds.

"Your groaning is a real turn-on," he said.

He gathered up the last crumbs and popped them into his own mouth, intentionally bypassing her with a smile. She'd had enough, but she had expected him to offer the last of it to her. Perhaps she was reading too much into such a simple act.

"Are you ready?" he asked.

"Ready for what?"

"To leave this place so I can do all the things you like to you. It's what we do so well together and what makes us happy. It feels so good that it can't possibly be bad. I want us to get back to that. To that special place where nothing else matters."

She nodded, knowing he was right. She needed to be reminded of how good it could be and stop dwelling on the what-ifs. Now that she'd successfully steered him away from all the marriage talk, they could get back to enjoying each other's company.

He pulled back her chair and assisted her to her feet.

She took a last glance back at their table and noticed the box was gone, probably back in Chris's pocket.

With his hand on her lower back, Chris propelled her to the lobby and out to a waiting car.

CHAPTER 25

Chris opened the door to their suite. The room was lit, and a massage table was set up in the center of it. A young man came forward and introduced himself as Jeffrey. He invited Tory to change into a robe in the bathroom.

Was this Chris's nod to the way they'd met, the first time he'd had his hands on her body (unbeknownst to her)? She felt a little apprehensive and wondered why. It was just a massage, and the young man was there to provide a service.

When she emerged, clad in nothing but a robe, fewer lights were illuminating the space. Chris was sitting in a club chair, still fully dressed. Waiting for her, she guessed. He looked like someone who had paid for a call girl and was waiting for the entertainment to begin. He was so handsome in his suit; he could have any woman he wanted. Suddenly feeling frumpy and older than her age, she stood still, not knowing what to do with herself.

"Do you need assistance getting on the table, ma'am?" Jeffrey asked.

"No." She hated being called *ma'am*.

"Lie down with your face here," he said, pointing to the round, cushioned opening.

She complied without comment, moving slowly and glancing at Chris to gauge his expression, which was unchanged. Jeffrey was expressionless. What had Chris planned?

She pulled open her robe, but she didn't remove it as she positioned herself face-down on the table. She didn't see a sheet she could cover herself with, and she refused to be naked just yet. Once she was situated comfortably, she heard movement behind her and shifted her head to see what was going on.

Chris had stood up and was removing his jacket. His movements were unrushed as he draped it on the back of the chair, unbuttoned his cuffs, and rolled up his sleeves. His measured steps drew him closer to the table.

He drew away the robe from Tory's body, sliding the sleeves off her arms, and positioned her head just as he had done so many years before. A cool cotton sheet was placed over her. He pulled her hair to the side, combed it with his fingers, and braided it loosely before securing the end with the rubber band that had been on his wrist all evening. Finally, he gently placed an eye mask over her face.

Chris began with her neck, applying slight pressure at first, and then he became more forceful as he worked his way to her shoulders. Her physical tension began to melt, but the mental tension did not. She was still in the dark about what he had planned for her.

The strains of classical music registered next. This all seemed odd. *What kind of person does this? Who rents a suite, orders a masseuse, and then takes over the actual work?* What was Jeffrey's role in all this?

"Stop thinking and relax," Chris said in that tone that never ceased to piss her off.

She moved to tell him so, but he pressed her head back down. She decided to let everything go: her anxiety, the questions, the internal struggles, and the fact that he wanted to control their time together. She pushed aside all of it to let him have his way. She would enjoy the massage. They rarely had these kinds of experiences anymore, and she knew he wouldn't hurt her. In fact, all he wanted was to please her.

When he picked up on her acquiescence, he said, "Good girl," making her teeth grind.

But she just sighed, not uttering a word, and was rewarded by broad strokes down her shoulders and back. The sheet slipped a little.

Another set of hands rubbed the tops of her thighs through the cloth, and then the sheet was removed and her legs were exposed to Jeffrey's touch. She sensed the roughness of calloused palms and briefly wondered what he did for a living besides this. His fingers were strong and dug into her muscles.

Tory had gone for a run the day before without warming up or cooling down properly. Her hamstrings were tight. She allowed herself the freedom to enjoy the attention of the two men without trying to guess what would happen next.

After a while, so relaxed she was half asleep, she realized that each man was massaging one of her hands and giving her a similar treatment. Their hands moved in unison, up her arms and down her back, grazing the sides of her torso and inadvertently touching her breasts. She tried not to jerk in response. When they reached her buttocks, she held her breath. The sensations were strange; the technique was a cross between pinching and pressure that made her skin burn.

On either side of her body, each man crept farther down her body toward her legs and feet.

"Roll over, baby," Chris said.

She was glad her eyes were covered because she did not want to see which man was where. It was better this way. Besides, she did not want to witness any possible revulsion in Jeffrey's face when he saw her chest. She still had scars, and even though Chris told her she was beautiful, she never fully believed him.

Once again, each man began on a different side. They made slight contact with the skin of her shoulders, causing a tickling sensation. Her arms were raised over her head, and they treated her to the same therapy along her rib cage, her underarms, her arms, and all the way up to her hands. It was a novel feeling.

They moved on before she was ready for them to, this time circling the base of each breast, slowly moving toward her rapidly hardening nipples. It was sinful, how good this felt, even though they barely made any actual contact.

They moved in unison down her abdomen, and her muscles rippled slightly; anticipation was making her body jittery. They reached her pubic area at the junction of her legs and torso, and her legs began to shake with excitement and a little anxiety. She had no idea what to expect.

Long, gentle strokes moved up and down her legs. When each man took a foot, it was pure heaven. Her legs were spread wide apart, and her groin was fully exposed. Tory soon forgot where she was, who was in the room, and even what was going on.

The next thing she knew, Chris was kissing her mouth—and hands were touching her everywhere. Both of her nipples were pinched at the same time. Fingers rubbed her clit, and others penetrated her vagina. She accepted that the digits did not belong to Chris. Her body began to float with the euphoria of supreme pleasure, and she heated up so much it made her a little uncomfortable.

"These are my hands on your body, Tory. My hands," Chris said into her ear, distracting her. *Why is he telling me this?*

The men played with her body, sensing when to slow down when she was close to coming and when to speed up when she had a ways to go. It felt like she was on a roller coaster without any option but to enjoy the ride. At one point, she was rolled to her side, and one leg was positioned over Chris's shoulder. Her anus was penetrated, and they finally let her climax.

"Jeffrey's going to fuck that pretty ass of yours, baby."

She was completely languid. They repositioned her so that she was crouched over the table. Jeffrey entered her from behind as one set of hands kept her buttocks spread wide and the other held on to her hips. At some point, the men had shed their clothing; she could feel coarse hair against her ass and her back. When Jeffrey was fully seated inside her, the burn dissipated and goo slithered down her leg. She presumed it was some type of lubricant since her own fluids were not as abundant anymore.

Somehow, they enveloped her with their bodies. Fingers thrummed her clitoris, and their weight combined with strength kept her restrained when she wanted to move. An intense heat fueled her need to writhe.

"Ah, my baby likes that, does she? Jeff, my man, speed it up." After a few seconds, he continued, "He's really enjoying this. His cock feels good, doesn't it, sweetheart? Is it as good as mine?"

She dared not answer. Hearing him laugh, she tried to tune him out.

"Do you know what I'm doing now, baby, besides playing with your clit in the only way that gets you off? My other hand is on his ass. I'm rubbing it now, but I'm going to smack him soon—and then fuck him with my finger."

Jeff and Tory groaned as presumably Chris accomplished what he wanted. Every slap Tory heard resonated within her as well. When it stopped, the slick friction became a frenzied race to the end as Jeffrey grunted his release. The muscles in her perineum began to contract, and she started to come when both men pulled away. She was left hanging and struggled to finish coming on her own, but they had other plans.

She was flipped onto her back quickly, and before she could do anything, a mouth was devouring her slit. Teeth nipped at the sensitive folds, and a tongue did wonderful things to her opening before teasing her clitoris. A pair of lips latched onto one breast and then the other.

Her lower body was tilted upward as the tongue fucked her. A finger circled her clit. Faster and faster, the actions gained momentum and were more forceful. It was almost painful.

Her mouth opened to protest and then was filled by a man's finger. "Suck!" Chris commanded.

She did so, tasting herself on his skin, and was rewarded with flicks to her nipples. Soon, she convulsed with an orgasm that seemed to go on forever.

She heard a door being opened, some murmurs, and then silence. Limp as a wet noodle, she didn't bother moving.

Someone picked her up, placed her on a soft surface, and removed her eye mask.

She was on the bed, and Jeffrey was nowhere to be seen.

Chris stood over her, the firm head of his penis rubbing against her lips. She opened her mouth, wanting to taste him. Chris's smell was so distinctive that she could have recognized him even if she were still blindfolded.

Sucking on the tip, she heard him moan. When he was completely inside her, he slowed the pace. His hands held her jaw and adjusted the angle of her head. Letting herself be used was small payment for what he had just given her.

As her strength returned, Tory felt revitalized. She used her tongue to narrow the space her mouth made and to give him more of what he wanted, but he denied himself, pulling out and taking a few deep breaths. He moved away and approached her from the other side of the bed. He grabbed her like a rag doll by the ankles, pulling her into him as he impaled her vagina with his jutting cock in one swift movement. No finesse about it.

Her breath caught at the impact, and he groaned. Her body welcomed the intrusion, despite how exhausted she felt.

He grabbed her arms and held them above her head. "Look at me!" he said.

"I am!"

"No, you're not," he said. He actually sounded angry. "You're not really looking at me. See me? The man who's fucking you, right now, right here!"

He pulled out and pushed back in forcefully.

Tory gazed into his eyes, trying to understand what he was telling her.

"I'm up to my balls in you, but you can't see it, can you?"

"I don't know what you want me to see!" she said, exasperated.

His voice went quiet. "Tell me what you see."

"I see the man I love."

"What else?"

"I see someone who wants me, wants me like no else ever has, who makes me want him to do all of the things that we do so well together."

"Tell me what those things are. I need to know." He looked as frustrated as she felt.

"The way we fuck. Is that what you want to hear?"

"Yes." He sounded almost relieved, but not quite. "What else?"

"The way we are when we're together. How good it is. I don't know how to describe it."

"Like it's heaven, a place where we can be *us*."

"Yes. Yes!"

"Right, so what don't you see? What are you looking for? Tell me, goddamn it! I'm not going anywhere and—"

"I don't know."

"Bullshit! You do! Now tell me!"

She yelled out the first thing that came to mind. "I don't know if lust and love are enough!" There. She had expressed her real fear. They were obviously good at sex, but she knew love faded. When they no longer worked together, where would she be?

His movements stilled. "You don't think what we have is enough?"

"It might not be to sustain us long-term. A long time ago, I thought I was in love with John."

"What else?"

Tory closed her eyes. Chris removed himself only to push himself into her again, deep and hard. "I said, look at me!"

"I don't want to hurt you. You mean too much to me."

"Tory, you can tell me anything. Nothing you could say would make me leave or want you any less or destroy what we have. Trust me, baby."

Her eyes began to water. "It's selfish and stupid. It may not even be rational."

"It doesn't matter. We'll deal with it, whatever it is."

She swallowed. "You might change your mind and decide you don't want to be with me and Zoey. Or you might want to see only Zoey—and not having you in my life would kill me."

"Why would you think that?"

"Why haven't you told the church that you want out yet? If you have, you haven't told me about it. I'm about to change my whole life, and you haven't even made the first move yet. Other than buying rings and telling Zoey, you haven't done anything toward making a change. At any point, you could decide to stay a priest, and where would that leave me? And I can't believe you have no problem renouncing your faith like that. You believed in this. You made a vow to God. How could you break that?"

"Even with the big house I just bought, you still don't believe I'm serious?"

"It's just a thing."

"What else?"

"How do you know there's something else?"

"What else? Spill it!"

"I can't take it!"

"What?"

"If you ever get sick, like John, I won't survive taking care of you! I didn't love John anything like the way I love you, and it would kill me to watch you die. Or if you left me!"

"Oh, honey!" He released her wrists and kissed her mouth with so much passion that she instantly began to get warm again. This time, it was not hurried. This time, it was slower, deeper, more meaningful, and actually better than before. They seemed to have gotten back in sync, and that helped her see what was right in front of her. Somehow, she had lost sight of that.

They were equally invested in reaching climax, just like they were equally invested in their life together. They rolled over so she could be on top. It was one of the most satisfying orgasms of her life.

She hadn't meant to lay it all out like that. In fact, she'd hardly known how to express her fears even to herself—until he'd made her face them. She wasn't upset about his placing her in a vulnerable position. It was not that way with them. He seemed to understand that she needed his help to expose her deepest fears.

And now, we can move on.

***

Tory was the most frustrating person he knew. She had been obsessed with the damnedest things. The good part was hearing that she loved him more than she had loved John. She had told him before that she'd stopped loving John long before his death, but he still wondered. He could see that she needed to feel more secure in their relationship. Somehow, she thought the worst of him. After all this time, she still didn't get that they were in it together.

His plan had been to give Tory a night to remember with a young man who had no trouble having several hard-ons in one night. He'd hired Jeffrey to make her climax while he watched. However, Chris had abandoned that plan as soon as he'd gotten Tory on the massage table. The need to feel her skin under his hands was too great to resist. He was driven out of his chair by the desire to feel her come apart under his hands instead of merely being a spectator.

He had been determined to use sex to torture away her objections to marriage. He planned to bring her to the brink of release over and over again until she confessed what was going on in that head of hers. He soon realized he didn't have the stomach for that. Instead, he tried to get her in the right frame of mind first, surmising that she might share what was bothering her under the right circumstances—and he had been correct. He had weakened her with a couple of orgasms and played his ace in the hole.

Now that he knew what he was up against, he could do something about it. At least, he hoped he could.

While they soaked in the tub, chest deep in the water with her back to his front, he said, "These are my vows to you—"

"Chris, no. You—"

"Shut up and listen." He moved her face so he could kiss her lips. "Can you do that?" He felt her smile against his mouth and finished kissing before he continued. *Here goes.* "I want you to know two things: You are part of me. And leaving you would be like cutting off my own arm. I'm pledging to love and cherish you all the days of our lives, starting today. I want to grow old with you and watch Zoey grow up. I'm not waiting to get married to pledge my devotion. We've wasted too many precious moments and too much time already.

"I've been working at several things that I haven't shared with you because I didn't want to get your hopes up. I also thought it might take a long time to get through all the red tape. I didn't want to put our lives on hold or make you worry. I guess I should have mentioned that I started the process. You seem to have a great deal on your mind these days, and I wanted to surprise you. I'm truly sorry about that. I promise not to keep that kind of thing from you in the future.

"Anyway, when we get out of this tub, I'm going to show you the letter I got this week. It acknowledges that I've left the church, and the judgment cannot be reversed. Tomorrow is my last official day as a priest, and—"

"Oh, Chris—"

"Hush! The second thing I want you to get through that head of yours is that I've got no intention of dying anytime soon. Genetically speaking, I have an excellent chance of living to ninety. No cancer in my family on either side."

She laughed.

"So you see, you're stuck with me," he said.

"Are you done yet?"

"I could be."

"Don't I get a say in this?"

"Nope. Do I look like an idiot?"

"Well, what if I don't think you've made your case? We haven't negotiated. I haven't even discussed terms and conditions!"

He proceeded to tickle her.

When the giggling ended, she looked him in the eyes. "Thank you for reminding me how it is with us, for always making me feel beautiful, cherished, and loved, for insisting I share my fears, which seem less daunting now, and for helping me trust what we have. My body and heart were yours already. Now my head is as well."

"Good to know, Mrs. Enns."

"You do know we might have to have a wedding reception, right? My mom will kill me if we don't."

"How old are you?"

"Old enough, buster, so watch it!"

"Fine! But nothing big, okay?"

"Nothing big. Justice of the peace and a reception of about three hundred."

Tory jumped out of the tub and raced out of the bathroom.

Chris made a show of trying to grab her arm but lost his grip on her slippery skin. He felt happier than he'd ever thought possible. They were back in business.

CHAPTER 26

Ten Years Later

"Zoey! You're going to be late for school!" Tory yelled up the stairs for the third time.

Finally, Zoey came bounding down as only the young can, without worrying about missing a step, looking beautiful.

Every day, Chris woke up and thanked God for his life. *There is so much more to life when you have love and family.*

"Turn right around, miss, and go change," Tory said. "You're showing too much cleavage and leg. The teachers will be calling me again."

"Mom!"

Chris grinned. Sitting at the table, he had a full view of the drama that was about to unfold, and he knew who was going to win this battle. His daughter had already learned how to play her softhearted mother.

"Don't start with me, Zoey. I don't care if it's the style or if everyone else dresses like that or if your group chose that as today's uniform. I've heard it all, and I'm not falling for any of it. Do as I ask."

"Okay."

As Zoey retreated, Tory looked at him as if to say, *That was too easy.*

He grinned, waiting for the next act. Within minutes, the girl was back, dressed in a one-piece jumpsuit that covered her completely, but left nothing to the imagination. He also guessed that she wasn't wearing any underwear. *Oh, this is going to be good.*

Tory took one look at Zoey and looked up to the ceiling. She knew she wouldn't be getting any help from Chris; his philosophy about clothing was that it didn't matter what you wore. Normally, she agreed.

"Okay, fine. You win! I can deal with the short skirt. I'll be in the car."

His daughter—God, would he ever get tired of referring to her that way? — shot him a grin and ran up to her room. Chris went outside to warm up Tory's car while she gathered her things.

Outside, she gave him a quick peck on the cheek. He made her give him some more.

"You don't deserve it, mister. Some help you were."

He grinned.

Their breath created small clouds of mist.

When Zoey made it outside, she found them still at it. "Ah, come on, you guys. Geez!"

Chris liked seeing her embarrassed. Their girl was growing up too fast. Boys had already begun sniffing around.

"I'll remember that when I catch you all kissy face with Jonathan Morgan," he said, teasing her.

"Dad, he's gross!"

She wasn't quite telling the truth. He'd seen how they looked at each other.

"Don't forget to pick up Jake at the airport," Tory said as she got into the car.

"I won't. We'll have dinner ready when you get home. Drive safe. Love ya!"

"Bye, baby," she replied.

In the passenger seat, Zoey made gagging noises, amusing him.

He watched the car back out of the parking spot and take off down the driveway before going inside to work.

These days, he was giving talks to youth programs at various associations and clubs. The subjects he delved into were predominantly sexuality and low self-esteem issues. He enjoyed researching and preparing for the interactive sessions and tried to make them relevant and current.

It was funny; it had all begun as a favor to a young pastor and a way to fill some time, yet be available to his daughter. When Zoey was younger, Chris had been looking for some meaningful work that would allow him to be home most of the time to live the life he'd come to love with Tory and the rest of the family. He'd been asked to do a speaking engagement for a church youth group. After that was deemed a success, word spread. Now he was in demand (especially since he charged only travel expenses) and drew large crowds. These days, his high-tech presentations had music, graphics, and funny images and characters on his slides. He considered each speaking engagement a new event and tried his best not to make his presentations appear recycled or cookie-cutter. This took some added effort. Jake and Zoey helped him with visuals and audio whenever he got stuck.

After a few hours, the alarm on his phone reminded him that it was time to go to the airport. He checked his e-mail for anything urgent and found one from Alice, asking him to pick her up on his way to get Jake. He was more than a little curious as to why she wanted to take the trip with him. Rather than inquiring, he replied that he was on his way.

As he and Alice waited on a bench in the airport arrivals section for Jake to emerge from the sliding doors, there was opportunity to talk which she did not take advantage of. She had been quiet in the car, and he wondered when she'd be ready to tell him what was on her mind. He hoped she wasn't going to inform him that she had some serious illness.

He checked his watch again. "We'll hit traffic on the way back. Jake must be waiting for his luggage."

"I guess."

When nothing more was said and he couldn't stand the tension any longer, he said, "So tell me. Why did you want me to pick you up?"

"I have a favor to ask. Actually, more than one."

"Okay."

"The first's a big one."

"Just tell me, Alice."

"I've lost my driver's license. It happened last week. My memory's not what it once was. I need to move to a place near amenities and I don't want Tory to know why."

He was certain there was a story behind losing her license, but he didn't push her for details.

"Why don't you come live with us?"

"I don't want to be a bother."

"Why do you think you'd be a bother? You could have your own section of the house, facing the lake. There are at least two empty bedrooms."

"I don't think that's a good idea, but thanks for offering."

"So, Alice, what do you need from me?"

"Other than keeping this between us, I need you to give me your word that you won't ever put me in a nursing home. Those places are like warehouses to store people who are waiting to die."

"Okay."

"Tory knows that. And I need help finding a new place. This part, she has no idea about. Since you're not working, I thought you might be able to help."

Because Chris freelanced at home, Alice—and many others—believed that he did nothing but lounge around all day.

"I definitely can. Do you have anywhere in mind?"

"Are there any decent places up where you and Tory live?"

"There might be. I'll have to check it out."

"Can you do that next week?"

"I guess so. Why the rush?"

"I'm being evicted."

"What?"

"Don't tell Tory. She'll get upset."

He laughed. "Okay. I'll try, but you've got to tell me why."

She turned pink. "I had a friend over, and ... the bathtub overflowed again."

He gathered that this was by no means the first time, and the landlord was fed up with all the flooding and related damages.

"Doesn't your insurance cover it?"

"It did the first few times."

"Um … why does the tub overflow?"

She sighed. "Ted and I fall asleep while the water's running."

It took a lot to shock Chris, but Alice had just managed it.

"Ted?"

"Franskey. I've been seeing him off and on since before Tory's dad died."

"Wasn't he the guy who used to be your neighbor when you were growing up? And you didn't get along with him? Tory told me about him. And that one time you got into a fight about something at a wake?"

"The man was—and still is—a pain in the ass. Thinks he's always right. We had a difference of opinion about who was related to whom on the Robinson side of the deceased woman's family. We don't fight much nowadays though."

He grinned at her, and she slapped his arm.

"Does Tory know you're seeing him? Do you need a place for him as well?"

"No and no. No one in either of our families knows. It's nobody else's business what we do. We've been close for a long time, but I couldn't live with him! Who wants an old man to pick up after?"

For some reason, it made Chris's day to learn that Alice was enjoying the company of a man.

"What are you grinning at, young man?"

"I'm hoping that your libido is genetic."

She laughed boisterously.

Chris spotted Jake at that moment, and the conversation ended. Ted and the eviction became Alice and Chris's little secret.

They hadn't seen Jake in person for a couple of years. He had filled out a little, but he looked good. Happy, even. Normally, the boy—no, the man—wore too serious an expression. The look of recognition and pleasure on Jake's face when he saw Chris was wonderful and reassured him that their friendship still existed.

Jake came closer. There was a young man following behind him, looking nervous. Chris brought Alice forward, shielding her from the other bodies.

Jake hugged his grandmother and kissed her cheek. "A welcoming committee!" he said. "How great!"

"And how's my favorite grandson?"

"I'm good. And since I'm your only grandson, I should hope I'm your favorite." He grinned.

Jake and Chris slapped each other's backs in greeting. Then he brought forward his companion. "Nana and Chris, I want you to meet Matt."

"Come here, young man, and hug the old lady." Alice didn't give Matt a chance to decline before grabbing him. To his credit, Matt never lost the smile on his face.

"Nice to meet you, Matt. Let's leave this zoo and start the trek home," Chris said.

He led the way to the parking garage, surreptitiously observing how Jake and Matt interacted. Jake catered to Matt, and they appeared to be very close. It might not be obvious to some, but Chris could tell that Jake had found someone special. Introducing Matt to the family was a big deal. No one had been expecting Jake to bring home his partner. Chris could hardly wait to see Tory's face when she met her son's friend.

At home, Alice helped Chris start dinner while the boys settled in.

A screech some time later notified him that Zoey had arrived home and was greeting Jake. Chris left them to it while he put the vegetables in the oven to roast. Shortly after, he heard Tory's car and went outside to greet her.

"Hi, baby!" he said, leaning in for a smooch as Tory got out of the car.

She kissed him, her cheeks flushed, looking lovely in a pink sweater. He could tell that she was anxious to see her son.

"Alice is here, and dinner's going to be ready in a little while."

"Thank you, Chris."

She took his hand and led them both into the house. She was on a mission and not interested in his delay tactic. She stopped when she entered the family room, her smile wide and welcoming, thrilled to see her son for the first time in ages.

Chris stood by, watching it all play out.

Jake stopped talking when he saw Tory.

"Hi, sweetheart!" she said.

"Oh, mom!" Jake jumped up and dashed over to her. He kissed her and they embraced.

It was really nice to see them together at last, Chris thought. He saw tears coming to Tory's eyes and rubbed her back, providing support. He knew she'd missed her son a great deal. He was anticipating the next part already. It wasn't every day that a man came home with his lover.

***

Tory pulled away slightly, her hands still on Jake's shoulders, and did a full head-to-toe assessment. "You look wonderful!" she exclaimed.

"So do you, Mom."

She looked up and addressed the other man in the room. "And who's this?"

"Mom, this is Matt." The grave look on her son's face made the significance of the introduction apparent.

Matt nodded to her and came over with his hand outstretched. When Tory hugged him instead, he seemed a little surprised before he eased into it. Looking at her son, she knew she had done the right thing.

"Have you all been waiting long for me?" she asked.

"Nope. The flight was a little late, and I was showing Matt around—until Zoey cornered us. My ears are still ringing." He grinned at his sister, and she smiled back at him. "Are you always this late from work?"

"Not always," she said.

"Your mother wants to work, and she works hard," Chris said. She knew he was trying to defuse what was coming. How she loved that man!

"I thought you'd finally considered retirement, but I see you're still hard at it."

And there it was. Why was everyone on her case about quitting? It was becoming more than a little annoying. Although perhaps it was time to think about slowing down a little. Tory knew herself well enough to know it would be quite a transition into a lifestyle that didn't require her to be anywhere at a certain time or to meet regular deadlines.

"What will everyone have to drink?" Chris asked.

He understood her need to work, and she was grateful for it. She glanced at him and grinned, hoping he was ready for a shocker. "Yeah, well, I've actually been thinking about it. Not full-time retirement, mind you."

Chris's left eyebrow rose.

"The commute is getting to me, and I thought I'd like to spend some time traveling the world with my husband. But enough about me. Let's all sit down, hear what you've been up to, and get to know Matt."

Jake laughed. It made her so happy to hear that.

"Sam's coming by with her gang for dessert," Chris said. "You'll want to warn the boys about that while I get drinks first and then put dinner on the table."

"Is she married yet?" Jake asked with a smirk.

"Still putting Tim through stuff, to hear him tell it. Last I heard, they were negotiating a contract," she said.

Everyone chuckled. For years, Tim had wanted to marry Sam, but she continued to refuse, even after four children had arrived on the scene.

***

Alice had been kind of quiet throughout the meal. Chris had wondered whether there was something she hadn't mentioned to him earlier. She barely contributed to the conversation or laughed at the silliness around the table.

After dinner, she helped him clean up. As they worked, Chris debated asking her if something was wrong.

He was about to put the question to her when Samantha arrived and the opportunity was lost. The twins had just turned two, and the two older kids, Jacob and Justin, had just started preschool and kindergarten. They were a rambunctious group of boys. The look on Tory's face when she greeted the small army was enough to make

Chris grateful for them, even on their worst days. How she loved those kids! He had to admit, they were pretty cute.

Tim came over and shook Chris's hand once all of the children were free of their outerwear and running around like wild animals. And they had yet to get a hit of sugar. Heaven help them when that happened!

He was thinking about Zoey and how quickly children grew. His daughter had gone out with friends, and he was hoping she would be responsible and not a typical fifteen-year-old.

Tory must have noticed his inattention and likely the cause of that because she came over and said, "She'll be home by eleven," she said. Sometimes, Tory seemed to sense when he needed her. Often, she even read his mind. "She's young, and her friends are more important to her than we are."

"I know."

After she had gotten herself settled in the family room, Sam said, "I'm pregnant!"

Jake howled. "Are you nuts? Tim, buddy, what are you doing, man?"

Tim shrugged. "She wants a girl. What's a guy to do?"

"How about making an honest woman out of her?" Jake said, trying to irritate his sister. It was like they were kids again. "Ever hear about contraception, Sam? Have you heard that all types are available now? You should try it."

Sam slapped him on the shoulder. "Mind your own business, you jerk!"

"I hear you're working on a formal agreement," he said.

Sam laughed and hugged him. "You can be such an ass. I love you anyway."

"Mommy said a bad word, Dad!" one of the kids said.

Tim responded like the lawyer he was. "It's in the dictionary and not something that you haven't heard me say before, so it's acceptable, Justin."

"Who wants cake?" Alice called from the kitchen.

All of the children ran in that direction. They were followed by most of the grown-ups.

Tory and Chris held hands as they joined the group.

***

Later that night, Chris found Alice sitting at the kitchen table staring at an untouched cup of tea. She turned as he approached.

"What's going on?" he asked.

"Just thinking."

"Have you been doing a lot of that lately?"

"When I can't sleep."

"Tory's the same."

"I know."

She remained silent for a moment before asking, "You're just going to sit there, aren't you, until I say something?"

"That's my plan, yes."

"It's just the imaginings of an old woman."

"Let me be the judge of that. Go ahead and tell me." He put on his stoic face, bracing for the news that she had a health issue or something equally grave, since something was going on. He began to think that their earlier conversation had been interrupted before she could get to what was the real concern.

"It's Jake."

At first he wasn't sure he'd heard correctly. What had he missed? His gut clenched with worry. "What about Jake? He looks okay to me. You think he's ill?"

"Chris, take it easy. I must say, I'm rather tickled you've gotten so close to my grandson that you'd get all bent out of shape thinking he might be unwell. But it's not that."

"What is it, then?" he said, sinking in a chair with relief. The women in this family were nuts. Why did they always yank his chain like this? Couldn't she just tell him what the hell was on her mind?

"It's Matt."

"Matt?"

"Yes. He's … he's not the one. Matt is using Jake, and it will end badly. I can tell."

"How can you tell?"

"Jake's doing all of the heavy lifting in that relationship. Matt just sits back and lets my grandson take care of him. Did you see how Jake even had to carry in their luggage and then bring it upstairs?"

"Yes. But maybe that works for them."

"Maybe. But I think Matt's too selfish to make it work long-term."

"You got all that from one evening?"

She nodded. "Our boy is going to get hurt by that man, and there's not a damn thing I can do about it."

"And this is the only thing that's keeping you up?"

She looked at him as though he were insane. "Well, yes. I worry about that boy. He's sensitive. Why?"

"I just thought it might be something more serious."

"Well, you thought wrong. Anyway, what are you doing down here in the middle of the night?"

He felt himself blush and realized it might not be such a good idea to have his mother-in-law living under their roof. He had snuck down to the kitchen for some black cherry ice cream so he and Tory could play, but that was not something he wanted to share with Alice. Instead, he replied, "Tory wanted something."

Alice grinned, probably enjoying his discomfiture. "Really? I can't wait to hear what that something is."

"Never mind. She's probably asleep by now."

"Uh-huh?"

He felt like a kid caught with his hand in the cookie jar. If Tory was still awake, she could come down and get her own damn ice cream for him to lick off her body.

CHAPTER 27

Another Ten Years Later

"I mean, where has the time gone?" Tory asked.

They were lounging poolside at a resort outside of Halifax, taking a break after Chris's latest speaking engagement at a conference and making use of the facilities.

"Doesn't it seem like yesterday we sent Zoey off to college?"

Tory grinned. Her daughter was determined to become a welder, and nothing would change her mind. Her goal was to get several trades under her belt, and her mother and father had no choice but to accept it. While Zoey waited for an apprenticeship for underwater welding, she was taking advantage of other programs. At the moment, she was enrolled in an electrical engineering course.

Whenever they spoke to friends about Zoey, no one was shocked to learn about her career path. It was common knowledge that Zoey made outrageous decisions. They were curious, though, about what had motivated such unorthodox and unconventional interests. Tory was proud that Zoey was doing what she wanted, regardless of what anyone said. Making inroads into male-dominated fields took courage.

"When's she coming home?" Chris asked.

She had told him the week before, but Tory repeated it. "At the holidays."

Zoey had a place of her own in the mountains near Coquitlam, British Columbia, and she was enjoying herself too much to return to Ontario.

"I'm glad that Jake is looking out for her. It's too bad things didn't work out with him and Matt."

"Where is Matt now?" he asked.

Jake had been with Matt for nine years before their recent split. The family had all gotten close to Matt, so it felt like they had all broken up with him.

"I'm not sure. I hate to probe. Jake's still bent out of shape by how it ended. Then again, maybe there's no easy way to walk away from a relationship when you've been together so long. But I think he left the continent. He might have gone back to the Middle East. You remember how he worked in Saudi Arabia before meeting Jakie?"

"No, I didn't remember."

"And Jake's met someone new. Actually, Zoey introduced them. His name's Randy, and he's a plumber or a pipefitter, something like that. Apparently he's built. She told us this week, remember?"

Chris didn't say a word, which meant that he had no recollection of it. Tory was going to have to stop reminding him of things like that. There would be no point in challenging his memory. It just upset him because he was probably realizing that he was having issues. She didn't need to drive it home.

She looked sideways at her husband. She was so worried about his declining health. His memory lapses were just one of the symptoms. He had become progressively worse since Alice had passed. At times, he was almost catatonic, staring off at nothing and she'd noticed that he had issues with short-term recall. Whenever she brought it up in conversation and suggested that it was time to seek other experts, he became very defensive.

Tory did what she could to keep them safe. She made sure that she was the one behind the wheel whenever they were in the car, and she covered for him in various other ways. Taking control of the finances and household responsibilities had been a gradual process that Chris seemed oblivious to. The kids—she still thought of them that way— had no idea what was going on.

She was convinced that Chris was intentionally missing doctor's appointments because he didn't want to deal with any more procedures or face any more bad news. They rarely argued, but lately, whenever the topic of his health came up, they fell into lively discussions that ended with the silent treatment. It was clear that nothing would be gained by attempting to talk about it today, but Tory became resolved to find other means to monitor him.

Whenever the opportunity presented itself, she would examine him for swelling, take his pulse, and check for any general signs and symptoms of heart or kidney failure. If he caught her at it, he would tell her to mind her own business. Sometimes, she resorted to methods that were very sneaky—what he might call *underhanded*—to gather information. By making him race up the stairs or do some other effortful activity, she could glean all kinds of information about how well his heart and lungs were functioning.

When Tory turned sixty-five and retired from her job, she convinced Chris to slow down as well. This would be their last conference time together. His last solo trip had been somewhat of a disaster, which was another reason Tory had decided to retire. She needed to accompany him to his speaking engagements to ensure that everything ran smoothly. She imagined that their travels abroad might also be coming to an end soon or diminish considerably. She never wanted to receive another call from Chris, telling her that he'd misplaced his passport and taken the wrong train. Getting him home had been a logistical nightmare.

Tory gazed at the young couple across from them, holding hands and fully enjoying the moment. She thought about her past and the paths she had taken. Recently, she'd begun reflecting on what she might have done differently had she known what lay ahead in her future.

She didn't have many regrets. The best decisions had been having children, making a life with Chris, moving away from the dense population of southern Ontario, changing professions from nursing to procurement, and continuing to work for as long as she had. She required mental stimulation and challenging activities distinct from her domestic life with Chris. Their independent spirits had kept their relationship exciting.

Engagement in meaningful activity had given her something to look forward to each day. She still needed it. Her strong work ethic and the difficulty she was having in keeping herself occupied were wearing thin. There was only so much cleaning, organizing, reading, and gardening she could do before boredom struck. Without purpose, she felt a little off-kilter. Setting up an office in their home where she could hide out or work on her own projects had helped a little.

"What are you thinking about over there?" Chris asked, interrupting her wandering thoughts.

She turned toward him and grinned. "I was thinking about all the good things that have happened, the ones I wouldn't change."

"I hope I'm on that list!"

"You are for sure."

When she looked at him, she still felt the connection, that special bond. So much more than she had ever experienced with John.

"What else are you thinking about?"

"What I'm going to do with myself now that I'm home."

"I'm sure you'll figure it out. We have lots to do."

"Really?"

"Sure. Travel. Spend time together. Sleep in until noon. Talk."

They grinned at each other, and she remembered him as the man he was. So capable and masculine. He still had that air of confidence about him, but he also looked tired all the time.

"Do you ever think about what you would do differently, if you could?" he asked. "I mean, I'm presuming you and I would still be a done deal."

Tory thought for a moment. "When John and I were together in the beginning, I used to search for him in a room, just to look at him, and our eyes would meet. It was that look that told the story. For me, it was the single most important thing we did to show each other where we stood. That we were important to each other. When we stopped looking for each other, stopped looking each other in the eye, I knew that we had lost it. That special thing between two people. I don't know when it happened, or even who began to pull away first. It seemed like one day we were okay, and the next we weren't—and I didn't care enough to find out why or try to fix it.

"With you, it's different. I still look for you when we're in a crowd. And when I get home, you still look at me that way, which tells me that we're okay. Most times, you're already looking right at me, like I'm the most important person in your life. I don't have to wait for you to sense me staring. You just do. It reminds me that we have a special connection even after all these years. If I had to do my life over, knowing what I know now, I would have left John before he'd gotten ill, and I would have pursued you instead of not trusting what we had as being real. I was lonely and miserable when I could have been happy."

"So you still look for me, do you?"

"All the time. Now what about you?"

"I would have gotten my sister some help."

He had become much more open with her over the years. She touched his arm to offer her understanding.

"I would have answered your texts and e-mails when you found out that you were pregnant."

"Yeah, tell me about it."

"Strike that. I would have broken the rules and made contact every week until I wore you down."

"Oh, I like the sound of that. Why? What would you have wanted?"

"To convince you to leave your husband and be with me. I knew that your marriage wasn't great or else you would have never had sex with me. And then I would have known you were pregnant with my child because you would have told me. There would not have been an option, since we would have spent more time together —not just by e-mail or phone—but really together. You would have gotten to know the real me sooner, and life would have been easier."

She nodded.

"I'd been looking for you my whole life, and I was an idiot to do what I did."

He didn't have to expand on that. They both had regrets, but nothing could be done about them. It was easy to rehash the past and fantasize about what they would have done differently. What neither of them would address on this trip, though, were the difficult topics of death and old age and what came along with them: declining health, decreased stamina, and less energy. Tory had no idea where Chris stood on some basic health care decisions. If they couldn't discuss those sensitive issues in the confines of their own home, there was little hope they'd resolve anything here.

It had only been four months since Tory had resigned from her position, and it was the beginning of the best years of her life, if you believed the commercials. She had planned well for her later years, and she would be assured of a comfortable lifestyle, at least where money was concerned, but there were other important considerations. Chris was rapidly deteriorating and she could no longer ignore that.

She was aware that at some point, maybe soon, one of them would need assisted or specialized care. It was more likely that Chris would be the one to require that type of support first. His refusal to discuss it troubled her. Dementia or behavioral problems would require them to alter their living arrangements.

Their property required a great deal of upkeep. Neither of them could manage the place on their own. They had a housekeeper who came by every week, a landscaping company to keep the yard clear and tidy no matter the season, and a handyman who made sure the house stayed in good shape. He acted as an overall contractor for small projects as well. Maybe they should look to downsize?

In the meantime, they could hire a live-in nurse or some other helper to keep an eye on Chris. He would need an assistant to drive him around and keep track of his schedule. It might be a little tricky to get him on the same page; Tory would have to play it off that the employee was her assistant as well. It would have to be plausible—or Chris would never buy it.

An idea surfaced, something she'd given up on a long time ago: owning her own business. The assistant could work with her to locate appropriate sites and investigate the types of businesses that might work up here. The more that she thought about it, the better it sounded.

She began to consider what she and Chris might require down the road. Even with the caregiver/assistant around, there would come a time when more help would be required. What if his personality changed or he needed more care than she could handle? This was a task for her to sink her teeth into once they'd returned home. She could start by engaging an agency to recruit someone while she researched facility options.

"That mind's still going," he teased. "You haven't turned a page in thirty minutes."

She laughed. "It's boring, and I'm contemplating all the things I want to do when we get back. How about taking a quick trip to see Jake and Zoey at the end of the month? Would you like that?"

He did not answer straightaway. "Yes. We should do that."

"Why did you have to think about it?"

"Oh, I was thinking about how you probably still need to fill your days with activities. Are you having difficulty adjusting to retirement?"

She could read between the lines. He was actually wondering if she regretted being home with him full-time, whether it was enough for her, and whether he was enough. His insecurities probably arose due to his awareness of aging and health issues. She tried to set his mind to rest.

"Sometimes. But I think I'm going to like being retired, now that you've decided to cut back. It will be a new adventure for us to take together."

He liked her response, she could tell.

"Are you worried about Jake?" he asked after a while.

This was how their conversations went. They could hop from subject to subject without any difficulty understanding each other or keeping up with the flow.

"A little. He calls every week or so, but I want to see him with my own eyes and let him know I care."

"Oh, I'm sure he knows that. It's Zoey I'm worried about."

"Yes, she's been a handful."

"Ha! She still is. She'll be the one to make my hair go grayer. She's the one we should be checking up on. I'm sure she's got a new piercing or tattoo, and God knows what she's been up to. I don't know if I can handle it! Maybe we can play on her sympathies and rent a wheelchair or something."

As if he would ever let someone push him around in a wheelchair! Chris could still make her laugh. Someone had once remarked about how he could press Tory's humor button with as little as a facial expression. The fact that he could still make her laugh after so many years was a testament to their strong and long-lasting relationship.

"If I thought that ploy would work, I just might. She is unique. Her hair was a hodgepodge of so many colors last time we saw her, wasn't it?"

"Ask her to send us a selfie in case she dyed it back to her natural color. Otherwise, we won't recognize her. I'd hate not knowing my own daughter!" he said.

"Good idea. Can we spend a few weeks on the West Coast? Maybe take some day trips?"

"Sure."

She went back to her book, and he dozed for a while.

Later, in the elevator, on the way back to their room, he pulled her to him.

"Why, Mr. Enns, are you looking to mess around? We've never done it in here."

He laughed. "An oversight, my love. No, it will have to wait. Since this is our last time at a conference like this, I have something planned."

The doors opened, and he took her hand as they walked to their room.

Wondering what he had organized, she got straight into the shower to get clean and get her head in a better place to enjoy the night. It was time for fun; luckily, she had already shaved and had brought a very expensive shift to wear.

***

Chris was trying to make this a memorable occasion for Tory. Since he could no longer trust his memory, he reviewed his extensive list of tasks. He'd almost forgotten to place the meal order that afternoon, and he had become a little paranoid. The piece of paper had been opened and closed so many times that it was wrinkled.

He squinted, blaming the condition of the paper and the low lighting for how difficult it was for him to read, and turned on another lamp. Even with bifocals, he still had to strain to see. He didn't want to mention it to Tory because she would make him an appointment with the eye specialist. He hated going to see doctors, hated the whole process. *You always have to wait for at least an hour, even if you have a fixed appointment time, and in the end, you only speak to the doctor for five minutes or less. And for what? No real help. So what's the point?* Maybe because it was his eyes, he would organize the examination himself, just to prove to her that he wasn't ignoring his health. Wouldn't that shock her a little!

The grin soon faded as his thoughts moved to another reality. It was a bitch, getting old, losing your ability to recall the simplest things. He knew what was happening to him, and he knew that she did too. It was good that she was taking a long time in the bathroom because he didn't want her to catch him with his list. His failing memory wasn't something he wanted either of them to dwell on tonight.

The attendant knocked on the door and set up the food and drinks.

Chris fiddled with the music, which allowed him to manage his nerves and control his pulse. He couldn't understand where his anxiety was coming from. It was a special occasion, nothing more.

He sat in a chair, waiting for her to join him. When she finally emerged from the bathroom, he watched her face as she took it all in. The best part was seeing her that way: completely impressed.

"What's this?" she asked, smiling.

He always appreciated that smile; it transformed her face. She walked toward him in a black negligee.

Fingering the silky fabric, he grinned up at her. "Something new?"

"Yes."

"I like it."

"I thought you might. You've gone all out: the wine, the meal, the lighting. What's playing?"

"A mix of your favorites and mine. Are you hungry?"

"Yes."

"Let's eat, then." They went to the bed, where the food was set on a very large platter.

They fed each other tapas as well as other finger foods. He so enjoyed being with her. She teased him about how he couldn't stand the taste of any food that was overdone, and he bugged her about her dining etiquette. Tory couldn't eat without a napkin. He had seen her use a towel if a cloth napkin wasn't available. Even when they were camping, she insisted on using serviettes at all meals. This woman would not lick her own fingers, but she thought nothing of cleaning the toilet without wearing gloves or using them on his body.

When they'd had their fill, he made a call for dessert. It took a little longer than expected, but seeing her eyes light up made the wait well worth it. The attendant arranged a chocolate fondue pot with various goodies on a small table near the large windows.

After dessert, they looked out at the illuminated city, feeling comfortably full.

He took out a small box and placed it squarely on the table in front of her.

"What's this?"

"An anniversary thing. And before you think I've lost my mind, I know it's not our real anniversary. But this is to remember the first time we met and made out like teenagers all those years ago in San Antonio."

"Oh, Chris."

"It matches the other two rings, doesn't it?"

"Yes."

"It's perfect! Thank you! But you shouldn't have."

"Well, I did. I want you to know that no matter what happens, I will always love you."

"I feel the same way," she said, and then she demonstrated it.

These days, their sex was more restrained, and he guessed that was normal. As he aged, he couldn't get it up as quickly or as frequently. Hell, he was lucky if it happened once a week. Tory didn't seem to mind. He had other body parts that worked just fine, even with the arthritis.

They fondled each other more now, he noticed. He had no trouble remembering how wild for each other they had been all those years ago. Tory called it the selective memory of the male mind, but he disagreed. Some memories could never be lost, he believed. Not the spectacular ones like the evening they'd spent at the sex club: seeing how free and unrestrained she became in front of others, losing all her inhibitions and giving herself over to his needs. The first time he sank into her welcoming body had been a revelation of just how good it could be with someone special. There had been no comparison to the women he'd known before her.

He had been beyond lucky to meet Tory and make a life with her. He'd always been certain that she was the one to fulfill his dreams of having a family and be his equal in every way. Her sexual appetites had been the same as his. She was one of those rare finds: unimpressed with the trappings of success and not obsessed with her personal appearance. Chris was all for self-improvement, but he was disgusted by the lengths that people went to rid their faces of wrinkles and such.

She rarely visited a salon or bought any new clothes. Her tastes were simple. The products and clothing she bought had to have quality and be practical. He'd liked that about her in the early days, and still did.

Tory continued to have no idea how attractive she was. She had matured into a better version of herself. At the grocery store, the mall, and restaurants, it was all the same. Men checked her out.

He understood her physical appeal since that was what had reeled him in from the start. From the moment he saw her walk past his window, he had known that nothing would ever be the same. That memory was so clear and special to him. He still remembered how he had felt that day. Before he'd even learned her name, his body had craved hers in ways that amazed him. Was it lust? Probably. At that point, it had been so long since he'd been sexually active with a woman that it must have been. Then, one taste of her, and he had been hooked. Once his hands touched her smooth skin, and he was lost. There had never been any doubt in his mind that their paths would cross again when he left her at the airport the first time. They were destined to be together.

His whole world changed when they continued to meet up. She was all he thought about in bed late at night. When he discovered Zoey's existence, he knew that fate had been nudging him toward Tory all along. It didn't matter that she had been married or that he had been a bishop or that the whole situation was not a standard romance novel plot. No, their story had already been written, and he had been helpless to change the sequence of life-changing events that propelled them forward.

He worried a little about what was in store for them. Would she stay with him when he became feeble or lost his mind? He expected that she would, but he was resolved to be institutionalized when it came to that. Those realities would not be discussed in advance; he preferred to leave the decision to Tory. After all, it was a forgone conclusion that she would survive him. Some part of him knew that for certain.

In the meantime, he wanted to continue enjoying their life together. It wasn't too much to ask, was it? That they remain intimate and close? He needed that more than anything. Just to be near her was enough.

He was rubbing her back, a sure way to keep her loose and mellow. Man, how she loved being touched. His healthy ego took credit for her response. It was all down to his skill and personality—or so he wanted to believe.

EPILOGUE

"The store looks great, mom!" Sam said as they hugged.

Zoey dumped a box on the counter and grinned at them. "What are you guys doing standing around? There's work to be done. The opening's in two days. Two days!"

Tory's dream was being realized. For a while, it had seemed as though it might not happen. It had taken her a long while to get over Chris's death. Right after he died, everything had come to a stop in her life. It was like a piece of her had died as well. During a rough patch, she had barely eaten enough to sustain her body and struggled with depression. Time and her kids had helped bring her out of the darkness. Her grown children were also responsible for the realization of this shop, a combination bookstore and art gallery.

Zoey and Sam had been by her side the whole way. It surprised her, sometimes, how she and her daughters kept growing closer as they aged. As a threesome, they dealt with the purchase of the property, its subsequent demolition, and the new building. In spite of all the permits, delays, and frustrating hurdles, they now owned a handsome building with a storefront and four rental units on the second level.

She and her girls were partners. They made all the decisions, big and small, with open dialogue and a dose of humor. It was working out so far, and Tory would ensure that it continued to.

The best thing about the new phase in her life was that she was doing something she'd always wanted to do. She could enjoy the process without worrying about turning a profit, earning a salary, or dealing with a boss.

Each of them had carved out a niche. Sam sourced the artists and consigned the goods so the store had a nice inventory of art. Zoey had so much energy; she took care of the practical aspects of the building and their tenants upstairs. She had changed over the past two years. Something must have happened while she was in British Columbia to trigger the transformation, but no matter how often Tory hinted for details, Jake and Zoey were mute on the subject.

The books were Tory's responsibility, and she truly enjoyed the task. Everything about that part of the business made her smile: ordering, negotiating terms, organizing the reading sections, and dealing with deliveries and distributors. She planned to establish a reading club and create some interactive promotions once they got through the first quarter of the year and things were running smoothly.

Grinning, she looked around at the half-filled shelves and cases. It was taking a while to make sure each object was displayed in a pleasing way. It was a satisfying process, even though they had so much more to do.

Happier than she had been in months, Tory resumed her work, knowing that she had made the right choices all along. Family, career, lover, retirement, and now this.

As a young woman, she had dreamed of owning her own business. Now it was really happening. With her daughters as partners, she was having such fun, and she felt younger than ever as she soaked up their enthusiasm. The bookstore/gallery would keep her mind occupied and her days full. She was looking forward to the buying trips, relationships with customers, merchandising, and making day-to-day decisions. Although, she would still have to consider what her girls thought.

They were expecting a visit from Jake soon, and hoping he'd bring his latest friend. What mattered most was that they were happy together. That was a life-lesson that she wanted to impart on her kids and grandchildren.

Her mind returned, as it often did, to Chris and what he would have thought of the store. She liked to think that he would have supported her in this venture. Toward the end of his life, he had changed considerably. Often, he seemed angry and uncommunicative, nothing like the man she knew. When he was finally diagnosed with prostate cancer and Alzheimer's, it seemed as though he gave-up. She surmised that it must have felt like a death sentence—if any part of his brain had actually registered the news.

The months had dragged on after that. Sam had been her rock, helping her with Chris in so many ways. His tendency to wander around in the nighttime had been overwhelming. He soon became bedridden and stopped eating or drinking. Tory had known what was coming, but it had still seemed like it couldn't be happening to her—and to them. When it came time to move him to a home where experts could manage his care, Sam had organized everything. When it was necessary to move him to hospice, it was difficult and painful to leave him each day, not knowing whether he would survive the night. Sam helped her through those difficult days as well.

The pain of losing him was almost too much to bear. To get through it, she began to daydream about having a shop of her own, something to occupy her after he was gone, a reason to get up in the morning. Maybe it would even provide the region with some much-needed employment and be a legacy for her family. Sam's children might like part-time jobs in the shop to give them time to figure things out before continuing their educations.

When her youngest daughter moved back home, she was so thankful. One less worry knowing that this child was nearby. Zoey and Sam ran errands, bought groceries, cooked, reminded her to eat, and tried to be helpful in any way they could. But no one could possibly understand how she felt, watching Chris slowly leave her. A part of her was dying with him. The longer it took for him to let go, the worse it got for her.

She wanted to prolong Chris's life for as long as possible; she was afraid to let him go. That was not at all how she'd felt when John was dying. Chris was a shell of a man, no longer the person she knew, but having him like this was better than not having him at all.

On a sunny day, she was reading to him from one of her romance novels when he said, "I know you, don't I? I'm with you, right?"

As soon as she answered him, he smiled and drifted off, just like that. No fanfare. Nothing more. Alone with him in the quiet room, she allowed the tears to fall. Death was personal and so final. In that moment, the sheer agony of losing him crippled her. She could not move. *This is it.* She arranged for last rites and should be reaching out to the priest again, and each of the family members were only a call away, but she could not bring herself to do a damned thing but sit there and feel that astounding pain. For months, she'd been trying to prepare everyone for the eventuality, but she couldn't practice what she had preached.

Sobs racked her body as she clutched his cooling hand. She had witnessed many deaths as a nurse, and she recognized the signs; she didn't need anyone else to confirm that he was dead. He was rapidly losing body heat, and that affected how he looked. The worst thing was knowing she would never see him again. Refusing to let her last memory of him be a corpse, she climbed onto the bed and wrapped her arms around her man. Eventually, someone would come by and see her with him, but she paid that no mind.

She stayed with him for a long time before summoning her family. It felt so strange to have him here one minute and know that he was gone the next. While she waited, Tory went over some of the details of their life together and tried to remember the good stuff: his sexy smile and his body that had always aroused her; his way of making her feel special. Now she would only have those memories.

Soon came the regrets. Why hadn't she ever agreed to get married? Why had she been so determined to have it her way?

Like Sam, who had never married Tim, despite his powers of persuasion, Tory had never married Chris. She had accepted the wedding band finally, during a very memorable bath, but they had never made it official. She had toyed with the idea once or twice, but after that time in Toronto, he'd never pressured her again.

Although Chris hadn't pressured her, he had on occasion griped about her refusal to marry him. He had performed many wedding ceremonies while he was a priest, and he wanted that for them. She had remained firm in her decision. It seemed silly to make a public declaration when most people already assumed they were married.

Besides, she had been married the conventional way once before, and that hadn't been as sacred as what she had with Chris. Perhaps her kids understood her sentiment; none of them had chosen to marry either.

She glanced at the three bright rings on her hand. Tory had no desire to remove them even now. They had kept their promises to each other and stayed together to the end. Their partnership had been better than any marriage she knew of. With all that she was, she believed that relationships like theirs did not come around every day.

In the bleak period following that day, not even the idea of a store helped her. It was all she could do just to make herself get out of bed. Knowing that her reaction was normal didn't make it any easier. She had always known that Chris's death would hit her hard, but she had expected herself to be stronger and handle it better.

It had been a hard time for them all—she had to remind herself of that. The rest of the family had suffered the loss as well.

One day, Zoey jumped onto the couch beside her, just like she used to do as a child, and showed her a property listing. That was when Tory had finally seen the light again. Her kids needed her to come back to life. Their energy made her realize that it was what Chris would have wanted. Besides, she had been acting more like a burden than a mother—and that was something she never wanted to become.

The business seemed like a good idea for many reasons, and then the reality of it began to surface. Money vanished as they purchased the old building, tore it down, and built a new one. Zoey claimed one apartment for herself.

Tory's plan was to sell the big house by the lake and use the money to add a small one-floor unit to this building that she could live in. They had room to expand out the back. Until it was built, she could live in an upper unit. There were numerous advantages to this: no commuting, being across the hall from her daughter if she ever needed assistance, and feeling less lonely. Maybe she'd do it the following year. She needed one more summer to look out onto the water and watch the loons. She needed a little longer to experience the peace of the place where she and Chris had lived together.

There was no pressure on her, but she did feel the need to get on with her life. At sixty- eight, she could have another twenty years—or more—left. She had to focus on that.

Zoey nudged Tory's arm, bringing her back to the present. She was so perceptive of the slightest changes in Tory's mood.

"I'm okay, honey."

"I know, Mom. He'd be proud of you."

"You think so?"

Zoey nodded, and so did Sam. Tory smiled. She wanted her daughters to return to their previous state of excitement.

"Come on, you two, let's have a look at that sign out front. You're sure you like the colors?"

***

They scheduled the grand opening for two weeks after the soft opening. There was even a ribbon-cutting ceremony with champagne. Zoey drank a little too much bubbly, but she liked the buzz too much to stop.

A strong arm suddenly wrapped around her shoulders and pulled her back toward a firm chest. Zoey recognized Mike by smell alone: car oil and lemon. The latter was probably the product he used to get the grease off his hands.

"Hey, babe," he whispered into her ear. "Have you told your mom yet?"

She shook her head.

She knew Mike was probably frowning at her. They had agreed to live together on a trial basis, but she was having second thoughts about that. He was rushing things. He actually wanted to get married, yet they hardly knew each other. *What is it with guys these days?*

"She won't be impressed about me dating a grease monkey, so don't push it!" she teased. "Besides, I'm not sure it's a good idea. You leave your shit around, and I like my space tidy."

He laughed. They both knew it was the other way around. The man was a neat freak.

Zoey wanted what her parents had and knew that Mike wasn't the one, so why would she entertain cohabitating? Tired of looking she was tempted to stop trying to find the one person who could count on and not be intimidated by her free spirit. There had to be someone who would appreciate her. Maybe she should try a different flavor? Sample the nerdy types, like that guy who just came in wearing geeky glasses that did nothing to hide his gorgeous eyes. What she could do to a man like that...

***

Jake watched his sisters and mother, feeling their excitement and soaking in the positive vibes of the new store. The craftsman style of the building suited the town, and the merchandise was pretty cool. He liked the combination of books and gallery-type items.

He admired his mom for having survived two spouses and bouncing back both times. How was she able to be so strong and capable?

He wanted to be like her: well-adjusted and happy. Was that too much to ask? His short romances were getting boring. It didn't help that each time a relationship failed, he took it as a reflection of his own inadequacies. Maybe he needed to be single for a while, to change his life in a profound way.

It occurred to him what was missing in his life: family. He considered, for the first time in years, moving back home. Sam had just told him that his mom might be ready to sell the cottage that was more of a house now. It had been completely redone years before and could use a refresh. His mom would need him in the future, so he should be closer. Plus, Zoey obviously still needed him around to set her straight on guys like the one who was hanging all over her. She wasn't all that into him. The signs were already visible. She had dodged his kiss and was disentangling herself from him now.

He spied one of his nephews, Justin, drinking a beer, and he couldn't help shaking his head. When had Sam's kids all grown up?

As if he'd conjured her, Sam suddenly bumped his shoulder. "New guy, I see," she said, indicating the guy with Zoey.

"Not for long," he responded. He knew he didn't have to elaborate. His ability to read Zoey was nothing compared to Sam's talent for

301

reading him. She still played the part of older sibling, telling everyone what to do.

"I figured. So, when are you moving back?"

He stared at her. It freaked him out how she did that. He had only just made the decision.

Sam looked at his expression and laughed.

***

Sam decided to talk to Zoey first thing in the morning about the creepy guy she was hanging out with. He was disgusting, in a crusty sort of way. What Zoey saw in him was anyone's guess. But right now, there was another guy not far off who was looking at her sister in that way that would make a woman melt, if she only paid attention.

Sam went over, took Zoey's arm, and pulled her away from the leech who had his hands (with dirty nails) all over her sister's back. *Yuck!* Then she marched her into the vicinity of the mystery man, who wore dark glasses and wasted no time introducing himself. Sam made a weak excuse about having to go and then took her leave. Her sister could have backed away if she'd had no interest in the man, but as it was, they were still talking.

Scanning the room, Sam located her brood scattered here and there. They were behaving for the time being. Then her gaze landed on Tim, who had obviously been watching her, by the look on his face. God, the man was getting sexier as he aged. She grinned at him and saw his eyes brighten at her unspoken promise that he was getting lucky tonight. All of the kids had plans, so they were free to spend the evening alone—unless they got a call from someone needing to be picked up.

She was looking forward to spending some quality time between the sheets with her man. She knew these were the times to remember whenever things got rough, and they always did. Good memories were what sustained a relationship. Her mother had told her that when Sam had inquired about how she could stand dealing with Chris at his worst.

Sam glanced at her mom; the woman was her idol. She was holding court with that calm manner she had that always seemed effortless, though Sam knew otherwise. Her mother was still grieving over Chris. It might take her years to get over that man. But she would. That was what a strong person did.

As if she knew Sam was watching, her mom made eye contact and came over to join her. "Everything's going really well!"

"It's like a party! We might have trouble getting people to leave."

They both laughed, but they stopped laughing when a police officer came in the front door. Sam heard her mother sigh as they moved in unison to greet the man. By the time they had wound their way through the crowd, Zoey and Jake had joined them. Sam didn't miss the look of interest that passed between her brother and the good-looking cop before the officer delivered the bad news: too many people were parked on the road, and now it was partially blocked. There had been complaints, and that meant that the opening-day celebrations were officially over.

Zoey stood on a chair, whistled to get everyone's attention, and asked them cordially to leave.

Sam addressed a more pressing matter: she asked for the man in uniform's information as though she might want to contact him about the situation. When he handed her a business card, without looking at it, she passed it straight to Jake, right in front of the guy.

"You owe me," she said, earning a slap on her behind from her brother before leaving them to it. When both men laughed, she knew it had been the right maneuver.

Now that the store was emptying out, Tim helped her gather empty food containers and dishes, and to tidy up so she could open the next day without the store looking like it had been raided. Some pieces of furniture needed to be repositioned and she was in process of doing that when she noticed an older man chatting with her mother as he helped her move an armchair. They looked cute together, she thought, but before she could do anything, Tim grabbed her around the waist.

"Don't you think you've done enough matchmaking today?" he whispered in her ear. "Time to lock up and go home."

She nodded, having recognized the old guy from the neighborhood; he wasn't going anywhere. There would be time to push them together if need be. But at the moment, she had her own man to enjoy.

***

Tory watched from the window as Gord Walker got out of his car and walked up to her door. They met a long time ago, when they were both attached to other people. Gord's wife had died a couple of years back. If he was looking to replace her, then Tory wasn't interested. However, if all he wanted was to continue spending time with her, then that was definitely possible.

Sam certainly seemed to like him as well. She had pushed them together at every opportunity since they'd chatted at the grand opening. (What was it with that kid? She had fixed up both Zoey and Jake at the opening.)

Tory was grateful for so many thing. That the pain of losing Chris seemed to be easing every day. That Zoey was seeing a nice boy for a change. That Sam was happy with her man and large family. That her son was moving back next month and that the business was finally up and running. That she was still active and healthy enough to enjoy these times. And that today, she had a very good-looking man interested enough in her to come calling.

She liked how Gord dressed and spoke. Furthermore, he had his own teeth, did not require a cane, and had a dry sense of humor. That last quality was essential.

The doorbell rang. Before answering the door, Tory did a quick check in the mirror. It reflected back the image of an old lady. *When did that happen?* Tory glared at herself. *When did these dark pigmentation spots, and wrinkles appear?* She rarely paid attention to her own reflection anymore; she didn't care how she looked. *Why am I suddenly preoccupied with my appearance? Silly woman!*

She patted down a wayward strand of gray hair and decided to pretend she was much younger than her age. She thought of Alice and grinned, remembering the reason her mom had been evicted. It had taken her weeks to get that information out of Chris. She remembered how they had laughed about it. Her smile was all the more genuine when she opened the door.

Gord didn't mind that her face was wrinkled or that she didn't have a youthful body. The first words out of his mouth put all her petty concerns to rest.

"Hey, beautiful, what are you up to?"

"The store's closed on Mondays. It's my day off. What did you have in mind?"

"Can we play?"

"Mr. Walker, you read my mind. Shall we eat before going to bed?"

"Depends what's on the menu," he said.

"I haven't planned anything…"

"Do you have ice cream?"

"Yes."

"Then we do both at the same time." It was a comment that both of them found highly amusing.

About the Author

Louise Loraine Conrad is a retired registered nurse and procurement expert. She lives in a small community in central Ontario, Canada, with her husband.